Praise for Meg Little Reilly

EVERYTHING THAT FOLLOWS

"A skillfully wrought tale of atonement in a frame of psychological suspense."

—*Booklist*

"A novel that stays surprising from beginning to end and refuses to provide easy answers for the moral quandaries at its heart… Riveting."
—Suzanne Berne, author of *The Dogs of Littlefield*

"Blockbuster fiction at its most thought-provoking and sophisticated."
—*Brooklyn Digest*

"Smart, taut, and seductive, Reilly's second novel immediately catches you in its grip and doesn't let you go."
—Michelle Hoover, author of *Bottomland* and *The Quickening*

"Taut with moral complexity and a subtly building tension, this is the kind of story that punishes you if you dare to put it down."
—Kim Cross, *New York Times* bestselling author of *What Stands in a Storm*

WE ARE UNPREPARED

"Timely and terrifying."

—*Publishers Weekly*

"An emotional and captivating journey."

—*Buzzfeed*

Also by Meg Little Reilly

WE ARE UNPREPARED
EVERYTHING THAT FOLLOWS

THE MISFORTUNES OF FAMILY

MEG LITTLE REILLY

mira

mira™

ISBN-13: 978-0-7783-6942-4

The Misfortunes of Family

Copyright © 2020 by Margaret Reilly

This edition published by arrangement with Harlequin Books S.A.

For questions and comments about the quality of this book, please contact us at CustomerService@Harlequin.com.

Mira
22 Adelaide St. West, 40th Floor
Toronto, Ontario M5H 4E3, Canada
BookClubbish.com

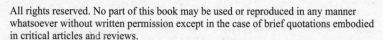

Printed in U.S.A.

This book is dedicated to my families

THE MISFORTUNES OF FAMILY

PROLOGUE

First among the seven deadly sins is pride, which encompasses vanity. All sins—whether you subscribe to this particular doctrine or not—are of excess. They are essential human impulses that we are advised not to overindulge. But how are we to know where the line between normal and excessive lies? We are left to rely on our own flawed judgment to figure that out and the examples of the flawed people who raised us.

The point here is: normal is whatever our crazy families say it is.

We grow up, leave home and try to recalibrate for the true north of normal, but by then it may be too difficult for many of us to locate it.

Such is the case with the Brights, a fundamentally good family of outsized pride, in a place and time that rewards the sinful impulse. They have everything but the ability to see themselves clearly. They are beautiful and terrible.

They are us.

1

"I can't believe we agreed to a month." Ian placed folded T-shirts into a neat stack beside his suitcase. "A month is too long."

Spencer emerged from the walk-in closet. "It's not a month. It's three weeks."

"Three weeks in July is basically all of July, which is basically half of our summer. By the time we get back, we'll be rushing to plan syllabuses."

"Syllabi."

"What?"

"The plural of syllabus is syllabi."

"I'll bet you a thousand dollars that it's not. I'll bet you three precious weeks in our short, precious summer—weeks that could be spent here in SoHo, reading the Sunday *Times* by a rooftop pool and drinking with our friends each night, instead of holed up in the woods with your family."

Spencer rolled his eyes. "It's a summer house in the Berkshires, Ian. This isn't *Deliverance*."

"No one would hear us scream."

"Stop."

Ian sat on the bed, the last T-shirt still in hand. "Sorry. I love it there. You know I do. It's just…a lot."

"I know it's a lot. They're asking a lot of us this year. And I'm asking a lot of you. So thank you."

Ian nodded at his folded pile, glad to have extracted some gratitude.

Spencer frowned. "Do I have to say thank you every day for all three weeks, or will that suffice?"

"I'll need a few more."

Spencer went back into the walk-in and began rifling through hangers.

Every summer, in advance of their trip to Spencer's parents' lake house in the Berkshire Mountains of western Massachusetts, Spencer had to do this. He had to say thank you and I'm sorry. Ian required it. It is not that a free vacation in the mountains wasn't a pretty good deal for two academics scraping by in New York. It is simply that Spencer's family was a lot, and Spencer was a lot when he was with them. And, after nine years of marriage, each knew what was required of the other to keep the peace. So Spencer dutifully said please and thank you each summer, and then they hopped into their rental car and drove to the country. Ian just needed an acknowledgment of his sacrifice, of his enormous deposit into the goodwill account of their marriage. He just needed to hear it.

That's how it usually worked, anyway. But this summer's trip was different because it was three times as long as their usual trips and there would be a camera following them around this time. It was the Bright Family times three, the movie! And it was going to be a lot for non-Brights. Ian knew that already. He'd attended enough of these family events, as the spouse to the second of four larger-than-life Bright brothers, to know what he was getting into.

"Thank you," Spencer muffled from the walk-in.

He was selecting blazers. Spencer always packed blazers for the country, which drove Ian mad. As if, at any moment, they might need to host a campaign rally or fund-raising gala from the woods. When you grow up with a US senator as a father, life is a stage for which one must always be appropriately costumed. Ian thought it was charming nearly all of the time—except when they were actually with all of Spencer's family. Then it was too much.

"Say it again," Ian yelled.

"Thank you."

"Once more."

"*Thank you*, you sadist!"

"You're welcome."

2

"I think this is exactly what we need, don't you?" Mary-Beth patted her husband JJ's thigh just as his foot pressed harder on the gas pedal. She could feel the muscles beneath his chinos shift in sync with the transmission.

JJ Bright nodded and smiled faintly, eyes on the road.

"What do you guys think?" Mary-Beth spun around and looked at her twin teenage sons, Lucas and Cameron, both deaf to her at that moment, their heads moving almost imperceptibly to the sounds coming in through their headphones.

Lucas nodded in her direction.

Cameron looked down at the screen of his phone and laughed.

They were enormous mirror images of each other, obviously formed from the same genetic clay as their father in the front seat. Sometimes Mary-Beth felt her breath catch when she took in the substantiality of these humans she'd borne and the man she'd married. Everyone around her was giant and hungry, fresh-sweat-stinking and throbbing with an energy that could build civilizations and start epic wars. All these overwhelming men relying on her, Mary-Beth.

"Yeah, this will be fun," JJ said finally. "Just what we need."

"Once the boys are on the plane for their soccer trip, we can just float on the lake, read books in the sun… When was the last time it was just you and me, without the boys?"

JJ looked in the rearview mirror and smiled. "Unfortunately, it's not going to be *that* kind of vacation, not with my parents, and brothers and their spouses there. Plus, there's this documentarian…"

"Oh, right, I forgot."

Mary-Beth hadn't forgotten the documentary. She'd been obsessing over it for weeks now, ever since her father-in-law told them that there would be cameras following them around at the lake house for a documentary series on the personal lives of political figures. She wanted to be cool about it—the Bright men certainly would be—but how to be cool when you know you're on camera all the time? It was thrilling and terrifying to imagine all the bad angles they'd catch, all the awkward moments. Bathing suits and puffy morning eyes. Exposed bra straps and chipping manicures. God, Mary-Beth wasn't suited for this sort of thing.

And yet she couldn't wait for it. To be watched all the time. It aroused something inside her that she hadn't known was there.

"I don't think it will be too imposing," JJ said with confidence. "Remember, the camera is really there for my dad. They want to get a peek behind the curtain and see what he's working on for a second act, I think. It will be a little weird, but we aren't the subjects. Just try to ignore it."

JJ knew about things like this, having grown up with some

degree of political celebrity. If anything impressed or intimidated him, Mary-Beth didn't know of it.

Her JJ (for "John Junior") was the oldest of the four sons of now retired senator John Bright of Massachusetts. JJ was the spitting image of his father—brawny and dark haired, a football player in his youth and still, at forty-five, a damn good fit in a tailored suit. Even among their friends in Washington, DC—a town of practiced extroverts and politicians—JJ stood out for his confidence and gregariousness. He impressed everyone, none more than Mary-Beth. And he loved her ferociously for it. Mary-Beth didn't need to stand out. She was content to simply bask in the light of her husband's glow. *And is there anything wrong with that? No, there is not*, she reminded herself from time to time. *There is nothing wrong with it at all.*

So JJ was good at things like being watched by cameras; he'd done it quite a bit. But he had never been in a documentary. Mary-Beth worried that JJ hadn't asked enough questions about this plan, that he'd been too deferential to his father, as usual. Details about this documentary were worryingly thin, and Mary-Beth suspected that there might be more to the story than they were privy to.

The production company behind the documentary was legitimate, as far as Mary-Beth could tell, if a little coarse. In anticipation of this trip, she had watched their docuseries on sweatshop labor in Bangladesh, which was impressive. *But why them?* she wondered. What was so interesting about John Bright Senior that someone would want to put him in a documentary? Mary-Beth had been around politics long enough to be wary of these things.

She flipped the car visor down to wipe the sweat-softened mascara smudges from underneath her eyes.

"I gotta piss," Cameron said from the back seat.

JJ nodded and looked at his wife. "We should stop for lunch, anyhow. We've got six more hours ahead."

Mary-Beth agreed. She studied her husband's face as he navigated their SUV through two lanes of traffic to a nearby exit. His index finger tapped the steering wheel impatiently. A small line of beaded sweat sat just below his hairline. Unlikely as it was, her husband seemed anxious about this trip.

3

Chelsea Thorpe pulled the hood of her sweatshirt up around her head and tried to sink deeper into the stiff seat. The sounds of flights delayed, lost people being summoned to their gates and airport employees whose expertise was needed elsewhere had been ringing in her ears for over two hours. The layover in Miami was supposed to be fast, but due to some security issue, all air travel was disrupted. The mood at gate sixteen was degrading quickly. Rolling suitcases smashed into knees, children cried, soda slurped through straws and aerophobics rubbed prayer beads to summon the patron saints of flight, which—it seemed clear to Chelsea—had long since abandoned them all.

Frigid air blasted down at her from a ceiling vent. It was cooling the sweat that had accumulated on her back when they humped their packs from a far concourse. Charlie Bright was somehow managing to sleep beside her, his heavy head pressing into Chelsea's shoulder.

She shifted intentionally and woke him.

He blinked and looked around. "How long was I out?"

The impression of her shoulder seam was pressed deep into his smooth cheek, tan now after months in the tropics.

Chelsea squinted at a nearby monitor. "I don't know, twenty minutes. How can you sleep in all this?"

A woman sitting directly across from them began noisily unwrapping a sandwich.

"How can you *not* sleep?" Charlie asked. "We haven't had a proper night in days. I think it's getting to you."

Chelsea rubbed her eyes.

"I should get in touch with my dad." He pulled out his phone. "I'll just send him a text to let him know we're delayed."

She nodded and looked over Charlie's shoulder as he composed a grammatically correct text to his father informing him of their travel complications and adjusted time of arrival. She'd never known Charlie—the most chill guy on earth—to be so formal. He seemed to be stiffening with each stretch of travel that brought them closer to his family. At that moment, he felt like a stranger to her.

And, in a way, he was. Chelsea and Charlie met six months before, in Haiti. The international development company that they had both been working for (from different corners of the globe) had brought them there for a road construction project. Chelsea had flown in from London for the project, and Charlie from Boston. Their desks were located side by side in the cinder-block project headquarters. They'd started talking on the first day, and the chemistry was instantaneous. They made dinner together the night after that. They slept together on the third day. The work was messy and hard and hot. The Haitian evenings were beer soaked and long. It was perfect.

But that wasn't real life. Chelsea didn't know Charlie's family or a single one of his friends from home. She regularly forgot which Boston suburb he'd grown up in, and his mother's name. They's fallen in love in an alternate universe. And now, suddenly, she was traveling back to real life with him. It was becoming unclear whether their romance could translate.

Charlie nuzzled into Chelsea, kissing her neck gently. A current of tingly electricity traveled from the place where his lips met her skin all the way down her spine.

The woman with the sandwich was watching them. Small globs of mayonnaise had gathered at the corners of her mouth.

"I'm so excited to introduce you to everyone," Charlie said into her neck.

Chelsea smiled. This trip might be a terrible idea—too much, too soon for a new and hardly road-tested relationship—but she couldn't bear the idea of being away from him. And so she was glad to be going, to meet his folks and all his siblings and their spouses and offspring. She was admittedly tickled by the idea of meeting a former US senator. Swimming in lakes, eating ice cream on a porch, lighting sparklers on the Fourth of July... It all sounded so wholesome, so *American*. It would be an anthropological adventure, if nothing else.

Besides, she had to go. They both did. It was a fact that—as of yesterday—both Chelsea and Charlie were, technically, homeless and broke. The international development company they had been working for had gotten involved in a local embezzlement scheme in Port-au-Prince and had to shutter immediately, sending everyone home without their last two paychecks. Chelsea couldn't go back to London because her parents were renting out their flat while they traveled, and she couldn't put a deposit down on her own place because she had no money. She was stuck.

It was vaguely embarrassing to be a professional in her early thirties without any long-term agenda or safety net. She could have planned better. But Chelsea tried not to think too hard about all of that. She certainly wasn't going to let it ruin this trip. The fact was that all of the traits that made her great at her job were also the things that seemed to inhibit her ability to embrace adulthood. Fearlessness, anti-materialism and a perennial restlessness were the things she *liked* about herself. They were also the things that made her and Charlie so alike! But those traits led them astray now and then. There were costs to living the adventurer's life. So today, they were on their way to the Berkshires of Massachusetts because it offered beds and meals and rich parents to catch their fall. It was unnerving, but at least they were together.

"Charlie, have you told your parents that I'm coming? Have you actually spoken with them on the phone about it?" Chelsea didn't love the sound of her voice as she asked.

"Of course I have," he mumbled into her neck.

"And that's it? Do they know how long we're staying? Do *we* know?"

He sat up. "I didn't tell them about our job situation, if that's what you mean. No point in stressing everyone out about it. I just told them I was coming back for the annual family gathering with my girlfriend. They were thrilled."

Girlfriend. It was true, she supposed. True, and heavy. The lightness of staying unnamed flew away with that word. She wanted the word, but she wanted the lightness, too.

"Chels, you're going to love them. I promise. They're going to love you."

"How do you know?"

"Because you're with me, and they love me. I'm their baby."

The feeling of sitting beside a stranger came back again, like a wave that washed over her and then retreated.

"But you're not really the baby. Don't you have a younger brother?"

"I do—Philip. But I'm still their baby. You'll see."

Charlie took her hand in his, both tanned and cold in the chill of the airport. "Don't worry. It'll be great."

4

"You should be in the far right lane," Spencer instructed from the passenger seat. "The Taconic Parkway is coming up."

Ian kept his eyes on the road, hands at ten and two. "We're already on the Taconic, hon. That was the last turn we made."

Spencer expanded and contracted the map image on his phone. "We are? How did I miss that?"

"It's fine. I know where we are."

Ian smiled at the mountains ahead. He'd forgotten to stay surly about the trip. It was all too pleasant, as they sailed along the highway at seventy, the hot, stinking pavement of the city behind them. He loved feeling the expanse of the universe open up to them, the rest of the world reintroducing its big self with outlet malls and factories, then fields and mountains. Town, and then country! They were, for a few weeks, anyway, among The Vacationers: the people who disappear to fashionable and remote places to recharge in the summer months. Good riddance to the steaming sidewalks and un-lucky urbanites who'd be trapped there all summer. They were vacationers.

Spencer was still examining the map on his phone.

Ian eyed him. "You seem weird."

"I'm fine. Excited, probably."

He didn't seem excited to Ian. He didn't seem half as excited as he would normally be at this phase of the drive. But then, it hadn't been a normal year for Spencer. And Ian knew that these summer visits with his parents were Spencer's private reckoning of the year's accomplishments. All the accounting was done in the Berkshires, the additions and subtractions of his worth, in the presence of his father who'd amassed too many accolades for it to be a fair competition. None of this was explicit, of course. They were too polite for that, too en-amored with each other. But Ian knew that Spencer arrived at the lake house with whatever pride or shame that he be-lieved he'd earned that year.

In the end, Spencer almost always arrived with a surplus of pride. It was a default mode for the Bright men, and Spencer had lived a mostly charmed adult life. This would be his first year without it. Spencer's most recent book—his fourth—had been poorly received in the foreign affairs community. He'd been too easy on Israel, they said, too conventional in his diagnosis for the Middle East, and lacking in new ideas. The *New York Times* review had used the word "unhelpful."

It was a good book, Ian thought. Not his best, but deserv-ing of publication, to be sure. The world and his academic field were shifting, though, and Spencer would need to shift with them to maintain relevance. That's what Ian would have told him if he wanted to be brutally honest, which he did not. He wanted instead to be a supportive partner to the person he loved more than life itself. He wanted to build this man back up to the charming and arrogant force that he was. So Ian happily proofread Spencer's fourth book and told him that the critics were bitter fools. That part, at least, was true.

"I hope you're not thinking about the book right now," Ian said, testing the waters.

"I've already forgotten about it."

"Good. You should. It's a good book."

Spencer smiled, wide and bright, and as beautiful at forty-one as ever. A lock of black-brown hair fell over one eyebrow, and Ian would have leaned over and licked it away with his tongue if it wasn't likely to cause a ten-car pileup on the parkway. Instead, he reached his right hand out and held firmly to the inside of Spencer's thigh.

Spencer let the hand linger there as organs stirred beneath denim, then threw it back and laughed. "You're an animal in the country. Please get us there alive."

Ian smiled. He knew how to do this, to make Spencer whole again. He didn't need what Spencer needed, and that gave him a superpower. Ian was a tenured professor with two highly acclaimed books of poetry under his belt. He loved his work. He loved his home life with Spencer. They didn't have much disposable income, but they had enough to live modestly on the island of Manhattan, which made them luckier than the vast majority of people on this earth. Ian never forgot that. He was content, so at times like these, it was easy to pour all this happiness into Spencer if need be. Even—especially—at the lake house.

5

The boys were both sleeping in the back seat, and if she closed her eyes, Mary-Beth could almost believe that she was ten years in the past, ferrying twin kindergartners to see their grandparents in the country. They had a smaller car in those days, and there was hardly room enough for the dog between them in the back seat. The Subaru had almost two hundred thousand miles on it by the time they finally traded it in. Barry (the dog) died a few days after that. It's possible Mary-Beth and JJ hadn't worn anything out to its natural end since then. The Subaru and Barry were their last old things.

The boys were bigger now. So, too, were the cars, the house, the needs and wants, and the can't-live-withouts.

It was almost exactly ten years ago that JJ left the environmental nonprofit he'd been working for to join a lobbying firm. He became a director within a year, and then a managing partner a few years after that. The trajectory of their finances changed so abruptly that they never had time to think about who they wanted to be in their well-funded life.

They moved from DC out to the suburbs after JJ's job change, to a big house in Bethesda. Then, of course, they needed all the stuff to furnish the big house. After that came the second car, the pool, the marble countertops and radiant heating. Somewhere along the way, they became people with real art hanging on their walls—not decorative impostors of art, but works with actual value. By then, of course, it didn't seem incredible to Mary-Beth, but rather overdue. And she didn't care about art, either way.

JJ raked a hand through his hair as he steered the SUV off the main road, toward the first of several quaint New England villages they would drive through on their way to the lake house. He was missing his regular haircut with Julio that day, and his hair looked shaggy. Mary-Beth considered scolding him for not rescheduling and getting an early cut—on account of the cameras—but she said nothing.

JJ's haircuts cost $140, which was still only a third of what she spent at the salon these days. She had forgotten to be appalled by it all. Ten years ago, when the boys were such a handful and every day a battle of wits, Mary-Beth didn't know people could spend so much money at a salon. She was blissfully ignorant of the multitude of treatments that fashionable Washington wives were expected to undergo in the interest of holding back time. There were so many things she hadn't known about in those days.

They drove slowly through a picture-perfect downtown, and JJ pointed at a cluster of families waiting in line outside a shop. "Good to see the gelato place is still there."

Mary-Beth smiled at her husband and he smiled back.

He should have gotten the haircut. God knows what kind of cut you'd get out here in the country. Once she knew what a $140 men's haircut looked like, she was pretty sure she could spot a cheap one. Not certain, but fairly sure. So much of their life together now was dictated by the demands of this *lifestyle*. They couldn't imagine living any other way, but they had lived another way, once. It was possible.

When Mary-Beth and JJ first started acquiring all the stuff, it wasn't about the stuff at all. The stuff was a proxy for their unbridled optimism for a future together. Buying a mattress, then an espresso machine and eventually a six-hundred-square-foot condo in DC's Columbia Heights. The condo overlooked a parking lot where homeless men congregated, and it was the most extravagant thing she had ever owned. It was wonderful. The condo and its furnishings were just projects into which Mary-Beth and JJ could pour all their excitement about their life together. And every new trip to Target was actually another proposal, a rededication of their love and hope. It was a sacrament, for a while.

Eventually, though, the sacramental vibes faded and the trips to Target together became solo trips to high-end stores. The condo became a house, and the futon became upholstered living room sets. They became trips of necessity, to fill in all the holes of their enormous life and demanding lifestyle.

And after a while, those gilded shopping trips become simply habit, a sort of occupation for Mary-Beth as the children grew older and needed less of her time. They produced neither pleasure nor sadness, just busy filler. JJ had no relationship to those trips anymore.

But at the start, it really wasn't about the stuff.

"I hope you take this time to relax," Mary-Beth said to JJ.

He flashed a small smile at her, then turned back to the road. "I hope *you* relax."

"You both need to chill out," Lucas said from the back seat, ever listening.

And then all four of them laughed, at exactly the same thing, at exactly same time. A person could live forever on that feeling.

Mary-Beth and JJ were still very much in love, but they were somewhat estranged from each other now. It was as if they were standing at opposite ends of a deep hole, still seeing each other, still wanting each other. But now they had to shout to be heard over all the complications of their life, and sometimes it felt like too much work to communicate across the distance.

The stuff hadn't done this to them, though Mary-Beth sometimes wished it had. A better person would have recognized the folly of her greed and the toll it would take on a pure life. But that's not how Mary-Beth felt about the stuff. It wasn't responsible for their estrangement. No, it was their anxiety about the possibility of losing all the stuff that was driving them apart. Insecurity about the precariousness of this lifestyle was keeping them from happiness and corrupting their marriage.

Did that mean the stuff was intrinsically evil? No, Mary-Beth would argue, if asked by her guilty conscience. Things are just things, and four-hundred-dollar trips to the salon are just that. Good people can have beautiful lives. They can wear designer pajamas, and bathe in Japanese soaking tubs, and still be moral humans. She was sure that hers was not an existential problem, but an easy, shallow, fixable one. If only she—they—could be assured that this lifestyle would always be there for them, then they could relax and come together. Their marriage wouldn't feel so fraught without the weight of their new worries.

JJ scratched his head again through thick hair, fingernails scraping audibly against his scalp. JJ's quiet anxiety was her own, though hers was even quieter.

Mary-Beth said a silent prayer for this trip: *Please let this documentary be the thing JJ needs. Please let this trip be the thing.*

JJ needed a boost. The lobbying firm that employed him had recently merged with another, and they were looking for redundancies, deadweight to cut across the company. Suddenly, everyone needed a new edge—especially the expensive people. JJ hadn't delivered any wins in a while, no legislative victories or measurable evidence of his political influence in months. There were discussions of buyouts for other managing directors, fat severances for people who left without making a stink. It was the kind of money JJ couldn't have dreamed of ten years ago, but now it would be barely enough for them to live on for six months. Most of all, JJ didn't want to get laid off in such a mealymouthed fashion. He didn't want to audition for new roles around town, knowing that everyone would know why he left. JJ needed to find his edge, reassert his juice and keep this lobbying job.

The documentary, Mary-Beth had suggested, might offer an opportunity to raise his profile a little and remind the world that he's political royalty. She imagined there'd be a Washington screening for it one day, and a round of press coverage. Something like this could give him a bump in name recognition and really secure his place in the ranks of Washington movers and shakers. She had seen this sort of thing happen to their friends. When their neighbor, a hack political strategist, appeared on an HBO series about the last presidential election, he landed a column in the *Washington Post* soon after. And then there was the time JJ's colleague—a subordinate!—was spotted by a gossip columnist at a Clinton fund-raiser and got promoted just days later. It was all a bit of a shell game, but you had to play it to win. And the thing about Washington is that the illusion of power and influence is the same thing as power and influence. JJ could at least create the illusion. Mary-Beth hated to be so crass about it all, but that was the truth of it.

Confidence was everything in this work, and JJ suffered from a secret lack of confidence that only Mary-Beth could see. They both knew—though they had never explicitly acknowledged it—that much of his professional success could be attributed to his last name as the son of a US senator. Because of this, JJ had never quite developed the confidence to match the job titles. He had ascended the ranks too fast to feel deserving of them. It wasn't a sad story, Mary-Beth knew, but it was the situation they were faced with.

Please, please let this trip be the thing, she prayed again.

6

"I can't believe they sent a limo," Chelsea marveled, with some disgust.

A suited man hoisted her worn-out frame pack into the trunk of a black sedan. A warm, welcome breeze whirled around the exterior of the Hartford airport.

Charlie threw his pack in on top of hers. "It's just a car service. But yeah, I'm not sure what we would have done without it." He put a firm hand on the driver's shoulder. "Nice to see you, Burt. It's been a while!"

Burt smiled, and he went from looking one hundred years old to about sixty. "One whole year, Charlie boy! How were your travels?"

"Fun. Long. Exhausting."

"You always were the adventurous one."

"Don't you forget it."

Chelsea watched her boyfriend as he did this thing she'd

seen him do countless times before: strike up a jovial conversation with anyone, anywhere. But there was something different about his tone in this conversation. He was projecting a sense of ownership now, a visible pride. Chelsea didn't love it.

They climbed into the cool leather of the back seat while Burt adjusted mirrors and air-conditioning in the front.

"Should take about eighty minutes, Charlie boy. Same as always."

"Okay, then. You mind raising the divider? We might try to sleep a little."

A shield of tinted glass went up between the front seat and the back. Charlie and Chelsea were alone. She buckled her seat belt and looked out at the swaying trees as Burt navigated out of the airport maze.

She stretched out horizontally across the bench seat, her head in Charlie's lap and her knees bent just enough to make herself fit. Charlie ran a finger through her tangled brown curls. His jeans smelled faintly like jerk rub and body odor. Eighteen hours of travel and they were both too ripe for civilized society. Charlie's finger ran softly along her hairline, down her neck and the length of her arm. She was nearly asleep, but still on fire. That's how it always was with them.

Charlie wasn't the smartest or the most accomplished man Chelsea had ever been with, but he was the most curious. He wanted to taste everything and feel everything. He certainly wanted to fuck everything. It didn't make him an animal in her eyes; it made him a connoisseur. He understood the inherent goodness of pleasure, as she did.

Chelsea had faith in lust—not only as a means to something deeper, but as the deep thing itself. Lust as the endgame. *Why*, she wondered, *should we not wish to suck all the jelly from the center of the donut and discard the rest? Why not a life of only jelly?*

Charlie was only jelly.

★ ★ ★

Chelsea fell in and out of sleep in Charlie's lap.

The black sedan drove north on I-91, then west onto I-90, where the traffic thinned and the road narrowed. Industrial parks gave way to rolling hills of lush green trees. The rest stops started looking like little faux villages, the fast-food joints camouflaged in tasteful muted colors.

Chelsea woke after thirty minutes. She sat up and rubbed her eyes.

Charlie's sleeping head was pressed against the window, his breath steaming a little patch of glass that evaporated instantly, over and over.

Chelsea knocked quietly on the divider. It lowered in response.

"Sir, where are we?"

"We're entering the Berkshire Mountains now, ma'am. About forty minutes from Senator Bright's lake house. You ever been here?"

She shook her head and leaned in closer. "No, I'm English. I've never been to this part of the US. I don't really know what I'm getting into."

Burt laughed. "I didn't think so. Well, it's real nice. And they're nice people. I've been driving for the Senator, on and off, for about twenty years now."

"Wow. Do you like it?"

Burt cocked his head, not quite nodding. "It's good work, and it helps me take care of my wife. She had to quit working a while back. So it's good for me. I don't know what's gonna happen now, though, now that he's retired."

Chelsea had no idea how to respond to this. She didn't know what US senators did when they retired, and she definitely didn't know what happened to their drivers. She'd never known anyone with a driver.

"So, if you've been working for this family for twenty years, you must know them pretty well by now, yes?"

Burt considered this. "I suppose I do, ma'am… I suppose I must."

Charlie stirred beside her and opened his eyes.

Chelsea sat back in her seat. He reached a hand across the seat and laced his fingers through hers. "Are you excited?" he asked.

Chelsea's eyes met Burt's in the rearview mirror and she took a breath. "I suppose I am."

7

Farah Dhaliwal turned off a quiet wooded road onto the long driveway that was—according to her directions—the entrance to Senator John Bright's summer home in the Berkshires. She was met by a closed gate.

Farah hadn't been expecting a gate at the end of the Brights' driveway, and she wasn't sure how to proceed. She could call the Senator, but they'd never spoken before, and it wasn't how she wanted to introduce herself. Was she supposed to have a passcode? Farah was sure that this had been her screwup somehow, and that it was an inauspicious start to this, her first solo project as a documentarian.

She pulled out her phone and called Wayne, her supervisor and executive producer of the *Domestic Affairs: The Real Lives of Elected Officials* series. It rang three times.

Finally, there was a click at the other end. "Wayne here."

"Wayne, it's me. I'm sitting in my car at the edge of Senator Bright's driveway."

"What are you doing there?"

"The gate's locked. Was I supposed to have a key or a passcode or something?"

"Oh, right. Shit. My bad. I have a code for you to punch in." Farah waited while Wayne riffled noisily through papers at the other end. "Okay, keypad is on the inside of the gate. Password is 7-8-9-10. Incredible! The people in charge of the nuclear codes, and they can't be bothered to think up a fucking password."

"I think the president has the nuclear codes."

"You know what I mean."

Farah looked out at the tall, leafy maples and the winding dirt driveway ahead. She shouldn't be here, she thought. This project wasn't for her.

Farah had been working for Torch Media for five years—most of her professional life—and in all that time, she'd assisted mostly in the production of climate change documentaries and cultural tourism. She'd recorded a C-list celebrity's tour of the best noodle bowls in Vietnam and did a series about gay-pride parades in Brazil. Their productions were vaguely political, culturally progressive series targeted at younger viewers. They had an edgy guerrilla aesthetic, even years after the independent company had been swallowed up by a media conglomerate. Torch viewership had been modest but cultish until a few years ago, when the appetite for fresh documentary TV started to take off. Suddenly, the streaming services couldn't acquire this stuff fast enough, and Torch was riding a wave. Now they were making more content with more of an explicitly political bent than they could keep up with: a documentary on the inner workings of the Trump White House, a day in the life of a neo-Nazi, voter suppression efforts in the South. *Domestic Affairs* was to be the next in that wave.

Domestic Affairs had been pitched internally as "a look inside the private lives of America's professional political class." Torch wanted to follow a handful of old political lions near the end of their careers to expose their expensive tastes, their disconnection from the constituents they served, and the relentless ambition that drives them. (To the subjects themselves, it had been pitched as "a humanizing biopic of America's most influential leaders.") If it was good, Farah was told, all the big streaming services would get into a bidding war over it. And if it wasn't, then it would be a financial boondoggle for a company that was, year after year, spending more than it was earning.

"I'm nervous," Farah said into the phone. "I don't really know what I'm doing out here."

Wayne sighed. "I know you're nervous, but you've got this. Just follow the guy around with a camera. Follow his kids around. Look for the incongruities, the indulgences. And keep an eye out for the weirdness."

"Right, the weirdness," she agreed distractedly.

"But don't call it weirdness. Call it *color,* if you have to call it anything at all. Which you don't. The point of this series is to pull the curtain back on these people to see what really makes them tick, good or bad. My guess is, this guy doesn't know what the fuck to do with his time anymore. He's been out of office a few months now, finally cleaned out his desk and got rid of his staff. He's already tired of playing golf and hanging out with his family. He's on the brink of either a new endeavor or an existential crisis. Hopefully both, for our sake. These guys fall apart when they don't have anywhere to go in the morning. That's what the Senator Bright story arc is, I think. Look out for that."

Farah sat with that for a moment. "Wayne, what does Senator Bright think I'm here for?"

"He thinks you're there because he's a dazzling and righteous elected official. We didn't tell him much because he didn't ask many questions. You have to understand, Farah, these people don't need to be convinced of why we want them on TV. They already know—or they think they know. Senator Bright thinks you're there for an inside look at the personal life of one of the Senate's great heroes and bipartisan negotiators. And you are! Sort of. Just don't let him steamroll you with a false show. Get the hidden stuff, the parts he doesn't want you to see."

"Okay, okay. I got it." Farah had been over this with Wayne before. She knew why she was there. She just didn't know why she was there *alone*. She had only ever been an assisting producer on these projects, never the person in the lead. "And you don't think I should have another producer here with me?"

"Sorry, the suits nixed it. They aren't completely sold on the premise of the series, so we need to do it on the cheap. If it works out and Netflix, or somebody, buys it, then you'll get all the credit. And you'll have a team at your disposal for postproduction. If it doesn't work out…well, then at least we're not too far in the hole."

"Assuming we still have jobs after that happens." Farah took a breath. "Wayne, is that really the reason I'm running this project—because the suits said no?"

"Yes, but not entirely. I gave you the Bright project for selfish reasons—because I don't want you to get bored and leave. You're overqualified for the work you're doing here now, Farah. You're not challenged. And one of these days, you'll realize that it isn't fun to be broke in New York…and your college loans will start to keep you up at night…and you'll decide that this isn't enough. Then one of those fuckers at Vice or somewhere will call you up and offer you something better for more money. So I'm giving you a push into the big leagues because I don't want to lose you. And if you do well with this documentary, it will make a good case for your promotion. That's what you want, right?"

"Yes, definitely." In fact, she'd been quietly plotting ways to approach Wayne about a promotion in the weeks before he gave her this project. "Yes, of course that's what I want."

"Good. Then act like you know what you're doing. You do. And when you don't know what you're doing, fake it."

"I can do that."

"Just don't go native, or fall in love with any of them."

Farah smiled. "Don't worry about that."

"I don't know... I hear those Bright men are dreamy."

"I hate you. But thanks."

"You're welcome. Godspeed!"

The line went dead, and Farah sat for another minute in her car. She could do this. She *would* do it. She would make an interesting documentary out of what sounded like a mostly boring idea. It would be so good that she'd forget all about that pilot for the show about Sherpas in the Himalayas—the show she *really* wanted to work on—and she'd learn to care about politics, or political families, or handsome Irish Americans or whatever this show was supposed to be about. She'd make this work and then she'd get a promotion.

Farah drove the car right up to the keypad affixed to the gate. She entered the number, heard a buzz, and the gate opened for her. She drove through it, then watched through her rearview mirror as it closed behind her. The gate bounced lightly against itself once, failing to latch, and then again. Finally, there was a click of the lock, loud enough to hear through her open window. She was secured inside the compound.

Farah drove along the winding driveway, through a thick canopy of mature trees. Cool air swept through the car from both sides. There were actual birds chirping.

About a quarter of a mile ahead, the trees opened up to

a sprawling lawn, at the center of which sat an enormous colonial-style home: the Bright lake house. It was a creamy white, with a perimeter of impeccable landscaping surrounding it. Americana-style bunting accented the doors and windows. Behind the house was the lake, shimmering.

Beside the house sat a detached garage that had been designed to look like a vintage carriage house with large barn doors. One of the doors was open, revealing a room filled with water floats, a small sailboat, paddles, life vests and bins of sports gear.

Farah parked in the gravel driveway and got out of the car. If she looked to the right or the left of the house, she could see the Brights' little private lakeside beach. There was a kayak resting at the edge and water lapping its nose. The smell of the air around her was aggressively different from the city. It was cut grass and freshly laid soil; she thought she could smell the cold water somehow.

Farah walked up the front steps and examined the old-timey iron knocker on the knotted-wood door. It didn't look functional, so she pressed the buzzer off to the side. It was clear now that this house was probably less than twenty years old, despite its vintage stylings. It was a jumbo reproduction of an iconic New England home, painted all the shades of the Benjamin Moore historical series. Through the window, chrome appliances gleamed beside custom cherry cabinetry. It was all a bit flashier up close.

Farah pulled a small notepad from her back pocket and began writing a quick note to herself about the details she'd need to get on camera. Her first impressions should be the viewers' first impressions. Chrome, cherry, sparkling water, American flags, manicured lawn, straw hat on Adirondack chair, birds in trees, potted peonies. Calibrated perfection.

The door swung open, and a slight blonde woman was

smiling wide before her. It had to be Patty Bright, the matriarch. According to Farah's notes, she was seventy, though she looked far younger.

"Welcome! You must be Farah."

Farah put her hand out. "Mrs. Bright? Thank you for having me."

The woman shook it with both of her hands and laughed. "Oh, call me Patty. Please."

"Okay, thank you, Patty."

This woman didn't look like the overly polished person in all the Senator's pictures. She wore sporty olive shorts with functional pockets. The purple cord of a bathing suit peeked out at the shoulder from beneath a white T-shirt. She was strikingly fit and emitted a youthful bounce. There was no makeup on her face, but she had the inexplicably poreless skin of a particular variety of wealthy women with the time and the will to maintain it.

"C'mon in and get comfortable. John should be back any minute." The Senator's wife put a hand on Farah's back and led her gently toward a grand kitchen. She smelled like sunscreen. She filled a water glass and placed it before Farah. "So it's Farah Dhaliwal? Am I pronouncing that right?"

Farah took a sip and nodded. "Yes, that's fine. It's Indian, from my dad's side."

"Oh, it's beautiful! I'm just embarrassed I have to ask. Really lovely."

Farah took another sip.

"So…do you want to bring your things in?"

Farah looked around. "Um, yeah. I should probably do that first. I have a few cameras and tripods that I'd like to set up around the house, if that's okay. They won't be in your way, I promise. And the rest of the equipment I'll just keep in my room."

"Of course. No problem," Patty assured her with a wave.

This was the problem with filming famous, or semifamous, people: they were too comfortable with the cameras. They *liked* them. And when people are that familiar with the cameras, their behavior on-screen could look too practiced—like actors playing the role of themselves in their own lives. It meant that she'd have to work harder and longer to capture authenticity. Farah hoped she was wrong about it, but she had good instincts about these things.

"I'll get us some snacks while you get comfortable," Patty said. She pointed back outside. "You'll be staying in the in-law apartment above the garage. There's a set of stairs around the back that lead up to a private entrance. It's small, but it has everything—bathroom, dinette, a large closet. I hope that will work for you."

"It already sounds better than my apartment in New York," Farah laughed nervously.

"Oh, I love New York…"

Patty looked wistfully out the window, and Farah was sure that whatever romantic vision she had at the moment bore no resemblance to her apartment in Bushwick, with its clanking radiators and peeling linoleum. Farah wondered if she'd remembered to tell her subtenant to jiggle the handle on the toilet and not to let the mail pile up in the entryway. She couldn't think about those things right now.

"Have you been doing this a long time, making documentaries?"

"For the last five years, yes." Farah nodded. "I usually work on the environmental and social justice projects, so this is a bit of a departure for me."

Patty ran a colander of strawberries with the greens still attached under tap water. "Well, it sounds like fascinating work. We're glad they sent you."

It was clear that Patty Bright either didn't know or didn't want to know the motivations for Torch Media's presence in her house, and the fact that this wasn't likely to be a glowing biopic about her husband. This made Farah feel slightly guilty, but it also made the work easier.

"Thank you again for having me," she said. "And, Mrs. Bright… Patty, may I ask, where's the rest of the family? I'd love to capture everyone's arrival, if possible."

"Yes, of course! Well, you're just in time. JJ, Spencer and Charlie should all be here within the hour—with their respective families, of course. And Philip is coming later this evening."

Farah pulled out her notebook and searched for the relevant page. "Great. And I have here that JJ and Mary-Beth are coming from DC…"

"Bethesda, yes."

Farah made a note. "And Spencer and Ian are coming from Manhattan. Charlie and—is Charlie arriving with anyone?"

Patty rolled her eyes as subtly as eyes could be rolled while still technically doing so. "Yes, I believe he's bringing a girlfriend. I'm afraid I can't remember her name, though. She's British, as I recall."

Farah made another quick note, then flipped the pad closed. She could feel Patty trying to peer down at the paper.

"And what about Philip? I don't have anything here about Philip."

A nervous laugh. "Yes, well, Philip is coming from Central America, by way of Boston. He's been traveling a lot lately."

Patty bit her lip, and Farah waited for her to say more.

"Philip is a roamer," Patty said finally. "It has taken him a little longer to find his calling… But he says he has some big announcement this week, so who knows, maybe he found it! Do you want lemonade?"

Farah smiled and pushed her notepad back into her pocket. She sensed there was something weird about this Philip brother from the way Patty spoke of him. Farah hadn't been able to find anything about him on the internet, and the Senator hadn't provided any biographical information about him beyond his existence.

Keep an eye out for the weirdness, her boss had said.

"Lemonade would be great. I'll just grab my stuff."

Farah let the screen door slam behind her as she went to the car. She could hear Patty Bright humming softly to herself through the open kitchen window.

Tripods, shotgun mics, three-point lighting kits, boom poles, cables, shoulder-mount rigs… Farah pulled them out one by one and laid them in the gravel. Packing for this had been scarier in the abstract: trying to imagine what she'd need for this project in an unseen location. But now that she was here, she could see it beginning to take shape, the beauty of it all. This inviting home on a private lakeshore. All the charmed Brights gathering together. It was exquisite—but that wasn't the only thing Farah would need to capture on camera. There was a feeling that she couldn't quite identify yet, like being on the set of a movie. Something about it all felt staged, artificial. There was something else here, too.

Farah carried her things up the stairs that ran up the back side of the garage to the in-law suite. From the landing at the top, she could see the lake and the lush border of trees that encircled it. A canoe was a speck on the water at the far end, the slightest mark of a painter's brush. She wasn't sure yet what she was supposed to see in it all.

8

The Brights were all standing together in the driveway when Spencer and Ian pulled up ten minutes later.

John Senior and Patty, JJ and Mary-Beth, their sons Lucas and Cam, and Charlie with his new girl, Chelsea, huddled in a spontaneous gaggle, their luggage still around them. It was everyone but Philip, who had not arrived yet. They were smiling and talking over one another, car doors ajar. Patty had an arm around Charlie's waist, who was beaming out at his hot new girlfriend. Mary-Beth was listening to John Senior as he spoke, a hand at her forehead like a visor in the afternoon sun.

"Here we go," Ian said as he pulled up behind JJ's SUV.

Spencer was out of the car before the emergency break was on.

"Look at this guy!" JJ yelled. He ran to greet his brother with a light punch to his hard stomach. "Making us all look bad, as usual."

Spencer smiled and threw an arm around JJ. "We'll do some hill sprints later and get you back into fighting shape, brother."

"No chance of it!"

Everyone laughed as Patty went in for a big hug from Spencer. "I'm so glad you're here."

Spencer kissed his mother and lifted her briefly off the ground. She squealed and demanded to be put down.

His father was next with a firm hug-backslap hybrid. "No trouble with traffic?"

"The only thing holding us up was my slow driver."

They all turned to Ian as he exited the car.

"Hey, Ian!"

"How can you stand this guy?" JJ joked.

Ian smiled and pulled suitcases, slowly, from the trunk of their rental car. He liked to hang back at this part, to let them all swoon over one another, the brothers punching and tussling like puppies. It was sweet, he supposed, but it was too much for him. He preferred to sidle up when things cooled down a bit.

"Nice to see you all," Ian waved, carrying two heavy suitcases toward the house. "I'll just bring these inside."

"Okay, you know which room is yours," Patty said.

And he did. Spencer and Ian always stayed in the same room, always with the same blue madras sheets and rugby-stripe curtains. An antique sailing flag was framed over the queen-size bed. Every detail considered by Patty. Each, on its own, tasteful enough, but ostentatious in the aggregate. Ian had long ago diagnosed their aesthetic as "aggressively WASPy," which seemed both showy and self-loathing for third-generation Irish Catholics. But the room was comfortable and familiar, with all the smells of vacation. Ian loved to hate it all. He loved it.

Through the screened bedroom window, he could see his

husband holding Charlie, his next younger brother, in a loose headlock. The boys. They weren't men in this house. They were Patty's boys, and boy oh boy were they. It was cute and fun and annoying as hell.

Patty caught his eye in the upstairs window. "You doing okay up there, Ian?"

"Be right down!" He waved and lingered at the window another moment.

Spencer released his younger brother in time to catch an incoming football from their father at the end of the driveway. It was like clockwork to Ian: the headlock, the football, the beautiful white people under the bright sun. In recent years, he had begun to feel that they were an advertisement for a product America wasn't really buying anymore, irresistible nostalgia.

Just then, as Ian was about to turn away from the open window, he saw a young woman, maybe in her late twenties, dressed in stylish but utilitarian clothing and a loose ponytail, joining the crowd of Brights. She held a camera in one hand and a collapsed tripod over her other shoulder. The documentary filmmaker.

Ian watched as John introduced her to the family. The woman shook each person's hand, then sprang back to her car to retrieve another item before setting a camera up by the front door.

The Brights went back to their conversations, everyone standing a little taller than before, now that the cameras were rolling. John Senior's voice got louder and his hand gestures more dramatic. Patty stopped talking altogether, smiling all the while. Mary-Beth smoothed the hair around her face self-consciously, and her husband, JJ, put a calming hand on her back.

Here we go, Ian thought.

He changed into a fresh T-shirt—because he was not impervious to the pressures of vanity—and went back downstairs to join the rest of the family.

Patty greeted him at the door with a tall Arnold Palmer over ice. "C'mon, everyone's moving to the back deck. The sun on the water is perfect right now."

"You're the best." Ian received his drink and kissed his mother-in-law's cheek.

She gave him a one-handed squeeze and kept walking with the tray. With or without the cameras, Patty's movements were balletic.

Outside, Ian found Mary-Beth talking to Charlie's new girlfriend. They were standing at the edge of the deck, looking out toward the water.

"I'm so glad you're here," he said, reaching out to Mary-Beth for a hug.

She held him for an extra beat. "God, has it been a year? I missed you. I can't survive these things without you."

It was true for Ian, too. They were allies at Bright family gatherings, necessary to each other's survival.

Mary-Beth turned to the pretty woman at her side. "Ian, this is Chelsea, Charlie's friend."

He put a hand out. "Great to meet you, Chelsea. You must really like this guy if you've agreed to be put through the gauntlet."

Chelsea smiled and cocked her head. She obviously had no idea what she was in for. "Ha, yeah, thanks. It's nice to meet everyone."

"So you and Charlie worked together in Haiti?"

Before she could answer, Charlie came up from behind and put an arm around her. "Don't you two go recruiting her just yet!" he joked. Or Ian thought he was joking. "C'mon, Chels, I have to show you something."

"Nice to meet you," Chelsea said as she ran off with Charlie toward the water.

When they were out of earshot, Mary-Beth raised her eyebrows.

"What do you think?" Ian said.

"Beautiful, as usual. She seems smart, too. Smarter than the last one."

"We can always use another extra in the family."

That was their secret word: *extras*. It's what they were here: the plus-ones, the non-Brights. Everyone who hadn't grown up with this father and mother, in this little cult of happiness and privilege, was just an extra at these events. They were beloved, by dint of their spousal titles, but they weren't *of* the Brights. They were extras.

Ian felt a presence at that moment and looked up: it was a camera. A small but intricate device had been mounted a few feet above them, to the exterior of the house. It appeared to be looking directly at them.

He nudged Mary-Beth with his elbow and gestured toward the camera with his head.

She was startled at first, then nodded resolutely.

They shared an intense and wordless exchange in which both acknowledged the new imperative: to be more discreet with their conspiratorial chatter.

At the other end of the deck, JJ set his drink down and called to Mary-Beth. "You mind if dad and I take the kayaks out, love?"

"Sure. See if you can convince the boys to go out with you, too."

JJ nodded and went inside, where the children were hiding out to watch English Premier League soccer on TV.

From another direction they heard Charlie laugh, pulling their attention to the glistening waterfront. He'd found a croquet set and was apparently recruiting Chelsea and Spencer to set it up with him. Charlie directed Chelsea where to put the wickets, while Spencer attempted several times to juggle the balls.

Ian and Mary-Beth watched them play. "It's kind of sad," Ian said quietly. "She doesn't even know she's an extra."

"Not yet, anyway."

Most families, it seemed to Ian, were bound by some combination of genetics, shared experiences, loyalty and the mutually destructive threat of their own secrets. The Brights had all those things, but they had something else as well: an unwavering belief that life was so much better as a Bright. They were sure of their own charisma and spent not a moment of their lives doubting the value of their genetic gifts. Somehow these men had lived decades—through adolescence, puberty and new love with non-Brights—and never entertained the notion that the Brights were flawed in any way. Which is not to say that they didn't have insecurities as individuals. Of course they did; they weren't sociopaths. But they believed wholly in this institution of the Brights.

It made them seem mildly delusional, but it also made their beliefs self-fulfilling. The Brights *were* happy and loving and eager to grab life by its beautiful balls. They were special in this way.

Down at the water, Charlie pushed the last croquet wicket into rough lake sand. Ian watched as Spencer gave up on juggling and attempted a handstand.

Mary-Beth turned back to Ian. "I wonder when Philip is arriving. Where is he coming in from?"

Ian looked around, as if the answer might be hidden in the swaying trees. "Boston or something? I think Spencer said he's coming later."

"I'm eager to see him."

"He always makes it interesting."

She laughed softly. "Poor Philip."

9

As the afternoon sun began to lower itself in the sky, Patty chopped vegetables rapidly at the kitchen's center island. Her posture was impeccable thanks to years of yoga and practiced poise in the public spotlight. Ever the senator's wife. *Ex*-senator now.

"Mary-Beth, would you pull out the carrots from the fridge," she said.

It was just the two of them now, Patty and her daughter-in-law, Mary-Beth. The three Bright brothers were out sailing with their father. Ian was reading in his room. The twins were kicking a soccer ball around outside. And Chelsea was scrolling through her phone on the back deck.

Mary-Beth didn't know where Farah-the-documentarian was, which made Mary-Beth a little nervous. Ever since she saw the camera mounted outside, she'd been feeling jumpy. She wondered how many cameras were hidden, and where—

if anywhere—she was safe from them. It made her feel dizzy to think about, but not in an entirely unpleasant way.

"You'll find the carrots in the bottom drawer."

"Carrots, right." Mary-Beth opened the massive refrigerator door and searched.

"And if you see any bell peppers in there, grab those, as well," Patty said.

"Okay."

Mary-Beth was happy to have something to do with her hands, other than sipping wine and readjusting her clothes, which suddenly felt like they didn't quite fit. She loved Patty and these trips, but it was unmooring to be a guest in another woman's kitchen, with no real purpose of her own. She'd never been the sort of person who enjoyed being waited on, but the real source of discomfort was the power imbalance inherent in this situation.

The thing they both understood was that, in this home, there was only really room for one chef, one comforter, one master of ceremonies, one keeper of secrets. There was room for only one mother in a house. All the other mothers were ancillary. So although Mary-Beth was grateful to Patty, she'd prefer to be head mother.

"Let's see…" Patty set a timer on the stove. "John and the boys should be back in fifteen minutes or so from their sail, so let's plan on dinner at seven."

"That works for me." Not that anyone had asked her.

Mary-Beth watched her children through the kitchen window as she sliced the carrots. Lucas dribbled a soccer ball around Cam's feet, and they argued about the rules of their scrimmage. In the distance, she could see the two Sunfish sailboats that the Bright men were steering.

Patty shook her head at the window. "Look at those boys."

It always took a moment for Mary-Beth to remember that

when Patty said "those boys," she was referring not to Mary-Beth's teenage sons but to her husband, JJ, and his brothers, Patty's grown children. "The boys" would always be Patty's own sons. At the lake house, all the men were boys, but the women were only ever women.

None of this was JJ's fault. If anything, Mary-Beth felt a little bad for her husband. With his parents' adoration came an impossible standard. Particularly for JJ, the expectation that he would follow his father was strong, if unspoken. John Bright had been a lawyer, a member of the Massachusetts House of Representatives, a US senator and a published author. He was more accomplished, more famous and wealthier than JJ would likely ever be. These were not the sorts of things that Brights articulated, but they were the things they measured their lives by. It seemed to Mary-Beth that the more things mattered to the Brights, the less they spoke of them.

There was a thud from the waterfront, and then a round of laughter.

Patty smiled to herself. "They're back."

Moments later, JJ, John, Spencer and Charlie burst into the kitchen, all dripping wet and laughing.

"Ah!" Patty yelled. "Get out, get out. We just had this floor mopped!"

"What happened?" Mary-Beth laughed.

"Your brother-in-law tipped us!" JJ yelled, pointing at Charlie.

Charlie put his hands up innocently. "It's your fault for forgetting what a lousy sailor I am." He laughed and retrieved a six-pack of beer from the fridge.

Then the men walked their dripping bodies back outside to the deck. Before leaving, JJ leaned in for a kiss from his wife.

Mary-Beth pressed her lips into his forehead and drank him in. Lake water dripped from his hair to her shirt as the smell of movement and sunshine emanated from his skin. He was happy. *This is why we're here*, she thought. *We are here for this feeling.*

John Senior slapped JJ playfully on his back as they left. The electricity of this family was something to Mary-Beth. Even years later, it continued to amaze her.

JJ looked more like his father than any of the Bright sons, which seemed to afford him a certain intimacy with John Senior, flattery being a powerful drug for the Brights. It wasn't only that they were both broad former football players, with big, toothy smiles and emerald eyes. JJ also worked hardest to cultivate similarity with his father. They wore expensive—but not overly fashionable—oxford shirts on weekdays, and golf shirts on the weekends. They kept the *Wall Street Journal* conspicuously tucked into their black leather briefcases and offered people good Scotch when there was something to toast.

Mary-Beth knew they weren't cool men. She'd never cared for cool. No, they were something better: they were impressive men. JJ and his father were the men who ran the world. They were the men fluent in everything Mary-Beth's father aspired to understand, but never achieved: politics, the stock market, global affairs and fine art. They were comfortable in every room, even the ones they didn't belong in.

Mary-Beth was smart enough to know that JJ and his father didn't really run the world. They weren't the most brilliant men she'd ever encountered, and they certainly weren't of the right pedigree or wealth to really count themselves among America's elite ruling class. But they passed and blended fairly well among that ruling class, which was important to them. And it was that fact—the fact of their vulnerability—that made JJ so wonderful to her. JJ needed Mary-Beth. He needed someone to reflect back at him all the greatness that he wanted to believe he was projecting out into the world. He really *was* great; that wasn't a lie. But Mary-Beth was sure that no one saw all his greatness as she saw it, and no one could make him feel as great as she could. Maybe wives aren't supposed to derive any happiness from such things anymore, but she did. She wasn't bothered by it.

It seemed to Mary-Beth that the best marriages are based on unspoken agreements to maintain wonderful myths about each other. Beauty, brains, power—whatever one needed to believe to get out of bed in the morning—a good partner could do that. She and JJ did that for each other. Without ever voicing this arrangement, they agreed to hold flattering mirrors up and offer beautiful reflections for each other. It was a lie only if one didn't believe that one's partner deserved to be flattered. But Mary-Beth was sure that JJ deserved it. She did, too.

"Okay, salad's done, and the chickens are in the oven." Patty looked at the clock. "Let's sit outside with the boys while things cook."

"Hey, Mom," Charlie called from the deck. "Can you make some of your famous guacamole?"

Patty dried her hands on a dish towel and, smiling to herself, began searching for the basket of avocados. "You go ahead, Mary-Beth. I'll get this," she said cheerfully.

Mary-Beth went out to join the guys, because, really, it wasn't her problem that Patty wanted to wait on them hand and foot. If her mother-in-law insisted on doing every damn thing for these grown men, well, what else was there to do?

Outside, the men were laughing and baking in the early-evening sun. JJ put an arm out along an open deck chair for Mary-Beth, which she gladly took.

Spencer was telling a long story about a bad student. Ian was smiling beside him, despite the fact that he'd obviously heard the same story at least once before. Chelsea sat right in

Charlie's still-damp lap, raising the libidinous temperature around the two of them by a thousand degrees. The evening sun pointed at their tanned faces from across the shimmering lake like a spotlight. In their bodies and in the world, the Brights possessed a laconic sort of belonging.

Mary-Beth wanted to match their contentment. But instead, she felt a familiar tugging inside her that came sometimes at the lake house. Sometimes it seemed to Mary-Beth that she was the only one among them who truly appreciated the value of these riches. Not just the house and all the stuff, but the great big, happy family—it was the thing she'd spent her whole life wanting. To the Brights, it was a mere birthright. They didn't appreciate it properly or ever bother to thank God for their good luck. She wasn't even a real Bright, and yet she often felt like she deserved Bright-ness more than any of them, because she'd been deprived of this and she knew what a gift it was to have.

Mary-Beth had grown up an only child, in a different time, to an Irish Catholic family that didn't believe in only children. As early as she could remember, people would ask her parents, "Is she your only child?" And this question had several other questions hidden inside it, questions like, "Are you selfish people?" and "Is it a medical problem?" Mary-Beth spent her whole life fantasizing about what her parents could have said in response to those questions. They could have said, "We got everything when we got our Mary-Beth," or "She's all we ever wanted." They never said those things. When Mary-Beth's parents were asked about why she had no siblings, they always said the same thing: "God only blessed us with one." It was a strange answer in that it confirmed both the idea of her miraculousness and the tragedy of their small family. She was a gift, but her aloneness was a punishment.

She was something, and nothing at all. It wasn't the only sorrow of her childhood, but it embodied everything.

Mary-Beth spent her whole life dreading those questions and her parents' tortured, tired answer. And she vowed to never again find herself in a small, wanting family. As a child, she pined for a family that demanded no explanation at all. Mary-Beth was always sure that it was the numbers alone that cursed her, not her family's inadequacy at appreciating small numbers. It wasn't a philosophical problem but a mathematical one. She wanted big numbers after that—and she got it with the Brights. She got a husband, two kids, three brothers and a set of famous in-laws. She got more bigness than she'd ever imagined.

And so it was with some repressed sadness that Mary-Beth had to acknowledge her status as an extra in this great big family. She'd been married to JJ for eighteen years. They had two perfect children together. And yet there was no denying that she wasn't a real Bright. (And she *was* a Bright! That had been her legal name for eighteen years!) But she couldn't stroll along for their long trips down memory lane. She never knew Gran and Pops, or the Labrador that died when JJ was ten, or the hilarious thing that Spencer said on Christmas morning in 1986. She knew the stories better than any of them by now, but they still weren't hers.

JJ squeezed his arm around her shoulders, and Mary-Beth came back to the beautiful, bountiful present. Spencer was still telling his story to a mostly rapt crowd while Ian looked at the water.

A car honked from the other side of the house, and Spencer stopped talking. There was a pause in conversation, then John Senior clapped his hands together and stood up. "That must be Philip!"

10

Chelsea stood at the doorway of the dining room, watching the Brights as the final dishes were brought to the table for dinner. It was a long table, made of a grainy wood that might have been part of a barn door in a previous life. On it sat two roast chickens, grilled corn, potato salad, wild green salad with carrots and peppers, and crusty bread. There were tasteful linens, heavy silverware and clear glasses running up and down the length of the table. Chelsea liked the lake house; it was impossible not to. And it emanated a very American flavor of optimism and class, available to anyone with the money and a few decades to grow into it.

People were pulling out chairs and pouring wine into glasses around her.

In the corner of the room sat a vintage hutch that was bursting with pictures of earlier summers. Boys in bathing trunks, dogs in canoes, s'mores over campfires and adults drinking cocktails in Adirondack chairs. Everywhere she looked, Chelsea saw bone-white teeth and smooth skin. They were like the stock pictures that come with new photo frames when you buy them at the store. It struck her as almost cartoonishly perfect, devoid of all irony.

"You're here, babe," Charlie said, pointing to a chair at the far end of the long table.

She smiled and scooted around the other bodies in her way to her seat.

Babe. It was probably the first time he'd called her that. It sounded rather nice, actually. Something about this place seemed to prompt it, as if their official coupledom was being rapidly reinforced by Charlie's family. Husbands and wives. Boyfriends and girlfriends. If you weren't one of those, you were nothing at all.

Chelsea sat and watched the rest of the group find their seats. Patty was passing bread while John Senior uncorked a bottle of something white.

Philip was there now, too, which made the circle complete. Chelsea hadn't really spoken with him yet, not one-on-one. He'd been swept up in the tide of family hugs when he arrived, lots of gentle ribbing and how-was-your-flight questions. He was seated too far from her now for polite conversation, but Chelsea was curious about Philip.

Just a few feet behind Philip stood Farah, the documentary filmmaker, as she adjusted knobs on a standing camera. Chelsea watched her put her face behind the machine and look through the lens, then stand back and change the height and direction. She was all business.

"Farah," John Senior said, coming up beside her. "You must eat with us tonight."

She looked surprised. "Oh, Senator, I was hoping to get some of this on tape. I assumed that would be okay…"

"It's just one meal. We'd love to get to know you a little first, before you disappear behind those cameras."

Farah looked unsure. The whole family was watching their exchange now.

"Do you mind if I keep it rolling while I eat?"

"Of course not!"

Farah forced a smile, made a few adjustments on the camera and found a seat out of its range of sight. She sat down beside Chelsea.

"Hi again," Farah said, putting a napkin in her lap.

"Hi, I'm Chelsea."

She nodded. "I remember."

The Senator stood up at the other end of the table and clinked a fork against a glass. "Okay, before we dig in here, I propose a toast."

Everyone quieted.

Chelsea noticed Farah looking longingly at her camera ten feet away.

"I would like to toast first to my lovely wife for making this incredible meal. I adore you, Patty."

Patty smiled, and the Bright men smiled, and everyone seemed thoroughly pleased with themselves. Chelsea felt like she was inside a movie.

He went on: "And I would like to thank my children and their partners for taking the long—in some cases, *very* long—trip up to the country. It means so much to your mother and me."

"Hear, hear," Charlie added, squeezing Chelsea's thigh under the table as he did so.

"And I'd like to welcome our guest," John went on, "the accomplished documentary filmmaker Farah Dhaliwal for joining us this summer. This is going to be a special vacation!"

"Cheers!"

Farah smiled. "I'm really not all that accomplished," she said, and everyone laughed politely. "But thank you."

They raised glasses and clinked, spilling white wine onto clean linens. The Brights resumed their boisterous conversation and began scooping food. After that, it was all pass the chicken, and who needs potatoes, and the corn is perfect, Mom, and so on.

Chelsea took a long gulp of wine and turned toward Farah. "So how does this work? Are you going to just follow everyone around for three weeks?"

Farah put her water glass down. "Well, I have stationary cameras set up around the house, and I'll be moving around with smaller ones for most of the day. There aren't any strict rules about how it's done. I just need to follow the action."

"What a cool job." Chelsea was impressed and slightly ashamed of her current unemployment status.

"It sounds more glamorous than it is." Farah's knee bounced beneath the table. "What about you? What do you do?"

"I work in international development," Chelsea said into her wineglass.

She didn't want to think about losing her job and leaving Port-au-Prince. She didn't want to think about being homeless and broke and somewhat reliant on this man beside her, whom she liked very much but didn't know how much. Thirty-six hours ago, she'd been sweating in the unrelenting Haitian sun, working her ass off as a liaison to the local infrastructure crew, arguing and bartering and loving every second of it. Chelsea missed the challenge. She missed the people, the language. She missed the sound of honking Mazdas and blasting compas music. She longed for the smell of fried cassava and aloe oil drying on her burnt skin. Chelsea's mind was calmest when the world was at high volume. But the Berkshire Mountains were very, very low volume. Even these loud men couldn't change that.

She was grateful that Farah didn't ask any follow-up questions.

"I'm considering drinking too much wine tonight. You should join me," Chelsea said to Farah.

Farah chewed potato salad. "I'd love to. But I'm supposed to be working."

"Just have another glass with me now. It will help you relax. I'll keep drinking for the both of us after that."

She laughed. "Okay."

Chelsea reached for a nearby bottle of white wine and filled each of their glasses right to the top.

"Cheers."

"Cheers."

Farah nursed her drink slowly while Chelsea finished hers and moved on to another round. Conversation in the room had settled into something mellower, lulled by food and the dimming daylight. Chelsea relaxed into the effects of the alcohol, quietly watching the Bright men in their element. They talked a lot, but they were happy to listen, too, inserting funny comments at every opportunity. The Bright men were slight variations of the same brand—the Senator, JJ, Spencer and Charlie—each different iterations of that dark-haired, green-eyed, sparkly smile gene. All but Philip; he was something else entirely.

All of Philip's physical attributes were similar to those of his siblings, but slightly askew, and, taken together, gave him a different look entirely. His eyes were green, but a darker shade of hazel than the rest. His jawline was prominent but, combined with his also prominent nose, made his features appear rather sharp and birdlike. His hair was thick, but of a mousier color. He looked exactly like his brothers, but entirely different. It was as if all the genetic excellence of their parents had been used up by the time it was Philip's turn to gestate. It wasn't that Philip was unattractive by normal standards, only that he was a striking deviation in this context.

Still, there was something about Philip that Chelsea found herself drawn to as she watched him from that distance through a pleasantly boozy filter. He was the most open among them all, the most vulnerable and the most sincere. He listened more and spoke far less. Yes, Philip was something else entirely.

Light was fading through the windows now as dinner lingered on. Someone had turned on the wrought iron chandelier above them, and the room was taking on a warm, yellow glow.

Chelsea pushed the chicken around her plate with a fork. It had an impressively golden crust and fine dusting of minced herbs, but she couldn't will herself to eat it. She was a traveling vegetarian, a moral-relativist-etarian. She avoided meat at home in London, but she ate whatever was available and customary when she was in the developing world. Chelsea was smart enough to recognize the cognitive dissonance of this rule. She knew it was the product of some combination of liberal guilt, romanticism and probably a bit of exoticization of foreign lands. And yet she stuck with it. Mostly, it just made her feel like less of an asshole, a feeling she hated more than anything.

Chelsea hadn't had a lot of rules growing up; her parents weren't big on them. Rules were for rubes, the ignorant masses who needed the state or, God forbid, religion to tell you how to live a worthy life. No, Chelsea had grown up in a ruleless world of rigid intellectual judgment. The message she received from her upbringing was that rules are horrible, except for all the politely unspoken rules of the erudite, which are ironclad. And so she decided early on that everyone needs rules, so you may as well pick them for yourself. Otherwise, someone will pick them for you.

Chelsea tried to hide some of the chicken under excess salad, realizing as she did that Charlie—her boyfriend-partner-lover to the right—didn't even know about this rule of hers. He was sitting *right beside her.* The fingers of his enormous hand were pressing at that moment into the flesh of her inner thigh, and yet he didn't know this fundamental thing about her. It was a small, dumb thing. But it was her.

Chelsea felt her heart rate suddenly rise with this realization. She reached for her glass, which had something red in it now, and took three long gulps in succession. *Who is this person? Where am I?*

"You okay?" Charlie whispered into her ear.

She must have been acting weird. Chelsea wished she hadn't had so much wine.

She looked up into Charlie's face and felt a little better. She didn't completely know who he was, and he didn't really know her, but there was an unmistakable intimacy between them. They had something that made all the other couples at the table look like mere acquaintances. They had a magnetic attraction, and maybe that was enough.

"I can't eat the chicken."

"Okay," he said easily, kissing the top of her head. "Just let me know if you want me to pass you something else."

She relaxed into her chair and looked to her left at Farah, who was now typing furiously on her phone. Chelsea wanted to talk more with her, to ask her how she got into this work and what the hell was so interesting about an old retired politician. But Farah had that serious look on her face again, and she seemed too preoccupied for small talk.

At that moment, Philip attempted to stand up, sending his chair nearly tipping over behind him. He caught it, knocking a wineglass over in the process. It was clear that he had something to say, but the pool of wine was holding everyone's attention now. Patty began blotting the spill with a napkin, and Philip apologized three times in a row. It was a gloriously inelegant sequence of events, beautiful in its normalcy.

When calm was restored, Philip straightened up again and announced to the room that he had some personal news.

"You're pregnant," Charlie joked.

"No."

Patty looked up hopefully from her wine-cleaning project. "You're moving back?"

"Kind of, I guess. But no."

"You're joining the circus," one of the twins chimed. (Chelsea didn't know which it was.)

Philip laughed. "Close."

"So what is it?"

He paused for a dramatic moment.

"I'm joining the priesthood."

Patty gasped.

The Senator expelled a puff of air, something like a laugh.

Charlie rolled his eyes. "Oh, c'mon, Phil."

But Philip was beaming now with excitement, looking around at his baffled family.

No one made another sound. Farah took her phone out of her pocket and quietly panned around the table to register everyone's reaction.

"I'm really joining the priesthood," he said again.

"Which one?"

"The Catholic one."

The Senator shook his head. "Jesus Christ, Philip. Are you serious?"

"Of course I'm serious. Why is that so hard to believe? We're Catholic, aren't we?"

Spencer grunted. "Yeah, but we're not *Catholic* Catholic."

Mary-Beth stared at the food on her plate.

"Philip, surely you're not serious about this," his mother said. All the color had left her face.

"Of course I am. I am entering the seminary this fall."

For a moment, no one said another word.

Lucas started to snicker, and JJ shot him a stern expression.

Chelsea held herself completely still. She could feel Charlie's hand slide mindlessly off her thigh.

And then the lights when out. The lights, the refrigerator, the ceiling fans, the digital clock on the stove and every electronic charger plugged into every device in the house. The low hum of energy ceased, leaving behind it a startling absence of sound. They were powerless, and no one was paying any attention to Philip any longer.

"Aw, shit," said one of the twins.

"Cameron!" Mary-Beth reprimanded.

"Everyone stay where you are," John Senior instructed. He stood up and went to the kitchen. "Must be a planned outage in the area. I'll just get my flashlight in case it lasts and see what I can find out..."

The sun was almost down outside, but a dim glow still came in through the windows from across the water and illuminated their ghostly faces just enough. The mood in the room had lifted slightly. No one was quite sure what to do with themselves at that moment.

"Game night!" Spencer finally announced.

Nods all around.

Charlie turned to Chelsea to explain. "It's a Bright tradition. Whenever we lost power as kids, we'd light a bunch of candles in one room and all stay there together playing board games until we fell asleep."

Chelsea's eyes widened.

"If it's winter, we make a fire," he went on. "And if it's summer, we eat all the ice cream in the fridge."

She smiled back at him, silently willing the gods of the electrical grid to resume order. She didn't want to play games tonight. She wanted to go to their private little room, have sex with Charlie and sleep for ten straight hours.

Chelsea turned to her left to find that Farah had quietly reclaimed her place behind the camera and was filming them again.

"Should we bring plates in?" Mary-Beth asked.

"No, let's leave it all for now," Patty said. "We'll sit out on the deck while John figures out what's going on."

And so they filed out of the dining room and regrouped on the back deck.

The twins found their soccer ball and attempted to kick it back and forth in the final whispers of daylight.

Patty and Mary-Beth took seats on the patio furniture, drinking wine and chatting. They looked like two versions of the same person in the dark, the ghosts of summers past and future.

John Senior was still inside, on hold on his cell phone with the power company.

Everyone else leaned against the deck railing, making uninformed guesses for why they would have lost power on a hot—but not *very* hot—summer night in rural Massachusetts.

Philip sat apart on a deck step and looked up at the sky. No one was talking anymore about his strange announcement, which made Chelsea a little sad for him.

"Might be a fallen tree," Charlie offered, putting a hand around Chelsea's waist.

JJ shook his head. "But there's no wind."

"Your father will get to the bottom of it," Patty said. "He'll have it all figured out soon enough."

"Should we eat the ice cream?" Mary-Beth asked. She seemed to know all the family traditions. A professional Bright.

It was difficult for Chelsea to imagine that there was ever a time when Mary-Beth wasn't a member of this family. She seemed to take such pride in knowing all these little rituals. Chelsea felt fairly sure that she didn't like Mary-Beth, a woman who exhibited nearly all the qualities Chelsea generally hated in other women. She was tidy and sweet, doting even. She looked to Chelsea like a helpful little lady-shadow, following all these men around as they enjoyed their lives. Women like that seemed to magnify all of Chelsea's unruly appetites. By comparison, Chelsea felt too large, too loud, too hungry. And because she didn't like feeling that way, she was almost sure she didn't like Mary-Beth.

Still, Mary-Beth seemed so *nice*. Genuinely nice. Chelsea couldn't fully dislike anyone who was that nice.

The back door banged open and shut as John Senior emerged from the house. "Well, the power company isn't answering its phones, so I don't know what the story is. Wi-Fi is down in the house. Is anyone still connecting on their phones? Service is terrible out here."

Before anyone could search their pockets, Lucas bounded up the deck stairs, with Cam behind him. "They say it's a cyberattack."

"What?" the Senator took the phone from his grandson and squinted into the illuminated screen while the others waited. "CNN is reporting that there's a series of outages across the Northeast… New York to Bangor…natural causes and grid overloads have been ruled out…looks like a targeted attack on the grid…no one has yet claimed responsibility…"

"That's not good," JJ said.

"So when's the power coming back?" Lucas asked.

At that moment, Chelsea became aware of Farah with her

camera, sidling quietly up to the group. Farah was following the Senator, who was obviously aware of it.

"Okay, no one panic," he instructed, handing the phone back to his grandson and putting a hand on the boy's shoulder. "I'll get on the phone with Washington and get to the bottom of this. In the meantime, have another beverage and listen to the crickets. You're all safe right here."

John Senior went inside and Farah followed him with her camera.

No one had suggested they weren't safe. The Senator seemed to be playing for the camera.

"Who's he going to call?" Chelsea asked.

"Dad's got plenty of people in Washington who can fill him in," Charlie said. "DHS, FBI, that sort of thing."

Ian looked at Spencer to his side. "What do you think?"

"Spencer's an international conflicts expert," Charlie whispered into Chelsea's ear, though she already knew that, and she'd seen all his published books on the shelf inside.

Spencer smiled at his husband, grateful to be asked. "I think this is just what we've been expecting for a while now. Attacks on our grid are the new frontier for fighting wars."

"Wars?" Cam said.

"I don't mean we're *at* war. I just mean that any number of antagonistic foreign parties could have attacked our grid. ISIS, Russia, North Korea…"

"I bet it's the Chinese," Lucas said knowingly.

"It's not the Chinese. But it's not an accident, that's for sure. This would appear to be a well-coordinated attack. Let's wait to hear what your grandfather learns."

"Good lord," Patty said to herself.

"It's probably nothing more than a massively expensive inconvenience," Spencer assured them. He sounded like a professor now, calm and all knowing. "It will be a good story for the boys to tell their friends when they go back home to DC. I wouldn't worry too much about it."

Ian raised his eyebrows. "You still have that bottle of Pappy Van Winkle from Christmas?"

"Excellent idea." JJ stood up and went inside to retrieve the bourbon.

Everyone relaxed a little, but they didn't say much.

The wall of trees that surrounded their private lakefront had begun to sway with the wind. The air was cooler now, and Chelsea wished she had a sweatshirt. It was officially dark. Only the fireflies and the abandoned soccer ball stood out in the blackness.

Mary-Beth watched her boys as they sat on the steps and scrolled through their phones.

Patty hugged her bare arms against herself.

Spencer and Ian stole a kiss.

Philip was there among them, but he didn't make a peep.

Charlie draped a warm arm around Chelsea's shoulders. It occurred to her that, in the dark, he could have been anyone. Without the light, would she know his scent? The contours of his arm? The sound of his breath?

Such a thing didn't normally matter to her. But now that she was thinking about it—now that they were marooned here together in the dark—she could think of nothing else.

11

Mary-Beth opened her eyes to the sound of the rising hum of household electronics. The alarm clock beside their bed was flashing 12:01, the fan was gaining momentum above them, and the specter of a prolonged period in a crowded house without digital distractions had lifted.

JJ woke a moment later. He rolled over to look at her.

"Power's back," she said.

"Mmm. That's good."

"What do you think it was?"

He rubbed an eye. "World War III? That's what my head feels like."

Mary-Beth ran a hand through his dirty hair. "You guys. You always drink too much the first night back. How late did you stay up?"

He squeezed his eyes shut in apparent pain. "Too late. We

found tiki torches in the garage and played boccie until Charlie finally won."

"So did you talk to Philip about his weird announcement? Is that for real? He can't possibly want to be a priest."

"Yeah, that was weird," JJ groaned, his eyes still closed. "But we didn't talk about it. I mean, no one brought it up."

"You guys spent hours alone in the dark and didn't ask your brother about his super strange plan? How does that happen?"

JJ opened his eyes and looked hard at his wife. "Do you think he was actually serious about it?"

"I think he was, JJ."

"Jesus Christ."

"Yeah, like, for real, though."

He laughed a little and massaged his temples. "I kind of thought it was like when he joined that band in Oakland. He just did it for a little while and then stopped doing it. Like everything he does. He's still a kid."

"I don't know. He never made a big formal announcement like that. And he's many years away from being a kid. He's twenty-seven! I think he might be serious about this."

JJ considered the plausibility of this theory. "Oh my God."

"I know. Maybe it's not such a weird thing. Maybe this is what he needs."

"What?" JJ sat up on his elbows and looked at her. "That's ridiculous. He's not going to be a fucking priest."

"He could. It's not *that* crazy. We're all Catholics."

"Mary-Beth, we're barely *Christmas Catholics* at this point. Christmas Catholics aren't priest material. It's gotta be something else. I mean, did his dick fall off or something?"

She shrugged. It didn't seem like *such* a crazy idea to Mary-Beth. Philip was forever looking for something purposeful, something to stick with. He'd had girlfriends in the past, but what did she know about those relationships? And for some reason, it wasn't so hard to imagine Philip in those robes, praying quietly. It was possible.

JJ got out of bed and angrily pulled a pair of shorts on. "I think you're wrong. I think this is one of his little whims, and I'm not indulging it."

"I guess we'll just have to wait and see." Mary-Beth could hear the sound of feet padding downstairs and the gas stove clicking on. A distant coffeepot gurgled enticingly. "Did your dad ever get an answer from DC about the power?"

JJ rubbed his temples. "Yeah, it was almost certainly an attack on the grid. Apparently, it was supposed to be more widespread, but it was thwarted before it could affect other regions. They think it's a terrorist organization working out of Europe. That's all I know."

"Oh my gosh, JJ. Is it safe to travel? The boys leave today."

He nodded. "I know. And my father assured me that there is no indication of other attacks planned. The threat level has been raised as a precaution, but no one seems to expect anything more. Security will probably be higher at the gates, but that's it."

Mary-Beth swallowed and studied her husband.

Later that day, Lucas and Cameron would be on their way to Barcelona with the rest of their varsity soccer team. They were joining high school teams from upscale suburbs around the world to participate in a weeklong soccer clinic with the promise of some one-on-one coaching from the FC Barcelona players themselves. It was the sort of thing that Mary-Beth still found ludicrously extravagant, but she wouldn't dare be the only parent at Our Lady of Mercy High School who denied her children the experience. And so, after coughing up four thousand dollars, they were preparing to ship their sons off to Spain.

"I don't like this, JJ."

He went to his wife on the bed. "I know. I don't like it,

either, but they've been waiting all year for this. The trip is still on. All their teammates will be there."

"Are you sure they're still going?"

"Yeah, the coach sent a confirmation email last night. They're going to Barcelona."

She nodded. "Okay."

"What time is the flight again?"

"It's this afternoon, but we should leave soon if we're going to get to Boston in time to get through international departures. The rest of the team is flying out of Dulles, but the boys will meet them at the gate in Madrid for the final leg."

JJ nodded apologetically. "Right. Sorry, I knew that. I'll go wake them up. You want me to take them and skip golf?"

What Mary-Beth wanted was for them all to drive to Boston together, to have a few more hours with her family intact before she sent her children to a foreign land. She was about to cut off two limbs and kiss them goodbye for ten days, and it didn't seem like too much to ask to have her husband there with her.

What JJ wanted, as usual, was to be accommodating. He hated to disappoint her. But they were already there, in the grip of the Bright family, and JJ's loyalty was divided.

"You go play golf with the guys," she said. "I'll take Lucas and Cam."

"You don't mind?"

"No, it's okay."

"I'll have breakfast with the boys now and give them a pep talk."

"It's fine. Maybe Ian will come with me."

"Perfect. Ian hates golf. Maybe invite Charlie's girl along, too?"

"Yeah, I could ask Chelsea." Mary-Beth didn't want to take Chelsea along. If she had to forfeit her husband, she at least wanted Ian to herself.

"Thanks again, honey."

"It's fine. Don't worry about it."

JJ pulled her in and kissed the top of her head. He smelled sour from last night's liquor.

As he left the bedroom, he yelled to their sleeping sons, "Airport shuttle leaves in an hour, guys!"

Mary-Beth showered and dressed in the upstairs bathroom. She could hear the house waking up around her. In her real life, she'd be the first person up, the one to start the coffee and get the paper. She liked having the quiet dawn all to herself in her clean kitchen. But here, she was little more than a ward, a kid at summer camp. She didn't have to worry about whether there were enough eggs in the fridge or the bagels had gone stale. She wasn't even sure she knew how the coffee machine worked. It was at once freeing and suffocating.

When Mary-Beth got downstairs, Patty was buttering toast at the counter while the rest of the group quietly nursed coffees at the kitchen table. Through the window, she could see John Senior stacking cut wood against the wall of the garage while Farah filmed. She was pretty sure that John usually paid someone to deliver and stack the wood.

Ian looked up from a newspaper. He was dressed and notably fresher than the others. "Long night for the party boys, apparently."

"So I heard." Mary-Beth poured coffee into a mug and then picked up the national section of the *New York Times*. There were apparently still hundreds of thousands of people without power in New England. The faces of children sitting on a city stoop outside an unlit apartment building looked back at her. The headline read: "Cyberattack Contained. Government Officials Say No Immediate Concerns in Aftermath."

Patty put a steaming platter of eggs on the table and sat down. "You're all still going golfing with your father, right?"

JJ, Spencer and Charlie nodded into their coffees. Philip had the largest bags under his eyes, but he was smiling. Chelsea was there, looking hungover herself, which meant that she had stayed up, too.

Mary-Beth remembered those early days, when she did that one-of-the-guys thing and went along on every Bright brother adventure. It had been fun and spontaneous, until it wasn't anymore. Eventually, she started to feel extraneous, nonessential to the fun. All the extras stop following the Bright brothers around eventually—not that Mary-Beth was sad about it. It was a relief, in fact, to stop pretending that she wanted to take the paddleboards out for a midnight adventure, or have another tequila shot or rent paintball guns on a Saturday afternoon. Being one of the guys had always seemed to her an annoying by-product of misguided feminism. Chelsea seemed like just the type to perpetuate it. But she didn't blame her for it, not in the early stages of this relationship. Everyone starts out that way with the Bright boys.

Lucas and Cameron walked through the kitchen with full suitcases and sleepy eyes.

"Guys, throw those in the trunk and then come have some breakfast."

They grunted and went outside.

Patty reached across the table and patted Mary-Beth's hand. "Don't worry about the twins. They're going to have a great time on this trip."

Mary-Beth nodded. "I know they will. I always feel nervous before things like this. They've just never gone *this far*. I'm entitled to be a little nervous."

"Well, sure. Especially with everything that's going on in the world."

JJ looked up from the sports section and caught Mary-Beth's eye.

She felt a lump forming in her throat.

Patty pressed on. "Especially given the power outage, and all this talk of terrorism. I just mean…it's understandable to feel nervous. I'm sure I would."

The lump in her throat was expanding to a grapefruit. Mary-Beth had been holding it all together, reminding herself of all the ways in which this was a great experience for her children and a worthwhile headache for her. She knew she couldn't keep them in her orbit forever. They were sixteen—a number that could sound shockingly high or low, depending on the context. But this, from her mother-in-law now, was almost enough to unravel her.

JJ put his fork down. "Did dad hear something new about the power outage? Has anything changed, Mom?"

Patty shook her head. "No, it's the same as it was last night. They don't know who did it, but it was definitely something nefarious."

Ian folded his section of the paper. "The world isn't any more dangerous today than it was yesterday." He gave his mother-in-law a pointed look. "And the FAA said flights are all on schedule, as usual."

Patty nodded and said not a word more. She listened to Ian more than she listened to Mary-Beth, which Mary-Beth suspected had something to do with a Y chromosome. She tried not to hold that against Ian.

Mary-Beth and JJ looked at each other from across the table. *Our children will be fine*, they silently agreed. She wished he was coming with her to the airport, but she wasn't going to make a big thing of it. *Our children will be fine.*

Twenty minutes later—after grandparent kisses, a run through the packing list, a round of preemptive warnings from JJ about drinking in foreign countries, and some unhelpful advice from Uncle Charlie regarding the liberated at-titudes of European girls—they were off, driving east along I-90 toward Logan International Airport.

Mary-Beth was at the wheel of the SUV with Ian beside her in the passenger seat. Chelsea, who had reluctantly agreed to come along at Charlie's encouragement, was in the back seat with the boys. Her forehead was pressed against the window, and her eyes were closed behind enormous sunglasses. Even hungover and asleep, she was maddeningly pretty.

Ian didn't say anything for a while, out of respect for Mary-Beth's apparent anxiety. They watched the hot pavement un-fold at high speed, listening only to the distant buzz of music coming through the twins' headphones.

"Tell me not to worry," Mary-Beth finally said as they passed Springfield.

"Don't worry."

She squinted into the sun.

"Really. There's nothing to worry about—nothing beyond the normal parent stuff."

Mary-Beth sighed.

"Would it make you feel better if we stopped at the little airport church and said a few prophylactic Hail Marys? You know—Our Lady of the Orderly Tarmac, or whatever."

"My mother always stopped in those airport churches. I loved them." She smiled. "Saint Ignatius of the Window Seat."

"Immaculate Heart of the First Class Lounge. The Cathe-dral of Complimentary Drinks."

She was laughing harder now. "Stop. Our brother-in-law is about to become a priest. I'm not sure we can joke about things like that."

"Then we'd better get it all out of our system now."

"Seriously, though. What did you think of Philip's an-nouncement? Do you think he meant it?"

"Who knows with Philip. He might be serious."

Mary-Beth looked in her rearview mirror to be sure the back seat wasn't listening. They were not.

"Well, is anyone going to ask him about it? JJ said it didn't come up last night. Can you believe that?"

"Are you really surprised?" Ian pressed buttons on the console until he found the air-conditioning. "I'm not. These people have Olympic medals in avoidance. They can go weeks before they say a word that means anything to each other. But I'll tell you, this Philip announcement isn't going away. He seemed really serious. And you know it's *killing* Patty. They're going to have to talk this one out."

Bouncing all this off Ian—a sane person, an extra—was a relief for Mary-Beth. The opacity of the Bright brothers' relationship was an enduring mystery to her. She had nothing to compare it to as an only child, but she suspected that most siblings had more beneath the surface of their relationships. There should be boundless loyalty, or simmering rage or cancerous regret. All of those things seemed like reasonable feelings for people with whom you shared a mother and father and childhood home. By her reasoning, the least plausible opinion for someone to hold about their siblings was uncomplicated contentment. No one just *likes* their siblings. But the Bright brothers all liked one another just fine, and it didn't seem right to her.

There had been moments in the past that served for Mary-Beth as little glimpses into darker corners of their familial memories, things that the Brights had edited from their canon of stories and their collective understanding of who they were. The Brights worked hard to ignore the dark corners, but they couldn't erase them entirely. Even if everyone silently conspired to forget them.

They couldn't erase the fact that one Thanksgiving, years

ago, Charlie had punched Spencer in the face and broken his nose. And they couldn't erase the fact that when they were in high school, JJ had walked in on Spencer engaging in a sex act with JJ's best friend. And it was still devastatingly true that JJ had once observed his father having cocktails with a woman who was not their mother at a Washington bar, and that when he reported this to his brothers they laughed off any possibility of their father having an affair, although it was utterly clear to JJ that an affair is precisely what he'd witnessed. Those things had all happened, and Mary-Beth wouldn't be complicit in their erasure.

All of those true stories—the multitude of stories she'd never know—should have been fodder for sibling angst, for the pain that accompanied all the joy. And that was sometimes what Mary-Beth craved from these people. Mary-Beth just wanted all of the trappings of a big, boisterous familial experience, and then she wanted to die feeling like she'd lived family life to the very fullest, and that the immense joy had made all the pain worthwhile. Without the pain, there was nothing to measure the pleasure against.

"These people..." Ian said, shaking his head. Only Ian understood how it was possible to love a human so thoroughly and also be driven to near insanity by his family's tendency to bury all unpleasantness. Ian knew.

"JJ was really mad about this priest idea," Mary-Beth said.

"Spencer was, too."

"Why do you think it bothers them so much?"

Ian raised his eyebrows conspiratorially. "I think it all seems a little too...ethnic."

"What on earth does that mean?"

"Oh, you know what I mean. The Brights, with their Anglicized name and their WASPy tastes...their *sailing*."

Mary-Beth burst out laughing, causing all three passengers in the back seat to look up at her briefly. "Are you serious?"

"I'm dead serious, Mary! Senator Bright might invoke his Irish roots on the campaign stump in Southie, but he hasn't been to Mass on a non-Christmas day since he was in high school. He's been kind of phasing religiosity out."

"That's basically what JJ said. But I just figured the church doesn't mean anything to him anymore. I thought it was kind of organic."

Ian shook his head, entirely sure of the point he was about to make. "I don't think that's it. I don't think John Senior even knows what he believes. He's too calculating about his image to believe anything. There is no inner John Bright. There is only John Bright the public figure. He is whatever he chooses to project. John Bright is the sentient version of his own resume."

Mary-Beth sighed in agreement.

"My point is," he went on, "it's unfashionable. Church on Christmas is fine, but it's unfashionable in certain circles to be too intense about it. The Brights think about things like that…even our husbands, whether they know it or not, are very aware of that stuff."

Mary-Beth had never relied on her own ability to recognize what was and was not fashionable, but the suggestion that her Catholicism wasn't came as a slightly bitter surprise. She didn't attend Mass regularly, either, but she still prayed. She still genuflected when an ambulance passed and avoided taking the Lord's name in vain. She still felt a little tugging in her heart when she encountered an old nun in a habit, and she made vague plans to give up meat each Lent even if she didn't do it. Catholicism was to Mary-Beth an old blanket that could comfort or itch like hell, but it was a part of her identity. And she liked the fact that her boys were at a Catholic school, even if the reasons for it were mostly academic. Her husband had no such relationship to the religion he'd passively inherited, but it hadn't occurred to her that he was embarrassed by it.

"I don't know, Ian."

He shrugged. "I don't want to overstate the point. I just think it makes them squirm a little... John and Patty just want four children with normal jobs that pay in social currency and actual currency. That's their religion—currency."

"That may all be true. But I have a different theory." Mary-Beth kept her eyes on the road as she passed a Subaru with the glad head of a golden retriever sticking out the window. "I think it also makes them nervous in the way that Philip has always made them nervous—he's too good. He's so kind and nonjudgmental and guileless. Worst of all, he has never been impressed by John and Patty's accomplishments or their stuff. There's something about him that makes John and Patty feel kind of exposed, by comparison. And I think that effect would be amplified if he was a clergy member...assuming he would be the good kind, which *of course* he would be."

"*Of course.*" Ian thought about this for a moment. "Yeah, that's not a bad theory. But what about our husbands? Why do they care so much?"

"I really don't know. Everyone just feels tenser this summer."

"They certainly do."

Twenty minutes later, they were standing in the long TSA line at Logan International Airport. Cameron and Lucas had their carry-on suitcases and tickets in hand. They were dressed up for the occasion in new soccer jerseys and sneakers. Both were bouncing on their heels, nervous and excited to be free in the world, unconcerned about any recent global events.

Mary-Beth checked and rechecked the flight number. Everything was on time.

Uncle Ian consulted with an airline steward about where, precisely, the boys could find the rest of their soccer team when they arrived at their layover in Madrid.

And Chelsea had volunteered to fetch neck pillows from a nearby kiosk.

There was nothing left to do but rip this Band-Aid off.

"You both have passports and boarding passes?" Mary-Beth asked (again).

"Got it."

"Yes."

"And you're sure that Coach Brett is going to wait for you at your gate in Madrid?"

Lucas held up his phone, with a confirming text message from Coach Brett.

"Okay, bring it in," Ian said, holding his arm out for hugs from his nephews. They were both taller than him.

Mary-Beth's eyes filled.

The boys hugged Ian, one after the other, as travelers jostled them from every side.

"Don't pick up any bad footballer habits," Ian instructed.

The boys smiled impatiently.

And then it was Mary-Beth's turn. She reached up to Cameron and put her hands on both sides of his smooth face.

He kissed her forehead and said, "Don't worry, Mom. It's going to be fine."

Lucas put an arm around her and pulled her toward him. She leaned into his strong teenage body, adult in every way but still smelling like the bath soap she'd been buying for him since he was a baby.

"We love you, Mom."

And then the tears came—not a lot, but enough to spill

over onto her cheeks and make Mary-Beth wish that she had the will to contain them, to save them up for only truly sad or miraculous moments. She didn't want to be the kind of woman who cried at all the mundane little turns in life, but she found herself crying fairly often these days. It was just that her boys were so big, and still so baby-faced, and she couldn't reconcile her helplessness in time's passing. And the sentiment itself was embarrassingly trite, but knowing that didn't mitigate the heartache of it one bit.

"I love you guys."

They turned and filed into the bustling security line, looking back once more for a final, half-assed wave.

"C'mon," Ian said, putting an arm around Mary-Beth and leading her back toward the sliding doors. "They're just going on vacation."

She laughed and wiped the running mascara from beneath her eyes. "I know, this is ridiculous."

Mary-Beth could feel Chelsea trailing behind them, trying to keep her distance from all this emotion.

As they were about to walk through the automatic doors toward the parking garage, all three of them turned to the wall of television screens to their right.

The CNN crawl read: "No leads yet in the North American blackout. US and European security officials in talks now."

Mary-Beth paused to read it again.

"That doesn't mean anything," Ian said, pulling her shoulders through the door. "Let's go."

They walked out into the hot summer air. Mary-Beth tried to breathe, but it felt too thick. Maybe she was making a mistake in letting the boys go. Maybe there really was something to be nervous about with these blackouts. And why would they put news programs on in airports? Aren't people nervous enough?

"Crazy world," Chelsea said to no one in particular. "I guess this is just the kind of thing that happens now."

Mary-Beth glared at Chelsea, who looked suddenly apologetic. She hadn't wanted to bring her, didn't want to make the effort to know Charlie's latest in an endless string of flings. And now Mary-Beth wished she'd spoken up and left her behind. She decided that she didn't like this Chelsea one bit.

12

The inside of the *gelateria* was cool and unhurried. An antique fan blew gentle air down on Farah as she paid for her salted caramel in a cup. She thanked the young woman at the counter and took her gelato back outside, navigating her way through the iron bistro furniture until she picked a private table at the far corner of the patio. She sat down under the shaded dapple of a tree and watched people walk up and down the main street of the little New England town. This is where she would be living for the next three weeks.

Farah took it all in as if through a lens for later viewing. She had become accustomed to seeing everything as an unattached outsider, even when she wasn't behind the camera. It afforded her a powerful sort of invisibility in the world, as a chronicler of the human condition, above and apart from it. It could be lonely at times, but more often it was a comfort to wrap herself in the job, the work, the invisibility.

From where she sat, Farah could see a handmade-jewelry shop, an art gallery and a home goods store. Flowers sat in pots along the sidewalk, and a banner hung across the main street announcing next week's road race. Distant baroque music was emanating pleasantly from invisible orifices along the street. Well-heeled retired couples, families and chic artist-musician types ambled by. So many unhurried people in this unhurried corner of America.

Who was working? Farah wondered. High school students were working at the gelato place, artsy middle-aged ladies were working in the bespoke shops, and passing men in six-hundred-dollar loafers appeared to be working as they spoke confidently into their cell phones. But still, Farah didn't see a single person doing a job here that would pay enough to live in this town. It was one of those places, she decided, where the money drifts down from the highest limbs of family trees. It gets made elsewhere and spent here. That was the view from Main Street, anyway.

At least in New York, people are honest about it all. Farah appreciated the honesty of the ambition, greed and raw materialism that turned New York's wheels. The money in this place (and places like it) was impenetrable and mysterious. No one here behaved like people trying to *make* money, and that was the difference: the money had already been made. It was now just old money growing new money. It was pretty, but Farah didn't think it was good. Maybe one day she would make a documentary about that.

Farah took out her phone and punched in her boss Wayne's number. She needed to touch base with him. So far today she'd gotten an hour's worth of footage at the golf course—useless, boring footage—and about twenty minutes of Patty's quest for the perfect cucumber at the farmer's market. None of it was worth much.

She needed some direction from Wayne because so far this

documentary was beginning to feel like a dead end. Save for a few moments of drama—the Senator taking charge of the blackout and the youngest son's peculiar dinner-table announcement about joining the priesthood—it all seemed too sleepy so far.

She'd worked on enough of these projects to know when something was about to go south. There had been a pilot show they'd done on lobstermen on Cape Cod, which sounded amazing until it became apparent that the sea spray would make almost all their footage useless. After that, there was a documentary about the steelworkers union that everyone was excited about, but none of the men wanted to talk while the cameras were on. You don't always know what you've got until you start filming, but Farah had learned that you have to be willing to admit when you've got nothing. Better to cut your losses early than try to sell a stinker after you blew your whole budget.

The receiver clicked on the other end. "Wayne here."

"Hey, it's me."

"Oh, hey, how are things going up there? You getting some good stuff on L.L.Bean's darker side?"

Farah sighed. "Not even close. Wayne, these people are sooo polished. They've been in the public eye too long for this to work. Plus, they're boring! All they do is golf and garden and do sporty water things." Farah pushed a scoop of gelato into her mouth. "The worst thing is that they're really nice to each other."

Wayne listened.

"They're polite, and for the most part, it seems like they're genuinely happy people."

"Hmm."

"There's *no way* all this niceness is real. There's definitely some tension surrounding their son Philip, who wants to be a priest. But so far, I haven't observed any family confrontation, weird habits, hidden secrets or hidden bodies. What should I do?"

Wayne readjusted at the other end of the line, and Farah imagined him putting his filthy sneakers up on his desk, the way he does. "Okay, first, chill out. You don't need to pin this all down in the first week. Just wait. Be invisible. Keep watching them. And take a deep breath."

"Yeah, okay."

"Keep your eye out for anything that hints of family discord or philosophical inconsistency—anything John Bright would want to hide from his constituents. That's what we want. And it won't just smack you in the face. These people are too practiced for that. You'll just get a whiff of something unsavory, and then it's your job to follow the scent."

"Follow the scent. Okay."

"Just capture it all. Don't worry about what it means yet or how it will be pieced together. The writers and editors will do that on the other end. Your job is the same as it always is—follow your nose and be everywhere. You know how to do this, Farah."

She took a calming breath and another bite of ice cream. She did know how to do this. If she got the right footage, took smart notes and listened to her instincts, she would go back to New York with all the raw material they needed to make this into something great.

"And Farah, you might try befriending them a little, in the interest of blending. Don't get too close, but you know, make them comfortable."

"I guess I haven't really done that yet."

"And maybe get some fresh air for yourself. Take one of those paddleboards out now and then, because you seem like you're wound extra tight lately."

She scooped gelato from the bottom of the cup. "I don't think I brought a bathing suit."

"Fine, whatever. But remember this—everybody breaks down eventually. Your senator is overdue for some kind of emotional response since his retirement. If you're there long enough, they will forget that you're there, and they will start acting normal. That's when you'll get the good stuff. Maybe— God willing—he's a secret gambler, or he's into bondage or he's leaking government secrets to the Russians."

"One can hope."

"And remember—we're just looking for human frailty. It doesn't have to be explosive. It just has to be genuine. That's not so hard to get. It will come out eventually."

She sucked the last drops of gelato from the cup. "Frailty, right."

"Just be patient."

"Thank you, Wayne. Promise me I won't get fired if these people don't turn out to be interesting."

"They will be. Everyone is."

"I don't know about that. You should see this place. It's like the opening scene of every horror movie. It's perfect."

He rustled papers, signaling the end of this discussion. "Farah, please try to relax. You're in a beautiful place in the dead of summer. Try enjoying yourself! Put on a pair of shorts, for fuck's sake."

"You know I won't do that. Even for you."

"You're the best, Farah. Gotta run to a meeting, though. Good luck!"

"You, too. Thanks, Wayne."

Farah put her phone back into her pocket and considered the ways in which she did and did not love Wayne. He'd been her boss for four years, and she wanted always to work with him. He was thirteen years her senior, and he was almost certainly a little infatuated with her. She cultivated his infatuation in fairly obvious ways, which afforded her a longer rope at work, but she'd also become a damn good videographer and producer under his guidance. They worked well together. At this point, Wayne was a mentor, friend and a back-burner possibility as a lover—but only on the *way* back burner. That would be a dumb path to go down, mainly because things were just right as they were now. Farah was glad to have Wayne on the other end of the phone for this project. And she needed him. For the first time since she started this job, she was genuinely concerned about screwing it up.

A teenage boy walked by with a fiddle under his arm. After him came a thirtysomething guy pushing a toddler in a stroller. Both were licking ice cream cones. Wind rustled an American flag above. *Jesus, this place*, Farah thought.

And then, walking right along the sidewalk with all the beautiful people, appeared Philip Bright.

"Philip, hi!" Farah waved from her table.

He turned, smiled and walked toward her. He was carrying a small shopping bag in one hand with a book peeking out.

"Hey there," he said. "Glad to see you getting some time for yourself. It's a nice little village, isn't it?"

"Yeah, it's really something. You want to sit?" She pointed to the seat across the table and he gladly accepted.

Farah hadn't really talked to Philip yet. Her focus had been on capturing the group dynamic thus far, and she hadn't talked with any of the Bright siblings one-on-one.

"So how long has your family been coming here?"

Philip thought for a moment. "Twenty-six years. My dad bought this place a year or two after I was born. He wrote a book about revitalizing local economies around that time, and it hit the bestseller list. They bought the lake house after that. It's a nice place to visit, but it's not really my cup of tea," Philip added, scratching a puffy insect bite on his forearm.

"Why not?"

"I don't know. This always felt like my dad's turf. What do you think of this place?"

"It's a little quiet for my taste." Farah pointed at the bag in Philip's hand. "What book did you buy?" she asked him.

"Oh, this is a book about soup."

She laughed.

"No, really. It's a book of soup recipes. At the seminary I'll be attending in the fall, we share cooking duties. I'm not a very good cook, but I thought soup might be a good place to start."

Farah studied him. "Yeah, it probably is. Casseroles, too. I bet you could really feed a crowd on casseroles."

"Ah, good thinking!"

Farah wanted to ask him more about these plans. She had no opinion on them, but it was clear from his announcement two days before that they were a source of intense family emotions. She decided to wait for it to unfold when the cameras were rolling.

"Can I ask you a question, Philip?"

He scratched his forearm again, and a tiny bead of blood appeared on the raw skin. He was utterly unselfconscious about it. "Of course. What's your question?"

"Why did your family agree to let me follow you all around with cameras? I mean, I understand why your dad did. No offense, but politicians rarely say no to things like this. And, to be clear, I'm incredibly grateful that he did agree to it. But what's in it for the rest of you?"

Philip took a long breath. "To be perfectly honest, I doubt most of us thought very hard about it. There's a certain amount of transparency that goes along with having a senator father, so it probably didn't seem all that novel. Maybe my brothers liked the idea of it a little, too. I get the sense that both JJ and Spencer are at career plateaus. And Charlie…" He smiled. "Charlie can't walk past a toaster without glimpsing at his own reflection."

"And what about you?"

"Actually, I didn't agree. I didn't know about it until I arrived."

Oh no. Had they forgotten a form or skipped over a legal requirement? This was a lawsuit waiting to happen. Farah wasn't in charge of these things, but she understood their necessity.

"It's okay, though," Philip assured her. "I don't mind doing it for my dad."

"Philip, if this was a misstep on our end, I'm really, *really* sorry. We can make this right."

"Don't worry about it." He waved it away with a hand. "It probably wasn't anything on your end. I haven't spoken much with my family over the past few years, and they might have just omitted it. I've just been kind of on my own journey. They give me space and I try to be accommodating. It works for us. Families are funny like that."

"Yeah, I guess they are." Farah wasn't sure how to feel about this information. Had Philip's father intentionally left him out of these discussions? It seemed incongruous with the Bright worldview. It seemed mean.

"I do have one request," he said, more serious now.

"Yes?"

"May I have a private place, a place where the cameras never go? For prayer, I mean."

"Yes, of course! I guess no one went over the parameters of this agreement with you, but we have all that stuff worked out. Bathrooms and bedrooms are off-limits unless verbal permission is granted at the time. You can make arrangements for private visits with outsiders if you need to. My personal rule is that kids get special treatment. If one of your nephews has a meltdown, I don't want to further humiliate him. Let me think...there are a few other exceptions."

"That's good, but I'm talking about some outside space. I was thinking maybe that big oak tree in the backyard, the one near the beach. Could that be a no-camera zone?"

Farah liked that tree. It looked good when she panned, and she envisioned it as part of the opening credits for whatever this thing turned out to be. But it was the least she could do, considering. "Of course, yes."

"Just when I'm under it, obviously. I'll just need privacy when I'm there doing my thing." Philip looked deeply apologetic about this modest request.

"No problem. The oak tree is—from here on out—the privacy tree."

He smiled. "Thank you."

"It's the least I can do." She stood up. "Anyway, I should get back to the house before everyone returns. Where are you parked?"

"Oh, I didn't bring a car."

"You walked here? It's, like, four miles."

He shrugged. "Yeah, nice day for it. But I'd be happy to accept a ride home."

"Great, my car's just up the road."

They strolled along the sidewalk to her car under the bluebird sky. Philip's arms swung jauntily at his sides. Farah liked the feel of his height beside her. She liked his openness and the pleasure he seemed to draw from nearly everything. He lacked a certain finesse that the rest of the Brights had mastered, and the absence of it was charmingly genuine.

"Oh, hey Philip?"

"Yeah?"

"Maybe you should look into pasta salads, too. You know, for feeding a crowd. Pasta salads could be good."

He thought about it and then nodded. "Yes, that's a great idea. Thank you for thinking of it."

"No problem."

They walked mostly in silence after that, under the bright sun, and Farah felt an inexplicable sense of gladness possess her.

13

"Pizza's here!" Patty appeared on the back deck carrying three large cardboard boxes of farm-to-table flatbreads and set them out before the group.

All the Brights and their partners were there, drying out in bathing suits and beach towels in the early-evening sun.

It had been a proper start to summer for all of them. After the morning golf excursion (for the Bright men) and the drive to Logan Airport (for Mary-Beth, Ian and Chelsea), they reconvened at the waterfront for hours of play. Mary-Beth had finally read her book in a lounge chair—fitfully, her anxiety over her children never abating. JJ, Spencer and Ian had taken the Sunfish out. Charlie and Chelsea had canoed to a semi-private sandbar at the eastern edge of the lake to "find some privacy." And Philip, wearing a floppy fisherman's hat and a copious slathering of zinc on his nose, went solo kayaking.

Farah had captured it all from behind her camera. It was a

nice place to spend her afternoon, though the quietness of the footage continued to stress her out. *Just wait*, Wayne had said. But she didn't want to wait. She imagined footage of these lovely people engaged in wholesome outdoor activities piling up like analog film ribbon in her mind, hundreds of hours of pristine country vistas, looping stock footage and screen saver material. It was beautiful junk, but still junk.

"Farah, put that phone away and have a slice," Patty instructed as she unloaded a tray full of ice teas.

"Thank you." Farah did as she was told. She was starving.

Patty smoothed the slim-fitting linen sheath she was wearing with one hand and addressed the group. "So this fundraiser shouldn't last more than a few hours. Sorry we have to leave you on your second night here, but as you know, this is one of the causes I work on all year. We'll be just a few miles down the road at Tanglewood."

Charlie took a chair at the table. "Don't worry about us, Mom."

"Mary-Beth," she said, pointing a finger, "keep an eye on these guys."

Mary-Beth forced an annoyed smile at her mother-in-law.

Minutes later, Patty and John Senior were off to their event.

Farah took her pizza and sat on a bench along the edge of the deck. She wanted to be there with them, but not *too* there.

At the table, tanned limbs reached for slices, napkins and cold beverages in ice-filled cups. People were talking over one another and laughing easily. They were kids home alone now, kids with faint crow's-feet. It was the regressive power of summer and fond memories. Farah didn't understand much about the Brights, but this energy she understood, and it made her pine for her own siblings and her childhood home in New Jersey.

"Okay, Phil," Spencer said, as he wiped his hands on a

napkin. "Mom and Dad are gone and it's time to get the real story. Are you seriously going to be a priest?"

Everyone quieted. Farah's handheld camera sat inert at the table, but the one mounted above them was still on. They seemed to have forgotten about that one.

Philip smiled and placed his pizza gently down on the plate in his lap. "Sure, okay. Thanks for asking."

Philip took a breath, and it was clear to Farah that he moved way too slow for this family. Their bated breath was noticeably impatient.

"Well, as you know, I spent much of the past year traveling with this international assistance group. It was actually a mission project, which I can tell you about, too, if you want to know. Anyhow, I got involved with a Catholic Workers group in Ecuador and had some pretty life-changing experiences in Colombia helping to build housing for poor families. We flew to West Africa after that for a hunger relief project, which is where I gave all my stuff away. Let's see, I did a month-long vow of silence in Angola."

JJ furrowed his brow and Mary-Beth put a quieting hand on his thigh.

"I did a lot of reading and a lot of soul-searching through all this and…well…" Philip looked dreamily at the water as everyone waited. "I figured a lot of things out. It was transcendent."

"And that means you have to become a priest?" Charlie asked.

Philip shook his head. "No. There are a number of paths I could go down from here. But this is the path I *want* to go down. I'm not coming to this lightly. I've done my research."

Farah quietly set her plate down and picked up the handheld camera beside her.

"Have you even read the Bible, Phil?" Spencer asked.

"Of course I have. Several times."

"And you agree with everything in it?"

"I'm not sure that's the right question. I do find inspiration in it."

Charlie jumped in. "But how can you square your political views with the church's? What about homosexuality, divorce and the rest? How are you going to defend all that?"

"I can't defend it. Those are the things about the church that I will resist and try to be a voice for change. But they're not the only things that define the church. I'm interested in serving the poor and comforting the afflicted."

Charlie snorted.

Mary-Beth, Ian and Chelsea all kept quiet. This interrogation was for blood only.

Then it was JJ's turn: "Well, what about sex, Phil? Sex for you."

"I've had sex," he said, a little defensively. "I enjoyed it."

"And you think you can just stop having it?"

"I think I might be able to. JJ, I'm not saying this is for everyone, but I think it's what I need."

JJ shook his head. "Abstinence will be harder than you think. It makes people do bad, perverted things."

"I've actually been abstinent for over a year now," Philip said.

Spencer smirked. "Voluntarily?"

Philip didn't bite.

"Don't you ever just want someone to…" Charlie elected not to finish the sentence before the camera, but everyone got the gist.

"Sure, but that feeling passes."

"Not for me it doesn't."

"Charlie, I don't think I ever wanted that as much as you do," Philip said. "It's probably an easier thing for me to live without."

"Well, what about jerking off?" Spencer asked.

"It happens. I'm not a saint."

Spencer nodded, closing his case. Ian gave him a stern look. Chelsea picked cheese off her pizza, her eyes down.

Farah was relieved to have the camera to hide behind at that moment.

Charlie leaned back in his chair and laced his fingers behind his head. "Vow of abstinence, my ass. You're just the same Phil you always were."

Philip smiled this time. "Yes, I am! That's the fucking point!"

And with that, they all laughed. JJ landed a brotherly slap on Philip's back, and the tension was broken again. Farah could see now what she hadn't seen before: the connective tissue of high standards and parental expectations, a shared anxiety about deviating too far from the mean. Also, love among brothers.

"I'm going for a swim," Chelsea announced, placing her oil-stained paper plate before her. She looked at Charlie. "You coming?"

Charlie nodded and stood up.

After that, the pizza party broke up. JJ and Spencer went inside. Mary-Beth and Ian began stacking greasy plates and consolidating the leftover slices. Philip took the extra pizza boxes to the garage.

"Why do they always do this to him?" Mary-Beth whispered when Philip was out of earshot. She seemed to have forgotten about Farah at the other end of the deck.

Ian shook his head. "Because it's easier, I think. They all turn back into insecure little boys around John Senior, and it's easier to take it all out on weird little brother Phil than to ever confront their father."

"Well, Phil isn't weird or little anymore."

Ian caught sight of Farah and gave Mary-Beth an expression of warning. "It's like they can't help themselves. And Philip makes it too easy."

Mary-Beth nodded and said nothing more.

Farah panned out toward the water, where Charlie and Chelsea were laughing and splashing each other. Her legs were wrapped around his waist, his hand down the backside of her bikini bottom. They kissed and whispered. Farah noticed both Mary-Beth and Ian watching them from the deck. It was hard not to. And it seemed impossible that the couple wasn't aware of everyone's eyes on them. It might have been, at least in part, for the audience.

For as long as she could remember, Farah had wanted to film people. She taped her siblings' school plays, holiday gatherings and dorm room shenanigans. She saved up for better cameras and pored over techy catalogs. Even now, when you can make a pretty good movie with a cheap little digital device, she preferred the technical variation and specificity that the high-end cameras allowed for. It was never about the post-production or the screening for her; it was about the filming. The power and control of being the one doing the watching was so alluring to her. She couldn't imagine why everyone didn't want to do it. But everyone didn't. Most people, Farah had come to realize, wanted to be watched.

Exhibitionism was a gross impulse to Farah, a contemporary sickness. But if it was a sickness, she was grateful to live through the epidemic. And if people were begging to be watched, she was ready to watch them. She liked the Brights already—it was hard not to—but their vanity gave her moral permission to record them.

She kept filming as Charlie kissed Chelsea's neck and she nibbled his shoulder.

The orange sun was moving down toward the tree line at

the western edge of the lake, casting a warm glow across the top of the still water. A lone kayaker from a different, less fabulous family cut across the liquid glass. Mary-Beth opened a bottle of wine and everyone made their way back to the deck. A thousand tiny sounds competed with each other in this, the quietest place Farah had ever been.

And then, on the other side of the house, a car barreled down the gravel driveway and skidded to a stop. They heard two car doors open, but never close.

JJ looked up. "Is that Dad's car?"

Patty and John Bright ran toward them from the driveway. John Senior got there first.

"Listen up," he yelled.

Everyone froze.

"There's been an attack in Spain."

Mary-Beth dropped the wine bottle with a thud on the oak planks.

"We don't have any details yet, but—"

"The boys," she whispered.

John Senior nodded. "They might be involved."

Garnet liquid raced across the planks of the deck, into the cracks and onto the virgin grass below.

14

Early-morning sun baked the bedroom that Mary-Beth and JJ had been tossing in, and the bedding had all been pushed to the floor. Twelve hours had passed since John Senior showed up at the house to inform them that there had been a terrorist attack at the Madrid airport. They had both aged a lifetime since then.

The boys were alive, but they were still so far away.

Mary-Beth wiped day-old mascara from the wet, tender skin beneath her eyes. She shook her head at her husband. "I can't go down there yet. Will you just sit with me for another minute?"

"I think they're waiting for us."

Mary-Beth didn't move. She kept returning to the moment the night before when they finally got the call from DC confirming that the boys were okay. They had been sitting around the horseshoe of couches in the living room waiting, crying and watching cable news. It felt like hours, but maybe it had been only minutes. John Senior took the call, and it was clear on his face within seconds that the boys were alive. He had put a hand on JJ's shoulder and squeezed, nodding. "They're okay," he'd said. "The bomb in the airport went off after their plane left the tarmac. They're alive."

Lucas and Cameron were alive. Mary-Beth had to say it to herself over and over again to remember that although it was unbearable to know that they were out in the world, this had been a good outcome. They were alive.

"Just sit another minute, JJ."

JJ nodded and sat back on the bed, the same one they always stayed in when they were at the lake house. It was the same bed the boys had been conceived in sixteen years before. They had been conceived on Christmas, after a long day of celebrating. JJ and Mary-Beth usually tried to avoid sex at his parents' house, but they were like magnets in those days, and resistance was futile. They'd exchanged gifts in private—a silk scarf for her and a knockoff briefcase for him—and then they slept together, within earshot of his brothers and their lovers, and that event cast them off on a new phase of life together. It was easy for Mary-Beth to remember how she'd felt that night, the levity of it all.

It was impossible to comprehend how they'd arrived at this point now, with her twin boys stranded in a foreign country after barely missing a terrorist attack, suited men from the FBI speaking in hushed tones downstairs.

What had Mary-Beth been thinking when she allowed her children to go on this trip? The physical tug of their absence suddenly pulled at her in a way that it hadn't in over a decade. It was the pain of swollen breasts that begged to be nursed, the panic of lost toddlers in a department store and the guilt of countless near tragedies that accumulate over a childhood.

Tumbles down a cement staircase, a sharp object in an electrical outlet, a bicycle veering into oncoming traffic—each one a searing reminder to never, ever take your eyes off your children for a second. The world is fraught with danger, and yet Mary-Beth had let her twins go.

She sat on the bed and buried her face in her husband's shirt. Mary-Beth just wanted to hear their voices, to have evidence that they were okay.

JJ held her tightly as muffled sobs shook them both. "They're safe, Mary. They're safe."

She came back up for air and rubbed her nose. "I know. I just can't stop thinking about everything that could have happened."

"Me, too."

She knew JJ was also suffering, reliving every horrible possibility they'd been forced to consider. They'd spent four full hours of the night losing their minds before anyone could tell them whether or not Cam and Lucas had still been at the Madrid airport when the bomb struck. When they finally got word that the soccer team was safely on its way to Barcelona by then, Mary-Beth was sure her heart would never beat regularly again. She was alive, but forever damaged.

"They're okay, Mary. They're at the hotel in Barcelona now. The boys' cell phones are in FBI custody for security reasons, but they're going to call with the landlines this morning. It shouldn't be long now."

She blew her nose into an overused tissue. "I know. You're right."

"For now, we should just go back downstairs and hear what the FBI agents have to say. I think they're waiting for us."

Mary-Beth had been crying on and off in the bedroom all morning. She'd held it together for a while after they learned that Cam and Lucas were okay, but eventually she needed to escape and purge all the emotion that had been building inside her through the night. Her children were alive, but the possibility of their deaths was still in her body. And so she'd cried and keened until it was all expelled. Now she was empty, but not recovered.

"But why are they here, JJ? Do you think it's a bad sign that the FBI are here?"

JJ had cried last night, too, wailed for a full minute. It wasn't as long or as loud as his wife, but it was terrifying for both of them to see him so unraveled.

"It's probably a formality or a courtesy because of Dad," he said. "Maybe that's all."

Mary-Beth didn't believe that and neither did her husband. She stood up from their bed and smoothed the wrinkled polo shirt she'd been wearing since yesterday. She again tried to wipe her smeared makeup from her cheeks. "Okay, I'm ready."

Downstairs, the rest of the Bright family was sitting on sofas, facing the two suited men in armchairs. Everyone was drinking coffee out of handmade mugs and engaging in strained small talk. No one had slept through the night, and everyone looked exceedingly tired.

The suited agents stood up when JJ and Mary-Beth entered the room.

"Mr. and Mrs. Bright," the first agent said, reaching a hand out for two quick shakes. "I'm sorry for the circumstances that bring us here. Very good to know your boys are safe."

JJ nodded. "Thank you for coming. So what's happening?" He sat at the edge of a couch cushion and leaned forward, elbows on knees.

Mary-Beth sat beside him.

The two men exchanged quick nods, and then the other agent jumped in. He was slightly younger, but with the same sharp haircut.

"Mr. and Mrs. Bright, we're from the National Security Branch of the FBI. Our primary function is to detect and disrupt threats to the US, both here and abroad. We have reason to believe that the attack in Madrid was politically motivated, that the perpetrators were targeting Westerners. It's still unclear who the specific target of this attack was."

John Senior put his mug down loudly. "You think Americans were being targeted in Spain? Are you talking about my grandsons?"

"Not necessarily, Senator. But we can't rule it out. Certainly, Europe was under attack here—there's little question about that. But organizations like the ones we suspect are responsible for this are always looking for the broadest possible reach. To hit Europe and the US with one strike would be highly efficacious from their perspective."

Spencer jumped in. "You think they were targeting the soccer team?"

"Possibly."

"So what does this mean for the boys?" JJ demanded. "Are they safe in Barcelona?"

"Yes, the whole team is on their way to the US consulate now, which is where they'll stay."

"For how long?" Mary-Beth asked, her voice hoarse.

"They'll have to wait until air traffic resumes in the region, which could be a few days. Could be a week. It's hard to say."

John pounded a fist into the coffee table. "Well, let's get a government plane in there!"

"I'm sorry, Senator, that's not going to be possible. We are working closely with Spanish and EU anti-terrorism authorities. These are close allies, and we defer to them on such matters. There can be no civilian air travel at this time."

"This isn't civilian air travel," John said. "These children are terrorism targets now!"

"We don't *know* that, sir. And until we do, they will receive the same treatment as the thousands of other air travelers who just missed this attack. There were a few other Americans on that flight, as well. They'll all be taking commercial aircrafts home, too."

John stood abruptly and walked to the kitchen to refill his mug. For as long as Mary-Beth had known him, he hadn't considered himself a mere civilian.

Spencer cut in again. "So I'm confused. Do you think this is a random attack on a group of American schoolkids? Is it a coincidence that two of them happen to be related to a former US senator?"

The older suit shook his head. "We don't know the answer to that. If the perpetrators didn't know that the Senator's grandsons were on this team, then it was probably a welcome surprise to them...no offense. But again—and I want to be clear about this—we don't know for sure whether US citizens or the plane your grandsons were on were being targeted. It's important that we not jump to conclusions. And it's very important that we not get out ahead of ourselves publicly. So, if you folks could be discreet about this for a while—try to avoid any press inquiries—we would appreciate it."

Mary-Beth, Ian and Philip nodded emphatically. The rest of the Brights made no such commitment.

Chelsea, who was at the far end of the couch looking tired, stared at her hands. She was as much a stranger to Mary-Beth as these FBI men.

Farah stood behind Chelsea, stick straight behind a camera on a tripod. The little red recording light was glowing out at them.

"Sorry, excuse me," Mary-Beth interrupted. "We should turn off the camera for now. Let's just keep them all off for the time being. Can we do that, please?"

Farah raised her eyebrows and looked at John Senior as he returned to the room. He shook his head and made a *don't mind her* look.

"Don't worry about the cameras," JJ said to his wife.

"What?"

"Mary-Beth, this was part of the deal. The cameras stay on," John Senior explained. "It's okay, Farah."

Mary-Beth made tight fists at her sides until her manicured fingernails were digging into the flesh of her palms. "I want the cameras off, JJ."

He turned to her. "I can't do anything about it, hon. We agreed to this. Let's just focus on Lucas and Cam."

Mary-Beth tried to breathe. Maybe it was true that they were contractually bound to have the cameras going, but it was also true that her husband and family could have stood up for her at that moment. They could have at least made an effort to request a moment of privacy on her behalf. They could have asked.

"Do we need some kind of security here?" Patty asked, moving on. "I mean, if this family was targeted in some way, are we in any danger?"

"We didn't say that you were targeted, necessarily, ma'am. And it's up to you whether or not to hire security. The federal government doesn't offer Secret Service protection to someone in your husband's position, but you might consider a private company."

"We'll get a few men out here," John said. He turned to the suits. "And let your bosses know that I am requesting a secure line of communication be set up with the most senior person in your division. I will want to speak directly with him."

They nodded politely, apparently accustomed to this variety of Washington bluster. "I'm sure *she'll* be happy to accommodate you."

"Fine, whatever," the Senator said. "Thank you for coming. Please keep me apprised of every development."

Spencer and JJ stood to shake the agents' hands and walk them outside.

Through the window, Mary-Beth could see her husband wipe sweat from his face with an open palm. Next to him, Spencer was talking with the agents and gesturing emphatically. It was a relief to have Spencer—a foreign-policy expert—here. He, and all the Bright brothers, could be trusted to fight for her family. They were good for things like that.

When the agents drove away in their black sedan, JJ and Spencer came inside, and everyone returned to their position on the living room sofas.

JJ sat beside Mary-Beth and rubbed her back forcefully. She struggled to keep from crying again. "What did they say?"

Spencer took the floor. "They don't know for sure, but this has all the signs of ISIS or a copycat group. They think the attackers made a last-minute attempt to change the location of the bomb once they learned that a bunch of American kids were passing through the airport. It wasn't part of their original plan, but in the end, they were likely targeting the soccer team. Thank God they screwed that part up."

"And what about Cam and Lucas?"

Spencer shook his head. "I don't think this has anything to do with them specifically. Given that the attackers didn't know there was an American team coming through until the last minute, it's almost impossible that they would have known the identities of the individual kids. No one would have had time to figure out that a former senator's grandkids were on the plane."

Mary-Beth exhaled. "That makes me feel a little better. Do you think it should?"

Ian nodded from another couch. "Yes, definitely. It means

no one is after them or their team in particular. It was just bad luck. Or, good luck, in a way."

Everyone quietly considered the direction of their luck.

"Does this have something to do with the power outage?" Philip asked.

"Yes," Spencer said. "They didn't realize it immediately, but now it looks like those were tests, to determine the most vulnerable targets."

"Oh no."

"Yeah."

At the far end of one couch, Chelsea began to snore. She'd nodded off with her head tilted back and her mouth wide open. Charlie nudged her softly and led her out of the room, upstairs to their bed.

"We should probably all try to sleep," John Senior said. "We can't stay awake forever."

JJ nodded. "You guys go rest. Mary and I will stay down here by the phone in case the boys call. We'll stretch out on the sofas for now."

Patty nodded and began walking around the room, pulling gauzy curtains together in an effort to block some of the morning light.

"This is going to be okay," Ian said, squeezing Mary-Beth's shoulder before he left.

She smiled weakly.

Philip went next, but instead of walking upstairs, he went through the back door, holding the screen carefully to prevent it from slamming.

When everyone else was gone, Farah turned off the camera. She walked straight up to Mary-Beth and JJ.

"I just want you to know that I'm so, so sorry," she said. And she looked it. Her large brown eyes—so exquisite up close—were red with exhaustion now, and puffy around the edges. "And also…if it's really important to you…I'll stop re-cording. This is real life. I get that. I'll turn the cameras off if you say so."

With this profoundly human acknowledgment, Mary-Beth felt the fat tears in her eyes spill over and down her cheeks. She leaned forward and, inexplicably, pulled Farah in, wrap-ping her arms around her for an awkward hug. She was sud-denly grateful to have this young stranger here with them, seeing her and her pain. And although she thought she should ask to have the cameras turned off until this ordeal was re-solved, she did not.

"Thank you," Mary-Beth said.

JJ nodded with her.

And then Farah was gone and they were alone together with their anxiety.

JJ went to the adjacent sofa and stretched out, his large head and mussed hair resting on an undersized throw pillow.

Mary-Beth tipped to one side and rested her own head on the tufted sofa arm. She pulled her legs up against her body. The softness of the couch against the massive weight of her exhaustion felt wonderful, but she didn't want to feel won-derful. She wanted to hear her sons' voices.

It was all so excruciating and also somehow expected. She had wasted all these years trying to power through her moth-erly anxieties and put on a brave face, when in fact she had been right all along: the world was fraught with danger. Her only mistake was in letting down her guard for a moment.

Mary-Beth had always understood that the depth of her love for her children was in direct proportion with the world's capacity to exact pain on her. The more she loved them, the more she could be hurt. The more joy she felt in their pres-ence, the more their absence would gut her. She felt sure now, as she looked directly at her pain, that this was the predominant experience of motherhood.

Sometimes, in their normal life in the suburbs of DC, Mary-Beth would walk down the street and look around at all the women who might be mothers themselves, and she would marvel at their collective functionality. All these mothers, just going about their day, chatting with each other, talking on the phone and strolling through the grocery store, as if they weren't haunted to a state of near paralysis by all the dangers that threaten to harm their offspring at every living moment. *Look at us!* she wanted to yell. *What a feat this is! We're alive and functioning!* She often thought there was no braver act than a mother waking up every day and pretending to live like an unburdened person.

Mary-Beth's eyes fluttered as she drifted in and out of a dreamless rest.

15

Mary-Beth jumped at the sound of the ringing phone. She banged her knee into the coffee table, hobbled to the kitchen and answered in a breathless panic. She had been asleep on the couch for just long enough to lose her bearings.

"Hello? Hello?"

"Mom?" It was Cameron's voice. "Mom, it's us. We're okay."

"Hi, Mom," Lucas said from beside him.

Mary-Beth gasped, the cordless phone pressed to her ear. "Oh God, I'm so glad to hear you guys. I love you. I'm so, so sorry about this."

"It's okay, Mom," Lucas assured her. "Don't be sorry. This isn't your fault."

JJ walked in and joined Mary-Beth on the floor, in a beam of late-morning sun. "Hey boys, it's Dad here, too. I love you both so much."

"Hi, Dad."

"We love you, too."

The boys didn't sound so bad. Mary-Beth thought this call would be worse, but they sounded okay.

"Where are you guys?" JJ asked.

"We're at the US consulate in Barcelona. It's a real fancy building, and there are guards out front. They have cots set up here for us to sleep on."

"There are guards out front?"

"Yeah, it's not so bad, actually. The food's okay, too."

"Oh, I'm so glad," Mary-Beth said. "Do you have everything you need?"

"I dunno. I guess," Lucas said. "We need to play soccer, but I don't know if that's going to happen now. No one will tell us what's going on with soccer camp."

"Honey, I don't think camp is happening anymore."

"Just stay inside and do exactly what the consulate tells you," JJ instructed. "We'll get you home as soon as we can."

There was a distant commotion on the other end, and Mary-Beth got the feeling there were others waiting to make calls.

"They took our cell phones," Lucas said.

JJ nodded. "We know. You'll probably get them back, but it will take a while."

"So we're all sharing, like, two landlines here. Actually, we should probably go. The rest of the guys are waiting to call their parents."

"Already?" Mary-Beth said.

"We'll call you tomorrow," JJ said. "Your grandfather has been in touch with the consulate, and they're going to make sure we stay in close contact. Boys, I want you to know that you're completely safe there and we'll get you home as soon as we can."

There was a pause.

"It was scary," Cameron said quietly. "We'd just taken off

the tarmac on the connecting flight when the bomb exploded back in the airport. We could hear it from the air."

"Everyone was freaking out on the plane," Lucas added. "Saying it was like it was 9/11 or something."

Mary-Beth closed her eyes and vowed silently to be strong, for at least as long as this call lasted. "You guys are safe, though. Remember that. You're safe and you're coming home."

"Yeah, okay. Well, we gotta go because everyone's waiting."

"We love you," JJ said. "You know how much we both love you."

He had never been afraid to say it; that was one of the wonderful things about JJ.

"Love you, too."

"Talk tomorrow."

"We'll get you home soon," she choked. "Be good."

"Bye, Mom."

And then they were gone.

JJ and Mary-Beth hoisted themselves up and hung the phone on its cradle. They looked around the kitchen. It was still littered with dishes from last night's dinner. Pizza grease shone in the sun streaming in from the windows. A collection of unused wineglasses huddled together. The clock said eleven, which meant that they'd been sleeping on the couch for three hours.

Mary-Beth still felt tired, but not as woozy and disoriented as she had earlier. Her boys were okay; they really were. She could breathe now.

JJ kissed the top of his wife's head, then went to the bathroom.

Patty and John Senior came down the stairs and looked expectantly at Mary-Beth.

"They're okay," she told them. "They're at the consulate and in pretty good spirits."

John Senior rubbed his face. "Good. I'm sorry we didn't get down fast enough to say hello."

"No, it's okay. They didn't have much time. It sounds like they're in good hands."

"They damn well should be," John Senior said, sitting down at the table and opening his laptop. His cell phone buzzed in his pocket. He glanced at it and dropped the call with one touch. Then it buzzed again, and he did the same. He was hammering away on the keyboard.

Patty started the coffee and began filling the dishwasher.

JJ walked past them, back into the living room, where he turned on the giant flat-screen TV on the wall.

Mary-Beth wasn't sure what to do with her useless body, so she went to her husband and the sounds of CNN voices in the living room. She sat down on the couch and looked up at the large TV screen mounted on the wall.

"Here's what we know so far," a smooth-haired woman said from a news desk. "Thirty-one people are confirmed dead from last night's terrorist attack at the Madrid–Barajas Airport. And that number is expected to rise significantly. The device used was a bomb hidden in a portable oxygen tank. It detonated in the main security line in the east wing of the airport. The man who detonated the bomb is among the dead. No terrorist organizations have taken credit for the attack yet, but officials say it has all the marks of ISIS. We'll keep you apprised of all developments as they come in."

The footage playing in the corner of the screen was a shaky cell phone video of a toddler dancing in an airport, followed by an explosion, and then a cloudy melee of debris and screaming people. They were looping it, over and over, playing it in real time and then again in slow motion.

Mary-Beth looked away, then back at the screen. The image of the dancing child, followed by the explosion, was like an electric shock that she couldn't stop administering to herself. She couldn't reconcile the mix of sweet relief at knowing her children were safe and the horror incurred by so many other families.

JJ rubbed his eyes over and over.

Finally, the video image was replaced by the face of a terrorism expert in a stark TV studio. Public transportation officials and Interpol were on high alert across Europe, he said, and air traffic in the region had been halted for now. The Madrid airport may not be functional for weeks or months. It was impossible to understand how much of this information pertained to Cam and Lucas Bright's safe return home.

Patty and John Senior were padding around in the other room, and Mary-Beth got the feeling that they knew all this already. While she'd been losing her mind, they'd been talking to John's contacts in Washington and getting up to speed on the specifics. This was a vague comfort to her. Surely, the grandchildren of a former US senator would get special treatment at a moment like this, some dispensation to come home on a private plane, or maybe additional security abroad. Everyone's children are worth protecting, but maybe hers were extra worthy of it? She cursed the thought and kept on thinking it.

At that moment, Spencer and Ian thudded down the stairs and burst into the living room.

"Turn to channel 244," Spencer instructed.

JJ did as he was told. He found the BBC.

And there on the screen were two faces—two almost matching faces—Lucas and Cameron Bright.

Mary-Beth gasped. "Oh God."

John Senior rushed in. "Turn up the volume!"

"Apparently, the grandsons of the recently retired US senator John Bright were among those who survived the attack," the BBC anchorman explained. "They were traveling with a high school sports team, on their way to Barcelona for football camp. The plane the team was on had just taken off, barely missing the detonation of the bomb. It made it safely to Barcelona. Some have speculated that these young Americans were targets of the bombing, but officials have declined to comment on that."

Lucas and Cameron's faces smiled back at the Brights in their summer home. They were wearing collared shirts, blue and red, respectively. It was last year's school picture, and they looked even younger than Mary-Beth remembered them.

JJ put an arm around his wife while they held their breath and watched.

The still photos of their boys disappeared from the screen, and two older men came on, their luggage by their side. They were fidgety and smiling for their on-camera interview. The newsman introduced them: "These travelers sat near the Bright boys on the flight from Boston to Madrid and got to chat with them a bit. Sirs, you were with these young men just minutes before the attack. What was that like?"

Mary-Beth knew what this was: disaster filler. News networks, forced to fill hour after hour of terrorism coverage, had run out of real information and were moving on to second-tier witnesses and unrelated hearsay. None of this had much to do with the actual attack, but that mattered less and less as time passed. It satisfied the world's beastly hunger for more discussion of the tragedy.

And that's how their sons came to have their faces on the screen of the BBC. It is why two old British men were recalling irrelevant stories about their proximity to boys who hadn't actually been present for the attack.

"They seemed like really nice lads," the one man said.

His friend nodded emphatically beside him. "Lovely."

"Just hoping to play some footy."

"Such a shame."

"Such a shame, but also a blessing that they are safe."

"A blessing indeed."

The two men nodded their heads together in agreement, so happy that the nice boys they didn't know at all had averted catastrophe.

The newsman took it from there. "Well, there you have it. America's Footy Fifteen were among those that escaped the attack by minutes, including two grandsons of former senator John Bright of Massachusetts. Remarkable."

All of the Brights were watching now with wide eyes. Charlie and Chelsea had come from downstairs. Philip appeared out of nowhere.

The tiny light on the camera in the corner of the room was on, recording them, but Farah wasn't behind it.

Ian pulled out his phone and scrolled social media.

JJ began flipping through the other news channels while everyone watched in silence.

It was more of the same on the other channels. Blurry cell phone videos and panicked voice mail recordings from the Madrid airport. Witnesses who hadn't gotten very close and experts who hadn't been there at all. Everyone had something to say about this event. And the longer cable news pontificated, the less it seemed they understood.

And then the story of Lucas and Cameron caught on like wildfire. Within two minutes, *Footy Fifteen* was trending online. They had a catchy name and a hashtag. Apparently all the news organizations had gotten their hands on the same photos, because the boys were suddenly everywhere. A team photo was circulating, too, the one the school used on their athletics page.

Chatter was already in full swing on social media as people sent thoughts and prayers, suggested all the ways in which this was the privileged parents' fault and concocted conspiracy theories about the former senator's support for terrorists. All the Bright family could do was watch it escalate, a perfect chemical reaction of bad luck and piping-hot culture war.

When Mary-Beth's own cell phone buzzed, she didn't immediately answer. It might be her cousin in Richmond, or one of the other parents from the soccer team. It could be someone she didn't know, calling to inquire about the boys they had seen on TV. She wasn't sure how to talk about this yet.

Then the landline began to ring, loud and alarming. It almost never rang at the lake house; no one but family and John's secretaries had the number. Hearing their secret phone ring now felt like a toppling of their last line of defense against the rest of the world.

John Senior answered it after two rings and took the call in the study.

Mary-Beth ran to the countertop in the kitchen where their devices were lined up, charging. Her phone and JJ's didn't work well at the lake house, and calls often went straight to voice mail. She looked down at her phone to see twenty-seven missed calls. JJ's phone had even more.

John Senior emerged from the study a minute later. "We need to issue a statement."

JJ nodded like he'd been expecting this.

"What kind of statement?" Mary-Beth asked.

"Something for reporters to use. It should be optimistic, grateful to authorities. It doesn't need to say much, but we need to have something out there now."

"I'll take care of it," JJ said.

Mary-Beth looked up at her husband. "But the FBI agents said not to talk to the press."

Her father-in-law shook his head. "Don't worry about that. We have every right to help shape this story. If we don't, someone else will. These are *your* children on TV. We want to make sure the media gets it right."

JJ nodded in agreement.

Mary-Beth looked at Ian and Spencer, who maybe weren't

as politically plugged in as her husband and father-in-law, but they had good instincts about things like this; *optics*, as the Brights liked to say. Both men nodded in assent.

JJ kissed her head. "It will be okay."

The momentum of it all was building fast. Mary-Beth felt left behind already.

"I need some coffee," Spencer announced.

The rest of the group nodded.

Mary-Beth wandered back into the living room and sank into the couch, the same place she'd been for most of the previous night, and Philip took a seat beside her. Neither said anything for a full minute.

She was aware of the camera still watching them from the other end of the room—with Farah now behind it—but she cared less and less about that. Farah had become a friendly ghost, sometimes visible, sometimes not, always watching them. It was inexplicably okay, a comfort even, to know someone was bearing witness.

Mary-Beth turned to Philip. He had little bags beneath his eyes and a streak of dirt across his T-shirt. She smiled weakly at him. "Hey, where did you go last night? Were you outside?"

He shrugged and pressed the fingers of his giant, bony hands together. They were nothing at all like JJ's hands. "I was under the big tree for most of the night."

"Maple or oak?"

"Oak. The one in the back, by the water."

"I like that one. You were out there all night?"

He laughed slightly. "Apparently, yes. I was thinking for a long time…thinking and praying for Cameron and Lucas. Eventually, I just fell asleep."

She took a breath. It was moving, but mostly horrible that her children were in a position to need prayer. Prayers were for desperation and lost causes. The boys were fine now.

"Thank you, Phil. Those boys love you, you know."

"I do know. And I know they will get home safely. This is probably over for them."

"Exactly." Mary-Beth nodded firmly. "But let me ask you, Phil—do you think it works?"

"Do I think what works?"

"Prayer. Does it do any good? I used to think it did, but I seem to have stopped believing that. I don't know what I think now."

He took a cautious breath. "I think it *might*. It definitely changes me when I do it. I haven't figured prayer out on an intellectual level, but I can't imagine *not* doing it at moments like these."

It was striking to hear Philip—sweet, perpetually lost, never-cool Philip—speaking so purposefully on a subject. And it was disarming to discuss something as earnest as prayer among all these skeptical Brights. Either Philip didn't know or didn't care how he was seen by the rest of his family. Mary-Beth was grateful to have him there.

"I'm glad my parents are dead," Mary-Beth blurted. "Today, I mean. I'm glad they don't have to live through this. It would have been too much for them. They were nervous people."

Philip nodded once.

"I'm sorry. I don't know why I said that."

"You don't have to apologize, Mary-Beth."

"Thanks," Mary-Beth said, and she patted his giant hand and they sat there for another moment.

Warm wind blew across her face from an open window, and Mary-Beth closed her eyes. She wanted to say a prayer for her boys—the formal kind, like she used to—but she couldn't do it. Once she prayed, it would become a desperate situation. This must not become a desperate situation.

Patty's head appeared from the kitchen just then. "Let's all have some breakfast."

Mary-Beth nodded but she didn't move. She looked out through the open window. "This family is never nervous. Have you noticed that, Phil? They don't freak out about things. This is a good place to be in a crisis, probably. Everyone here always knows what to do."

He shrugged. "We've had it easy, Mary-Beth. It's easy to know what to do when things are easy."

Of course, Philip was right.

The tiny light on the camera kept glowing, and she wondered briefly if their conversation would sound profound or idiotic to an observer. Then she wondered if her mascara was smeared (it was, left eye) and if her hair looked stringy (it did not). A new kind of worry had been creeping into the edges of Mary-Beth's psyche in those hours—the worry that perhaps she wasn't performing this role of panicked mother properly. Did it look more sincere for her to be composed or unraveled? Mary-Beth *was* sincere in her maternal concern. She always was. But the presence of the cameras made her feel different, like someone watching herself from the outside, and that made her want to behave differently. She wanted to tweak her performance here and there, edit out the goofy comments and stupid questions. She just wanted to look like the good, scared mother that she really was, just in case it wasn't believable.

"You're welcome to come out to the oak tree anytime," Philip offered.

She smiled. "Thanks, Phil."

She wondered if she still knew how to pray, and to really believe it. She wondered, too, if it was the sort of thing a bereft mother should do if the cameras were rolling.

16

John Bright's full statement was all over the news within minutes of its release:

> By the grace of God, our sons Lucas and Cameron arrived safely in Barcelona with the rest of the Our Lady of Mercy High School soccer team last night, following the tragic attack in Madrid. We are deeply grateful to Spanish and Catalonian authorities; to the US consulate; and to the public for their concern. Our hearts go out to the victims of this horrific attack and their families.
>
> We will be working closely with US government officials to ensure the safe return of all the children as soon as possible. Until then, we ask that you respect our privacy.
>
> Thank you and God bless America,
> Mary-Beth and John Bright II

Once it was out there, it belonged to the world. The story of Lucas, Cameron and the Footy Fifteen was public property after that. Social media mined the internet for personal details of the Bright family, dredging up every photo and minor bit of DC gossip available on them. Left-leaning media lionized the former senator for his history of progressive(ish) votes and causes, making a hero out of a man they had been ambivalent about for most of his political tenure. And right-wing media seized on the beautiful irony of the offspring of globalist elites traveling to Europe—for *soccer*, no less—and only narrowly surviving the ubiquitous scourge of Islamic terrorism. The story wrote itself.

From Mary-Beth's perspective, as they sat around the living room watching TV and scrolling through their phones, none of the Brights were particularly bothered by these disinformation campaigns. Every version of who the Brights were was a-okay with them. The relatable white American family, the privileged brats, the political powerhouses—it was all untrue. Everything Mary-Beth saw was a simplistic reduction of a small part of who they'd been at one time or another, but none of it was right. And yet she seemed to be the only one who cared. *Anything to get the boys back*, is what JJ told her. And he was right about that, though it wasn't clear to her how the media frenzy was getting them closer to having their children home.

JJ and Mary-Beth's phones pinged, and they looked down from their posts on the couch. It was an email from the consulate. John Senior had convinced officials there to set up a generic address on the secure State Department server to allow the children to email their parents during this time. It was intended to complement the twice-daily phone calls the kids were allowed, and probably to keep pushy DC parents at bay for a while.

It was from Lucas.

Hey Mom and Dad, it's Lucas. They said we could email you on this computer but it's weird because we're all using the same account. Everything's fine, but I'm really tired of being inside and I'm tired of those long skinny sandwiches. They said they'd bring in some sushi or Thai, but that hasn't happened yet. There's a TV here that gets the Premier League and some reruns of American shows. I guess that's better than nothing. Hope we can come home soon. Love you.

Another email arrived right behind it from the same address.

Hi it's Cam. This sucks. I'm glad to be with the guys on our team and at first it was kind of like a party, but now everyone's getting restless and pissed off (sorry) and I hope this doesn't take much longer. Have Grandpa get us out of here! We'll call you tomorrow morning. Love you both.

"I'll write them back," Mary-Beth said. "You go help your dad."

JJ nodded and left the room.

She considered telling him to go take a shower, to change his clothes and brush his teeth. They'd been at it all day, and it was taking a toll. But neither of them wanted to stop watching the news or reading the internet. With nothing useful to do, monitoring the chatter felt like something.

Mary-Beth got to work at the thing the Brights were best at: putting on a brave face. In an email, she told the boys that they were working hard with government officials to get them home soon. She advised them to be polite and remember that they were representing their country abroad. She suggested that perhaps they should employ those yoga breathing skills she'd told them about for stressful situations, which they would roll their eyes at, but maybe eventually use. She was upbeat and assured because that's what everyone needed. And from across the ocean, she could still sense that they weren't buying it.

The truth was that Mary-Beth had no idea what was really going on. Her father-in-law had been on the phone with dozens of people that day. He was paying a private security company for two guards to hang around outside, which seemed wholly unnecessary. He'd also alerted the local police, whose expertise seemed to be primarily over-capacity jazz concerts. JJ and John Senior were taking all the media calls, directing people to their statement and providing terse on-the-record responses to the follow-up questions. The volume of incoming calls seemed to be increasing.

Mary-Beth stood up and turned the TV off. She went into the kitchen, where Ian was preparing two vegetable tarts. (Of course, only Ian was allowed to commandeer the kitchen from Patty.) Spencer was hovering around him, drinking a beer and talking excitedly about coordinated anti-terrorism efforts between the US and Europe. He didn't notice Mary-Beth come in.

"I spent all of chapter twelve elaborating on the idea that if we removed some of those bureaucratic barriers, we could do counterintelligence sharing much more efficiently among Western democracies."

Ian nodded as he arranged a fishtail design of sliced squash in a pie crust. It was unclear whether he was interested in this. If he wasn't, he was doing a convincing job with the nodding.

Farah angled a wheeling camera closer to the couple and pointed the lens at the vegetables, then back up at Spencer as he talked.

"And that's what we need to be focusing on today. This is an ideal moment to push for the counterintelligence legislation again." Spencer paused and studied his husband. "Do you think I should send out a media avail? Just let the shows know I'm free for cable appearances?"

Ian caught Mary-Beth watching them, and he gave Spencer a *not now* expression.

Spencer smiled at her and popped a cherry tomato into his mouth. "Mary-Beth! How are you holding up? You need a glass of wine." Spencer filled a glass with something white while the Bright household buzzed around them. He put it on the counter beside her. "Here, drink this."

She smiled and took a sip. It was instantly calming, but it also made her aware of her empty stomach and fried nerves. She couldn't drink now.

Patty walked in. "Ian, how long do the tarts need?"

"Thirty minutes."

She set the timer on the stove and looked out at the dimming sun. "Let's have a sit on the deck while they cook."

Just then John Senior and JJ burst into the room. "Little schedule change, guys. We're doing a sit-down."

"What does that mean?"

"It's a brief on-camera TV interview," JJ explained. "It will be someone of our choosing, someone friendly from a major network."

"What? In DC? Why?"

"We can do it right here. They'll send a producer. Dad's done them before in the study. He thinks it's important to address all the incoming questions in one swoop."

"But why does anyone have questions for us? What can we answer?"

John Senior popped a cucumber slice into his mouth. "The shows want us because it's a very personal angle to the terrorism story. And it's a good move for us because it will help keep public pressure on federal officials to get Lucas and Cameron back on home soil. Trust me, Mary-Beth, you don't want the public to move on from this until the boys are home safe. It could be a week before seats are available on commercial flights. But if we keep the squeeze on the administration, they'll cave and send a military plane in a day or two."

"I think it's smart," Spencer said.

Ian agreed.

Mary-Beth wasn't sure that she believed them, but she was at a disadvantage when it came to things like this.

"Okay, then."

Everyone nodded, and the planning for their television appearance commenced. (Mary-Beth suspected it was already locked-in.) They ate the vegetable tarts with goat cheese on the back deck. No one had much to say at dinner. There was some casual conversation about the mild evening temperatures. JJ squeezed Mary-Beth's hand twice under the table. Philip said a quiet prayer to himself before he ate a bite. No one joined him, but they waited patiently before digging in.

A windsurfer glided across the surface on the far side of the lake. From that distance, he seemed to be going so slow that you wouldn't know he was moving at all. And it occurred to Mary-Beth that, most of the time, she couldn't perceive life's progression until she was looking back at the distance she'd covered.

17

By 8:05 the next morning, they were all back downstairs.

Mary-Beth leaned against the doorway of John Senior's office, watching her husband and father-in-law get fussed over by young NBC News producers.

The study had been arranged like a live television stage, with two armchairs side by side in front of a bookcase filled with legal volumes. John Senior and JJ, both in navy sport coats and oxford shirts, talked excitedly to each other as a woman with purple hair applied pressed powder to their foreheads. Big white umbrellas were open above them, and a fuzzy boom microphone kept bumping into John's head. They maintained sober expressions, but it was clear that they were enjoying themselves.

Mary-Beth was supposed to be with them in the study. That's what NBC had requested. A producer had said that "the audience always wants to see the mothers," but she couldn't do it. She couldn't keep from bursting into tears and looking like a fool in front of the whole world, not after another sleepless night without her children.

They're just fine, JJ had assured her. And they were. Lucas and Cameron had called earlier that morning, and they were indeed fine, if grumpy. But everything else around her suggested that this was still a dire situation. The tone of the press calls and the volume of incoming thoughts and prayers were alarming. The fact that NBC sent a camera crew up to Massachusetts just for them suggested that things were definitely not fine. The fact that networks wanted to put her on TV to talk about her absent sons was precisely what made her incapable of doing it.

And, amid it all, Farah was filming. She was still there, peeking out from behind her big cameras in the corners of every room, following them with smaller ones when things got interesting. Somehow, though, the ubiquity of her presence had become a comfort to Mary-Beth. Something about having Farah there made Mary-Beth feel less likely to be drowned out by all that Bright noise. The fact of her existence was irrefutable with a camera there to prove it.

"Almost ready?" a man with a protruding belly asked from behind his own big camera.

The lady with the makeup nodded and readjusted an umbrella. "Hang on. There's still some glare."

They installed small earpieces in JJ's and John Senior's ears, testing audio levels and chatting with the NBC News personality at the other end of the line.

The Senator had done scores of TV interviews in the years he'd been in office, and he looked almost relieved to be back at it. But JJ had been on TV only twice. Both times were just brief appearances for unflattering news features about Washington lobbyists—"how the sausage gets made" stories, as JJ had put it. Mary-Beth could see that he was nervous.

Spencer padded down the stairs in his pajamas, looking briefly into the study with a scowl. He was disappointed to be left out. Mary-Beth had heard him arguing in his bedroom with Ian the night before. He was insulted that no one in the family or the news media had asked for his expert opinion on the Madrid attack. From what Mary-Beth gleaned through the walls, Spencer wanted to pitch himself more aggressively as a talking head to the shows, and Ian wasn't so keen on the idea. It sounded like they'd gone to bed mad, not that it was any of her business.

"We'll go live on one," the camera guy said. He held up his palm and counted down with thick fingers.

JJ breathed in and out audibly.

Five, four, three, two…he made a shotgun signal with his hand, and then they were on.

Someone at the other end of their earpieces spoke to JJ and John Senior. They nodded and smiled in response.

"Thank you for having us," JJ said.

"It's good to be back, though I wish it was under different circumstances," John Senior added.

Mary-Beth couldn't hear the questions coming from NBC. All she got was the stilted one-sided conversation, the Bright responses.

JJ: "Yes, our hearts go out to the people of Spain and all the victims of this attack."

Heads nodded. They listened intently.

John: "I'll defer to the FBI on that one, but I think it's an important question for the weeks ahead."

More listening. A little smile.

JJ: "My wife, Mary-Beth, is here with me, and we're just so grateful to know that our sons are safe."

After that, John seemed to take over: "Well, Peter, we've been here before, and one thing is for sure—Americans come together in times of crisis."

Listening.

"It's true, we don't have all the details yet, and I'll defer to the administration on that one."

Nodding.

"Peter, an attack like this is an attack on Western values. It's an attack on the liberties that our servicemen and women give their lives to protect. Freedom of speech and religion, among them."

Emphatic nodding.

"Yes, well, we don't know yet if the Our Lady of Mercy soccer team was *specifically* targeted, but it may prove to be the case that faith played a role in this. We just don't know yet."

Listening.

"I'm not saying that, *necessarily.* And I don't believe Our Lady of Mercy High School has weighed in. I'm simply saying…to these radical terrorists, the Footy Fifteen represent Western, Judeo-Christian values. And any attack on people of faith in this country should be taken seriously."

People of faith? What was going on? Mary-Beth looked back into the kitchen where Spencer and Patty were drinking coffee at the table, listening. Patty shrugged at her, unconcerned.

This made Mary-Beth nervous. All this "faith" and "Western values" and the possibility that their sons were targets despite the FBI's assertion that they were likely not. It was all too much. It was too much, and Mary-Beth should have seen it coming. This interview had been a bad idea.

Charlie bounded down the stairs at that moment in swim shorts, and Patty put her finger to her lips to preempt his noisy arrival. He nodded and went to the coffeepot. Chelsea came down after him in a bikini that insufficiently contained her top half. They filled two mugs with coffee and escaped through the back door, bound for the water. Through the window, Mary-Beth saw Charlie take a quick squeeze of her exposed left butt cheek.

Mary-Beth looked back at JJ and John Senior as they offered pleasantries for the conclusion of the interview. JJ was smiling now. *God bless America* and all that. He was enjoying himself. They both were.

Mary-Beth felt a little sick. She'd had this feeling many times since marrying into the Bright family: the feeling that she was watching something strange, but everyone around her was so obviously sure of its normalcy that she could only assume she was mistaken. But she didn't think she was mistaken; they were laying this on thick for the cameras, exploiting a tragedy for their own ends. But what were the ends if not getting her children home safely?

It wasn't only that John Senior and her husband were at that moment preening patriotically before the cameras. It was Patty, too. She had been floating around all morning in tennis whites and lip gloss, serving iced coffee to the NBC News team. Spencer was sulking about not getting his time on TV. And Charlie was probably at that very moment feeling up his girlfriend in plain view of the whole crowd. They were shameless, all of them.

None of this had anything to do with *her boys*. And, until their fate was resolved, she hated them all for their selfishness. She hated how they made her feel like a hysterical stranger, forced to bear all the weight of this frightening episode. Her legitimate anxiety would be validated if anyone else really felt this fear with her. Instead, they were merely performing fear. And maybe this TV appearance would work. Maybe the rest of the stupid world would believe the Brights, and it would pressure the federal government to get her boys home sooner. But Mary-Beth knew better. *She* knew what they were. And at that moment, she hated them all for it.

She hated her husband most of all, but not because she actually hated him; it was because she loved him, and she knew that he really *was* frightened for his children. But he was playing along with the rest of his monstrous family. He was doing this brave-faced-patriot nonsense because his father told him it was the right thing to do. God, she loved JJ. She only wished, in her weaker moments, that she didn't have to share so much of him with these people.

These people. His people, not hers. She didn't like thinking this way, but this is what they did to her.

"And that's a wrap! Thanks, guys."

The cameraman unplugged electrical cords and looped them around his arm. The lady with the purple hair retrieved the earpieces.

John Senior took his jacket off and laced his fingers behind his head.

JJ rubbed his face several times and then looked at his wife expectantly. "How was that?"

Mary-Beth blinked. "If it brings the boys back, then it was great."

18

"My favorite producer." Wayne yelled through the phone.

"That's what I like to hear. How are things back in civilization?" Farah reclined in the Brights' deck chair and looked out at the sparkling water. She was alone on the deck.

"Let's see… It's ninety-five degrees here today, and New York City smells like piss. But I spent all weekend on my brother's boat, so I'm feeling pretty good. How are our movie stars?"

"They're not so great, Wayne. I assume you've heard about the Senator's grandsons."

"Of course I have. I left three messages on your phone this weekend."

"Yeah, sorry about that. It has been nonstop here." Farah looked out at the lake. The blue water sparkled under a lightly clouded sky. She could see Charlie and Chelsea at the far end, tiny specks on paddleboards. Philip was under the oak tree, reading a book just out of earshot. The rest of the family was in the study with the FBI agents, who had returned for the second day. For that moment, the lake view was hers alone.

"So what the hell is going on there?"

Farah took a breath. "It's been crazy. We all stayed up straight through the night into yesterday, waiting to hear about JJ and Mary-Beth's boys. That part was scary. I felt terrible for these people, Wayne. It was hours before they knew whether or not their kids were safe. I had to retreat to the bathroom a couple of times just to have a cry and to pull myself together."

"Did you catch the drama on camera?"

"Yeah, most of it," she said, a little reluctantly. She sighed. Farah had been there with the Brights through the horror of that night. She'd stayed up and gotten all the good angles. She had hopefully managed to do it with compassion. It was a dubious accomplishment.

"Farah, this is, like, an international incident now. It's a *thing*." Wayne was hammering audibly on his computer. "Does it feel like a thing from your perspective?"

"Yes, definitely. I mean, the Bright kids are fine, but the Senator and his son JJ are doing kind of a media blitz with it. They went on TV. It's really something."

"Yeah, I saw it. And I was thinking—maybe *that's* the story you need to be telling. Their appetite for fame, the lure of the cameras for a former politician. I mean, it's about the Madrid attack, too, but for framing purposes, maybe this is what it's really about. Man, we lucked out...all due respect to the victims."

"It's not quite that simple, though. I don't know..." Farah suddenly felt queasy about this conversation. The Brights sounded vain from the way she'd described them, but everything she'd seen in those thirty-six hours was genuine and loving. It was real—or, as real as these people got. "I'll think about it, Wayne. Anyway, that's not why I called. I called because I want to make another plea for production help. I need another body here to help with the cameras. Even if it is just an intern. There's too much for me to watch and manage at once."

"No can do, sorry. We're over budget already."

"But how am I supposed to handle all this new action on my own? This is not what we thought we were getting into. It's bigger. Let's invest in this and make it something good." She stood up and began pacing around the deck with the cordless phone.

"I hear ya, but I just can't do it. That's way above my pay grade, and it's a dead end. Farah, you have, like, six tripods there. Follow the most important moments with your handhelds, and we'll supplement it with all the stationary footage. I'll have the team help with the edit when the assignment is done. It's going to be fine."

"I don't think it's going to be fine, Wayne! I think I'm going to miss something! And then we'll just have a bad documentary that doesn't get picked up and will cost the company too much money. And then I definitely won't get this promotion."

"You won't blow it, Farah, because you're obsessed. I know you, and I know that you won't sleep or eat if it means missing something. That's why I picked you for this. You want it."

"Yes, I do. But do you really think I can get this promotion?"

"I don't know. It's not my call. But I think so, later. After this works. Just make it work."

"I'll try. I gotta go, Wayne."

"Okay. Keep me posted, Farah."

Then he was gone.

Farah put the phone down on the patio table and looked across the water again. She thought about her crappy apartment and her dwindling bank account. She tried to imagine herself as a managing producer at Torch Media, as someone who got to pick the projects and the places she went. Her only way in was through the Brights.

Farah pulled out her cell phone and tried to check for news updates, but her phone had lost the connection again. So she walked down from the deck, across the grass, toward Philip at his privacy tree.

"Hey there. Sorry to bother you."

He looked up and squinted into the sun. "No bother. What can I do for you?"

"I, um, was hoping you could tell me the Wi-Fi password."

Philip looked around, confounded. "Sorry, I don't know it. I suppose I should probably find that out at some point, but I'm never here long enough for it to matter."

"No problem," Farah said. She hesitated, trying to think of something more. "So why aren't you inside with the rest of the family for this FBI briefing?"

He shrugged. "They don't really need me in there. Besides, someone will fill me in later. I'm more useful to everyone from out here, I think." A pause. "Do you mind me asking why you're not filming the FBI briefing? Aren't you supposed to capture everything?"

"I set up a stationary camera, but it didn't feel quite right to be in there myself."

"That's very decent of you."

"We'll see about my decency…"

"What?"

"Nothing. Have you been in the water yet today? Looks nice."

"Not yet. I was thinking about going for a dip in a little while. Do you swim?"

Farah shrugged. "I do, but not here. I'm supposed to be working while I'm here."

"You should go in at some point. It's really clear. Warm, too, for New England."

Farah nodded like she might consider it, but she knew she probably wouldn't. The thought of being in a bathing suit on assignment in front of this crowd seemed, at best, unprofessional.

"You should come swimming with me right now." Philip looked up at her and waited. "Do you have other plans?"

Farah was trapped. "No, but… I don't even have a bathing suit with me."

"How about a paddle in the canoe, then?"

She got the sense that she couldn't escape this conversation without agreeing to some outdoor activity with Philip.

"Yeah, okay."

Philip grinned from ear to ear, and she was instantly glad that she'd agreed to it.

Farah emptied her pockets on the porch, slipped her shoes off and pulled her ponytail through the hole in a Yankees hat.

Two minutes later, they were casting off. Philip was in the rear, steering the canoe gracefully away from the sandy beach, out into the bright, open water. Farah sat in front, awkwardly gripping the paddle with both hands. She spun around in the webbed seat to watch Philip for a few minutes as he stroked effortlessly with his whole arm, pushing against the calm waters on one side and then the other, propelling them forward with ease.

"The lake is so calm today, you really don't need to paddle at all," he said. "Kind of a one-person job."

"You sure?"

"Absolutely. Relax."

She put her paddle down on the floor of the canoe.

Philip looked different to Farah now from when she met him a few days before. For one, he was sunburned, after all the time he'd spent outside. His skin was a pleasant pinkish brown now, and there was a spray of brown freckles across his face. He was still gangly, but she could see the fine muscles in his arms animating and shifting under his skin with each stroke of the paddle. He smiled into the sun, and she liked the way his sparkly eyes crinkled slightly at the corners each time.

"Do you want to go to the far end?" he asked.

"How long do you think that will take? I shouldn't be gone from the house too long."

Philip nodded. "We'll go halfway."

She reached her hand over the edge of the canoe and let her fingers drag in the water as they tacked north.

"May I ask you a question?" he said.

"Sure."

"What do you think of us Brights? You've been observing us for a few days now and you must have an opinion."

She knew she shouldn't answer the question. And she didn't quite know how. Farah wasn't sure what she thought of this family of beautiful, smart, vain and magnetic men.

"I think it's clear you love each other very much."

"That's all?"

She pulled her fingers up out of the water. "As a group, I think you're all exceptionally confident. But you're also just a family like any other...loving and complicated."

Philip stopped paddling and they glided in silence.

Farah went on, despite herself. "I also think you are each quite different. You all seemed so alike on first impression— not so much *you*, but the rest of your family. But I soon realized I was wrong about that. None of you are as alike as you originally seemed."

He nodded and resumed paddling. "That's a pretty good description. This family is a mystery, even to me."

Philip moved the paddle from his right side to his left, sending a spray of water across Farah's shins.

"Really?"

"Kind of, yeah. I go away for a long time, and when I come back, I always think, *I don't understand these people at all*." Philip laughed. "I'm sure that's what they say about me, too."

She chuckled. "That's probably the most normal thing about the Brights."

He smiled wider, satisfied with that assessment, and kept paddling.

Neither one of them said anything for the remainder of the trip. Farah closed her eyes and let the hot afternoon sun press down on her eyelids. She could feel the rhythm of the paddle entering and leaving the water as Philip moved them along.

The canoe bumped up against the shallow lake floor just as Charlie and Chelsea were returning from their latest adventures in not-so-hidden-lake-sex.

"Hey," Charlie smiled. "Nice out there, huh?"

"It's perfect." Philip nodded as he and Farah climbed out of the canoe.

Chelsea twisted her long hair into a bun on the top of her head as the Bright brothers dragged the two watercrafts up onto the shore.

"You guys looked like a postcard out there in the canoe," Chelsea said to Farah. "Just like an old Victorian painting of lovers on the water."

Farah laughed and Philip laughed, but neither looked up from their feet in the sand.

19

Spencer looked at himself in the bedroom mirror as he rubbed moisturizer on his face, a little too aggressively for Ian's liking. It was late and he had been quietly fuming all day.

"You could have stood up for me with NBC News this morning."

Ian looked up from the bed. "What was I supposed to say?"

"You could have reminded them and my father and JJ that I wrote a book about the rise of terrorism in the West and am considered by some to be an expert, that I have spoken to every major news outlet on my tour for that book. You could have—nicely—implied that I know a shitload more about this issue than either of them." Spencer frowned at his reflection in the mirror. "I should have been in that interview."

Ian sat up on his elbows. He was dead tired. "I know that. But what does it matter now? The logistics are mostly resolved, as far as Cameron and Lucas go. What would you have been able to contribute to the process?"

Ian immediately regretted saying the last part. None of Spencer's anger was about the concrete problem of getting their nephews home. It was about being recognized for his accomplishments before his father. It was about beating JJ at something. It was about the current fragility of Spencer's ego.

But it was true that, at that moment, Cameron and Lucas were already on their way home. The FBI had confirmed that afternoon that the government would be sending a military plane to retrieve the whole team from Barcelona. JJ and Mary-Beth were on their way to DC to meet them when they arrived. It was the best possible outcome, but Spencer was pissy because he didn't get to go on TV. Ian couldn't muster much sympathy.

There was a knock on the door. "You guys need anything in there?" Patty turned the knob and peeked inside before they had a chance to answer.

Ian forced a smile. "We're good, thanks, Patty. I think we just need to turn in early and catch up on some sleep."

"Of course."

Spencer, in only boxer briefs, moved on to his shoulders and arms with the moisturizer. "Are JJ and Mary-Beth gone?"

"Yes, they left about an hour ago. They'll get there late and stay in a hotel so they are ready to meet the boys' plane in the morning. After that, all the parents and kids have to do a debriefing of some kind with the FBI."

Spencer nodded. "That makes sense. They'll need to know if any of the boys on the team saw or heard anything useful. Is Farah with them?"

"No, she decided to stay here to keep the cameras on your father." Patty lingered. "I just want everyone home safely again."

"Me, too, Mom." Spencer crawled into his side of the bed. "Okay, goodnight."

"Goodnight, boys," Patty said.

"Goodnight, Patty," Ian said.

She frowned. "Ian. It's 'Mom' to you, too."

"Right, sorry."

Spencer turned off the light, and Patty closed the door behind her.

The couple lay in silence for a few minutes, gauging the level of disharmony between them.

Patty had been reminding Ian to call her "Mom" for almost a decade now, and still Ian could manage to do so only about 30 percent of the time. It felt strange and a little disloyal to Ian to call someone other than his own mother "Mom," but it meant so damn much to her that he forced himself now and then.

Ian knew he had things easier with Patty than Mary-Beth did. Because he was male, he folded into this pack of boy cubs that Patty wanted to play den mother to forever. She seemed relieved never to have to relinquish her role as the primary woman in Spencer's life, which infuriated Ian when he allowed himself to think about it. Ian had to remind himself that Patty's intentions were mostly good, and that at least some of the blame fell to his husband, and the rest of the Bright men, who were content to be mothered forever.

But all the wonderful things about Patty were also the things that made Ian feel as if he were being slowly smothered by a down pillow. While they were at the lake house, Patty tended to their every need, determining when they ate and where they slept, how they spent their time and with whom they interacted. They were liberated from the rushing hose of adult life when they were there. It always felt wonderfully weightless for a while, until it didn't.

"I don't know why you can't just call her 'Mom.'"

"I don't know why we have to talk about this right now." Ian turned over and closed his eyes. Exhaustion had him feeling almost feverish.

Spencer sighed. His bare chest was pressed up against the back of Ian's T-shirt. "You know I'm not really mad at you. I'm just mad."

Ian rolled back over. "I know. I'm sorry things didn't go the way they should have today. I should have said something on your behalf. You'd do it for me."

He could feel Spencer softening before him, melting into the mattress and coming back to his side. They needed to be on the same side when they were at the lake house. It was awful to lose Spencer to the Bright family dynamic on those summer visits, leaving Ian alone on the island of extras.

Spencer inched closer until their foreheads were touching. He pressed his soft lips and minty toothpaste breath into Ian's. They still kissed well. After so many years together, they still kissed, on the lips, well. There may be no greater defiance of time and familiarity than a commitment to real kissing, with hungry, open mouths.

Ian pulled him in closer and felt his body come alive.

Spencer reached into the warmth of Ian's boxers, but Ian pushed him gently away. He went to the bedroom door and dropped the small eyelet hook into the little loop—not a foolproof lock, but a deterrent, anyway.

Ian pulled off his T-shirt and underwear and bounded back into bed.

They had the sort of sex that starts as a hurricane and ends as a mist. All the anxiety and desperation of the preceding two days were purged in a few ferocious minutes, and then they were free to just be there with each other, warm bodies and wet mouths and bare skin. Skin! Parched, browned summer skin. The distinctly delicious taste of vacation sex.

When it was over, they were relaxed and on the same team. But they were also back in reality.

Ian unlocked the door and went into the bathroom.

Spencer went next.

When he came back into the bedroom, he sat down on the bed and looked out the window for a long while. "Sometimes I just hate JJ."

"You don't hate him," Ian said, nearly asleep. "But I know."

"He's such a self-righteous prick. And why? He's a *lobbyist*, for Christ's sake. Let's not pretend like that's on par with being a US senator, or an expert on anything. He's a peddler of bullshit."

"Let's talk about this tomorrow."

"Did you see them on TV? All that God-bless-America shit? What a couple of phonies. This has nothing to do with them, but they're eating it up!"

"I know."

"Sometimes… This fucking family, you know? This family…"

This was something new to Ian: Spencer expressing genuine doubt about his people, seeing them with clearer eyes.

Years before, when they were a new couple, Ian had asked Spencer, "Where are the wounds?"

They were at the lake house for Christmas with the whole family. Everyone had a fine, festive time. But Ian found the Brights to be unknowable still.

"So where are the wounds?" he had said to Spencer when they were back in their bedroom, the same one they were in now.

"What wounds?" Spencer had been baffled.

"*The wounds*, Spencer. The ones we all incur from the large and small acts of cruelty we inflict upon each other over a lifetime in a family. The marks from arguments that went too far, birthdays forgotten, quiet judgments and passive-aggressive gestures. Where are they?" Ian hadn't meant to be pushy about it, but the more he said, the more the Brights confused him.

Spencer had thought about it before attempting an answer. "I don't think we hold on to those aggressions the way other families do."

"But you commit them?"

"I don't know...probably. I mean, surely we do."

Ian had the feeling that Spencer was trying to answer in a way that sounded sane and honest, but he didn't believe that Spencer believed it. It seemed possible at that moment that Spencer secretly thought his family simply didn't have any wounds. There was a willful ignorance to it that Ian envied, as if the secret to a happy family may be as easy as believing you're happy, truth be damned. But Ian still saw the wounds. Even before Spencer allowed himself to see them, Ian knew they existed.

And now, as Ian fell asleep, it seemed possible that a fog was lifting and Spencer was seeing things more clearly.

20

Everyone slept late the following morning. Three days had passed since the attack in Madrid. Mary-Beth and JJ were with their sons in Washington, DC. And the rest of the house was free to just sleep. When the Bright men and their extras finally emerged from their bedrooms around eleven, the spirit of their summer vacation had returned.

"We should do something big today," Charlie announced as he piled onions and capers onto a cream cheese and lox bagel.

They were sitting around the kitchen table—Charlie, Chelsea, Spencer, Ian and Philip—satiating their returned appetites and feeling like children without chaperones. John Senior was on the phone in his study, while Patty weeded in the garden. Farah and her camera watched them from a corner.

"I was thinking about doing that hike at the east end of the lake," Philip said.

Ian reached for the cream. "I'd love a hike."

"Too short," Charlie said. "Let's do something that really makes us sweat. How about the Notch. Anyone up for that?"

Spencer nodded emphatically, his mouth full.

"Sure," Chelsea said.

Philip shrugged.

"You coming, Farah?"

She pressed a button on the camera and looked out from behind it. "Sorry, no. I should stay with your dad here. And I'm not much of a hiker. I probably don't have the right gear for it."

"Chelsea can lend you something. Right, babe?"

"Totally."

Farah hesitated. It was clear to Ian that she didn't want to go, but these were not cues that the Brights understood easily. Declining a family outing *and* an outdoor activity were two sins too many.

"Do what you want to do, Farah," Ian said.

"But the view is amazing. You can't miss this. You can bring one of your little cameras."

"We'll find you some shorts after breakfast," Chelsea said.

And poor Farah just smiled, ambushed.

Ian tried to send a sympathetic look her way, but she was back behind the camera. In his experience, people eventually resign themselves to move with the Bright tide instead of resisting it.

Two hours later, they were huffing up a knotty trail, two by two, under a canopy of evergreens and lush maples. The sun could barely reach them through the overhang, but they were dripping with sweat. Spencer and Charlie Bright were at the front, going way too fast for the rest of the group. Ian and Philip were behind, with Farah and Chelsea bringing up the rear. Farah took her camera out intermittently to capture the scene.

The pitch was steep, and Ian's thighs burned, but it felt good to be out and moving his body. He would have gone faster if he didn't feel an obligation to put a drag on things for Farah's sake. She looked fit enough, but she wasn't in the kind of shape that Brights expected. These people had completed triathlons, hiked the Swiss Alps and rafted the Zambezi. They didn't know what it felt like to occupy an average American body.

"Please feel free to go up ahead without me," she puffed from the rear.

Philip looked back. "We never leave a crew member behind."

Farah rolled her eyes and smiled.

It sounded something like flirtation to Ian. His eyes met Chelsea's then and it was clear that she saw it, too.

Chelsea and Farah began chatting from behind. They shared a love of documentaries and travel writing. They'd both lived in a bunch of different cities. It was impossible not to eavesdrop, so Ian and Philip didn't bother resisting. They'd jump in now and then when they had something to add, but there wasn't a lot of airspace between the two women. Ian heard both of them say more on this hike than in the previous days put together. That was the effect of the Bright household: it could shrink normally large personalities. He wondered what they were like in the rest of their lives.

"Water break!" Charlie stopped the train, and the rest of them caught up.

They passed around two water bottles and wiped sweat from their faces.

Ian leaned against a tree and rubbed his lower back.

Spencer turned to Charlie. "So how'd you swing a whole month off from work, brother?"

Farah quietly resumed recording.

"It wasn't so hard, actually." He sat down on a nearby log.

"What do you mean?"

Charlie sighed. "The Haiti project is over. For good. It's a long story, but there was some malfeasance, and the State Department rescinded the contract. My boss is probably facing criminal charges. We were all sacked immediately."

"Charlie, that stinks," Philip said.

Spencer nodded. "Hey, man, I'm so sorry. I had no idea." His voice was quieter now, and he seemed to have forgotten about their race to the top of the mountain. "You, too, Chelsea?"

She nodded. "Yeah."

No one said anything for a minute.

"So what are you guys gonna do?"

Charlie shrugged. "I guess I'll send my résumé around to some of their competitors, see what happens. I don't really know."

"I might look at a few NGOs back home in London," Chelsea said.

Charlie looked at her. "You didn't tell me that."

"It's a new idea."

Ian took the water bottle back. "Well, at least you guys have a little time to figure it out, right?"

"Yeah, sure." Charlie scraped dirt from the underside of his boots with a stick. He didn't seem to want to talk about it. "Should we keep going?"

Spencer started walking and everyone fell in line behind him. "You could always become a man of the cloth. Like Philip here."

Philip kept hiking.

"That still your plan, Phil?" Charlie asked.

No answer.

They were goading him, trying to get him to bite. Ian had seen this before. All family deflections landed on Philip. There was a direct relationship between the anxiety the men felt in their father's presence and their aggression with Philip.

Philip usually took it in stride and laughed it off, but there was a bite to it now.

"Is that still your plan?" Charlie asked again. "Philip, can we talk again about how you're still planning on taking a vow of celibacy, of telling people not to get divorced or use birth control?"

"No, let's *not* talk about it," Ian said.

Chelsea and Farah hiked quietly from the back of the hiking line. The camera was rolling.

"Yeah, Phil, I was thinking about that," Spencer started.

"Guys, stop," Ian tried.

"Does that really make sense to you?" Spencer went on. "Don't rules like that give you pause about the whole enterprise?"

They all kept walking, waiting for his response. Even Ian, who wanted to stop the teasing, also wanted to hear the answer.

"Sometimes it does," Philip finally said. "But I'm comfortable with my skepticism. The work is good if you do it right. How does anyone commit to anything that's flawed?"

"So you're like JJ, then," Charlie said.

"How so?"

"JJ does the same calculation about his work," Charlie explained. "It's the *net-positive* argument. You think he's lobbying to get solar panels on household rooftops all day? No way. I bet he spends at least half his time working for oil companies and mountaintop mining. He doesn't want to admit it, but he does."

"I've wondered about that," Philip said quietly. "But JJ isn't here to defend himself."

Charlie went on. "And the thing is that JJ believes that the net result of his work is good—or more good than bad. And that's how he lives with himself. So in that way, you're just like him."

Philip stopped walking, and then they all stopped with him. "It's not the same thing," he said softly. "I don't think some arcane ideas about human sexuality are as bad as defending massive oil spills."

"But it is, Phil!" Charlie was yelling now. "It is! Because *you're* lobbying on behalf of shame and repression—two of the most destructive forces in human history!"

Philip's hands formed tight fists at his sides. "Why do you care so much about this, Charlie? Don't you have bigger problems right now? Didn't you *just* tell us you're unemployed?"

The two brothers stared at each other while the others watched. Finally, Charlie started walking and Philip followed. Everyone else fell in line. Charlie's unemployment, of course, was the point.

Ian wished that Mary-Beth were here with him, to witness whatever it was he had just seen. It was the same old brother stuff, but with a sharper edge this time. There was a new fraying.

They huffed and dripped and hauled their aching bodies up the rest of the mountain in silence. Leaves swayed in a gentle breeze, and chipmunks darted across the path.

At the top, everyone collapsed on their own private patch of grass or flat rock. The view was glorious. Each tiny Berkshire town was now just a cluster of dollhouse figurines with a church steeple at the center. Their own lake was a blue puddle in a series of oddly shaped puddles, surrounded by cartoon-perfect trees. A miniscule paper sailboat floated across the largest.

"This is one of the prettier things I've ever seen," Farah said as she zipped her camera into a pocket. Her face was blotchy with heat and exhaustion.

Charlie handed out apples from his backpack. "It's worth it, right?"

"I wouldn't go that far."

Philip laughed to himself.

Spencer looked at his phone. "We got a note from Mom. Apparently JJ and Mary-Beth are going to be on *Good Morning America* tomorrow with the boys and a couple of their teammates. Dad's going to be on, too. They're all meeting in New York tonight."

No one seemed surprised by this information. They nodded, as if appearing on national television twice in one week was the most normal thing in the world.

"We should head back," Philip said.

Charlie stood up and readjusted his baseball cap. "I'll take the lead."

"No, *I'll* take the lead," Chelsea corrected. "This isn't a race."

He smiled and kissed the side of her sweaty head.

The walk down was mostly quiet. It went faster, but because the steep descent engaged a whole new set of unprepared muscles, it was still difficult. Their thighs wobbled and threatened to buckle every now and then.

This was one of the things Ian thought the Brights always had right: the impulse to walk it off. They pushed their bodies until uncomfortable thoughts dissolved in the exhaustion. It wasn't a sophisticated theory of emotional well-being, but it worked more often than it should. It had gotten them this far in life.

When they got to the bottom, Spencer stopped and looked around at the group. "With Mom and Dad gone, we're on our own for dinner. What should we do?"

Philip stepped forward without hesitation. "I think we should get drunk," he said. "I think it's time for that."

21

The first round was margaritas—not the good kind Farah was hoping for, but the cheap chartreuse mix, left over from some party years ago and forgotten in the basement. They were all still in their rank hiking clothes when Charlie started mixing them up and passing them around. They'd brought a full pitcher down to the lake and arranged folding chairs in the shallow water, just deep enough to soak their aching calves.

Cold, sweet and synthetic, the margaritas went down quickly.

Farah leaned back in her chair and closed her eyes. The sun was beginning its descent behind the tree line at the west end of the lake. She could feel the water dissolving the film of dirt and dried sweat that coated her legs. Everything hurt, but in a kind of pleasant way now. She was proud of herself for having survived the hike.

Two drinks, she told herself. *You're only allowed two.*

Farah was stressed about all the action she must have missed while they were on that mountain. She should have been back at the house when John Senior and Patty made the decision to go to New York for *Good Morning America*. She should be driving there with them right now, documenting the Senator's every move.

Farah pulled out her phone and sent a text to Wayne.

Senator Bright and wife on their way to NY for GMA. I screwed up and missed my chance to travel along.

Wayne wrote back immediately.

Just be sure to get reaction from family when it goes live. That might be the better angle anyway.

Will do.

Farah put her phone back in her pocket and stood up. She felt wobbly on her feet, as much because of her sore muscles as the two strong drinks.

"I should get back to work."

Charlie, who was pouring more green liquid into Philip's cup, looked up. "No, stay for another."

"I really can't."

"Just set some cameras up out here." He gestured vaguely toward the house.

"Charlie, relax," Chelsea said. "She said she has to work."

"Well, we're going swimming," Spencer announced. He pulled Ian out of the chair beside him.

Ian pushed Spencer backward into the water, sending a small wave over the rest of them. The group laughed and splashed, and the focus again shifted away from Farah, as it should be. She walked back to her apartment above the garage.

Inside, Farah switched out batteries in two of the cameras. She uploaded hours of footage onto her external drive and wrote up accompanying notes for the files she thought might be useful later. The sound of men laughing floated up through the screen window of her temporary bedroom.

She'd spent almost no time in her room since arriving there. She hadn't used the little electric coffeepot or turned on the TV. She hadn't noticed the little basket of hand towels or the soaps shaped like trout. Now that she was looking around, she realized that Patty's little touches were everywhere.

Farah walked to the window and looked out. It was just Charlie and Chelsea on the beach now. No sign of the others. Charlie was sitting in his chair, and Chelsea was standing before him. He was stroking the outside of her right thigh, looking up at her. Water lapped around their feet.

They were even more beautiful from that distance, both of them. Even in their sexless hiking clothes, they were bursting with erotic virility. It seemed to rise up from their skin as an invisible steam. Farah was reminded of a moment on the trail earlier that day, when she'd turned and bumped into Chelsea, accidentally inhaling her spicy sweat. It was the scent of ripe, new, interesting lust between two people. Something so private, but in clear view of everyone.

Charlie began kissing Chelsea's neck. His hands moved up her shirt. She rocked softly in his grip, and her hair fell around them.

It all happened in the span of a few seconds—Farah watching the couple from the window as the clear moon illuminated them from above. That was all. And then, with his hands still beneath Chelsea's clothes, Charlie looked directly at Farah.

In a stunned paralysis, she held his gaze there. Charlie

smiled—maybe, it was difficult to tell in the distance—then turned back to Chelsea.

Farah closed the curtains and felt her face go red. She felt as if she'd been caught in the act of something shameful.

An hour later, Farah stood under the showerhead until the water changed from warm to cool. She rinsed the shampoo from her hair, shaved all the necessary parts and got dressed again.

Farah had to get back to her cameras, to keep watching them. That was her job. But she dreaded seeing Charlie after that strange moment of being caught in her voyeurism. Farah wasn't attracted to Charlie or Chelsea—not really, though they were both undeniably attractive. It was this place, these men and their sureness that the world exists only to be enjoyed.

She dressed quickly and headed downstairs, checking herself in the mirror on the way out. She was flush from the cold shower and the hot day. Even with stringy wet hair soaking into her faded T-shirt, she looked good—a little pinker and brighter somehow.

Farah's body didn't feel particularly good as she walked down the back stairs and across the gravel driveway. Her legs were stiff and there was a blister on both of her heels. She knew she wasn't in great shape, but the aftermath of the morning's hike was ridiculous. The pain was her penance, she decided, for going on the hike and letting her guard down. It was her punishment for watching Chelsea and Charlie, for yesterday's canoe with Philip, for feeling things.

Farah's phone buzzed in her pocket as she entered the Bright family kitchen.

It was a text from Wayne.

GMA is promoting this like crazy. Could get interesting. Get everything you can from your angle.

"Farah's back," Philip announced cheerfully. He was sitting at the kitchen table working on a jigsaw puzzle with Chelsea. He seemed drunk.

She put her phone into her back pocket and tried to smile. "Do you guys mind if I turn the TV on in the living room?"

"Nope."

In the next room, Charlie, Ian and Spencer were sprawled out on the sectional couches, drinking beer and watching an English Premier League game. They'd all showered and changed since Farah last saw them.

"You need the TV?" Charlie asked, eyes still on the television.

"I was hoping to just take a quick look at ABC, if you don't mind. Apparently, they're promoting the *Good Morning America* piece pretty hard."

"No problem."

Charlie changed the channel and Farah went to the camera at the corner of the room. Nothing more was said between the two of them.

A cat food commercial concluded with a jingle about wild-caught salmon, and then the faces of Lucas and Cameron Bright appeared on the screen.

"Coming up tomorrow—our exclusive interview with the Bright family and several members of the so-called Footy Fifteen. We'll talk about their narrow escape from the terrorist attack that has rocked Spain, and what's next for former Senator Bright and his family."

Spencer sat up. "This should be interesting. I would love to know what's next for the Bright family."

Charlie laughed in agreement.

Ian shot Spencer a give-it-a-rest look, and Spencer ignored him.

"Anyone want more margs?" Philip yelled from the kitchen.

"I think the last one is burning a hole in my gut," Charlie said.

"Just one for Chelsea, then."

The feeling in the room was oddly friendly. Philip appeared to harbor no hostility about his brothers' coordinated attack on him from earlier that day. Everything was just fine now. More than fine; they seemed bonded over a new shared resentment for JJ and their father, which had been reignited by their forthcoming TV appearance.

"Here." Chelsea appeared beside Farah, holding a margarita out in her direction. "Drink this. It will help with the boredom."

Farah looked away from her camera. She wasn't bored, but she took the cocktail. "Thanks."

"Leave the camera running and come sit outside with me, okay?"

She wouldn't have agreed, but for the desperate look in Chelsea's eyes. "Sure."

They carried their drinks through the living room and out the back door.

"So how's it going with all this?" Chelsea asked as the screen door slammed behind them. They relaxed into deck chairs. "How's your documentary coming along?"

The sun was down, but there was still a glow on the lake. Peepers were screaming in concert around them.

"It's fine, I think. I don't really know what this is going to be yet. *If* it's going to be something. That part is hard."

"Are you bored? I'm sooo bored."

Farah swatted a mosquito. "Um, not really bored, no. I'm kind of stressed out, actually. A promotion at work kind of hinges on this. You're bored?"

"It's not boredom exactly." Chelsea ran a hand dramatically through her long hair, and it was clear that she was drunk. "It's just too intense here. The Madrid thing, and the TV cameras, and now all of us just holed up together here. Like, I know what *you're* doing here. And I know what *Ian* is doing here. But what am *I* doing here? I barely know Charlie."

"Really? I thought you guys…" Farah felt her face go red again and she took a sip of her drink.

"Well, I *know* him, but we're not exactly at a meet-the-parents stage in our relationship. This is way more than I signed up for…not that I had any other options."

Farah nodded, unsure of how to help.

"Sorry, I'm just blabbing on like this. I don't really know you, either."

"It's fine. I'm glad you are."

"You're just the only person here who isn't…one of them, you know? I feel like we'd hang out in the real world." Chelsea suddenly looked embarrassed, like she'd been coming on too strong. "Sorry, I've had a few too many of these."

"No, we would. I agree."

"Will you get drunk with me tonight? It will make me feel so much less alone and bored."

"I can have another, at least. But we have to avoid the cameras. The shots that I'm in are unusable."

"Deal." Chelsea gave her a little squeeze.

A light came on and Ian appeared a few seconds later. He walked to the grill and started turning knobs. "You guys want tuna steaks? I'm gonna do seared tuna and corn on the cob."

Farah and Chelsea said yes, then went back inside to join Philip at the table with the puzzle. Farah was careful to make sure the two nearby cameras were running and to seat herself as far outside the frame as possible.

Charlie went outside to help Ian with the grilling.

Spencer made a salad.

They left the TV on in the other room to be periodically reminded of their family members in New York.

And the margaritas flowed until they reached the end of the dusty Jose Cuervo liter. It was beer after that.

The group ate a late dinner on top of the partially finished puzzle, then got back to work on it when the dishes were cleared again. It had 1,500 pieces and, when completed, illustrated the most common bird species of the White Mountains. It smelled like mildew and fireplace.

The puzzle was just the pretense for sitting around drinking, telling (or listening to) stories about the funny things the Bright men had done as children and teasing one another in sweet, harmless ways. It made Farah miss her own family, her parents still in New Jersey and two siblings with their own families on the West Coast. They'd all followed their professional ambitions, and it led them so very far away from one another.

Farah was sitting beside Philip at the table, and it was no mistake. Ever since their canoe ride, she had been hoping (despite herself) to talk more with him. Philip reached across the table to fit a piece into the far end, pressing his shoulder against Farah as he did. His closeness felt purposeful to her.

"You're no help at all," Philip teased.

Farah blinked. His face was inches from hers. "What do you mean? I did that whole corner section."

"That's like five pieces! You're going to have to apply yourself more if we're ever going to finish this."

"Philip, this isn't a hazing." Ian pushed a piece in from across the table.

Farah laughed. "Isn't it, though?"

Philip smiled wide, his canines peeking out. "Maybe it is."

It was definitely something.

"Is that the last of the beer?" Chelsea asked.

Charlie stood up. "Nope, I'll grab more."

He returned with a six-pack of Long Trail, handing the first one to Farah. "I knew we'd get you drunk with us eventually."

She laughed and took a sip. And as she drank, Farah realized that she'd been charmed, snared in the Bright net. Whether for sincere or manipulative reasons, the Brights had brought her to their side. She had barely resisted at all. It was precisely what Wayne had warned her about. *Don't go native and don't fall in love with any of them.* That's what he'd said.

And here she was, doing both.

22

"They're on in ten!" Spencer announced from the kitchen.

Charlie got out of bed and put on a T-shirt that had been lying on the floor. "We should get downstairs if we're going to catch my brother on *GMA*."

Chelsea blinked from under the covers. She wasn't even awake yet.

"You coming?"

"You can go ahead without me."

"What?"

"Charlie, I think I should leave today." Chelsea had been practicing the statement over and over in her head since she made the decision the night before.

"You're serious?"

"I am. This has been good—the being with you part. And I'm glad I came. But Charlie, this adventure may have run its course."

"You mean us?"

"No, not exactly. I mean, this adventure in premature co-habitation. Siblings and parents and everything. It's a *lot*. And I'm so grateful that you took me with you, but I think it's time for me to go now."

Chelsea didn't have much of a plan, but she had something. Her parents had agreed to buy her a plane ticket back to England, where she could sleep on her aunt's couch for a while, until she found a job and saved enough for her own place. It wasn't an ideal scenario, but it was preferable to the Brights in the Berkshires.

Charlie looked stricken, panicked. Chelsea was almost touched by it, but she knew him well enough to know that his panic was as much about his fear of being alone as his affection for her. Still, she didn't want to hurt him. This decision wasn't about getting away from Charlie. It was about getting away from this place, his people. She needed to start putting her life in order.

What Chelsea really didn't want to do was talk about it right then. She didn't want this to turn into something decisive like a fight or a breakup. She just wanted to not be here anymore. And she wanted Charlie to understand that it didn't have to *mean* anything beyond its face value. She had been here too long and she couldn't stay another day. That's all it meant.

"You can't go." He shook his head. "No one goes. We agreed to three weeks with my family. That's the plan."

"But so much has happened here, Charlie. Your nephews were involved in a terrorist incident. They're on national TV today! Don't you think the agreement is kind of void at this point? Isn't your summer vacation already screwed up? Let's just adapt."

"No, I disagree. I think you should stay. I would like you to stay."

Chelsea didn't know how to disagree with his disagreement. The more she thought about it, the more the absurdity of his argument came into focus for her. Why were any of them still there? Why were JJ and Mary-Beth planning on bringing the boys back up to Massachusetts after all they'd been through? Why was Philip still allowing himself to be taunted by his siblings about his future plans? Chelsea suspected that it had something to do with Patty and John Senior, their quiet control, which served as an invisible force field around the compound, keeping everyone inside.

"It's starting!" Spencer yelled from downstairs.

Charlie opened the bedroom door. "Let's talk about this later."

"Fine." But Chelsea was even surer now that staying was a dumb idea. She had an exit plan, and she knew she should use it.

"C'mon."

They went downstairs and joined the rest of the family on the couches. The smiling faces of John Senior, Patty, Mary-Beth, JJ and the boys appeared on the large screen.

Farah was in the corner recording Brights as they watched Brights. She gave Chelsea a little wave.

I could just leave now, Chelsea thought.

But she didn't. And she suspected that she wouldn't. Because there was just so much going on with these people, she felt illogically invested in the outcome of whatever the hell this was. And what was waiting for her on the other side of this? A couch at her ailing aunt's house? Weeks or months of staring into the abyss of unemployment? Maybe this was better than that. Maybe it wasn't. She didn't leave.

George Stephanopoulos smiled at them from the screen. He was perched on a stool beside the six Brights, who'd been arranged in a cluster on the tiered production stage.

"We're here with former senator John Bright, his wife, Patty, their son JJ and his wife, Mary-Beth, and their sons, Cameron and Lucas. Thank you all for joining us."

The Brights smiled and thanked George like he was an old friend, and maybe he was.

"Cameron and Lucas—you narrowly escaped a devastating terrorist attack in Madrid earlier this week, along with the rest of your soccer team. We'll talk to a few of your teammates tomorrow, but today, I'd like to hear directly from you guys about what it was like to be caught up in this event. Lucas, can you tell us what you saw?"

Lucas nodded and gulped. He was dressed in a stark blue shirt and had brushed his dark wavy hair back from his eyes. Despite his size, Chelsea thought he looked about ten years old.

"Well, ah, we didn't really know that anything was happening until our plane took off. We had just left the ground, I think, and then there was this explosion from the airport. We couldn't see it, but the plane kind of vibrated, and then everyone started freaking out."

George shook his head. "Terrifying. Cameron, tell us what happened next."

Cam looked to his brother at his side. "After that, we just had a pretty panicked ride to the Barcelona airport. It was short, which is good, I guess. But none of us knew what was going on. The pilot said there had been an explosion and then a few people cried. One guy on our team threw up. When we landed, all these cops were there, and they took us to the US consulate and explained what had happened."

"Were you scared?"

Both boys nodded and Cam spoke. "Yes. But, um, we should also say that all of the Catalan authorities were very nice to us and made us feel safe. We'd like to thank them for taking great care of our team." He looked up at his father, and it was clear that he'd been instructed to say that part.

George shifted his attention to JJ and Mary-Beth. "You

must be proud of these young men and how they've represented the US in a moment of crisis?"

Mary-Beth smiled shyly.

JJ elaborated on just how proud he was, and how brave the boys had been. He restated some of the messages from their press release and his gratitude to the troops who'd escorted the team home.

Chelsea looked back and forth, from the screen to the people sitting there with her on the couch, watching it all like there was nothing remarkable about having half your family in the living room and the other half in George Stephanopoulos's fake TV living room. She was keenly aware of Farah's camera lens, which made a faint buzzing sound as it zoomed in and out from their faces as they watched.

Charlie put a hand on Chelsea's thigh and squeezed.

"Senator Bright," George said more seriously, "I'd like to turn to you now and discuss the broader political implications of this tragedy. EU officials haven't confirmed which extremist group is responsible for this attack, but experts are speculating that it was ISIS related. You've alluded to the possibility that your grandsons were specifically targeted by these terrorists. Why do you believe this to be true?"

John nodded. "George, I can't say for sure that they were targeted, and I don't want to get out ahead of our security agencies on the matter. But what I do know is that, in my long career in the United States House, Senate, and Massachusetts state government, I've championed issues that are central to the values we stand for in America—the very same values that religious extremists in the Middle East oppose. I'm talking about freedom of expression and freedom of religion."

"Well, let's talk about that, Senator. You've been a long-standing advocate for Israel in your time in office. And now your grandsons attend a Catholic school in the suburbs of

Washington, DC. How has faith played a role for your family during this crisis?"

Cameron and Lucas fidgeted.

Mary-Beth looked at her hands clasped in her lap.

And John Bright forged ahead. "George, we found great solace in our faith in the time that the boys were away from us, for sure. Prayer and contemplation got us all through, as well as an abiding faith in the values of the United States of America. I'm fiercely protective of those values at moments like this—when the US and the Western world are under assault."

George smirked. "Senator, you sound like a man running for office. Are you sure this retirement is for good?"

John laughed a big, happy laugh and put an arm around Patty. "That was the plan, George, but who knows. I don't have any announcements to make today."

Patty looked at her husband, and Mary-Beth looked at hers.

George raised his eyebrows and looked directly at the camera. "Well, there you have it, Senator Bright is *not* denying the possibility of another run for office! You never know when we're going to break news here on *GMA*." He turned back to the Brights. "I'd like to thank you all for being here and sharing your experience. Lucas and Cameron, best of luck to you and the whole Footy Fifteen. We'll be back after the break."

Ian turned the TV off.

Spencer leaned back into the couch. "Well, fuck."

Farah's lens zoomed in and out.

"Are you surprised that he wants to run again?" Charlie said. "I'm not."

Ian stood up. "Me, either. I need some coffee."

"You surprised, Phil?"

Philip shrugged and frowned. "I guess not. It's what he does. Though I think it would be a good idea for him to figure out what *else* he does."

"He didn't actually *say* he was running for anything," Chelsea volunteered.

Spencer, Charlie and Philip rolled their eyes, and Chelsea understood that it was too late for all that. Apparently, something was already underway. What a strange language these people spoke. Announcing you're running for office by announcing you're not running, or not *not* running.

"Who else wants coffee?" Ian said from the kitchen, and the Bright men all got up.

Only Chelsea was left in the living room, with Farah watching her from behind the camera.

Farah pressed a button, and the recording light went dark. She looked out at Chelsea. "So are you gonna leave?" she said quietly.

"I don't know."

"I hope you don't. I'll be here all alone if you do."

Chelsea smiled. "I probably won't. I don't have much to go to at the moment. I *should* leave."

"Yeah, I get it."

Chelsea rubbed her temples. She'd had too much to drink the night before. "So this is a new twist in your movie, huh? Another campaign, maybe."

"Could be." Farah looked worn-out, too.

The idea of following this family around all day seemed so tiring to Chelsea. Then again, at least Farah was getting paid to do it.

Charlie popped his head in. "Canoe regatta starts in twenty minutes. Grab your suit, Chelsea."

Chelsea nodded in assent. She'd probably put her bathing suit on and follow the guys out to the water. She'd probably pop a Tylenol and chug a seltzer, and spend the rest of the day with this hangover and an acute awareness of her own weakness. She didn't know why she was there, but she couldn't think of anywhere else to be.

23

When they returned to the lake house that afternoon, Mary-Beth gasped, "Look at this place."

Wet swim trunks and towels were slung over kitchen chairs. Lunch plates were stacked in the sink. Two flies buzzed around margarita goblets that were still sticky with old drinks.

The house was empty but for the flies. Everyone was down at the waterfront, lounging in beach recliners and bobbing in inner tubes. Three canoes were beached at cockeyed angles in the grass.

JJ, Mary-Beth, John, Patty and the boys scanned the house.

"I guess vacation is officially underway," John Senior laughed, already headed outside to join them.

Cameron and Lucas plopped onto the couches and pulled out their phones.

Patty shook her head and got to work on the dishes.

"Patty, relax," Mary-Beth said. "Let them clean this up."

Patty ignored her, so Mary-Beth headed upstairs without another word. If Patty wanted to wait on these adults like a servant, that was her choice. Mary-Beth wasn't going to do it.

Things weren't like this at their home back in Maryland. JJ was a thoughtful partner, grateful to Mary-Beth for handling the vast majority of the housework and happy to pitch in where he could. But when he was with his mother, JJ and his brothers were like spoiled children, content to take full advantage of her amenities. In turn, Patty felt entitled to a level of intimacy with her sons that seemed wildly inappropriate to Mary-Beth. It was the kind of thing that drove her nuts in the early years of their marriage. She'd pick fights with JJ about it when they were back home, which only made her appear threatened and petty. Somewhere along the way, Mary-Beth stopped bothering with the arguments. She knew who her husband was. She wasn't going to do the damn dishes, but neither was she going to shame Patty for doing them. She was exhausted and overwhelmed, and she had no interest in competing with her mother-in-law's martyrdom.

Upstairs in their bedroom, Mary-Beth slipped out of her shoes, crawled under the covers and closed her eyes.

Three minutes later, JJ came in. He lay down over the top of the comforter and put his arms around her blanketed form. He sighed. "They're home, honey. We can relax now."

She breathed and let the weight of her body sink into the mattress. Her children were home with them. They were unharmed, and only a little traumatized. Cameron and Lucas had spent the majority of the drive back to Massachusetts recounting stories of silly, dumb ways in which they'd passed the time while they were stuck in the consulate with their teammates. They'd laughed and slept and complained about the length of the car trip. Things felt wonderfully normal all of a sudden, and Mary-Beth was beginning to believe that they *were* normal again, that she could relax. Still, she wished they were at home in Maryland, just the four of them.

"Can we leave the lake early, JJ? Let's just go home."

He kissed her forehead. "We talked about this already. I don't think we should. I feel safer with my dad's security detail around, just in case the attack really did have something to do with us. Plus, we made a commitment to the documentary people."

"But we could probably get out of that now, don't you think? I'm sure there's some fine print in the agreement for extenuating circumstances. Let's just go home and finish the summer together."

"We might be able to get out of it, but I'm not sure that we should. If my dad is serious about running for office..."

Mary-Beth pulled back from him. "Do you think he was serious about that? What would he run for? His senate seat won't be up again for three more years."

"The governor's race is next year, though." JJ paused. "I think he should go for it."

"God, that's the last thing your father needs. You're encouraging this? I thought that was just talk for the cameras, his usual stuff. Why would you encourage this? Your father needs to figure out how to be a retired person. If not for himself, then for your mom."

"This is what they do, Mary. They like this life. And I think he could win that seat. Democrats are ready for someone with national security experience in the governor's office. All these attacks make people hawkish." JJ looked sheepishly into his wife's eyes. "And I may have suggested to him that I could take a leave from work and be his campaign manager."

Mary-Beth shot up in bed. "Are you serious? Were you going to ask me?"

"Of course I was going to ask you. This is all just talk right now. It doesn't mean anything yet. I wouldn't do anything without your blessing, or the boys'. Let's just forget I mentioned it and get some rest, together, just the two of us."

JJ peeled the covers back and tucked his large body underneath with his wife's. He wrapped his arms tightly around her.

Mary-Beth wanted to sleep. She wanted only to feel him enveloping her and holding her until sleep washed over them both. This new talk of a campaign was too much to wrap her head around right now.

But JJ wasn't tired; he wanted more of her that day. It was so rare that JJ wanted more than Mary-Beth. Their desire was usually mutually reinforcing; she was aroused by his arousal, and vice versa. Even when things felt distant between them, they could find each other in bed. Their bodies could span the distance first, then their minds.

But it suddenly felt as if there were too many Brights in bed with Mary-Beth and JJ at that moment, as he pressed himself against her. They weren't alone. Senator John Bright was with them in bed, running the show; and Patty was there keeping things tidy; Spencer was competing with them; and Charlie was teasing them; Farah was recording it all; and George Stephanopoulos was breaking news about it. Mary-Beth couldn't have sex with her husband without feeling like she was sleeping with all of them, all at once. She wanted to be home, in private, with *her* family.

"JJ, I have to sleep."

"Okay, I love you." He kissed the back of her neck.

JJ stayed with her until she could feel the hazy fog of afternoon sleep pull her away from reality. When she had almost succumbed to it, she heard him creep quietly out of the room.

When he was gone, Mary-Beth tried to fall back to sleep, but she couldn't stop thinking about JJ. She had the disturbing sensation that his arousal had nothing at all to do with her. It was this moment: the television appearance and documentary film cameras, the onslaught of social media attention, and now the possibility of John Senior throwing his hat in a gubernatorial race. It all excited him. JJ's ego—which had been so bruised in recent months—was recovering with all this new possibility.

It was all Mary-Beth wanted for her husband: to feel appreciated and purposeful again. But she didn't want it this way. She didn't want the tether connecting her family to her in-laws growing shorter, the remaining boundaries dissolving. The reason Mary-Beth could come to the lake house each summer and enjoy it was because they had their own life far away for the rest of the year. Distance was essential to this formula. Without the distance, these trips lost their usefulness. So while JJ was mistaking this campaign idea for a professional win, Mary-Beth couldn't help but feel that it was a regression—or worse, a coup led by John and Patty.

She fell asleep in her in-laws' bed, surrounded by people, and utterly alone.

When Mary-Beth awoke, the sun was low in the sky and her stomach was growling. It must have been dinnertime, though she heard not a peep from downstairs.

She slipped into flip-flops and went down to the kitchen. It was sparkling clean again. A bowl of peaches sat on the counter, a handwritten note tucked beneath it.

Went with Dad and the guys to the wine store. Mom's at yoga. We'll get takeout for dinner on our way home. Love JJ.

Mary-Beth fished her book from her purse and decided to head down to the waterfront to do the only thing she wanted to do at the lake house this summer: read in peace. But when she walked through the back door to the deck, she saw Chelsea standing down at the shore. She sighed to herself and kept walking toward the water.

"Is everyone gone?" Mary-Beth asked as she approached the shore.

Chelsea jumped and turned. "Jesus, you scared me. Most of them are gone, yeah."

"Sorry."

Mary-Beth stood beside Chelsea and tried to see whatever it was that she was looking at on the water. "It's nice when it's quiet here, huh?"

She hated how square she felt beside Chelsea, how neat and orderly her appearance seemed against Chelsea's messy coolness. It felt like a false advertisement for the person Mary-Beth was. She wasn't as prim as she seemed. And yet here she was, dressing and speaking and acting like a middle-aged prude. How, Mary-Beth wondered, does a person get so accidentally swept up in a tide that she doesn't know she's in? She didn't mind aging, but she hated to think she'd been passive in the trappings of age. Seeing Chelsea made her feel that way. Chelsea made her aware of all the old-person habits she'd mindlessly adopted over the years without questioning their necessity.

Mary-Beth was about to sit in the lounge chair and open her book when Chelsea turned to her.

"Mary-Beth, I feel like I need to say..." Chelsea looked at her toes in the wet sand. "I'd like to say that I'm sorry."

"For what?"

"Just for being here. I know that what happened to your boys is a big deal, and I feel like you deserve some privacy now that you're all back together. You don't need some random outsider here right now. And, for whatever it's worth—which probably isn't much—I'm working on leaving. Anyway, I'm just sorry for crashing this private family thing."

Mary-Beth smiled slightly. Chelsea had apologized for precisely the thing that Mary-Beth had been resenting her for. But as she articulated her apology for the non-crime of her presence, Mary-Beth realized that Chelsea wasn't the impediment to her privacy. Her husband was—he and the rest of his family. Because privacy was the thing that none of them wanted, even under these circumstances. They were the ones who'd invited a documentary filmmaker there, and gone on *Good Morning America* and answered the phones to dozens of reporters. If Mary-Beth was going to feel mad at her open-book family life, it shouldn't be at Chelsea.

"Thanks for saying that…and don't worry about it. I'm kind of glad you're here, actually."

The sound of bare feet padding through grass approached from behind, and both women turned around.

"Nice evening," Philip said. He was smiling in swim trunks.

"Hey Phil," Mary-Beth said. "You didn't want to go with Farah and the guys to get wine?"

"Actually, I was looking forward to a little quiet time."

The faint sound of children splashing in water drifted down from the east side of the lake. Mary-Beth imagined those children as JJ and his brothers not so long ago; it wasn't hard to do.

Philip heard it, too. "Do you remember that time we went skinny-dipping here, Mary-Beth? It must have been ten years ago. Lucas and Cam were so little."

"Actually, *you guys* went skinny-dipping. Only the Bright men were naked that night."

He nodded. "Yeah, that makes more sense. I must have forgotten."

They stood three abreast at the water's edge, listening to the sounds of someone else's children. Chelsea drew circles in the sand with her big toe, and eventually the sounds faded to silence.

"Of course *I* hadn't gone skinny-dipping on that day," Mary-Beth said to no one in particular.

Philip and Chelsea studied her face. She could feel their eyes on her as she watched the indigo water ripple in the dusk light.

A small fury was growing inside Mary-Beth at that moment, for all the time wasted on modesty and discretion and a practiced, ladylike smallness. All that privacy had left her only alone. Whether here or at home, her reward for it all was always just a shrinking self.

Chelsea turned to walk back to the house. "Anyway, I should…"

"No, wait." Mary-Beth reached out and held her forearm. "Let's go swimming."

Chelsea's eyebrows rose. "Okay."

Mary-Beth stepped out of her shoes first. Then she pulled her shirt off. Shorts went next, leaving only her bra and underwear, both formerly pretty items that had done too many rounds in the washing machine. Frayed threads at the waistband fluttered in the wind. And then she took those off, too.

Philip and Chelsea hesitated for only a moment, to be sure that Mary-Beth was proposing what she seemed to be proposing. And then they joined her, letting shorts fall to puddles at their feet and tossing shirts off in one stroke. They were both entirely comfortable in their bodies, but in different ways.

Mary-Beth stood naked for a moment beside her brother-in-law—the maybe future priest—and this pretty woman she barely knew. A breeze moved past them, and she became aware of the parts of her body that hadn't felt a breeze in decades—her breasts, which she still liked a lot; her stomach, which remained disappointing no matter what she did; and the tuft of hair that she didn't know what to do with as she approached middle age. It all felt surprisingly lovely in the wind. Parts of her body were enjoying the exposure without waiting for her permission.

"Do you think those cameras can see us?" Philip wondered.

All three of them looked back at the house, where a camera mounted to the deck was doing the work of recording them in Farah's absence.

"I don't know," Mary-Beth said, still naked.

Philip and Chelsea, and even the sounds of nature around them, waited reverently for her to initiate the next move.

And then Mary-Beth ran straight into the water, laughing along the way.

It wasn't particularly cold, but the chill hit some parts of her body harder than others. She swam out farther and let the work of treading water warm her muscles. Her unobstructed skin was silk against the water's pull. Heavy limbs transformed to something weightless and gossamer. Nothing was old; everything was new and vital.

The other two followed and swam out to meet her. Moments later, the three of them were bobbing in a perfect triangle in the lake.

"We should do this every day," Mary-Beth said.

"Definitely," Philip agreed.

Chelsea went under and came back up like a seal. "I'm in."

"I knew you had this in you," Philip said.

Mary-Beth laughed and shivered, and she felt at that moment so deeply in love with her extended family, these Brights and their extras. They might never do this again, but forever and ever, it will be a thing that they did.

The screen door squeaked open and through it came JJ, Charlie, Spencer and Ian. Farah and her camera were a few steps behind.

"What the hell?" someone said.

There was a whoop and a laugh as the men approached. Mercifully, her children were nowhere to be seen.

Mary-Beth closed her eyes and went under once more,

holding her breath for ten seconds in that dark other world. And then she came up. Her hair was slicked smooth against her head, water falling from eyelashes and lips. Mary-Beth swam to the shore and emerged from the lake renewed, still herself but lighter.

24

The waitress set tall glasses of cold lagers before each of the men at the table while they looked out at the rolling hills of the golf course. Another day, another male-bonding experience with the Bright boys.

Ian hated golf. He hated the environmental costs and the arcane club rules, the stupid clothes and the old conservative men. But at that moment, he didn't mind the cold beer and picturesque views. John Senior had invited all the men out for a round on the links, followed by happy hour beers, to discuss "next steps for the family." Ian probably could have gotten out of the activity on the grounds of not being a biological Bright son, but he had come along for Spencer's sake. Spencer loved golf.

A group of passing men recognized John Senior and stopped to shake his hand. They told him they'd voted for him and hoped he was enjoying retirement. John Senior stood up from the table and pumped each of their hands before rejoining his family.

"So let's talk about the thing we're here to talk about, Dad," Philip said. "Are you running for governor?"

John took a sip of beer. "Well, son, I'm not sure yet. What do you think I should do?"

"I think you should retire."

Spencer balked. "Don't listen to him. You should run, Dad. This is your moment. You've always said you wanted to try for governor, and I'd be willing to bet that you poll through the roof right now. Security and immigration are going to be huge issues in the next gubernatorial."

"Through the roof," JJ agreed. "I can get poll numbers done for you in two days, no problem. They'll be rough indicators, but something."

John nodded. "What do you think, Ian?"

Ian didn't really want to say. "I agree that you probably poll well right now, after the whole Madrid thing. But I think next fall will be a tough year for establishment Democrats. I just read a *New Yorker* piece about all the money pouring into progressive candidates right now. Sounds ominous for the old lions."

John Senior loved to consider himself an old lion.

"Charlie, what do you think?"

"I think you should do what you want to do, Dad. What do *you* want?"

"You know what I want?" John took a deep breath and looked out toward the mountains. "I want to run for governor of Massachusetts. And I want to do it with my family this time. What do you think, John Junior—you want to be my campaign manager?"

JJ hadn't worked on a political campaign in fifteen years, but that wasn't the sort of fact that got in the way of Bright men. He smiled proudly and waited for his father to continue with this soliloquy.

"And I want Charlie running the boots-on-the-ground operation—wrangling volunteers for door knocking, signs, flyers, robocalls. Charlie, I know you've never done a campaign before, but you have lots of project management experience that would be directly useful here. Seems like this might be a good transition moment in your career to take advantage of, right?"

Charlie nodded, adding no details about the state of his career.

Ian knew what was going on here. John was sparing all of them the awkwardness of having to articulate their professional stumbles. Charlie's employer had dissolved, JJ was stalled at work and Spencer was suffering from a severe case of underappreciated genius. John Senior intuited all this and wanted to save them. It was an act of kindness, but it came with rewards for him, too. Ian suspected that this had always been his father-in-law's vision: to have his offspring all working for him, selling his brand. John Bright Senior wanted his children to be successful in the world, but what he wanted even more than that was to feel like the infallible patriarch to his brood. With this move, he could come to his children's aid and avoid ever being unseated by them. It was perfect.

"And Spencer, I'll need you to be my head of policy. I assume you're committed to another semester of classes, but it could help keep you busy while you're in between books."

The Bright men all looked at one another—all but Philip, who had snuck off to the restroom, unnoticed.

"When would something like this start?" Charlie asked.

"Well, we could do some polling this month. We'd have to get all the signatures and paperwork in as soon as possible. And we'd need to get a few big names signed on for early endorsement. I've already floated the idea with leadership at the Democratic Governors Association and am pretty confident they would get behind me, which would unlock some major donors. My primary concern is that it's getting late to jump in, so I don't want to wait long. Probably your official start dates would be next month. After that, we could work on building out staff and setting up a proper operation."

"Here?" Ian said.

"No, we'll have to rent space in Boston. I've got a guy, a developer, who owes me a favor and could probably get some reasonable space for us. You could work from your respective homes through the fall and join me there in the winter, once you've wound down your other obligations."

"I'm in," JJ said first.

"I might be, too," Charlie said.

Spencer looked at his husband, and Ian sighed in a sort of helpless, resigned signal of permission. "Me, too."

"It's decided then!" John stood up with his beer raised high. "We're running for governor!"

The men all clinked glasses and onlookers turned toward them. It occurred to Ian that John had planned it this way, to get the rumor mill churning about a possible run for governor. It was a trial balloon, as the Brights called it. If the political gossips mocked the idea, John could still scrap it; but if there seemed to be an appetite for a Governor John Bright, then he could confirm the rumor. Nothing was an accident with these people.

Philip returned to the table and looked around. "Looks like you've already decided. Are you doing this, Dad?"

"I am, son. Will you help me?"

"I will *support* you. But it's not my line of work. What does Mom think of the idea?"

"She thinks it's a great idea, of course."

And that was that. They drank their beers and enjoyed the views overlooking the golf course. Strangers approached the table to say hello to the former senator, and he shook their hands and looked into their eyes like they were the only people on earth. John Bright Senior was a politician in every waking second of his life.

"What do you think of it all?" Mary-Beth asked Ian later that night.

She was lying across his bed reading a magazine while he folded laundry. The rest of the family was playing Pictionary downstairs. Farah was presumably capturing it all.

Ian sighed. "I don't know. I have no opinion about whether or not John Senior runs for governor. I honestly don't care. But I'm conflicted about whether Spencer should be involved. He loves the idea, of course, but I'm worried that it won't deliver in the way that he thinks it will. I'm not sure working with his father will make him feel more accomplished in the end. It could do the opposite."

Mary-Beth nodded. "I know. I was thinking the same thing about JJ. But I'm not sure we have a choice. He hasn't said it outright, but I get the feeling JJ's being layered at work. Things aren't good. We could certainly use the extra money from a campaign."

Ian stopped folding. "You guys need money? I don't believe it."

"It's true. We went too fast with the new house renovations…the swimming pool and master bath and everything. It's the dumbest reason to be broke, I know. It's so embarrassing. God, I shouldn't be talking about this. Don't tell JJ I said anything, okay?"

"Of course not. You know me."

Ian folded T-shirts into a stack. He wanted to say more, but he didn't know what to say. He loved Mary-Beth. She was one of the best things about these summer vacations: the quiet camaraderie of being extras together, finding sanity in the validation of another non-Bright. Sometimes it felt to Ian that they could have been siblings in a different life, both trim and fair. Either one of them would stand out in a normal family, but not in this one. Their beauty was too muted and wispy for the stark contrasts of the Brights' dark hair and emerald eyes.

"The truth is," Ian said, "I just don't think I can handle a whole year of Bright family interactions. It's going to be constant. You realize that, right?"

"I can't even think about it. Are they getting started right away? JJ didn't have any details when I asked him."

"I think the plan is to map out the campaign messaging and strategy over the next few weeks, while we're all here. Then they'll make a plan remotely in the fall for what comes next. It sounds like we'll all be back together by Christmas if this is really happening."

"Oh, God help us." Mary-Beth laid her head down on the comforter.

She looked especially pretty in that moment to Ian, with her hair uncharacteristically messy and her face free of makeup.

"I should probably get back on my therapist's schedule before then," Ian half joked.

She laughed. "Hey, what about Philip?"

"John Senior barely even asked if he wanted to join the campaign," Ian whispered. "It was like he wasn't there."

"What?"

"No. It was so rude. John Senior just waited until he was in the bathroom to pitch this to the rest of them. I mean, it's a good thing Philip isn't interested in working on the campaign, but it was still pretty shitty. Anyway, he's still gung ho about seminary school."

Mary-Beth thought about this. "I'm kind of glad for him... for having his own thing. It's healthy."

"That's true. He's his own man."

"He really is."

Through the window, they could see Philip under his oak tree, sitting with his legs folded beneath him, eyes closed. A book was open beside him. He had logged dozens of hours out there already, under his tree, while the rest of his family talked and played and competed. His capacity for stillness was astonishing.

"We should go downstairs," Ian said. "Charlie's doing his annual slideshow of his international travels at four."

Mary-Beth rolled her eyes but got off the bed.

"It could be worse."

They both laughed, knowing that was true. And also knowing that it wasn't so bad at all, to be a member of this club. These Bright vacations were like cruise ships with twenty-four-hour activities aboard. It was a cheery sort of torture.

25

"Do you mind me asking what you're doing?"

Farah didn't look away from her camera, which was focused on a bee as it landed on the bud of a lavender plant in the Bright family garden. They were alone outside. "I'm getting b-roll."

Philip didn't say anything from behind her.

"B-roll." She turned to look at him. "Get it? Bee roll?"

He frowned.

"Never mind. I'm trying to get some extra footage of atmospherics—shifting clouds, babbling brooks, hummingbirds in flowers, that sort of thing. You have any ideas?"

Philip thought for a moment. "Actually, I have the perfect spot. You want to go for a little hike?"

Farah turned off her camera. "Not if it's anything like the *little* hike your brothers forced me to go on a few days ago."

"No, it's nothing like that. Just a flat trail around the west side of the lake. It's beautiful in the morning."

Farah knew she'd go with Philip no matter where he invited her, even if it was back up that mountain. Ever since the night they all stayed up drinking, she'd been falling fast down a rabbit hole of infatuation. It didn't make any sense that she was suddenly obsessed with Philip. The idea of it almost embarrassed her. But there it was: she wanted Philip. Among the various handsome and charming men at that house, she wanted him. And he was planning on becoming a priest! That was the dumbest part. He was *officially* off-limits.

Ten minutes later, Farah was walking behind Philip along a narrow trail that looked out through the trees at the shimmering lake on their right. Beneath their feet, roots jutted and crossed in an arthritic web. It required vigilance not to trip. Farah could feel sweat beginning to soak through the back of her shirt and into her backpack. The sun was gaining strength above them. And, to her great surprise, she didn't mind it. The muscles in her legs had healed since their last big hike, and she was becoming reacquainted with the feeling of her body in the wild outdoors. Bugs and sun and dirt and sweat. She was surrendering to all the things she normally avoided.

Philip talked from up ahead, his ears rising and falling slightly as he did.

"So this used to be a big mill town. Paper production, I think. Anyhow, the river and lakes got so polluted for a while that no one could go in them without getting sick. Eventually, the mills closed down, and they launched this big watershed cleanup initiative. It took years, but it worked. Today, it's considered one of the cleanest lakes in the state, which is just amazing to me. I saw these pictures from, maybe, the turn of the century, and it looked as black as soot then." He stopped and looked back at Farah. "Pretty great, right?"

"Yes, it is."

"Sorry if I'm boring you." He started walking again.

"No, it really is interesting."

A mosquito landed on the back of his neck, and Farah had to resist the urge to reach out and brush it away; she was afraid he might somehow sense her desire through the tips of her fingers.

"Here it is," Philip said, turning off the trail and toward the water. "This is what I was thinking of."

To their right, a winding creek spilled down its rocky riverbed and into the lake. Moss carpeted the edges of the creek, peppered with small purple flowers. If anything had ever been enchanted, Farah felt that this was it.

"Oh, this is perfect." She pulled off her pack and took out a camera. She made a few adjustments, then put her finger to her lips, indicating to Philip to stay quiet.

They were still for two full minutes while Farah collected footage of a falling leaf as it moved along the surface of the creek. It went around wet, black stones and through swirling little pools, catching occasionally on the fuzzy hairs of the moss, until it eventually reached the lake. These were the visual metaphors Farah liked to stock up on early. She wondered which brother's life this footage might eventually help explain, which metaphor it would need to carry.

As Farah filmed, she could feel Philip's immobile presence just a few away.

"Just another minute," she whispered. "Thanks for waiting."

He nodded, content in his stillness.

Farah wondered, *How does someone born of this Bright world manage to become something so different? How does uniformity spawn deviation?* It was particularly baffling in Philip's case because the Bright family identity was so reliant on their sameness. Farah thought she'd never met a family with such a strong notion of "us." She wondered if Philip had been willfully defying the rest of his family all this time or if he was simply incapable of imitating them, a miraculous mutation.

The cold water gurgled on.

"We should have brought snacks," Farah finally said. "For a picnic."

"Great idea. Next time, I guess."

"Yeah, next time."

"C'mon, there's a little waterfall farther up the creek. You should definitely get that."

They climbed through the dense woods, away from the lake, grabbing hold of hanging branches to avoid slipping on the wet rocks. At the waterfall, Philip put his hand out and pulled Farah up the last step to a flat boulder. They had to stand close to balance their bodies on the small space. He held on to a fat tree limb above while her shoulder pressed into his armpit.

Farah laughed awkwardly. She wanted to look up at his face, but she couldn't trust herself.

Philip stood and smiled.

Kiss me, she thought.

He didn't move. The smell of his summer body, so thoroughly male, was all around her.

There was a rustling at that moment from the trail below, and they both strained to see what it was. An animal, maybe. Farah wondered if she could pull her camera out from that position if she needed to.

Philip squinted and then let out a puff of air. "It's only Charlie."

"How do you know?"

And then she smelled it: pot, the faint skunky, sweet smell of quality weed.

"Charlie!" Philip yelled.

He appeared twenty feet farther down and looked up at them. "Oh, hey guys. What are you doing up there?"

Philip dismounted the boulder, helping Farah down with one hand. "We're hiking. What are *you* doing?"

Charlie squinted at them and sucked cannabis oil from a small contraption. "Taking a little personal time. You want some?"

Philip shook his head, and they walked down to the trail. "Farah?"

"No thanks, I'm working."

Charlie shrugged. "Your loss."

"Everything okay?" Philip asked.

He took another hit. "Yeah, I guess. Chelsea seems pissed at me, though. C'mon, walk me back. I'm supposed to meet Dad in ten minutes."

Philip looked at Farah. She nodded.

"Sure."

They walked back along the trail, this time with the water to their opposite side and the sun much hotter and higher in the sky. Charlie explained that he and Chelsea had been fighting for the past two days, that she wanted to go home, and she felt confused about their relationship. Farah knew all this already.

When they got back to their private beach, Philip said, "So why not just let her go, Charlie? I can understand how she'd want to get on with her life right now."

Charlie was incredulous. "Because what am I supposed to do with her gone? We've got, like, two more weeks here? Who am I going to play with?"

He laughed at himself and stuffed the vape pen into his pocket.

A phone rang inside the house, followed by the sound of Patty's voice from a window. "Philip, it's for you!"

Philip thanked Farah for the hike and bounded off toward the house.

Farah wondered what sort of calls he received and from whom.

Charlie lowered his eyebrows and looked at her suddenly. "Hey, what were you guys doing out there, in the woods?"

"Oh, I was just getting some nature footage." Farah reached into her backpack to pull out her camera again, remembering that she needed to change a scratched lens. She wanted to end this line of inquiry. Ever since Charlie had spotted her watching him, she wanted to avoid Charlie completely.

"Just getting footage, huh? You looked pretty close up there on that rock."

She laughed nervously and fidgeted with the camera. "That's ridiculous."

"I thought so, too."

Farah focused on her hands, and as she did, the new lens dropped from her fingers onto the toe of her right sneaker, rolling ten inches along the sand and landing in shallow lake water.

"Oh no!" Farah grabbed the submerged lens and held it up to the light. "This is a two-hundred-dollar part."

"Just dry it off. Here…" Charlie went to reach for the camera lens in her hand, but she pulled it back from him, stepping on his toe as she did.

"Ouch!"

"Oh God, I'm sorry."

He laughed and stepped toward her.

She dried the wet lens with the edge of her shirt and smiled nervously.

And then Charlie's face was right above hers, moving closer. His eyes were inches away. *Don't do it*, she thought. Farah froze. It was too late. Charlie's lips were pressing down onto hers.

"No," she said, pushing him back. "I'm sorry. I'm so sorry." Farah grabbed her backpack and ran.

Charlie said something—sorry, maybe—but she kept going. She went around the house, to the garage and up the stairs without looking back.

In her room, Farah locked the door and sat down on the edge of the bed, listening to the sound of her strained breath. What had just happened? Her first instinct was to blame herself, but the more she thought about it, the less it felt like her fault.

She walked into the bathroom and splashed water on her face.

What if Chelsea had seen them? What if Philip had? Really, anyone could have seen them right out on the waterfront in the middle of the day. It hadn't been her fault, but none of that mattered now. To anyone who might have looked out the window at that precise moment, she was just an unprofessional, unoriginal girl, kissing Charlie Bright.

And then Farah's panic changed to anger, and that's where it stayed.

26

The back door slammed and Charlie walked into the kitchen. He filled a glass of water at the sink and drank it down.

Chelsea, Ian, Spencer, Patty and John looked up from their sandwiches at the table.

"Hi, love. You want lunch?" Patty stood up to fix her son a sandwich, because apparently grown men aren't responsible for sandwich assembly here. "Where've you been?"

He shrugged. "I went for a hike."

Chelsea knew that he'd been smoking pot and seething in the woods. They'd argued that morning about her desire to leave. She'd said she needed to get out of here and figure out what she was going to do next. She needed to find a job and a place to live. Charlie asked her again to stay with him, to make her plans from here. It had gone back and forth for a while like that: not quite fighting, but more contentious than anything their relationship had ever known. He'd tried to take her clothes off. She said she wasn't in the mood. That's when he stalked off to the woods.

It was a dumb exchange. Neither was quite mad at the other. They were just annoyed, consenting hostages stuck together. It was becoming clear to Chelsea that maybe they didn't have quite as much in common as she'd originally thought. In Haiti, with a shared professional challenge and zero vestiges of their origins, they'd been perfectly aligned. They worked and played and drank and had sex. They had everything in common because neither of them had anything else in Haiti. But Charlie looked different to her now. With his family, in this coddling place, he looked less like the fearless man she'd fallen for and more like a petulant and helpless child. It's not that she thought she'd marry him or anything crazy like that. But now she didn't even want to hang out with him.

Patty put a turkey-cheddar sandwich on a plate and set it on the table.

Charlie took a beer from the fridge and sat down before the sandwich without a word for his mother's efforts. The rest of the Brights kept reading the paper.

John dropped his section of the *Boston Globe* and looked up. "Well, this story couldn't have been better for us."

The headline read: "'Draft Bright' Movement Picks Up Steam. Will He Run?"

Chelsea hadn't read it and she wouldn't read it, but she understood the moment. John Bright Senior and his sons were basking in the glow of the anticipatory gossip. Ever since their *Good Morning America* appearance, calls for John to run for office again were mounting in political circles. He'd been making coy statements to reporters for the past day, neither confirming nor denying the possibility of a run for governor. With each call, John Senior and his sons got a visible charge. They all did.

It was interesting, in a way, to see how these things worked.

Chelsea had never known anyone in politics, and she'd never thought much about it. But seeing the early stages of this whisper campaign up close was fascinating because of how unnatural it all was. John Bright had performed well on *Good Morning America*, where he denied any interest in running, which inspired voters to ask him to run, which he would decline until his declines drove the public (some of them) to begging, after which he would dutifully accept the call to public service. It was diabolical and impressive. Chelsea was kind of sad to know it all.

Spencer cleared his throat to read a passage of the article to the table.

"'Former senator John Bright insists that he is not planning another run for public office, but his supporters argue that he's just the man for this moment—pragmatic, experienced and civilized at a time when his party seems intent on tearing itself apart over ideological differences.'"

John Senior smiled and bit into his sandwich.

"Amazing, honey." Patty set her salad fork down. "So when do we announce?"

Spencer shook his head. "Not yet. Make them beg for it."

A car pulled into the driveway. It was Mary-Beth and JJ.

"Great story!" JJ boomed as he came through the screen door. "Great story for us."

The men began talking at once after that, all bursting with ideas and energy.

Chelsea stood up and put her plate in the sink. She had to get out of there.

As she was leaving, Cameron and Lucas ran in.

"Mom and Dad, we have an announcement to make."

Everyone turned to them. "Yes?"

The boys waited until they had the full attention of the room.

Chelsea stopped and waited, too.

"We want a dog."

Mary-Beth frowned. "Guys, we've talked about this. Now is not the time."

"Your mom's right," JJ said.

Cameron folded his meaty arms. "Dad, you asked us what might help us heal after Madrid. This would pretty much do it."

Chelsea watched from the sink while the little shits made their case. It had taken less than a day for her to recognize these boys for what they were: privileged progeny, genetically blessed, and starved for any opportunity to develop real integrity and perspective. Mary-Beth and JJ seemed like nice people, but their niceness was obviously not enough to counter the easy, rarified air these boys breathed in their everyday life.

Mary-Beth shook her head. "Guys, we said no."

"Well, wait a second, son." John Senior raised his hand. "A new dog for a healing family…a playful puppy in the wake of tragedy… It's a good look, don't you think?"

Spencer nodded. "Yeah, it's the right optics."

"No," Mary-Beth said again. "Optics aren't a good reason to adopt a living thing. The answer is *no*."

JJ turned to his wife. "I don't know, Mary. Maybe we should consider it. What if it was a shelter dog?"

"It *has* to be a shelter dog, if you're worried about optics," Patty added.

Lucas and Cameron stood expectantly, waiting for their mother to be overruled by the room. Chelsea wondered if perhaps the whole scene was premeditated, if they'd planned on ambushing her in this context all along.

Mary-Beth shook her head and exhaled. "Whatever," she said finally. Then she walked loudly up the stairs and disappeared into a bedroom. Farah's lens followed her up for a moment, then turned back to the rest of them.

JJ nodded at his sons with a stern look that said, *You won; don't rub it in.*

"Yesss!" Cameron and Lucas high-fived each other and went back outside without so much as a thank-you.

JJ looked guilty for siding with his parents over his wife. And, although this moment had nothing at all to do with her, Chelsea felt surer suddenly that she needed to be rid of Charlie. No matter how much she liked him, she didn't like all this. She didn't like the look of marriage in this light, and she didn't like their collective rationale.

When she'd first arrived at the lake house, Chelsea thought the Bright men were just chauvinists, old-fashioned woman-haters. But she'd been wrong about that. Maybe John Senior was a bit of a pig, but not his sons. No, the offensive mood in the room had nothing to do with gender, but with blood. These people stuck together at the expense of every other relationship. Theirs was an impenetrable club that left everyone else on the outside. Chelsea felt bad for Mary-Beth, but ultimately, it had been Mary-Beth's foolish choice to try to compete with these people.

Two hours later, Chelsea was hunched down low at the dog shelter, looking in through a wire cage at a sheepdog mix. He was old, and, unlike all the other barking dogs around them, he was in no mood to perform for this audition. It was as if he had already resigned himself to an orphaned life. Chelsea loved him.

Charlie squatted down beside her to pet the dog through the wire cage. "Did you have dogs growing up?"

"One. A little terrier named Roxy. She wasn't very nice, but I loved her. She died when I was ten, and my parents vowed to never get another dog after that."

"You should get one now... I mean, as an adult."

"I always thought I would. Not sure when."

"I probably will, too, someday."

They petted the old man's nose through the cage and sat with the unwritten possibilities for their future, or futures.

From another room, JJ yelled, "I think we have a winner!"

They'd been at the Humane Society for over an hour already. JJ, Mary-Beth and the boys had stopped at the cage of every photogenic dog under the age of two. An accommodating young woman with a large ring of keys at her hip was walking them through the halls, taking each of the puppies out for the Brights to pet, take selfies with and discuss over. Farah captured it all on video from a few feet away.

Chelsea wasn't sure why she'd agreed to come along for this task, but the idea of getting out of that house into the world had appealed to her. And she hadn't been wrong; the dogs were a kind of temporary therapy for her ennui. Their noisy physicality—even the strong canine odors mixed with astringent cleaning solutions—it was a relief, a respite from the unmitigated perfection of the lake house.

"C'mon," Charlie said gently, and they walked toward the sound of his nephews laughing. He was treading lightly with her now, afraid to push too hard.

"How awesome is this dog?" Lucas asked.

Chelsea walked up to the small, caramel puppy in the boy's arms and began scratching under its chin. The pup rolled its head around and chomped its needle teeth on her fist.

"We believe she's a Labrador-rottweiler mix," the woman with the keys said. "Her disposition is all Lab, though. She tests well with children and other dogs. She's four months old, give or take a week. And she's going to keep growing. You folks sure you want a big dog?"

Cameron nodded emphatically. "Will she do Frisbee?"

"I can't promise you that. But she'll be an athletic dog. She'll need a lot of outside time and a bit of space."

Mary-Beth turned to JJ, and Farah's camera turned to

Mary-Beth. "I don't know, hon. Is the backyard big enough for a dog like this? How will she get to run?"

JJ put a hand on her back. "If she needs more exercise, we'll hire a dog walker. The Yangs love their walker. We'll get his name."

Mary-Beth pursed her lips and said nothing more.

"Can we, Mom?" Cameron took the puppy from his brother and let it lick his face.

"Please?"

Mary-Beth exhaled and nodded almost imperceptibly at her husband. Surrender.

"Yes!" the boys yelled.

And with that, it was settled. Mary-Beth and JJ followed the woman with the keys to a cluttered desk where they received information about vaccinations and neutering, Lyme disease and heartworm. They got a book of coupons to a local pet store and a purple collar with the dog's name on it. "Minnie," it said in glittery embroidery.

"Obviously, we'll change the name," Cameron announced when they were back in the car.

"Obviously."

The puppy was in the middle row of seats with Lucas and Cameron, behind a silent Mary-Beth and JJ in the front. Charlie and Chelsea were in the farthest row of seats at the rear of the SUV.

"What about Athena?" Lucas said. "It's like a Greek goddess."

"No way, dude. No Greek goddesses. How about Rocky?"

"For a girl?"

The boys argued while Chelsea looked out the window.

Charlie pulled out his phone and distracted himself.

Behind them on the road, Farah followed in her Prius. Chelsea envied her, with a private sanctuary all her own, a place to escape from these people. She wished she were in the passenger seat of Farah's car at that moment, and not beside a boyfriend whose presence was becoming more irritating than charming.

A phone rang from somewhere in the car. JJ pressed a button on the console and then a Bluetooth voice was speaking to them all. "Um, hello?"

"JJ Bright here."

"Mr. Bright, this is Meghan at the Human Society. I'm so sorry to inconvenience you, but we need to run a different credit card. This one isn't working. I'm sure it's, um, just a technical glitch on our end."

"Can I give you a number over the phone now?"

"No, sorry, we can't do that. Can you come back? Again, I'm so sorry."

"Fine," JJ grumbled. He hung up on Meghan.

Mary-Beth looked at her husband as he turned the car around in a driveway. "What card did you give them?"

"The Amex. It should be fine. I don't know what the problem is."

"The Amex is the one we put the bathroom renovations on."

"I don't think it is."

"It is."

Neither of them said another word. The dog barked. Chelsea felt as if she were witnessing something exceedingly intimate.

When they pulled up in front of the cinderblock-shaped building, JJ jumped out and slammed the door hard behind him.

Mary-Beth exhaled in the front seat of the silent car.

The windows were open, and above the sound of yipping dogs, they could hear the conversation between two men just around the corner of the building. They were leaning against the exterior wall, smoking cigarettes and watching a pen full of energetic dogs. Chelsea could see one of their hands extend out now and then to flick the ash. No one in the car was listening exactly, until they heard their name.

"You know who that is, right? That's Senator Bright's son."

"The Madrid bombing guy? No shit."

"Yup. Looks like he's gonna run for governor now, too."

"The son?"

"No, the senator…well, *former* senator."

"He any good?"

"I always thought he was a good enough guy. But did you see the *Herald* today?"

"Nah, I don't read that right-wing stuff."

"Well, apparently, he's got baggage. *Girls.*"

"More than one?"

"At least one. Maybe more."

"It's always girls with these types, isn't it?"

"Always."

The front door swung open, and JJ jogged back to the car, apparently in a hurry to be done with this episode. They all were.

"All good," he announced.

Mary-Beth forced a smile. She rolled up the windows and turned on the air-conditioning.

The boys were suddenly red-faced. They played with the puppy and avoided eye contact with their father.

Chelsea tried to look at Charlie, but he pretended to read something on the screen of his phone.

JJ pulled back onto the main road and they drove in silence for the twenty-five minutes back to the lake house.

The twins named the dog Messi and decided to make her an internet star.

27

"*This* is the documentary," Wayne declared. Farah could almost hear him salivating from New York. "It's all about this now. You know that, right?"

Farah put her phone on speaker mode and opened her laptop. She was sitting on the bed in her private room above the lake house garage, trying to catch up with what Wayne was telling her. Her stomach growled and she wished for dinner. "Hang on, it's loading."

A pause.

And then there it was. On a local politics blog of the *Boston Herald* site: "Is Former Senator John Bright Hiding a Sex Scandal?" The story itself was thin: an unnamed woman claimed to have had an affair with John Senior years before, and she suggested that there had been others. The rumor wasn't verified by other sources, and it wasn't the work of staff reporting. It could be nothing at all.

But it didn't seem like nothing at all to Farah. When the Brights finally returned from the dog shelter, she'd watched John Senior come out to the car and whisper something to JJ. Then the two of them walked quickly to the study and shut the door. Everyone else had gone directly to their rooms. Something was up.

"Wayne, this could go either way, I think. Could just be a smear campaign."

"Could be… But it could be real, too. And if it's real, it's a big fucking deal. This guy is always held up as the moral conscience of his party, a God-fearing family man. His image has been squeaky-clean. If he's having affairs, that's a big deal."

"I need to get back in there with the family. I should be recording them."

"Yes, you should. Farah, they're going to try to keep this quiet. Your job just got harder."

"I know. I'm ready for that."

"If they close doors and ask for privacy, you gotta remind them of the deal we made. Full access—that was the agreement."

"Right, full access."

"I know you can do this. Just…resist the urge to be nice. That's not your job."

"I'm not actually that nice, anyway. But Wayne?"

"Yeah?"

"If there's no affair, then this is probably going to be just another documentary about a political race. It seems like that's where the drama is going now. Is that what you want?"

He exhaled. "Just follow the family dynamics. Whatever happens from here on out is about all of them—John Bright's marriage, his sons, his blind ambition. It doesn't matter what's true and what isn't anymore because the accusations will open something up with these people."

"I agree."

"Good. Call me tomorrow."

"Okay, bye."

Farah hung up and leaned back against a pillow. She agreed with Wayne on the strategy, but she also felt a little sick about the Brights now, too. Ever since Charlie had tried to kiss her earlier that morning, she was terrified of being approached by Chelsea, or Philip or anyone who may have seen them. She was angry with him for crossing that line; it was professionally compromising. Worst of all, she just wished it had been Philip. If she was compromised, she wanted it to be with him. And that made her feel like a fool, too.

Farah went to the line of cameras laid out on the carpet and selected a midweight device, with a good lens for evening light. She changed the memory card and put extra batteries in her pocket. It would be dinnertime soon, the first time they would all be in the same room since word of John Senior's affair went public.

Downstairs, Farah switched out the new camera on the mount and adjusted the curtains in the dining room for glare. As she looked through the lens at the empty farmhouse table, Charlie walked in. He stopped dead in his tracks when he realized she was there.

"Oh, sorry," he muttered and turned around.

"Charlie, wait."

He looked up.

"It's fine, okay?"

It wasn't fine, but she needed to move on from the attempted kiss if she were to do her job. There couldn't be weirdness.

He shrugged. "Okay."

"It's really fine."

"Okay."

He was annoyed. And his annoyance bothered her. This was a problem of his own making.

"What I'm saying is I accept your apology."

Charlie stepped toward her. "Are we done?"

"Almost. But I want to know why you did that."

"I don't know *why*. I just did it. But clearly, I misread things. You just seemed sort of...open to something."

"Well, I'm not. And you have a girlfriend here."

"It's not like that with Chelsea and me." He looked around, nervous and uncomfortable. "I don't know what I was thinking. I'm sorry. Are you going to torture me over this?"

She didn't want to feel bad for him, but it was true that there was a lot going on in his family at that moment. "No. I'm over it."

"Thank you. And I really am sorry. Things are kind of blowing up right now...but you probably already know that." Charlie looked up, toward the second floor, where his parents and siblings were hiding out in bedrooms.

"Yeah, I get it."

"Thanks, I guess." Charlie walked out.

Farah stood in silence for a moment, then headed to the back porch to wait for them all. As she opened the screen door, Chelsea appeared before her.

"Hey!"

Chelsea grinned. "Hey, I've been trying to find you." She didn't seem like she knew anything about Charlie's advances, but Farah was still wary. "Wanna go for a walk later? After you're done with your work."

"Ah, sure, maybe. So you're staying, then?"

"At least for another week. I can't go to my aunt's place yet, so I kind of let Charlie think I decided to stay for his sake. No point in hurting his feelings."

"Right. Well, good!" Farah didn't think Charlie would try

anything again, but she liked the idea of having Chelsea there as a deterrent just in case.

"So are you going to this dinner?"

"What dinner?"

Chelsea leaned in and whispered. "The guys are apparently going to some bar tonight, to discuss the rumors about their dad. I wasn't invited—thank God—but I thought maybe you'd be there."

"No one said anything to me, but I'm not surprised they'd prefer not to be recorded."

"That would be a first."

Farah turned back toward the screen door. "Okay, I'm sorry to run off, but I need to make sure they take me with them. I'll find you later."

"No problem. Good luck."

Farah ran back up to her room above the garage, tucked her camera into a backpack and changed into a clean shirt. As she freshened up, she considered if and how to tell Chelsea about the kiss—the *attempted* kiss. She owed her that much. She'd expect another woman to do it for her. On the other hand, Chelsea was leaving soon. And the kiss never really landed. Maybe, in the interest of their immediate sanity, she should wait and tell Chelsea after she'd gone. Yes, that's what she would do. It was a selfish choice—because Farah couldn't risk becoming part of a story that she was supposed to be observing—but it was mostly harmless. She wouldn't let Charlie ruin this for her.

And so Farah tucked the kiss into a sealed box in her brain and chose to forge ahead. She laced her sneakers, lifted her backpack and left the bedroom.

In the driveway, JJ, Spencer, Charlie and Philip were talking quietly around JJ's SUV. They noticed her presence and began quickly loading into the car.

"May I come?" Farah immediately regretted having framed it as a question.

Charlie looked away. Philip looked at his feet. JJ and Spencer exchanged glances.

"That was the deal," she reminded them.

"Fine," Spencer said. He turned to his brothers. "There's nothing to these rumors, and we have nothing to hide. Better to get this all on camera."

No one objected, though the other three seemed less sure.

So Farah got in her little car and followed the SUV down the driveway, through the gate and into town behind the Bright boys.

"This is just par for the course," Spencer assured his brothers as they waited for their drinks.

A sign above the bar said The Wagon Wheel in burned wood on thick cedar. It was a surprisingly interesting bar, the kind of place Farah would have chosen. Dark and a little dirty. It had, inexplicably, Western paraphernalia mounted on the walls and autographed pictures of B-list celebrities hanging. Actual drunks sat at the bar, and the only wines listed on the menu were "red," "white" and "pink." Farah liked them all just a little more for picking the spot, though she suspected it might have been chosen as an unlikely hideout for their famous family. If anyone knew who they were at The Wagon Wheel, they definitely didn't care.

The Bright men were seated around a small table in a quiet corner, with Farah recording them from several feet away. It wouldn't be quality footage with all the ambient noise, but it would be something different.

"Every campaign deals with this," Spencer said. "It could have been made up by the opposition. It could have been exaggerated by some scorned ex-employee. This will pass."

A waitress put beers down in front of the men, and JJ began drinking immediately.

"But do you think he did it?" Philip said.

Spencer looked offended. "Did what?"

"Had an affair. Do you think Dad would cheat on Mom?"

"I don't think so," Charlie said. "I mean, you never know, but I don't really think…"

Spencer shook his head. "He didn't do it. We would have known. It would have come out in a previous campaign. And c'mon, this is Dad we're talking about. Do you think he's capable of that?"

No one said anything, and Farah imagined that they were watching reels of their respective childhoods unspool behind their eyes. Every interaction their father ever had with babysitters, friends' moms and pretty teachers. Every look and comment was suspect now. They were trying to understand the things they'd witnessed in this new light. Did Senator John Bright's integrity hold up?

Farah had seen John Senior with several women in her short time with this family. He was vaguely flirtatious in a way that she dismissed as old-fashioned and harmless. He called waitresses "honey," but he didn't stare at their breasts. He complimented Charlie on his taste in Chelsea but didn't insinuate anything lewd. He was like a lot of men his age, which meant that he absolutely could be—or could not be—a cheater.

"But why would somebody say it if it wasn't true?" Philip asked.

Spencer rolled his eyes. "There are, like, ten good reasons to make something like this up, Phil. This woman could be on the payroll of a primary challenger. She could be looking for a payout. She could be a run-of-the-mill fame whore. This is just what happens."

The waitress returned and put two large plates on the table: one fries, one chicken wings. "Careful, they're hot."

"We need to find out who this bitch is," Charlie said.

The waitress frowned and walked away.

"We probably will," Spencer said quietly. "The truth is that Dad's senatorial campaigns weren't all that competitive. I'm not sure anyone has ever done any serious opposition research on him."

"Has Dad said anything to anyone about it?"

They all looked at JJ, who was understood to be the closest to John Senior on all things, campaign related and otherwise.

"Not to me," JJ said, finishing his beer. "He's been in his office ever since we got back from the dog shelter."

Philip leaned in toward his brother. "But JJ, what do you *think*? Do you think Dad did it?"

JJ looked sick. He looked like the pint of Miller Lite that he'd just inhaled was churning inside him and considering coming back up. "I don't know. I don't know anything for sure... But I did see something once."

"Oh no."

"Yeah. Remember ten years ago at Christmas? I told *all of you* that I'd seen Dad having a drink with a woman at the Four Seasons."

Spencer waved him off. "That doesn't mean anything."

"That's what you said ten years ago, Spence. And I told you it looked like something. I can't really explain why...it just did."

"I remember," Philip said. "We got mad at you."

JJ signaled for the waitress and pointed at his empty pint glass. "May I have another?"

"I'll have one, too," Charlie added.

JJ looked angry now. "None of you believed me then. Do

you think I'd bring it up if I wasn't fairly certain? Don't you think I know what a big deal this is?"

No one spoke for a moment. Farah panned her camera around the table, registering the tortured looks on each of their faces. She felt bad for being there and having to memorialize their pain, but she didn't stop.

Philip turned to her. "Do we have to film this?"

Farah looked at JJ, who looked at Spencer.

"It doesn't matter because it isn't true," Spencer said. "Keep recording."

Farah wanted to apologize to them all, but instead she focused on the small screen in front of her and plowed ahead.

"I believe JJ," Charlie said softly.

"What?"

"I heard something once. It was years ago. I was just a kid. I picked up the phone at the same time as Dad and he was talking to a woman. I don't even remember what they said, but I remember thinking it didn't seem right. I just tried to forget it."

"So it's true," Philip said quietly.

Spencer shook his head. "Unbelievable. You're all just going to throw Dad under the bus like this? There's no proof of anything yet!"

JJ turned to him. "Look, you haven't been around Dad as much as I have. We work in the same city. We run in the same circles. I have more to lose from this, but I also can't pretend he's someone other than who he is. It seems possible. And it fucking kills me to say that, but it does."

"Do you think it's still going on?" Charlie asked.

"No. I haven't seen or heard anything in years. I doubt it. But who knows…"

Spencer began eating fries, one after another. He was livid. Farah watched him as he struggled to weave this new information into the things he already knew and the things he wanted to believe.

"I think it's true," Philip said again.

"Okay," Spencer started. "So maybe it happened in the past, but it probably isn't happening now... We can work with this... Infidelity doesn't derail political campaigns anymore. You just do a public apology... Make it a redemption story. Yeah, we can work with this."

JJ nodded. "I think we can, too. And there's still the possibility that we can discredit this woman, whoever she is."

Spencer ate more fries.

"Guys, this isn't about the campaign," Philip said. "Who cares about the campaign! This is about our father. Doesn't this *matter* to you?"

He looked back and forth at his older brothers, who were blank at that moment. His expression changed from appalled to comprehending. Farah watched as Philip began to understand the desperation of his brothers. In his attempt to see the best in everyone, Philip had missed a lot about his family.

"Oh," he said finally. "You guys need this campaign, don't you? Is that it?"

JJ nodded. "I need it. Fuck it! I'll say it. *I need this campaign.* You happy, Phil? Our firm is merging with a bigger one, and I haven't had any wins in over a year. I need something else right now to make the case for myself. People are going to lose their jobs. Plus, we're a little underwater financially."

A pause.

Then it was Spencer's turn. "I don't have a publisher for my next book. The reviews were brutal for the last one, and now I don't even have a chance to redeem myself with a new one."

"But you're still tenured, right?" Charlie asked.

Spencer laughed bitterly. "And yet I still feel like shit. Go fucking figure."

"You need a shrink," Charlie said. "I'd be thrilled to be a tenured professor."

"It's not enough for me. It's not enough for Dad, either. You know it. JJ knows it."

JJ nodded.

Charlie slumped. "Well, Jesus, then I can't imagine how much of a disappointment I must be to him."

No one said anything.

Charlie looked around the table. "You think I'm a disappointment? You think Dad thinks that?"

Spencer leaned in toward his little brother. "It's not right. It's just how he is. You've been gone so long, you've forgotten what it's like to have him watching. He doesn't say anything directly, but he lets you know whether you're meeting expectations."

"You need this campaign, too, Charlie." JJ said it regretfully. No one was enjoying this.

Philip leaned back and put a hand on Farah's knee. "Can you turn it off...just for a few minutes?"

Farah held her breath for a moment, and then she stopped the camera. She put it down in her lap. *This isn't about them*, she told herself. *I don't need to humiliate everyone in the family to do an honest profile of one man.* Wayne would want the footage, but Wayne couldn't know what it was like to be there with them. Watching these paragons of confidence and success confess all their failings, one after another, was like watching towers fall. All of them sitting around those soggy fries in that sad, weird bar as they exposed the humiliations endured at the hand of their father. Farah was shocked by how much it gutted her. These men weren't victims. These men were the lucky winners in a rigged world. Their failures were illusions, minor setbacks in otherwise blessed lives. They deserved no one's pity.

And yet the shame on their faces was real. The Bright men weren't archetypes in some abstract class war. (She missed thinking that they were.) The Bright men were small, soft humans.

The waitress returned with a second beer for Spencer, but he didn't drink it. Instead, he got up and brought it to Farah. It was a thank-you. She drank.

"Well, what about me?" Philip said. "What does he think of me, then?"

There was a pause.

"It has always been a little different with you, Phil." JJ searched for the most delicate possible phrasing. "Dad expects different things from you."

"He lets you be you," Spencer added.

They suffered another twenty seconds of silence. A group of men playing darts at the other end of the bar erupted in cheers. Pool balls clanked against one another. A soda gun sprayed.

Finally, Philip said, "It's true. Dad has always been different with me. I don't know why he has, but I try to think of it as a lucky break. Hearing you guys talk about Dad... I never knew it was like that for you."

Everyone nodded. Some drank. Suddenly, the power imbalance between all the beautiful, natural, cool Brights and quirky Philip was teetering back to the center. Something equalizing was happening. All the petty, demeaning humor was gone as JJ, Spencer and Charlie looked at Philip, wondering why things had been different for him. And how he maintained the courage not to care.

"I think you should do the campaign," Philip said.

Charlie looked up. "You do?"

"Definitely. If you guys need this, then I think you should do it. Even if he doesn't win, it will be a professional win for each of you. Dad's the only person with something big to lose. What I'm saying is…*use him*. That seems fair to me."

"What about the women?" Charlie said.

Philip shrugged. "If it's true, and it comes out, it's his past to reckon with."

This wasn't a happy answer. They wanted to win, as Brights do. But it seemed that in receiving Philip's approval for this plan, they were somehow absolved of their impure motivations for doing it. If Philip could bless their selfishness, then maybe it wasn't so selfish after all. That's what Farah heard, anyway. And who else could grant that absolution but Philip?

"We have to talk to him about the women," JJ said. "First thing when we get back. We need to get out ahead of this."

"*If* it's true," Spencer added, weakly.

"Right, if it's true."

"Poor Mom," Philip said.

JJ drained his third glass. "What an animal."

Spencer stood up and wiped his eyes. He looked down at each of his brothers and shook his head. Then he walked through the bar and out the door.

Farah and the rest of them could see him leaning against the car in the dark. They looked around at one another with sullen expressions. Nothing left to do at The Wagon Wheel now. JJ dropped two twenties at the center of the table and everyone stood up.

They went home to face their father, as he really was.

28

Mary-Beth cried when she heard. She was at brunch the next morning with her family—*her* family: JJ, Lucas and Cameron—when JJ told them that his father had admitted to having an affair with a woman who worked for him years ago.

John had explained it all the night before, when the guys got back from the bar. He'd been waiting for them with a neat Scotch and bloodshot eyes at the kitchen table. Her name was Lisa, and she was his secretary in the early 2000s. By his account, the affair had been brief, consensual and the biggest regret of his life. John Senior reportedly cried when he told his sons, which Mary-Beth couldn't picture. JJ and his brothers cried, which Mary-Beth could. Patty knew about the affair, and they had since done couples counseling. He could never make it right, he'd told his sons, but they were in a good place now. It didn't need to be a "liability."

That's when Mary-Beth started crying at the Pink Radish Café, over lobster eggs Benedict with her family. "He said that? A *liability*?"

JJ slumped. "He is who he is."

"Jesus," Lucas mumbled.

"Watch it, Luke." JJ straightened up and turned to his sons. "I want to be clear here. What your grandfather did is inexcusable. It's not the way for a man to behave. I have never, and will never, do something like that to this family. And I will not make excuses for your grandfather. But we're running a campaign now and we need to handle this strategically. It doesn't mean I endorse any of this. I don't want to hear any jokes or innuendo of any kind on the matter. No mention of this—or anything at all having to do with the campaign—on your little internet videos."

"We know, Dad."

"We wouldn't, anyway."

Cameron and Lucas were mostly preoccupied with hash browns at that moment, looking away to take furtive glances at the smartphones in their palms. Ever since their national TV appearance, the boys were experiencing their own flash of fame on various social media platforms. Mary-Beth kept meaning to crack down on that.

"Good."

Mary-Beth dabbed beneath her eyes where mascara was starting to run. "I'm glad your mom already knows and they've had counseling. This would be worse if she was just learning about it."

Mary-Beth was sickened by it all. It was as if a thread had come loose in the weave of everything, and now it was just hanging out there, daring someone to pull harder, to see how much more could unravel. She felt this way not because she'd thought John Senior was incapable of infidelity but rather because she always suspected he was. And now that it was known and public, his tawdry story was theirs, too. She had to discuss it with her children and watch her husband strategize around it. And she had to wonder—she really didn't want to wonder this—how alike were JJ and his father? How badly did JJ want to emulate him? With this thread loose, so many other aspects of her life were subject to the unraveling.

"I'll take your mom out," she announced. "Shopping or antiquing or something. She deserves at least that today."

JJ nodded. "That would be nice. Actually, we're making a formal announcement of the campaign this afternoon, in an effort to get out ahead of the gossip, so maybe you guys should be out of the house for that. The press calls will start pouring in immediately."

"You're announcing today? Isn't that early? You guys don't have anything in place. There's no staff. Have you even submitted anything to the campaign finance office?"

"It's not ideal. But we can't hang back any longer. This information changes everything. Better to just make the announcement, offer an explanation and apology and stay in control of the narrative. It's actually better that this is coming out now and not two months before election day. This timing is… I don't want to say *good*, but it could be worse. You know what I mean."

Regretfully, Mary-Beth did. "How are you going to do it?"

"We're going to release a video, with Dad and Mom, where he makes a very apologetic statement and they hold hands and reaffirm their commitment to each other and Massachusetts… that sort of thing. Spencer's writing it now. Mom will probably need a little escape after that. She's a trouper for going along with it."

Mary-Beth nodded. She understood. This affair was years ago, and John Senior had atoned for it, so she supposed that it was possible for a marriage to recover from things like this.

God forbid, of course. But she understood the world these men operated in. She knew Washington by now, and though she hated this sort of moral relativism, she'd grown surprisingly numb to revelations of powerful men and their sexual indiscretions. She was no longer capable of horror at the men nor disappointment in the women who forgave them. Everyone's home life is an unknowable balance of things sacrificed and permission granted. Marriages are mysteries.

"Brian's dad had an affair," Cameron offered.

Lucas nodded. "Liam's, too, I think. That's why his mom got the house in the Outer Banks."

The idea that her children saw it, too—the ubiquity—chilled Mary-Beth.

"That doesn't make it right," JJ said.

Cameron dropped his napkin onto his plate. "Got it, Dad. Can we go?"

They paid and left the restaurant, walking out into the scorching summer sun toward their car. As they drove home, Mary-Beth went around and around in her head about how to protect her own family from this contagion. She didn't think JJ would ever cheat on her; that wasn't her (primary) concern. But she didn't like how flip her sons had been in discussing their friends' parents' affairs. The crassness of who did what to whom is exactly the sort of thing that she could usually rely on the Bright family to avoid. John and Patty's world had always been a sanctuary of civility. But now the ugliness was on the inside, infecting them all.

As they drove through the gates at the lake house, Mary-Beth made an announcement to her children. "Hey guys, looks like we're going to be here for a few more weeks. Let's find you a summer camp. I think there's a volleyball one at the park. You need more to do."

Lucas looked up from his phone. "I don't even like volley-ball."

Cameron didn't look up. "We're too old for camp, Mom."

"Fine, then maybe you can be camp counselors!" She was shouting suddenly. "You're doing something for the rest of our time here. No more lying around and looking at your phones. You're doing *something*, for godssakes!"

The house was clean and quiet when Mary-Beth and family returned. Spencer was working in the study with his father and Charlie; Farah was nearby with cameras rolling. Patty was clipping herbs in her garden. Chelsea, in a teeny bikini, was floating on a raft on the lake with a magazine in her hand. There was a note from Ian on the counter—he had gone to the library to do some work. Philip was reading under his tree. It was like nothing had happened at all. Mary-Beth didn't know what she'd been expecting, but this wasn't it.

"You guys have two days to make a plan," JJ said to his sons. "Mom's right. Find something to do."

Lucas and Cameron retrieved the puppy from the couch and took her upstairs to their room.

JJ joined his brothers in the study.

Mary-Beth went outside in search of Patty. Their yard was unbearably hot all of a sudden. The water was so still that you could see reflections of the puffy clouds on its surface. The only movement around them now came from the fat bees in the garden.

When Mary-Beth approached, Patty was bent over chives in an enormous straw hat.

"Hey there."

Patty stood primly. "Hello, Mary-Beth. What can I do for you?"

She wiped her palms on her shorts. "I was wondering if

maybe you wanted to check out that antiques shop in Lenox with me later."

"Thank you. But no, I have too many things to do today." Patty plucked her gardening glove off her hand, one finger after another. "Listen, I know what you're doing, Mary-Beth, and you don't have to. This doesn't need to be a tragedy. John and I have worked through our troubles, and we're just fine now."

"Of course! I just… I just wanted you to know that if you ever want to talk about anything, I'm here."

Patty knelt back down and began pulling clovers of wood sorrel from the soil. "Well, thank you. But I highly doubt that day will ever come. Marriages are long and complicated. You forget that I predate the modern ethos of oversharing— a trend with few benefits, as I see it. The world could use more secrets."

Mary-Beth nodded. This had gone precisely as she should have expected. The only thing to do now was return to the original script. "Well, then, how about I make dinner tonight? Something light in all this heat?"

"That would be great. I have salmon in the freezer if you want to defrost that. Thank you." She didn't look up from her weeding.

And that was it. The entirety of their heart-to-heart in the wake of her father-in-law's affair revelations had unfolded as a brief exchange about salmon.

Mary-Beth wandered away from the garden and toward the water. She had that familiar feeling of floating away that sometimes set in on these long visits with her in-laws. With no house to clean, groceries to purchase or laundry to fold, her day was a formless sprawl. The scaffolding of responsibility that measured time in her real life wasn't there, and so she wasn't really there, either. Even Patty's silent misery refused to become a chore for Mary-Beth.

She looked toward the lake. A cloud passed in front of the sun, putting Chelsea in a pocket of shade on the water's surface. The curve of her perfect and substantial behind didn't bother Mary-Beth as it had before. Ever since their impromptu skinny-dipping, a door of understanding had opened between the two women. Their lives were profoundly dissimilar. But at the lake house, they were both just extras.

And anyway, Mary-Beth didn't want to waste any more time envying the parts of Chelsea's body that were smooth and pert. Rather, she wanted to emulate her ability to relax and surrender, to just float. There may be no other way to survive the summer.

Philip stirred beneath his tree nearby, and she wandered toward him.

"Hey, Phil. How's it going?"

He closed his book and looked up at her from the grass where he sat cross-legged. "It's going okay. Do you want to sit?"

"Thanks." She slipped out of her sandals and found a soft place nearby.

"So you talked to JJ about my father?"

Mary-Beth nodded. "Yeah. I'm so sorry. This is hard on you guys."

"It is." Philip squinted into the sun and thought for a moment. "And surprisingly, it also is not. You know what I mean?"

"I guess. I don't know. It's not like I expected this from your dad."

"No, maybe I didn't expect *this* exactly. But something was always amiss."

"With your dad?"

"With all of us. It's hard to be disappointed when I've always been aware of a… I don't know, a dissonance among us. Don't you think so?"

Mary-Beth didn't think so. For her, the Brights had always been a model of the great American family, the kind of family she wished she'd been born into and hoped to make for herself. They avoided uncomfortable topics and kept things fairly shallow, perhaps, but she figured it felt different if you were a real Bright.

Philip picked up his book and began to open it, then set it in his lap again. "Maybe that's what I'm doing right now, with the church. Maybe this is a search for closeness."

"I have to say, Phil, celibacy seems counterproductive to that."

"Forget that part for a second. I'm talking about *family*. Maybe I'm looking for a new one, or a closer one. Is that a bad motivation?"

"I don't think so." Mary-Beth watched Patty pull weeds at the other end of the yard. Pluck, pluck, pluck. What had she said? *The world could use more secrets.* "No, I don't think it's bad, Philip. Isn't that what we all do in adulthood? It's the same reason most of us get married and have children, I suppose. To start anew."

Neither of them spoke. Because it was true, Mary-Beth thought, that most of us do look for a new family in adulthood. Most, but not Bright men. Bright men branch out, but they don't start anew. Their mandate had always been about carrying on, not starting over.

"Imagine how devastating this must be for my brothers," Philip said. "To have to see my father as he really is."

Mary-Beth didn't know what to say.

"Of course, they've always had the choice to see Dad—and all of us—with clear eyes. They just didn't choose it."

Mary-Beth reached out for Philip's hand and gave a quick squeeze. "You're a good brother, Phil. I know they don't say it much, but your brothers love you."

"I know they do. Thanks."

They sat for a moment in silence. (Philip was the only person she could do that with, without the nagging urge to make small talk.) Mary-Beth didn't really know what had happened last night when the brothers went out for drinks; JJ hadn't told her much. But she knew that something had changed among them. The brothers had woken up that morning as more serious men, less eager to please their father.

"I think I'm going for a swim," she said finally.

Philip smiled. "Good day for it."

Mary-Beth stood up and walked away from the oak tree toward the house. She held her sandals in her hand as her feet stepped through the dense grass. Inside, she went past the study filled with buzzing Bright men, up the stairs and past the closed door of the bedroom where her sons were playing with the puppy.

In her own room, Mary-Beth fished around in the drawer that held all her modest, tummy-firming bathing suits in slimming colors. She searched for the floral bikini she'd been bringing with her to the lake house year after year, the one she'd bought in a delusional wave of hopefulness and never once worn.

She put it on and looked in the mirror. Clusters of rosebuds met at the knotted center of her chest, pushing her breasts up into pleasing little hills. Mary-Beth sucked her tummy in and let it fall out again. She pulled the bottoms down beneath the softest part of her stomach and over it again. The skin was loose and puckered, still shocking to acknowledge despite the fact that it had been that way for years. But two humans had grown beneath that skin, and the corporeal price for that marvel seemed smaller and smaller as time passed. It was possible that she no longer had any opinions about her soft stomach at all, only the shadows of past opinions.

Mary-Beth walked back downstairs like that, in nothing more than her never-worn rosebud bikini. She went through the kitchen and out the back door. The day was hot and heavy, but also pleasant for the way it seemed to press down on them, forcing slowness.

She took a floating raft from the grass and carried it to the lake. Chelsea looked up at the sound of splashing and gave a little wave. Mary-Beth smiled and waved back as she climbed aboard her raft.

She let the sun bake her skin as her fingers dragged through the cool water. In its stillness, she could see right to the bottom of the lake.

Everything was becoming clear.

29

Farah could barely keep her eyes open by the time she returned to her room. She pulled two thumb drives out of her pocket, wrote the date in black Sharpie across each and dropped them into a shoebox of thumb drives. Her bounty. As the shoebox filled with Bright family footage, her anxiety mounted with it. There would be so much video to watch and sort and cull later. But of course, the more she had, the more potential there was for something great. Much of the footage she'd shot herself with a camera in hand, but almost as much of it was recorded passively while she was elsewhere, so who knows what treasures were hidden there. And now that things were really happening with these people, the likelihood of making a story out of their lives was improving.

Not that Farah liked to think of it that way. She wasn't *writing* stories, but relaying them, finding the most salient plot in the overwritten, unedited jumble of real life. She would never describe herself as someone who composed fiction. But of course, she was. It was easy to hide behind the reality of live footage, but the assemblage of that footage was only as real as the filmmaker chose to make it. Her job was either real-ish fiction, or fiction-y real life, depending upon the project. It was never completely true.

Farah peeled off her clothes, which were damp with sweat after a full day of ninety-five-degree heat, and fell into the unmade bed in her underwear. With her head on the pillow in the dark bedroom, she pulled out her phone and began scrolling through email.

It had been only three days since John Bright formally announced his run for governor, but it felt like a week had passed. Since then, he'd done in-person editorial meetings with three state newspapers, hosted a dinner for major donors at the lake house, recorded four robocall messages and conducted two conference calls with grassroots volunteers. Farah had been with him for all of it.

Patty was in and out constantly, as the unofficial head of the fund-raising operation. JJ traveled with his father for most of the outside events, while Spencer handled all writing and policy platforms. Charlie was in charge of list-building, whatever that was.

Most of what the Brights talked about was meaningless to Farah—a coded campaign-speak that excited them. But she understood the broad strokes of their efforts and the wild energy it imbued.

She understood that John Bright Senior had thrown his hat into the ring of the governor's race before he had a proper campaign apparatus established. It was plainly clear that he had a lot of fund-raising connections, but as far as Farah knew, he didn't have any major commitments for donations yet. Funds had to be shifted from here to there, and promises made for later payment in order to hire a website manager, pollsters and a printing company for all the paraphernalia. Unpaid interns would be hired in the fall, and Spencer had said, "Thank goodness for that cheap labor pool." There were so many calls to make to people who felt entitled to calls. They didn't have enough of anything and had to beg for it all. It was exhausting just to watch. It seemed to Farah that campaigning was primarily an exercise in ass-kissing and apologizing.

And there had been a *lot* of apologizing in those three days, a lot of contrite explanations about lessons learned and family values restored. John Bright Senior had admitted to his past affair, and Patty Bright assured the world that he was a changed man, that she loved him more than ever. They were falling over themselves with this redemption story and the press was eating it up. Even Farah found herself accidentally believing it. She almost felt bad for the man.

The new busyness of their lives made the days pass faster. She woke early, filmed all day and felt exhausted each night—just the way Farah liked it. Another benefit to the frenzied energy at the lake house was that it effectively neutralized most of the weirdness between her and Charlie. If he was still hurt that she'd rebuffed his advances, he didn't show it.

Earlier in the day, Farah had traveled with John and JJ to a local newspaper bureau, a senior center and a greasy-spoon diner for a highly staged lunch with local laborers. Each campaign stop was the same, whether John Bright was talking to cops or senior citizens or college unions: (1) speech about the need to strengthen law and order at the state level (peppered with some lefty issues); (2) marriage redemption story; (3) roll up the sleeves and answer some hard questions with folksy wisdom. With young audiences, he'd spend some time on social justice. With old audiences, he'd talk more about tax reform. Jobs. Middle class. Massachusetts values. Progress. Pride. Security. Terrorism. Reforms. Safety. He didn't sound much like a Democrat to Farah, but JJ said no one does in the wake of a big terrorist attack. And suddenly, it seemed, an attack was occurring every other day in some part of the Western world.

Remarkably, John's strategy appeared to be working. Since making the premature announcement of his campaign and admitting to the past affair, no news organization had pursued the story. The woman in question refused to speak to the press, and it seemed possible that they had neutralized the threat, as Spencer would say. Someone had just attempted to bomb a movie theater in the Netherlands, and according to Patty, that had "helped," too. What a dumb, fickle place—this world of politics, Farah thought. Everything big is small the next day, forgotten in a week. Why bother? Her job, on the other hand, was getting better all the time.

Reclining in bed, Farah answered a few emails from friends back in New York, one from her dad and six from work. She ignored a reminder for a teeth cleaning and a long string of angry emails on her apartment building group chat regarding someone's barking pit bull.

She was almost free to turn off her phone and sleep when a new email came in. It was from a name she hardly recognized at first—and then it hit her. It was her old roommate's boyfriend, from several years ago. She didn't really know him at all.

Hi there, Farah. I hope you're well. I'm actually writing in a professional capacity. I don't know if Liz told you but I'm in Boston now. Anyway, I heard that you're embedded with the Brights these days, which is very cool. I'll be covering his campaign for a new investigative outlet and I've got a scoop that I wanted to run by you if you're interested. Could be something we can collaborate on. Mutually beneficial, I promise.

Would love to chat further about it. You can call me anytime on my cell: 555-347-9822.
Cheers, Jeff.

Farah remembered Jeff clearly now. He'd been in and out of the apartment for the three months he dated Liz. He talked fast, slept little and fancied himself the smartest guy in every room. She remembered not liking him at all. He was at the *Daily News* then (or was it the *New York Post*?) and then somewhere else after that. Good for Liz for breaking up with that guy. Farah couldn't imagine what he had that would be beneficial to her.

It was almost 11:00 p.m., but the email had come in seconds ago, so he was probably still working. She dialed the number.

"Jeff here."

"Hi, Jeff, it's Farah Dhaliwal. I just got your message."

"Farah! Thanks for calling me. So, ah, how are you?"

"I'm fine. What's up?"

"All business, as always, Farah. So listen, I'm following a lead that could turn into something big, and I was wondering if you can help me. Or actually, if we can help each other. You interested?"

"I don't know. What do you have? Who do you work for?"

"Right, sorry. I work for a new political news site called the *Electorate Informer*. We're about a year old."

Farah googled it and found a link to a site that looked legitimate, if low budget. She was already pretty sure she wasn't going to help this guy.

"So anyhow, I've got some information about John Bright's personal life...his affairs."

"You'll need to go directly to John and the campaign for a statement on that. They're taking all those questions."

"I already asked them, and they declined comment. But this isn't about the lady he had an affair with. It's something new."

"Seriously, this isn't what I do." Farah sighed. "But what's the story?"

"How about you get me on the phone with John Bright Senior and I'll tell you both."

"That's not my job, Jeff. I don't work for the campaign. And I can't imagine how that would be useful to me. I have to go to bed."

"It's useful to you because you get to be there, recording the exact moment at which John Bright realizes that he's been made." Jeff was getting excited at the other end of the phone, his voice growing louder. "We have something significant. This is going to be huge, Farah."

"Jeff, I can't get John on the phone with you. You've got to use the proper channels for that. Again—not my job."

"You're missing out here, Farah. I'm telling you…"

"Actually, it sounds like you don't have much. If you had this supposed information verified, then you'd just publish it. You don't need me or John for that."

"Fine, that's true. But we're close. And, with or without Senator Bright, we'll get it eventually. The offer stands if you want to change your mind."

"I'm good, thanks." Farah put her head down on the pillow. "Jeff, I have to go to bed."

"Your loss. Call me if you change your mind."

"Bye."

She placed her phone on the floor beside the bed and closed her eyes.

Jeff what's-his-name probably didn't have anything. Not that she'd put it past John Bright Senior. No, she'd done the right thing in declining his offer.

On the other hand, Farah thought, *I should stay close, just in case.*

30

The sun was low on the lake house lawn. The Brights were one week into their campaign.

Patty clinked a fork against her champagne flute and the party quieted. "Pardon the interruption! We're cutting the cake on the east patio if you'd like to join us."

Heads nodded approvingly. The music came back up, and the well-dressed crowd went back to mingling among themselves.

Ian ignored the directive and went to the kitchen to refresh his gin and tonic, wading through smiling faces along the way.

Spencer was already there, doing the same. He put his glass down and his arms around his husband's neck. "How're you holding up?"

Ian smiled weakly. "I couldn't do it without my friends G and T here."

They were halfway through one of Patty Bright's fabulous garden parties. This particular event was a fund-raiser masquerading as a double birthday for Lucas and Cameron, whose actual birthday was two weeks away. John and Patty had manufactured a plausible enough reason to invite nearly one hundred wealthy (and very wealthy) residents of the Commonwealth of Massachusetts, along with some big names from Democratic super PACs, on the promise of fine food, high profile socializing and A-plus ass-kissing. Among them were also socialite bloggers and political gossip columnists, a photographer from *Town & Country*, and two tabloid reporters waiting just outside the front gate.

If Cameron and Lucas were offended by the sham of a birthday party, they didn't show it. The boys seemed content to canoodle as the semicelebrity spokespeople of the Footy Fifteen, all while making videos for their expanding social media fame. The campaign life suited those boys just fine.

A woman in a flowy dress breezed into the kitchen, pulled a bottle of white wine from a tin bucket and gave Spencer a little squeeze on his arm on her way back out.

Ian leaned against the kitchen counter and waited until she was gone again. "So is this working? Are you going to get some big donations from this?"

Spencer poured vodka over ice. "I think so. Most of it will come later, if they feel adequately flattered. But we might get a few big checks today."

"Well, happy birthday to Cam and Luke!"

Spencer frowned. "Oh, c'mon. You know how this works. It's just what you have to do."

"I know, I know."

Ian did. And he didn't really care about the party, which was undeniably lovely. He wasn't thrilled, however, with the ease with which Spencer had manipulated his father's admission of infidelity for their political gain. He wasn't attracted to the apparent pleasure his husband took in this victory. They were making lemonade out of lemons, but they didn't need to enjoy it so much.

No one in the family had spoken of John's infidelity since it came out several days earlier. Every day now was a new whirlwind of activity, leaving no room for what Ian's therapist would call "processing." And, although he wanted to be happy for Spencer, for his resilience in the face of this devastating family news, he couldn't. What the Bright brothers were demonstrating didn't look like resilience so much as avoidance. That's what it had always been with them.

Ian reached for the Tanqueray. "Are you really okay with all this? Don't you want to talk about your dad?"

Spencer rolled his eyes. "We've been over this. I really am fine. We're all fine."

"I don't know if Philip is fine."

They looked through the window at Philip, who was sitting in a lawn chair down by the water. He'd been there for the duration of the party.

"Maybe you should talk to him, Spencer."

"I will. Listen, I've gotta get back out there and introduce myself to the new DNC chair before she goes." He leaned in and kissed Ian. "After that, I'm all yours."

"Fine. Get your drink and meet me down at the water in five minutes."

"Deal. Five minutes."

Five minutes would probably be ten, which is why Ian had said five. He put a cube in his glass and walked back outside, through a scrum at the cake table, past a game of croquet and two men arguing about the latest Fed chairman appointment.

Ian usually liked parties like this. He liked being among the educated and concerned, people who cared about things and knew what was going on in the world. But not today. Today, he was a bored extra, wholly unnecessary.

He found Mary-Beth collecting dirty plates from the grass, and he whispered in her ear. "Drinks on the water in five."

She smiled and nodded.

He continued to the lake.

"What's up, Phil." Ian dragged a beach chair up next to his brother-in-law's chair.

"Just reading." It was unclear whether the book in his lap had been cracked. "Perfect day, right?"

"Indeed. Hey, um, are you okay, Philip? You seem kind of distant."

Philip turned to him. "I'm fine, but thank you for asking. I guess I'm not in a party mood."

"I understand that."

Philip paused. "It just feels like something has changed here. Or like it *should* feel like something has changed. It's weird that nothing has. You know what I mean?"

"I absolutely do."

Mary-Beth came up behind them with her own beach chair. "Hey guys. Are we officially done being polite to strangers?"

"Yup, I'm calling it." Ian reached his glass out to clink with hers.

And then Chelsea came up behind her. "Do you mind if I join?"

"Please do!"

She dragged her chair next to Mary-Beth's. Ian was struck by how the dynamic between the two women had changed in the past week, from quietly adversarial to almost conspiratorial. Ian liked the idea of having Chelsea in their court, maybe forever. She'd be a good one for Charlie to hold on to, if he was inclined to such a thing. It was difficult to tell where this relationship was headed.

"We're glad you're here, Chelsea," Ian said.

She smiled and sipped from a beer bottle. "Thanks. To be honest, I've been trying to leave. But I don't have any money, and now the place I was going to stay in London is falling through. No offense, but I'm kind of stuck here."

"Well, I'm glad for it."

"Me, too," Philip said.

"Me, too," Mary-Beth said.

Chelsea smiled sadly, and Ian realized she really was stuck. He'd been thinking that she was an extra-in-training, but she wasn't. Chelsea could still get out.

Vivaldi's third season was playing from the stereo, and someone had turned it up to match the rising, increasingly intoxicated voices of the party.

The caterers, who'd been walking around with trays of crudités and champagne, began collecting dishes around the partygoers. They had loosened their ties and sweated through their shirts. The sun was a low fireball glaring onto everyone's overexposed skin just above the tree line. Abandoned shoes littered the grass. Everyone was so beautifully disheveled in the summer heat.

"It's exactly like what people think it is," Ian said.

Philip turned to him. "What is?"

He sighed. "People like this. Parties like this. This life."

"No, it's better," Mary-Beth said. "Not because it's more opulent or elegant than you might think…" She paused for a long time and they waited. "It just *feels* better. Before seeing it for myself, I could never have imagined how great it feels to be in this life. The ease of it all."

"People would be so much angrier if they knew what it felt like," Chelsea said.

Philip looked baffled. "Which people?"

"Everyone else," Ian said. "Regular, working people."

Philip nodded slowly, digesting. "Inequality is a reasonable thing to be angry about."

Mary-Beth shook her head. "But what I'm saying is that it's more different than just the scale. It's the sureness, the sense of ownership. Those things were surprises to me when I met JJ years ago. I could picture bigger houses and better wine before I saw it for myself, but I didn't have an imagination for this feeling. And it's actually the best part."

Philip said nothing.

It could be easy to forget that Philip was, in the end, entirely Bright. He was different from the rest of his family, but not so different to have grown up oblivious to his own luck. Even Philip couldn't quite appreciate it.

"I wonder if it's better not to know," Chelsea said.

Mary-Beth closed her eyes.

Ian wondered if Mary-Beth and JJ were really broke. He wondered if she understood that John and Patty weren't as wealthy as the old-money people who attended their parties—that they just blended in well. Not that any of this mattered. (But it did.) He'd never ask.

"I'm tired of this party," Mary-Beth said.

"Me, too."

"Me, too."

"Me, too."

No one moved.

Farah walked up and panned their row of chairs with her camera. Then she pressed a button and put the device in her bag. "Mind if I sit for a few?"

Philip stood. "Here, take my seat. I'll grab another."

"You sure?"

He nodded.

She sat down and pulled out her phone.

Ian dug his bare toes into the sand and felt the cool wetness just below the surface. He glanced at Mary-Beth to his right, who had her eyes closed and her head tipped back.

Then he looked to his left and caught an unintentional glimpse at Farah's phone. Ian wasn't snooping, but he couldn't *not* see the text message that appeared at that moment on her screen.

We're close, it said. Senator Bright is done.

Ian tried to stay steady and avoid looking directly at Farah, because whatever he was seeing, he felt sure she wouldn't want him to. So he stared at the water while she typed a quick response into her phone, glancing back just in time to catch what she'd written. Leave me alone, it said.

Farah wiped her brow and put her phone into her pocket. She stood up abruptly, knocking Chelsea's half-full beer bottle into the sand as she did.

"Oh God, I'm sorry! I'll get you another."

"No, it's fine. I've had enough."

"You sure? Ugh, sorry." Farah gave one more apologetic smile and hurried off.

Ian watched her go, disappearing through the sea of seersucker and linen.

He saw John Bright Senior holding court in a circle of men and women; Patty Bright topping off glasses with a bottle of Moët; and Spencer laughing with Charlie and JJ. Spencer looked so happy and confident at that moment. He was glowing. And although he'd forgotten to meet Ian at the water, as promised, Ian wasn't angry. The setting sun and beautiful people, the bubbling spirits and fine food—Ian wasn't capable of forgetting about the rest of the world and enjoying this rarified universe without complication, but neither was the pleasure of it lost on him. And Spencer couldn't help where he'd come from.

From across the lawn, Spencer smiled at Ian, and they held

each other's gaze long enough for Mary-Beth to blush and look away. It was all worth that feeling.

Hours later, after drivers in black town cars had taken everyone away—back to Boston, and local inns and the airport—it was just the Brights again in the big lake house. The caterers clattered around as dishes were stacked and silverware organized. The residual vibrations of a party still echoed on the grounds, and it would be days before all the forgotten sunglasses and abandoned cardigans were found in the grass.

As a final curtain on the festivities, a dark cloud settled in above them around eleven. Fat rain drops saw the last guests out.

Ian and Spencer were in their bedroom upstairs, which was sandwiched between Mary-Beth and JJ's room, and Charlie and Chelsea's room. All three couples were talking in voices hushed just enough to maintain an illusion of privacy in their family dormitory.

Spencer moved excitedly around their room, pulling off his shirt, then pants, detailing the various commitments they'd gotten over the course of the night.

"The former attorney general gave us a soft yes, which means we need to do a little more wooing there. But I think we've got at least two of the House members on board."

Ian was dead tired in bed. "That's good."

"And the Democratic Governors Association seems like they're hedging right now. They want to make sure we're really viable before they go all in, but I'm pretty confident. Ian, are you listening?"

"Kind of. Sorry. I'm so tired."

"Yeah, me, too." He didn't seem tired.

"Hey, have you noticed anything weird about Farah?"

Spencer climbed into bed beside Ian. "No, why?"

"Because I accidentally oversaw a text message she got during the party that looked fairly ominous."

"What did it say?"

Ian took a breath. "It said 'Senator Bright is done.' That's all."

Spencer froze. "Well, who was it from? What was the context?"

"I really couldn't tell. And Farah left before I could say anything. It's probably nothing at all. But she seemed rattled by it."

"Senator Bright is done?"

"That's what it said. Senator Bright is done."

He frowned. "Maybe I'll ask her about it."

"I'm not sure you should. I definitely wasn't supposed to see it."

"Fine, then I'll just poke around a little. I'm sure it's nothing, though. There are plenty of people whose job it is to make sure my father loses this race. They are going to come at us from all angles, so it's not impossible that someone has contacted Farah. I'll remind her of the terms of this agreement."

"Which are?"

"She can't talk about anything she has seen here. All the footage is fair game once the documentary is out there, but she can't leak anything about Dad in the meantime. It's boilerplate language."

Ian studied his husband's face. "She seems like a professional. It's probably nothing."

"I agree. And anyway, the truth is out there now. There's nothing left to uncover."

"Right."

"Oh, I forgot to mention the Petersons—the people who run the opera house—they were totally smitten with my mother and…"

Spencer continued on about the successes of their day—

their "kills," as the Bright men put it. And Ian was trying to listen, but he was overcome with irritation. It was a particular irritation he had only with his in-laws, usually after a few days among them all, when he started to feel adrift from his husband. He wanted to listen and care about this boring story about the opera-house people. But more than that, he wanted to take Spencer back from his family. He wanted to reclaim their time together, their identity apart from these people. Ian nodded along half-heartedly.

"What is it?" Spencer finally said. "You seem annoyed."

"It's nothing. I'm listening."

Spencer moved in closer and put his arms around Ian's body under the covers. "What is it?"

Ian kissed him. "I just miss you."

Spencer softened to his lips, and it seemed for a moment that he was going to abandon this endless thread. But then he pulled away and plowed on. "So anyway, we're thinking about testing some messages in south Boston..."

Ian put his hands firmly on Spencer's shoulders. "No."

"No?"

"No." He pushed him down into the pillow and hovered over him. Ian was slighter than Spencer, and his force was only a performance, but they were both into it. "Stop talking."

Spencer was instantly aroused with this order. He quieted and waited.

"No more talking," Ian whispered into his ear.

Spencer moaned in anticipation, and Ian made love to him with the angry, possessive force he reserved only for those angry, possessive nights on Bright family vacations.

Surrounded on every side by kin, Spencer belonged only to Ian for ten furious minutes.

31

Farah woke to the sound of her ringing cell phone. It was almost nine o'clock on the morning after the party.

"Hey, uh, hi, Wayne."

"Hey. Are you asleep?"

"No, of course not. What's up?"

"I just need a quick update before I go into this senior staff meeting. The corporate overlords are going to want an update on this project. What can I tell them about our progress?"

"Ah, well…" She jumped out of bed and pulled the curtains back. Outside, Lucas was trying to teach the puppy to roll over in the wet grass while Cameron recorded it. Farah's mind raced as she tried to think of something substantive. "So there's the Senator's past affair, and they had this big fundraiser birthday party yesterday, and…"

"Do you have anything new, though?"

"Not really, Wayne. I'm not a breaking-news reporter. All

I have right now is hundreds of hours of video in a shoebox. It's getting interesting, though. You can tell them that."

"I know. Sorry. I'm just feeling their impatience to pull the plug on this. There's a new series in the works about home-grown terrorism, and accounting thinks that's where our resources should all go. They want to start pulling people from other projects for it."

"Don't let them pull me off this, Wayne. Please. There is still the potential for some very interesting stuff to happen here. I don't think Senator Bright's affair is totally resolved."

"Okay, that's good news. Can I tell them that?"

"I don't know, I—"

"I'm going to tell them that the drama is just getting started. We have to keep you on this because things are really heating up with the Bright family scandal."

"Well, I'm not sure that's the story."

"It's the story today, Farah. And if you want this project to be your breakout, then pray for more scandal."

"Okay."

"Good, thanks. Later."

"Later."

Farah plugged her phone in and went to the bathroom. She took a quick shower, brushed her wet hair and pulled on clean clothes. She grabbed a shoulder-mount camera and ran out the door, down the garage stairs and into the overcast morning.

As she stepped through the door to the lake house, Farah could hear John Senior speaking in a commanding voice, his media voice. She followed the sound to the study and panned in to see JJ, Spencer and Charlie watching silently as John boomed into the phone, his eyebrows pointed inward. This was a serious discussion.

"Yes, Eileen, I believe state preparedness for terrorist attacks has a long way to go," John Senior said. "Ultimately, city police forces are the first line of defense in situations like these. State governments have a responsibility to give them the resources and authority they need to thwart incidents at the local level, before they become national threats. And as governor of Massachusetts, I'll make terror preparedness a top priority."

John stopped talking and nodded along as the voice on the other end spoke. Farah captured the looks on his sons' faces, which were serious, but also glimmering with excitement. Farah put the camera on a nearby tripod and pointed it back at John Senior, then left the study to find out what was going on.

In the kitchen, Patty was rolling out pie dough while Philip read the newspaper at the table. Farah walked over and picked up the front page.

"Terrorist Plot Halted in NYC."

Philip looked up at her. "What a world."

"Yeah." Farah wanted to know what neighborhood it had been and who had been targeted. She wanted to know how close it had been to her apartment (not close) and whether subway transportation had been halted (briefly). She had done this before.

"Scary," Philip said. "I'm glad you weren't there."

"It was blocks from my place."

"Still…scary stuff."

Farah put the paper back down on the table. "There are almost nine million people in New York City, Philip. It's probably statistically safer than the Berkshires." She walked outside and sat on the front steps, leaving the screen to slam behind her.

It may or may not have been true, about the Berkshires, but the spirit of it was true, and she hated having to remind people of it. She wished to be home in New York. She wished to avoid having one more of *these conversations* about terrorism and cities and fear. And she wished to not be here, listening to the faint voices of Bright men in another room, discussing ways to weaponize that fear for their own political gain.

Farah took two deep breaths and resolved to not make this moment about her, the invisible documentarian.

Instead, Farah pulled out her phone and called Jeff, the reporter.

"Farah, what's up?"

"Hey, so, that thing you were telling me about? Why don't you tell me more and I'll see if I can help."

"Really? Well, sorry, you're too late. It's showtime. We've confirmed the story and it's ready to go. Would have run it today, but we didn't want it to get buried in all this terrorism stuff."

"So when does it run?"

"Maybe tomorrow. Maybe the next day. Hard to say." It was clear that he enjoyed being the one with the power.

"Well, can you tell me what the story is?"

"Nope, I cannot. You'll just have to learn about it when the rest of the world does."

Farah felt foolish. She should have bitten when she'd had the chance. The fate of this documentary was hanging by a string, and she'd demurred because...why? Because she felt some sense of loyalty to these people, exactly what she wasn't supposed to do. And now it was too late, which meant that she would need to follow John Senior around for every waking second until the news broke to be sure to record his response at the very moment it hit him. Whatever *it* is.

"You know, Jeff, you're exactly as I remember you," Farah said bitterly.

"Really? You're not. I never took you for such a softy." Jeff waited for her response, which did not come. "Farah, can I ask you why you changed your mind?"

"I guess I just remembered what I came here to do."

No one said anything for a moment. Their usefulness to each other had run out.

"Okay, well, good luck with things."

"Bye, Jeff."

Farah ended the call and walked back inside.

Philip jumped up as soon as she came in. "Hey, Farah. Look, I'm sorry. I didn't mean to sound ignorant back there. I was just trying to think of something to say."

"It's fine. I know. Sorry if I was weird."

"No apology necessary." He looked around, searching for something else to offer her. "Hey, um, do you want to take a walk along the lake path while the rain is stopped?"

She did, despite it all. And she wasn't mad at Philip about the thing he'd said, which was perfectly innocuous. She was just exhausted by the world, which he'd surely understand because it was the sort of person he was.

"I wish I could, but I can't. I'm sorry."

He nodded. "No worries. Another time." And then he reached out and put his hand around her arm, just above the elbow, in a soft squeeze-hold. "Again, I'm sorry for sounding like an idiot earlier about the New York thing. I'm often an idiot."

"You're really not."

And then Philip's hand was gone and the moment was over.

Farah was aware of Patty's presence at the other end of the kitchen where she was slicing peaches and piling them high in a bowl. They had nothing to hide from her, and yet the moment felt too intimate for observers.

Farah went back to the camera on the tripod in the study just as John Senior was finishing his phone interview. She smiled wordlessly at his sons and adjusted the settings on the machine. It was good and right that she'd declined Philip's offer; she was proud of herself for it. And it was appropriate that she'd called Jeff and tried to seize on this professional opportunity. Farah was there in only one capacity, to work. It was showtime.

32

The next morning, Mary-Beth ducked under the front gates and jogged up the driveway to the lake house. It was raining again and her clothes were soaked through. Her sneakers made a squishing sound each time they hit the gravel. But it felt good to be out of breath, to be away from the house and alone with her thoughts. The wet nylon of her running shorts was sticking to the parts of her thighs that she'd long ago decided were too abhorrent for the world to see. As of this trip, those parts were declassified again, and Mary-Beth was enjoying the sensation of wet air on tender pink flesh.

When she got to the top of the driveway, she stopped and stood still in the rain, watching through the window as her husband and his brothers moved around inside. A television was on, set to one of the cable news networks…the soundtrack to their summer.

A light glowed upstairs where Cameron and Lucas were

playing video games. Neither Mary-Beth nor her husband had pursued the idea of the boys finding something constructive to do in those weeks, which she regretted now. She felt like she was losing the boys to the force of the Brights. Ever since returning from Spain and going on national television, they had come to fancy themselves as young internet celebrities. They spent most of their time adding content to their multiple social media platforms, which Mary-Beth knew she should police more aggressively, but she didn't have the will. Most of what they posted was harmless and stupid: videos of the boys arguing about soccer players or trying to teach tricks to the puppy. They had tens of thousands of followers—most seemed to be girls—and Mary-Beth cringed to think about how that was changing them, inflating their egos and warping their understanding of their role in the world. Most disturbing to her was that they never even asked to leave the lake house. They were teenagers with no apparent desire to drive around, or buy booze or talk to live girls. All the things Mary-Beth had feared about raising teenage boys had become the things she most wanted for them now.

Not that the boys were entirely to blame for it. No one seemed to leave the house since the campaign began. For all the Brights' love of being recognized, sometimes it felt as if they were afraid to leave the compound. Mary-Beth wondered if perhaps the world itself had become something frightening for the family, not because they were too famous, but because there was always the possibility that they weren't really famous at all. These people weren't Hollywood starlets or Red Sox players. They weren't recognizable faces to most Americans. They were just political stars, which made them barely stars at all. And to face that truth—to go out into the world and walk freely, unmolested by the public—might be the most emotionally catastrophic fate they could meet. Their isolation was a kind of self-preservation.

Mary-Beth took her soaked shoes off on the front steps and went inside.

JJ was at the door. "How was your run?" He kissed her wet forehead.

"It was great. I'm going to take a shower. Everything good here?"

"Yeah, huge day so far." He looked back toward the study where Spencer was talking loudly. "Dad's already done four interviews about yesterday's terror attack, and we just got invited to a national security forum in New York for next week."

"Next week?" Mary-Beth squeezed the rain from her ponytail. "I thought we were leaving next week."

"Babe, we talked about this. We might need to be a little flexible on timing for the rest of the month."

She sighed. "Okay, but the boys need some time at home before school starts, so we can't stay much longer."

"Of course. Don't worry about it. I only bring it up because things are really picking up steam today. This campaign actually feels viable now, you know?"

"I guess so." Mary-Beth shook her head and left JJ in the kitchen.

Upstairs, she peeled her clothes off in the bathroom and stepped into the shower. It was good to see her husband so energized. It was what she'd hoped for from this trip. Usefulness! He'd been suffering without it, and she understood why. Motherhood is, even at its worst moments, the living embodiment of usefulness. It's the lowest you can expect of someone—to be useful—and yet it's as essential as oxygen. The only place Mary-Beth felt starved for usefulness happened to be here, in the place where JJ had found it.

As the hot water rained down on her, there was a knock on the door.

"You have clean towels in there?" Patty yelled over the clatter.

"Yes, thank you!"

"Okay, dear."

Mary-Beth could see from the shower six white towels stacked neatly in a cupboard above the toilet. She had the feeling that Patty knew they were there, that Patty couldn't resist intruding on her moment of privacy to remind her whose house they were in. Or maybe she was wrong about that and being unfair to her mother-in-law. Maybe it was just a thoughtful gesture from a gracious host. That was the problem with being there: she could never tell if it was she who was losing her mind or them.

Mary-Beth washed her hair and shaved her legs. She lay naked in bed for ten minutes while she checked her email. And then she dressed and wandered downstairs with a ferocious appetite.

The kitchen was buzzing with lunchtime family energy. Cameron and Lucas were filling their plates with sushi rolls from a large take-out platter on the counter. Ian and Spencer were laughing beside them. Farah filmed it all. And everyone else was at the table already eating—everyone but John Senior and Patty.

"Where's the candidate?" Mary-Beth asked as she helped herself to seaweed salad.

Spencer nodded toward the lake. "He and Mom are outside with a photographer from *Redbook*. They're doing a feature on political spouses."

"She might be on the cover," Ian added.

Cameron got a seltzer from the fridge and carried it out of the room with his full plate. Lucas took the puppy and followed him. Mary-Beth knew she should tell them to eat in the kitchen, with the rest of the family. Instead, she let them go, and took her own plate to the table and sat down beside Charlie. As she ate tuna rolls, Mary-Beth watched her in-laws through the window. John was holding an umbrella above his wife while a photographer moved around them. With her own camera, Farah watched them all from a greater distance. Everything was soggy.

John looked down at his much shorter wife and kissed her forehead. She put her arm around the sturdy trunk of his body, and they smiled in the way that they'd been practicing for decades, two perfect magazine-spread smiles. They knew just what to do, but it still looked remarkably real to Mary-Beth. If they were acting, they were happy to be acting. It wasn't the version of love that Mary-Beth aspired to, but it was *a* version. There are worse ways to be in a marriage, she supposed.

"This will be helpful," JJ said from across the table. "Putting Mom out there will be good for the campaign."

"They look good," Mary-Beth said.

Charlie nodded. "I think they are. They seem fine."

Philip swirled a cucumber roll in soy sauce around and around on his plate.

Chelsea looked away from the window and back at all of them. "How do you think it works?"

"How does what work?" Philip asked.

"One married person having an affair with another married person… Like, how does it start, I wonder. You can't just proposition someone, right? You have to somehow know that they're in the market for it. How do you make that first move?"

No one said anything. Mary-Beth wished she would stop talking, but Chelsea went on. "Like, do you actually tell someone that you're planning on cheating on your wife, and that's why you'd like to invite them out for a drink? Because some-times a drink is just a drink. Is there some kind of code so the other person knows what you're after?"

For a moment, no one spoke.

"I think you know if it's you," JJ said finally.

Mary-Beth looked at her husband. "What does that mean?"

He made a strained throat-clearing sound. "I just think there's probably a way to say to another married person, 'I see you.' I don't *know* this, obviously. I'm guessing." JJ spoke slowly and cautiously. He looked like he wished he'd never set out on this path, but for some unknown reason, he continued. "I think that's how you send the signal to another person, by making them feel seen. Because that's what affairs are about, probably. Am I here? Do you see me? Have I disappeared?"

The room was silent. Ian and Spencer, who'd been talking quietly at the counter, were watching now, too. Mary-Beth could feel her face turn red.

JJ went on. "And if the other person says 'I see you, too,' well then, you're defying invisibility together."

"And that means sex?"

"Maybe. I don't know, but maybe."

Chelsea shook her head and went back to her sushi. "Jesus, that bums me out."

It didn't offend Mary-Beth to hear her say it. JJ's argument would have bummed them all out before they were married, before they knew what they knew now. It was impossible for Chelsea to see it all from where she sat. Their lives were something denser, more complicated and less sexy, but immeasurably rich, too.

Charlie stood up first from the table. He went to the sink and started the dishes, granting all of them permission to end the tense moment.

Mary-Beth carried her plate to the sink. JJ followed her

and did the same. They stopped together at the counter and looked at each other. JJ was amazing in this way, his ability to stop and look at her. He had somehow always known that this was what Mary-Beth needed. She looked at her husband and smiled. And to her surprise, he reached for her hand and led her out of the kitchen. They walked hand in hand to the door, down the hall and up the stairs. The camera's lens, probably, followed for as long as they were in sight.

The sound of Mary-Beth's bare feet on the wood steps was louder than she'd ever heard it before, and she wondered if the rest of the family thought so, too.

Through a closed window at the top of the stairs, Mary-Beth could see John and Patty outside. They were sitting in a small rowboat at the water's edge, side by side, in a manner that you'd never actually sit if you needed to navigate. High above their heads, a professional umbrella had been set up to block the drizzle and create the illusion of clear skies. Months from now, Mary-Beth thought, no one looking at that photo in a magazine will ever know that it was raining on this day, which made her strangely sad.

JJ led her to the bedroom and locked the door behind them.

Inside, they sat down on the neatly made bed, and he began to take off his wife's clothes, one article at a time. He looked at her face while he did it. And sometimes he looked at the parts of her body where the clothes had been. He kissed her knee and her shoulder. He bit down gently on her hip bone, which used to be more prominent than it was now, but wasn't hidden entirely, either.

It was midday and the room was bright. Their children were mere paces away, and his siblings were talking loudly downstairs. These were things that Mary-Beth had to acknowledge as she lay naked across the bedspread her mother-in-law had selected for them, because normally they would deny her the ability to enjoy the moment. But she *was* enjoying the moment, and she didn't care about those things today.

JJ saw her. And in seeing her, he was asking to be seen. He was giving her the things he wanted to be given because it was easier to do that than to ask for them. Mary-Beth knew how to bear witness to her husband's quiet suffering, which had become their shared suffering. Through professional failings and his father's relentless presence in everything, she could lose the place where his pain ended and hers began. They had become so entangled that it was impossible to know with whom each sadness originated. But when he bit down on her hip bone, hidden below the flesh of her foreign adult body, she knew how to salve them both simply by bearing witness to their shared pain. And they found each other.

Always, they could find each other.

33

The news broke before dawn, so it was everywhere by the time they woke up.

John Senior and Patty—always the first downstairs—saw it all first. They saw the original story in the *Electorate Informer* and held their breath, because the *Informer* was a partisan rag bankrolled by the political right, and so there was still hope that it wouldn't catch fire in the mainstream. But it did. And by the time the coffee was ready, the *Washington Post* had verified the story of the two women; and then CNN put their pictures on TV. And by the time the rest of the Brights emerged from their bedrooms with bleary eyes, the truth was already breeding conspiracies, and everyone had a take.

Farah, with bed hair, moved swiftly about the house as she tried to catch each of the Brights waking up to their new reality.

That was when Patty Bright took her coffee mug back up

to her bedroom without a word to her husband, her children or their partners. She didn't yell or cry. She just left.

From behind her camera, Farah watched them watching Patty leave. It was remarkable to Mary-Beth that no one protested being filmed at that moment, but they didn't. No one said a thing, not even her.

"It's just two women," Spencer finally said as he poured cream into his coffee. "That's all they've got, right?"

His father nodded. "Right."

"There are no other bombshells we should expect?"

"No, no."

But what Spencer obviously meant was, *Is that all there is?* He wanted to know what the actual truth was, but all John could tell him was the known truths, as if the rest was unknowable.

Mary-Beth was glad the boys would sleep until noon on that day (as they always did). She looked at her husband, who gave her a small smile because the mood in the kitchen was sad but he was not sad about her. They were okay.

"When do we turn our phones back on?" Charlie asked.

"Not yet," JJ said. "We need to have a plan before we start commenting."

Spencer ran his hand through dirty hair and leaned against the kitchen counter. "I think we should go dark for a day. Acknowledge nothing. Don't add fuel to this fire. Just wait for the next news cycle."

"It might last longer than one cycle," JJ said, and then no one said anything. He had the final word on the media strategy.

Philip, who'd been sitting at the kitchen table reading the story on Mary-Beth's phone, looked up at them. "So there were three women in total. Is that how many women you had affairs with, Dad? Is it three?"

"I believe so, yes."

And with that, everyone knew there might be more. Mary-

Beth hoped they knew this, anyway. She hoped that her husband and his brothers would allow themselves now to see what was plainly obvious. Their father was capable of things they wished he wasn't.

"And it was years ago?"

"Yes, *many* years ago. All of them." John made a broad time-sweeping motion in his pale blue pajama pants. He looked unusually old and frail before them. "This is all decades behind us. I made mistakes years ago. It was a different time, which doesn't excuse it, but it's true. And there are no secrets anymore between your mother and me. She and I worked through all this."

His tone and confidence suggested to Mary-Beth that perhaps the last part was true.

"Excuse me," Philip said, sliding his chair back against the hardwood floor. He refilled his coffee mug and went out the back door, toward his tree. It was partly sunny now, but the ground was saturated from yesterday's rain.

Briefly, it seemed as if maybe this was going to be the moment at which the Brights really went for it, the moment of real confrontation with their father—yelling and crying and true catharsis. But it wasn't; of course it wasn't. And Mary-Beth felt foolish for thinking it might be, but not for wishing it.

"We should monitor things" is all Charlie said, and he went to the living room to turn on the TV.

Mary-Beth realized that Chelsea wasn't there, and she hoped for her sake that Chelsea's escape plan could be executed soon. If you were going to leave the Brights, now was a good time to go.

JJ, Spencer and their father joined Charlie in the living room. Farah followed them.

It was just Ian and Mary-Beth left in the kitchen.

"This has to be the end," Ian said. "Right? I mean, this campaign has to be over."

She shook her head. "I don't know. It should be, but it doesn't seem like it's going to be."

He rubbed his eyes.

"Maybe I'll take the boys with me back to Washington."

"I was thinking about going back to New York. Spencer won't like it, but I don't need to be here for this."

"We all have to go back eventually." Mary-Beth looked out the window. "God, this is a terrible vacation."

Ian laughed a small laugh. "Is that what this is? Vacation?"

They listened to the voice of the TV news anchor from the other room as she brought all of America up to speed on the developments.

"As of this morning, two more women have admitted to affairs with former Democratic senator John Bright, who recently launched a bid to be governor of Massachusetts. The Senator did not respond to our request for comment, and both of the women have asked for privacy at this time. It's unclear still how this may affect his gubernatorial campaign, though we do have a statement from his challenger in the race…"

"Someone should talk to Patty," Ian said. "Ask her if she still wants this campaign."

Mary-Beth nodded. "Her kids should. She doesn't want to talk to us about this. Or, she doesn't want to talk to *me*. I already tried."

"Maybe Philip. He's better than the rest of them at things like this."

Philip was still outside, under his oak tree. He seemed to be taking it the hardest of all of them.

"Philip has been really quiet. He's been spending so much time under that tree. I don't think Philip's okay."

"No, I don't think so, either."

34

Farah's phone buzzed in her pocket, alerting her to a new text.

Are you getting all this?

She checked the levels on the camera, smiled at John Senior, who was working on his computer, and quietly excused herself from the study. She didn't dial Wayne's number until she was out on the front steps.

"Hey!" he yelled excitedly into the phone. "So are you getting all this? The women?"

"Yeah, I'm getting it. The story broke in the middle of the night, but I've been with them all since dawn, basically." It was nearly three o'clock.

She didn't tell him that, as of forty minutes ago, the Bright men and their partners were staging some kind of protest at the oak tree. She didn't tell him that she couldn't hear what they were saying or see the expressions on their faces. It hadn't raised any alarm bells at first. The oak tree was a camera-free zone; she'd agreed to that for Philip's sake. They'd gone out there to check on him, which wasn't a thing anyone normally did, but it wasn't a normal day, and any person could see that he was having a hard time with the news. So they'd all gone out there—JJ, Spencer, Charlie, Ian, Mary-Beth and Chelsea—ostensibly to check on Philip. That was forty minutes ago. No one had left the tree yet, and it was beginning to seem like they were hiding out there together. They were hiding from her cameras.

Through the window, Farah could see their mouths moving. Sometimes it looked like they were laughing. Other times, they were all just sitting around saying nothing. Yes, they were definitely just hiding from her.

"There's gotta be more bad news coming for these guys," Wayne said. "I want you on them nonstop. No way is this over. What's the wife doing?"

Farah drew a line in the driveway gravel with a stick. "She's been in her room all day. I haven't seen her."

"You gotta get in there, Farah!"

"I know, but bedrooms with closed doors are off-limits. I have to wait for her to come out."

"Fine, just make sure you get the confrontation, the real blowup. They might be waiting for you to be gone, so you can't disappear for even a minute."

Farah could feel her heart in her chest again. This was the feeling she waited for. In all the documentaries she had worked on, there was always a moment when she could sense the purpose of the film coming together, nearing a crescendo. It could be an animal approaching its prey or a dam about to break. She would have experienced this moment as unadulterated pleasure if not for the fact that she was watching a family fall apart. *This* wasn't her job.

But there was no one else there to do it, and so it was.

35

"So what's the verdict?" Spencer asked his siblings as he leaned against the oak tree.

JJ stretched his legs out into the grass, which was drying quickly with the returning afternoon sun. "I say we leave this decision to Mom."

Mary-Beth made a face.

"What?"

"I don't know if your mother will tell you what she wants. She might say she wants to continue with the campaign as long as your father does. I don't even know if she *knows* what she wants."

The Brights considered this possibility as they sat together in the shade of Philip's tree.

Charlie stopped massaging Chelsea's shoulders. "This is going to make Dad really mad."

"I don't care," JJ said. "The only way I'm staying on this

campaign is with Mom's blessing now. After everything he has done to her…"

Spencer nodded. "Me, too. It's the least we can do."

Ian was incredulous. "You guys could just *quit*. That has always been an option. It's probably unwinnable at this point, anyhow. Just quit for fuck's sake."

"No," Spencer said. "It has to be up to Mom. And I don't think we can assume that she wants us to quit."

"I think that's right," Mary-Beth agreed. She looked around. "What are we going to do about the cameras?"

They looked back at the house where Farah had a camera pointed at them. She surely couldn't hear them or see anything interesting from that distance. But the camera was still there, watching, waiting for their return.

"This looks worse," Spencer said. "The longer we stay out here, the longer it looks like we have something to hide."

"Who cares what it looks like?" Philip said. "We haven't done anything wrong. This is Dad's problem."

Charlie stood. "Let's just talk to Mom. We'll know what to do after we talk to her."

Everyone nodded and got up, brushing the grass from their behinds and stretching their legs.

Mary-Beth walked back toward the house with her husband. She was proud of them all, for coming together and facing reality.

As they approached the deck, Lucas dribbled a soccer ball over. "What were you guys doing out there?"

"Just talking," she said curtly. "Stay off the internet today, okay? Tell your brother."

"What did we do?" he whined. "Are you serious about this?"

"You didn't do anything wrong. Just try, Lukey, please."

Mary-Beth knew that she couldn't keep her boys off the internet and away from their personal promotion campaign, but she had to try. She was almost glad—on this day only—that their own vanity might shield them from some of the ugliness of the internet. She thought perhaps that their preoccupation with their own brand management might diminish the perceived size of this news about their grandfather. They seemed to exist in an entirely different cyberuniverse from her own. Today, she hoped it.

Mary-Beth and JJ were intentional with their parenting, to the extent that anyone could be. They'd done everything they could to create a safe, stable and predictable environment. They'd been explicit about their values and expectations in an effort to present a sort of moral map for their children, devoid of guesswork. More than anything else, they showered the boys with genuine affection. Mary-Beth said every day all the things that she'd wished her parents had said to her in a lifetime. *I love you* and *I'm interested in you* and *I'm lucky to have this job of being your parent*— all the things that Mary-Beth's parents probably felt but couldn't say because they were of a different generation and disposition.

It wouldn't have occurred to Mary-Beth to feel cheated by her parents' lack of affection—until she met John and Patty Bright. It was from John and Patty that she learned that parents from prior generations could be effusive in their love and that, contrary to her training, such affection didn't rot one's soul like candy in dental work. John and Patty had told the Bright boys that they were loved and special every day since the day they were born, and even if it had perhaps contributed to their inflated sense of self, what better by-product of misguided parenting could you hope for? As long as there would be unintended consequences, Mary-Beth decided long ago, let them be of the self-love variety. JJ and his family gave Mary-Beth permission to parent in the way that her soul begged to parent—not only for the boys, but for her younger self.

But there had been unintended consequences to this approach—the risk of raising children with outsize egos. It wasn't the worst thing you could do to your kids, but it was a thing she felt she needed to acknowledge having done.

"We'll try to stay off the internet, Mom," Lucas said.

And she smiled, knowing they would not.

Upstairs, JJ knocked on his parents' bedroom door, with all his siblings and the extras behind him. Farah was with them now, too, cameras rolling.

"Mom, can we come in?"

There was a pause, and then the door unlatched and cracked open. JJ, Spencer, Charlie and Philip filed in first, in birth order, followed by Mary-Beth and Ian. Chelsea stayed outside, which Mary-Beth thought was wise, given her tenuous stature in the family at present.

The door closed abruptly.

Inside the bedroom, JJ got right to it. "Mom, we'll quit the campaign if that's what you want. We'll just end it today. It's up to you."

Patty stood on the other side of the made bed. It was piled with throw pillows decorated with embroidered knots. She folded her arms across her chest and looked sternly at the group. "Is that what this little ambush is all about?"

"It's not an ambush," Spencer said. "We're trying to just do what's right here, Mom. We know you don't want to talk about any of this…stuff…which is fine. But you do need to tell us whether it's gotten to be too much for you."

"That's a decision for me and your father."

JJ shook his head. "Not to us, it's not. You get to choose here."

Mary-Beth thought their adamancy was sweet. She'd assumed Patty would think so, too.

"Well, you're being ridiculous," Patty said. "I've been doing this longer than some of you have been alive, and I'm perfectly capable of handling a little bad news."

Her sons were taken aback.

Patty went on. "You think any of this happens without my permission? Your father may be the candidate, but he's not the only one running this show. I'm always in it, even if you don't see me. So while I thank you for your chivalry—or whatever this is—I don't need your help. No one's quitting the campaign." Her voice quivered for a moment at the end, betraying something more. "But thank you. I do love you boys."

Charlie stepped forward. "But Mom, we'll probably lose this, anyhow. Is it worth it?"

"I don't know about that. Has anyone seen the news in the past hour?"

They shook their heads.

"There was another attack on the electrical grid. It was on the West Coast this time. Most of Portland is powerless right now. Your father's got the strongest security platform in the race, and he's pulling some moderate Republicans to his court right now. This could be enough to bump all that other stuff off the news pages and refocus on substance."

Charlie looked at his brothers. They nodded. This cyberattack could, maybe, reclaim media attention and provide an opportunity for John Senior to pivot back to the issues. Everyone seemed to agree, it could be good news for them.

And so the Brights left the bedroom and went on with the campaign.

The sons joined their father in the study, where they made fund-raising calls and assiduously avoided the press. They wrote a speech for the national security summit that John was still scheduled to attend, and Patty picked out his shirt-tie combo for it. Farah's video cameras followed because the show must go on. And no one said another word about the three women whom John Bright had long ago (but not *that* long ago) slept with.

36

"I'm going to miss you so much," Charlie said as he rolled onto his back. His skin was coated in the coarse sand they'd been tumbling around in.

The little beach in the cove was all theirs.

Chelsea put her head on his chest. "I know. Me, too. But I obviously can't stay here."

Charlie didn't say anything, probably because he knew that she was right. They couldn't keep sneaking out to have sex on a hidden beach. She couldn't stay trapped, unemployed and friendless, on this strange family vacation indefinitely. He thought he wanted her to stay, but he'd soon be bored with her. It hurt Chelsea to think that, but it was true. They were in something like love, but probably more like lust. There was no one else, but that wasn't enough exactly.

Charlie spun a lock of Chelsea's sand-soaked hair around his fingers as she lay upon him. Around them they could hear bullfrogs calling and water lapping gently against a log. Under different circumstances, it would be a kind of paradise.

But the circumstances were what they were. The centrifugal force of the Brights was pulling Charlie away from her and closer to them. The world outside was burning down and no one here seemed to care except for the ways in which it could help them. Charlie wasn't so craven as the others, perhaps, but she didn't love him in the way that she thought she had.

"When is your flight?"

"Friday," she said. "My aunt should be back from her hip surgery before that. It will be a help for her to have someone around. I'm kind of looking forward to feeling useful again."

"You're useful to me."

"I know, but it's not the same thing."

"Is it a direct flight to London? I can drive you to the airport."

"That would be really nice, if you don't mind."

Charlie sat up and rolled her around so she was beneath him in the sand. He kissed her stomach and hips. The wet tips of his shaggy hair brushed against her breasts. "I might have to sneak onto the plane and escape with you."

Chelsea smiled and enjoyed the moment, because she knew he didn't really mean it, and that was okay.

37

They decided to go minigolfing. Spencer and JJ had convinced the rest of the family that it was important, while they were declining to comment publicly on the matter of their father's sexual affairs, to make a show of family unity. The entire plan was premised on the assumption that someone would recognize them, take a picture and post it on social media. Then that picture would circulate on the internet and offer proof of their strong family values and John Bright's electability. It seemed far-fetched to Ian, until it happened.

They were still picking out their little clubs when the young man at the soft-serve window on the other side of the green spotted them. By the time they were teeing up at the mini windmill, he'd posted the picture online.

"Mom, you're up next," Philip said, and Patty stepped ahead of them to tap her ball under a small bridge.

John Bright put a gentle hand on her arm, and she leaned in to receive his cheek kiss.

Charlie and Philip smiled hopefully, children desperate to believe.

The soft-serve-stand guy took another shot from afar.

It seemed a little over the top to Ian, too obvious a rebuttal for the world to buy it. Their public affection couldn't possibly be an effective counterweight to the ceaseless buzz of John Senior's multiple affairs. But its obviousness, he suspected, would be the reason it would work and he would be wrong. Spencer told him it would work, and Ian had to admit that his husband was very good at this campaign business. It was always assumed that JJ was the political brother, the one most likely to turn into their father. But Spencer was at least as comfortable with it as JJ was, and possibly hungrier.

The most remarkable thing about this campaign arrangement was how well the brothers were working together. It wasn't just JJ and Spencer; it was all of the Bright men. Even Philip, who was usually a reluctant tagalong on this strange summer adventure, was no longer an object of their teasing. It was as if the revelation of their father's impropriety had galvanized all that long-suppressed Bright brothers energy toward the campaign. They wanted to win for themselves, together, but not for John Senior.

Mary-Beth came up behind Ian and whispered in his ear. "Just one big happy family."

He rolled his eyes. "It's unbelievable."

"Like nothing ever happened."

"Is this what going crazy feels like?"

"I believe it is."

Patty Bright turned back at that moment, and her eyes locked on Ian. He stopped laughing. Even as the Brights did this happy-family show, Patty seemed especially stiff. Something had hardened in her over the past few days. And although Ian wanted to stay sympathetic, all the things about his mother-in-law that had long bothered him were now on display. The calculating way she moved through the world, the unvarnished self-interest. Was it possible to behave like a good mother while still being a bad person? Was it possible for morally compromised people to raise good offspring? *Of course it was.* It had to be. Ian had married one of the good ones.

Ian and Mary-Beth let the group go up ahead as Cameron sent his ball into the mouth of a painted moose. JJ said something funny to Spencer, and Farah directed her camera at the laughing brothers. It looked particularly artificial from that distance.

"What do you think is going on with Patty?" Ian said.

Mary-Beth shook her head. "Who knows. I'm running low on empathy, though. She wants this campaign as much as John does, so why should we care? It seems kind of ridiculous now that we all tried to step in on her behalf. I'm done trying to protect her."

Ian looked up at the high sun. "I have to admit, Mary-Beth... I hope they lose. I know I shouldn't, but I do. I hope Spencer at least gets to stay involved with this campaign from New York, stay occupied while he's in between books, and then I hope they lose and we all go back to our lives."

"Me, too. I'm nervous about what all this is doing to the boys, being in the spotlight. I want them to have a normal life."

Ian didn't say anything more about that. He thought Lucas and Cameron were becoming spoiled with all the public attention. He'd heard Lucas describe their newfound popularity as *our brand*—not a good look for two well-connected white boys on the fringes of a family sex scandal.

Ian watched Mary-Beth as she watched her sons goof around. She probably saw something different when she looked at them, he thought, and who could blame her. They were hers, and she was probably blind to their flaws.

John Senior took his turn with the pink golf ball. They watched him swing his club gently as the ball rolled forward and fell with a plop into the hole.

The group cheered self-consciously and the soft-serve-stand guy took another picture.

John Senior picked the ball out of the hole. "Now, who's up for oysters next?"

They were only midway through the short minigolf round, but nobody expected to finish. They'd already been spotted and photographed doing happy-family things, and so the purpose of the outing had been realized.

Mary-Beth and Ian applied smiles to their faces and joined the rest of the group.

Oysters at The Huckleberry Inn were always a grand affair: sitting outside, looking out at the horses grazing in the rolling hills. It was easy to forget about the ills of the modern world and just bask in a sort of antiquarian memory of American greatness.

But the ills were still out there, and on that clear day, the Brights were plowing through chilled rosé at an accelerated pace to forget them.

"To family," John said, raising a stemmed glass.

They clinked and drank. "To family."

The waitress came to replace a platter of empty Wellfleet shells on ice with fresh ones. She adjusted the umbrella above them, just so, to account for the shifting sun. A woman approached from a nearby table and asked to have her picture taken with John Bright, which he glowingly obliged to. (If she knew of the affairs, she didn't seem to care.) Farah was there, holding a camera with one arm and propping that arm up with the other. She looked tired.

None of the Brights, or their extras, said anything about

anything throughout lunch. They spoke of the lovely weather and the verdant pastures. They tried to remember the last time they'd been horseback riding, and JJ reminded them of the Montana vacation from ten years before. That had been a nice trip, everyone agreed. *We should get out the old photo album from that trip. And maybe we need to plan another vacation out West.* It went around and around like that for a long time. It was perfectly fine for Ian, but at a certain point, it becomes more exhausting to avoid a topic of conversation than to simply sit in silence. He would have been fine with silence.

"I have a toast," Patty finally announced. "I'd like to toast to Philip."

Everyone turned to Philip, who looked the most surprised of them all.

"In all this campaign activity, I don't think we've properly congratulated you on your upcoming…studies. We're proud of you, Phil. It's good to have something you care about."

With some hesitation, the table nodded and brought their glasses together. No one made any jokes. They just toasted.

"Thank you, Mom. That means a lot."

"So when does school start?" JJ asked. "Is that what we call it? Graduate school?"

"Sure, or seminary. I start the first week of September. I'll head to Boston the week before that to move in."

"I'm so glad you'll be close," Patty said.

And Philip's face lit up. His chin lifted slightly and his eyes sparkled. Why Patty was giving him this gift of her blessing now was entirely unclear to them, but it was apparent that he'd been desperately awaiting it.

"Yeah, it's cool, Phil," Spencer said. He looked to Ian, who smiled in assent.

The rest of them all agreed. It was cool enough for Philip to become a priest. Not entirely understandable, but cool enough.

Their father's face, however, was blank. "I support whatever you want to do, son. We're certainly glad to have you back in the area. But tell me again, why the priesthood?"

Philip straightened in his chair. "I'm happy to tell you. In fact, I don't think I've had the opportunity to explain any of this to you guys."

Everyone waited.

Philip set his water glass down slowly and looked up at them. "I've come to realize that the things I've been doing all this time have one thing in common—trying to get closer to our shared humanity."

No one budged. Patty blinked twice. Farah moved closer with her camera.

"Let me be more specific. I wanted to help people, so I joined humanitarian missions. While I was traveling with those folks, I learned about Mandela, Gandhi, Mother Teresa. I also learned about Doris Day and the Catholic Worker Movement, which affected me the most. I started looking at the teachings that had inspired her, and I kind of fell in love. From that angle, the church felt like the culmination of all the disjointed turns I've taken in my life. It felt like I had been walking toward this one thing all along."

The table listened intently as he struggled to find the right sequence of words to explain this meaningful, intangible desire inside him. He was straining.

Philip took another sip of water and wiped his brow with his hand. "Look, I don't think I have many talents. I know I don't—not compared to you guys. But I have this one gift that it seems most people don't have—the ability to listen well. I can pretty much listen to people forever. I *like* listening. And I can listen in a way that allows me to almost feel what another person is feeling as acutely as they do. I don't *know* that this is exactly true, but I feel it is... It's not, like, magic. It's just an ability to focus my energy on making people feel seen and heard and understood. It might be my only talent."

Philip waited for their reaction, but nobody recognized this as his final point. This was his argument for becoming a priest: he wanted to be a listener in a sea of talkers.

To Ian, it was exquisite and important. It was the best argument, perhaps, for doing anything in life. But it also seemed painfully misplaced in this world. It was certainly misplaced in this family. He was speaking a language that no one among them understood, defending a talent that no one appreciated. With or without the blessing of these Brights, Philip was a marvel.

Mary-Beth fought back tears.

Philip's brothers exchanged glances and smiled.

And Ian noticed that Farah, who'd been recording this exchange from several feet back, had a pained look in her eyes and two worry lines across her forehead.

"I think it's great, Phil," Spencer finally said. "It's great."

"I agree," Mary-Beth said.

But John Senior seemed unmoved. Philip's plan made no sense to his worldview. Perhaps Philip made no sense to him.

The waitress returned and asked if they'd like another bottle of Cinsaut, and John Senior nodded enthusiastically, for the wine and the distraction.

Cameron announced that he was going inside to pee.

JJ clapped a hand on Philip's shoulder and gave it a firm squeeze.

Beneath the table, Ian put his own hand on Spencer's knee, and he held it there. He was proud of Spencer for seeing Philip as he deserved to be seen. Spencer was not his father, no matter how much time he spent with his family. Maybe none of them were.

Patty drank from her glass and smiled sadly at her boys.

Something was ending.

38

Farah lay back in her bed and let her freshly washed hair soak into the pillow. She scrolled through the messages on her phone while late-night comedians made jokes about the day's headlines. John Senior featured in each of their monologues. It was low-hanging fruit: an unfaithful politician and the contradictions of his life.

Farah couldn't shake the feeling that she was a living cell in this sick media organism now. She hadn't intended to be. Documentary filmmaking had always afforded her a certain distance from popular culture and gossip. But as a function of luck and location, she was in it now. The best possible outcome at this point—to make a searing documentary about a beloved public figure—would implicate her in all the muck.

"I can't believe the Brights haven't asked you to leave," Chelsea had said to Farah three days before. "I just can't believe they're still allowing the cameras to roll, as all this terrible stuff comes out." She'd shaken her head and looked at the lake, astonished that sane people would ever allow for such a thing.

But Farah could believe it. Her presence at the Bright house was the least surprising thing about this project. Because in her experience, people—not all, but most people—would still rather be filmed than not, even in the face of humiliation. The camera becomes a sort of oxygen once you've been breathing it, and taking it away can induce existential death.

She flipped from one network to the next, her phone still in her hand. Farah couldn't turn her mind off, and it wasn't only the work. It was Philip. It seemed that the more she observed him, the more she found herself wanting more. She wanted to know more about him, what went on in that inscrutable head. But she also wanted to know what he smelled like first thing in the morning, what the fuzzy hair below his navel felt like to the touch and what the little hollow between his pectorals would taste like if she put her tongue in it. All of which made her feel foolish and unprofessional and perpetually distracted by her own physical wantings. This was work and Philip was unavailable. Farah kept flipping through the channels.

Bzzzt. Her phone vibrated beside her, and she looked down. It was Jeff, the reporter. Farah watched her phone ring over and over as she contemplated what to do.

She should answer it. Jeff had been right about the last scoop, and he might have something new to share. But she didn't want to hear his voice, and she didn't want to get pulled into his murky world. She was still a documentary filmmaker, not a Jeff.

Finally, it stopped. No voice mail. Then a text message.

Farah, things are happening. Turn on the news RIGHT NOW. This one's a freebie.—Jeff

She found the remote in the sheets and started flipping. There it was: on the first cable news network she crossed, a picture of John Senior. At the bottom of the screen, it read: "More revelations for former senator John Bright?"

It was a question, not a statement. And when Farah turned up the volume, the newscaster merely said that one of the previous women he had already admitted to sleeping with was talking now. She suggested there were further secrets to come out.

After that, the camera cut away from John's face, to shaky footage of a woman holding a grocery bag at her front door. She was trying to unlock it and get inside, away from the TV cameras.

The woman looked as old as John. She had white hair and was wearing a velour tracksuit—not the mistress image Farah had been picturing. She was shaking her head and trying to ignore the questions being hammered at her by reporters. Then, finally, the door opened and she slipped inside. And, just before she closed it again, the woman yelled back: "Why don't you go bother Patty Bright! Ask *her* the real story! It's not as simple as you think!" Then she slammed the door and closed the curtains.

When it was clear that the anchorperson had nothing more to report, Farah turned off the television and sat still for a moment.

This one's a freebie. That's what Jeff had said. Surely, he was chasing this story—whatever it was—along with every other political reporter in America right now. Someone would find whatever this woman was alluding to, and it would probably be sooner than later. All of which meant that this night was not over for Farah. Things could still happen tonight.

So she pulled her leaden body out of bed and searched for her jeans. She tucked a pillow under her arm and grabbed the smallest camera she had. This was the moment that Wayne was talking about, the time *not* to fall asleep. And despite all the ways in which she hated this project, she liked the tingle of excitement that these events stirred in her. She wanted to be there for *the thing*. She didn't always know what the thing was, but she had a good sense of when it was coming.

Farah padded down the back stairs of the garage, into the clear black night, then along the driveway to the front door of the house. Gravel crunched beneath her unlaced sneakers. She knew the door would be open—they kept it that way for her—but she'd forgotten about the fussy latch on the screen, which required some jiggling and tugging. Every sound she made seemed to echo above her and across the surface of the lake.

When finally it opened, Farah stepped into the dark house and slipped out of her shoes. She walked slowly up the stairs, past the boys' room and Philip's room, past Charlie and Chelsea's room, Spencer and Ian's room, and then JJ and Mary-Beth's room, until finally she was outside the master bedroom, John and Patty's. Farah was struck by how cavernous the house felt now, illuminated by a bar of moonlight from the window at the other end of the hall.

She could hear someone snoring from a distant room. There was a sneeze from a different location and the ruffling of bed sheets. Farah held still for a full minute to be sure that everyone was really asleep. When it was quiet again, she placed her pillow on the floor, just to the left of John and Patty's door. She checked that her camera was charged and set it to rest mode. Then she curled up on the floor with her head on the pillow and waited.

In the hours that passed before dawn, it wasn't sleep that claimed Farah's body, but a sort of semi-alert recharging mode. Her eyes were closed and she hardly moved, but there were no dreams that night, just the blurry melding of subconscious thoughts with the real-life sounds of a creaking house and sleeping family.

When Patty Bright gasped the next morning, Farah was already on her feet.

39

The sound of something falling to the ground outside her room shook Mary-Beth from sleep. She gave JJ a wake-up shove and ran out of the bedroom toward Lucas and Cameron's room, because that's where her instincts took her first. But before she arrived at their door, Mary-Beth realized the danger wasn't with her sons, but at the other end of the hall, with her in-laws.

Mary-Beth turned at that moment, just in time to see Patty Bright emerge from her bedroom and snatch a small camera from Farah's hands. She was wearing a pale blue nightgown with a halo of furious bed hair. Patty threw the camera to the ground and stomped her delicate bare foot onto the device, over and over. The small sound of cracking glass and breaking plastic crunched with each new stomp.

Farah was frozen for only a moment, just long enough for Patty's foot to break an external microphone and send it sailing across the floor. Farah stepped back, away from Patty, and pulled her cell phone from her pocket to resume recording.

"Leave this house," Patty said. Her voice was low and hoarse.

Farah said nothing. She held her cell phone out before her.

"Leave now."

JJ emerged from their bedroom. "What's going on?"

Patty glared from Farah to JJ to Mary-Beth. She swallowed and clenched her fists at her sides.

Spencer's door swung open. "Mom, are you okay?"

Patty's lips pursed together and her body began to shiver. She crumpled to the ground all at once as a lacy, formless ghost. She began to sob.

JJ and Spencer ran to their mother and held her.

Philip and Charlie were there now, too, hovering around Patty while the rest of the family looked on.

Mary-Beth walked toward them to peek into the bedroom. And there, sitting on the bed with his face in his hands, was John Bright Senior. He wasn't crying or speaking, just holding himself motionless, in shock or fear. He must have heard his wife's sobs, but he didn't go to her.

Mary-Beth felt all the blood in her body drain away as she watched him. Nothing shook John Senior or Patty. In her eighteen years of marriage to JJ, she'd never seen them respond to anything with such dramatics. Not the public revelation of John's affair, and not the revelation of more affairs. Whatever this was must be worse.

Ten minutes later—after Patty collected herself and was pulled off the floor, after John asked everyone but his children to go downstairs and the sun finished its ascent from behind the mountains—the original Bright family gathered in their parents' bedroom.

This meeting was for Brights alone, not Brights-by-marriage or Brights-by-association, just blood. Only John, Patty, JJ, Spencer, Charlie and Philip were in the bedroom. Farah was left to lurk in the hallway. The rest of them drank coffee downstairs and speculated in the meantime.

"I can't even imagine…" Mary-Beth said to Ian from across the kitchen table.

He shook his head. "It's got to be something bad. I've never seen her like that."

"No one has."

Chelsea looked up from her phone and back down again.

Every now and then there was a creak in the floorboards above them, like someone was pacing in the bedroom. Mary-Beth thought she heard a pounding—maybe a fist, though it could have been her imagination.

Lucas smeared cream cheese onto a bagel at the counter, while Cameron played with the puppy in the living room. Even they knew to stay quiet and agreeable that morning.

Birds chirped outside, and they could smell the dewy grass as its scent wafted through the open windows. A Weedwacker buzzed from another corner of the lake, apparently unaware that the world was ending somewhere else.

"Guys, come in here!" Cameron yelled from the living room. "Guys!"

Ian frowned at Mary-Beth and they rushed in.

Cameron was pointing the remote control at the TV screen, adding bar after bar to the volume.

The chyron was clear as day: "Bright family sex scandal update: former senator's wife had alleged affairs of her own."

A young man in a suit and tie explained it all. One of John Bright's previous mistresses was claiming that Patty cheated, too, and that she had proof. Nothing had been substantiated yet, but this woman—tired of being hounded by media about her affair with John—promised to produce it soon. She said the fact of their affairs was an "open secret" between the Brights, some kind of agreement.

"Turn it off, Cam."

He did as his mother said.

Mary-Beth, Ian, Chelsea and the boys stared at one another in silence.

"This is gossip," Mary-Beth reminded them. "We can't believe everything we hear right now."

Cameron and Lucas nodded, and then they took their bagels and their puppy out to the back deck to escape the tension.

Mary-Beth fell back into the couch.

"This is what they're talking about upstairs," Ian said. "It has to be. Do you think it's true?"

Mary-Beth didn't know if it was true. She couldn't imagine that it was. Not Patty. But, then again, why not? Was it so impossible to imagine that a woman married to a serial cheater would seek closeness—or revenge—with another man? Patty Bright may have been the model politician's wife, but that's why it was plausible: she was just a model. So much of what they modeled was revealing itself to be little more than a performance now, and Patty's authenticity suddenly seemed as unlikely as her husband's. So why hadn't it occurred to her that Patty Bright might be capable of an extramarital affair? They were both, apparently, capable of anything.

"I don't blame her, if it's true," Chelsea said. "Who could blame her?"

If Chelsea were her child, Mary-Beth would have reminded her that two wrongs don't make a right, and that marriage isn't measured by a scorecard and infidelity harms a whole family. She would have said "wrong is wrong"—an inane phrase she used far too often with the boys. But Chelsea wasn't her child, and she agreed with her, in a way. It made intellectual sense, and a shallow kind of feminist sense, too. Why should we expect goodness and purity from Patty but not her husband?

But still. Mary-Beth couldn't imagine a mother doing such a thing to her family...*if* she had done it. And she probably had.

They heard a door unlatch and footsteps upstairs.

Mary-Beth, Ian and Chelsea stood up and exchanged glances, waiting.

JJ appeared in the doorway of the living room first. When Mary-Beth saw his face, she felt as though she might burst into tears. His eyes were red and his head was hanging low. He was still in the old basketball shorts that he liked to sleep in, and his T-shirt had wet spots on it.

JJ shook his head and went to his wife, who put her arms around her husband. He curled his body around hers and buried his face in her neck. Neither of them said a word.

Farah followed, cameras rolling.

Upstairs, a door slammed. And then another. Ian and Chelsea left to find their partners in their respective bedrooms.

Philip was the next one to come down. He looked the worst of them all. His face was blotchy and wet, his eyes wide and unblinking. With slow, robotic motions, he walked through the house and out the back door. Mary-Beth wanted to say something to him, but she didn't know what to say.

Through the window, they watched him march straight to his oak tree, where he curled up in a fetal position and hugged his arms around his legs. It seemed to Mary-Beth like he was rocking slightly.

She looked up at JJ. "What happened up there? Is Philip going to be okay?"

JJ shook his head. "I don't think so."

"This is about your mother's affair?"

"It's worse than that. It's about Philip, too."

★ ★ ★

Patty Bright's statement was released to the press within the hour. She'd typed it herself in her husband's study. JJ sent it to their press lists, and Spencer turned off the phones. As soon as it was out there, Patty disappeared upstairs for a long time.

Hardly anyone said anything.

Mary-Beth went back upstairs and got into bed with JJ. She could hear the shower running and the sound of two bodies moving about in the master bedroom nearby. She heard Patty's closet door open and close and John Senior's bare feet pad around. Mary-Beth heard Ian and Spencer's voices grow distant as they went downstairs and out the back door toward the lake. She heard the sound of her own car ignition turn over, and of Charlie and Chelsea drive away in her SUV. And she heard the heavy rise and fall of JJ's breath beside her in bed as he slept, the hoarse rasps of a man who'd surprised himself with his capacity to cry.

It was barely noon.

A digital machine gun fired in the distance, and Mary-Beth was grateful to have her sons preoccupied with video games at that moment. She'd have to talk to them eventually, of course. She'd tell them some of what JJ had told her, but not all of it.

Mary-Beth would tell her children the parts that were factually true and irreversibly public by now: that more than twenty years ago, Patty Bright had an affair with a man, and that man was Philip's biological father. She'd tell them that their grandmother and grandfather had made a choice when Philip was born to keep this secret from Philip and the rest of the family. She'd remind her boys that families are complicated, and adult choices are sometimes difficult.

She wouldn't tell them most of what had happened in John and Patty Bright's bedroom earlier that morning, though.

She wouldn't tell them that Philip had scratched long tracks of grief into his forearms when he learned this all from his mother. Or that Patty had moaned like she was dying as she stroked Philip's head. Or the blank way that John Senior just sat there while everyone cried and raged around him. JJ had explained the entire scene from his parents' bedroom to Mary-Beth, knowing that she'd know which parts to pass along to their children.

Mary-Beth imagined that she'd shake her head in astonishment as her sons listened to the facts of the story, and she'd remind them that, while this was all very shocking and sad, they were still a family and would get through it. She'd repeat the same line she'd used when their close friends adopted a baby from China, about how family is something you *do*, not something you get. All of that would be true and easy enough.

But the *why* of it all would stump Mary-Beth as it stumped her heartsick husband. Why had Philip been denied the opportunity to know his biological father? To know the truth of his identity? Why had they all, even in adulthood, been lied to? Mary-Beth understood the appeal of the lie; it was tidy and uncomplicated. It was peace. But it came with such catastrophic risk and potential pain. And it wasn't *true*. Doesn't truth have inherent supremacy over untruth, even if it's messy? If Philip had gone his entire life never knowing what they knew, would they have been vindicated in withholding the truth?

Mary-Beth went to the window and looked out at Philip as he lay flat on his back under his oak tree. The leaves of the tree, which were as broad and green as they'd be all year, kept his body in complete shade. He'd been out there for hours. Mary-Beth wanted to bring him something to drink and a snack, but she decided to wait just a little longer. Philip was doing what he needed to do, she supposed. She couldn't imagine the depth of his pain and confusion. She didn't know what he needed.

Everything was different now, too. Mary-Beth couldn't stop thinking about all the things that made Philip unlike the rest of his family. There were so many: his facial features, his placid temperament, his slow way of moving through the world, the distance he'd always maintained from the rest of the family. Was it all explained by divergent genes? She didn't want to believe that it was. These were the things about Philip that Mary-Beth most loved, and she realized now that she'd always found hope in the idea that a person can become something entirely new. It meant that her husband's and sons' fates had not been sealed by the men who preceded them. She wanted to be surprised by these men.

JJ stirred and opened his eyes. He looked like a worn-out child with his face pressed into the pillow and the covers pulled high. He slept exactly the way Lucas always slept; or rather, Lucas slept as he did.

"How are you feeling?"

JJ rubbed his face and sat up. "I feel bad for Phil."

She nodded and glanced again at her brother-in-law through the window.

"I'm angry, too," he added. "I'm really angry."

"That seems right."

"What kind of people do this, Mary-Beth?"

"I don't know."

"You know the craziest part? I think my dad is still planning on continuing this campaign."

She gasped. "What?"

"Yeah. I mean, he didn't say it, but I could tell. No one has said anything about it, but I bet you he's thinking right now about a way to salvage this."

"Well, that's just nuts."

"It sure is." JJ got out of bed and rolled his stiff neck around twice. "This is all so messed up, Mary. I don't even know how to talk about it yet. My head is pounding. But I'll tell you this, we're packing our stuff and leaving later tomorrow. You and me and the boys. We're going back home to our life. I can't be here anymore."

Mary-Beth walked over and put her arms around her husband and rested her head on his chest. He ran a hand through her hair and held her there. And, although it seemed petty and she was ashamed of herself for thinking it, Mary-Beth was a little bit happy in that moment. She listened to the thrumming of his heart and smelled the funk of his old T-shirt. JJ belonged to her and the boys. As much as he admired his father and needed this campaign job, there was no question at all about whether he would stand by them after all this.

JJ's moral compass was sound. He wasn't made up entirely of this Bright material.

He kissed the top of Mary-Beth's head and squeezed his arms around her so tight she could hardly breathe. Like his brother—his half brother—all the words seemed to have drained from him. He was only the soft flesh of a body, and his hurt, wrapping itself around another, tight enough to blur the lines between them.

40

Clouds moved in that afternoon, bringing an air so thick that their clothes felt wet as they hung on their bodies.

Mary-Beth made a spinach lasagna that would sit on the counter uneaten. JJ carried the canoes, kayaks and paddleboards that had been strewn across their beach into the garage, one by one. Ian and Spencer walked along the lake until the sun was almost down. After that, they drank cold beers on the deck together. Charlie and Chelsea returned from their long drive and then disappeared to their room with takeout. The teenage boys took a break from their phones. Lucas actually sat in a beach chair and read one of the books he'd been assigned for the upcoming school year. Cameron did solo soccer drills in the grass while the puppy tried to bite his heels. Everyone seemed aware of the ripples their bodies made in the world.

And Farah was working to achieve total invisibility, as the cameras rolled.

Patty and John Bright skulked around the lake house, staying out of the way of the others and saying very little. They unplugged all the phones and double-checked that the gate was locked. The couple didn't appear angry with each other. Rather, they seemed closer somehow, bonded together in their avoidance of their children.

On two occasions, Patty walked out to the oak tree and tried to speak with Philip. She looked like she was pleading the first time, down on her knees, begging for her son's forgiveness. The second time, she kept her arms folded at her chest as Farah watched from afar. Patty didn't go back out there again.

All the while, Philip stayed alone under his tree. He drank from a water bottle that Mary-Beth refilled for him throughout the day. He shifted his position every now and then and wiped sweat from his brow before it fell in heavy drops to the dirt. The sun set around him and the mosquitos multiplied in the soupy darkness.

The previous days had been flying by at record speed. But now it seemed that time was barely moving.

That night, Farah watched Philip from her bedroom above the garage. The glow of a porch light illuminated his form in the cloudy black. He looked so vulnerable out there, his hand flicking at a mosquito, his legs folding and unfolding in a restless fever. Farah had the terrible feeling that Philip was offering himself up as a sacrifice under that tree. It was the hopeless, wilted form of his gangly body that made her fret. He was an overgrown weed returning to the earth, losing its will to fight.

But Philip did live through the morning. At the first crack of dawn, Farah went to the window to find him sitting cross-legged, looking out at the lake.

She couldn't wait any longer to see him, so she slipped her bare feet into sneakers and walked quietly down the steps of the garage and around the house to his tree. She ran her hands through her hair along the way, wishing she'd taken a moment to pull herself together. She left her cameras behind.

He looked up as she approached and smiled sadly. "Good morning."

"Good morning." A streak of dewy dirt went across his cheek. "Did you sleep?"

"Not much. A little, I guess."

Thirty feet away, water lapped at the shoreline.

"Philip... Are you okay?"

He looked toward the water. "I don't know. I came out here to clear my mind, but it doesn't feel any clearer. I feel angry. I really don't like feeling angry. I just thought that maybe if I stayed out here long enough, God would reveal himself to me and I'd understand something about all this."

"Did he?"

Philip shook his head. "No."

Farah sat down beside him and rested her back against the trunk of the tree. It seemed a terribly uncomfortable place to spend any amount of time.

Philip scratched a bug bite on his thigh, and she could feel his upper arm moving against her own.

"What's going on with everyone else?" he asked. "Is the campaign over?"

"I don't know. I haven't heard anyone mention it. Seems like it must be, but I don't know for sure."

"This must blow things up for my father."

"I would think so."

To describe the campaign as blown-up would be an understatement. Farah had watched TV and read online news for hours after the rest of the family had gone to sleep the night before. News of their drama was everywhere. Patty's statement confirming the affair, and the identity of Philip's biological father, had inspired a new round of public moralizing. People who'd never met the family were on cable shows talking about them; late-night comedians had a new batch of jokes; and other candidates were already weaponizing the news for their purposes. John Bright's political friends and former supporters were calling for him to drop out, while a small group of loyalists maintained that this storm could be weathered. If he wasn't political toast, he seemed to be cultural toast.

But Philip didn't know any of this—or any of the other things that had occurred on planet Earth in the preceding twenty-four hours—because it was possible to shut everything else out at the Bright lake house, if that's what you cared to do.

"Are you going to reach out to your father…this, other man?"

Philip looked at Farah. "I don't know. Not yet. Probably eventually, but not now."

She nodded.

Philip swallowed and kept his eyes fixed on Farah.

She felt all the muscles in her stomach clench into a fist and her breath stop.

"What do *you* think I should do?" he finally asked.

"I don't know, Philip. I'm sorry."

And then he leaned down toward her, so their foreheads were touching.

Her heart was racing as she held her body completely still. She could feel their humid skin sticking together. Philip blinked. His long lashes came up like curtains, green eyes still on her. He seemed as surprised as she was, to be so close and looking at her in such a way.

Then Philip tilted his head, and with utter astonishment, he kissed her.

Something surged from their hot mouths down into Farah's stomach and through every extremity. She thought she might faint, but instead she reached out and held on to the hard flesh of his upper arm. He tasted sour and hungry to her. She wanted all of it.

It was not a long kiss, but neither was it short. Farah couldn't perceive its length. There was nothing more to it—just a tender, long-enough kiss while they leaned against the trunk of the oak tree. Soft lips and hot breath. They felt alone with the lapping lake water, though anyone could have woken and seen them then.

When it was over, Philip pulled his head back and smiled at Farah. His expression was inscrutable. She looked away and let herself sit with the expansive joy of the moment. She wanted never to stop feeling that way.

"I don't know what's going to happen," he said finally.

"I don't know, either."

They sat for another few minutes in silence as the sun rose and the lake house woke up. Through the windows, they could see lights come on and bodies move about. The faint breeze that had been pushing the water against the shoreline in predictable heaves ceased. The surface of the lake turned back to glass. That day would be as wet and heavy as the previous one, maybe more so.

Eventually, Farah stood up and brushed off her shorts. She looked down at Philip. Would he come in? Would they, and could they, kiss again? Philip smiled up at her, but he did not move. She understood his paralysis to be about more than simply her.

So Farah walked inside and went about the usual business of watching them all through her cameras. She did her very best to divorce her body from her thoughts, to ignore the churning of her insides and the sour taste still on her tongue.

She didn't feel right watching them anymore, if she ever had. Now that it was real—with this vindication of her feelings for Philip—she couldn't will herself to go on filming the Brights, exploiting this vulnerable moment. But she also couldn't see a way out for herself. This assignment was her job, which was her paycheck, which was her survival, her career, her identity.

Farah kept working.

41

Chelsea and Charlie were back at their private beach for one last roll through the sand. They hadn't noticed it before, but the beach wasn't so private. The people living in the house just around the bend could see them if they knew what to look for. And anyone with a pair of binoculars could have found them from across the lake. Suddenly, Chelsea felt keenly aware of the exposure of their naked bodies. Two weeks before, they were the first geniuses to consider having sex on a semipublic beach; now they were just adults behaving like children. A spell had been broken.

The shift in their feelings about each other could be attributed to any number of things: Charlie's family trauma, the intensity of the public spotlight or too many days spent alone together. It shouldn't have surprised Chelsea to learn that their bond wasn't strong enough to endure all that, but it did. Even as she wished to be anywhere else, she didn't really wish to be through with Charlie.

Chelsea couldn't discern how Charlie felt, for they hadn't really discussed it. In lieu of emotions and words, Charlie was just dealing in bodies for the time being. He seemed incapable of understanding the breadth of the bomb that had just exploded in his family, and instead of working through it, he was burying his head in the soft parts of Chelsea's body.

This was a relief to her. Chelsea hadn't the slightest idea how to comfort a person in Charlie's position, but she knew how to do this. She was tired and sore and sunburned after the better part of the day spent in depraved congress on a sandy beach. But talking about it would have been worse.

Charlie sucked the last of their water bottle down in one gulp. "What time do you have to go tomorrow?"

"I should leave for the airport by eleven. You sure you don't mind driving me?"

"Of course not. I just wish you didn't have to go yet." He kissed her shoulder. "We should probably get back. I think JJ and Mary and the twins are leaving soon."

Chelsea nodded. "I'm starving. Are you hungry?"

Charlie reached for her hand and pulled her toward him. He kissed her forehead with parched lips. They pressed up against each other until she could feel fresh sweat accumulating between her breasts. Neither could think of a way to say what this was: an end, but not an angry end. And so they said nothing. They were alike in many ways, but none more than this.

Twenty minutes later, Chelsea and Charlie emerged from the lakeside trail and walked toward the back side of the house. Despite the fact that it was an objectively perfect summer day, there was almost no sign of human life outside. JJ had put all the watercraft away and the twins had folded up all the beach chairs. The cushions from all the deck furniture had been returned to storage and the grill was covered. The only evidence of the Brights on that sprawling lawn now was Philip, sitting on a cushion, reading a book under his tree. He had a different set of clothes on from the day before, and a little cooler beside him (courtesy of Mary-Beth). He had hardly moved in over two days.

They smiled at Philip as they passed, and he smiled back. No words were spoken among them. Chelsea wondered what Charlie thought of it all—his brother (half brother) camping outside indefinitely—but Charlie wasn't up for questions, so she kept quiet. He just nodded at his brother, who nodded back, as if all the new rules of this strange new arrangement were as normal as could be.

Inside, Ian and Spencer were having a whispered conversation in their running clothes.

"Hey, aren't you guys leaving today?" Charlie asked.

Spencer shook his head. He had large bags under his eyes. "Tomorrow. No one's leaving today, actually. Dad's doing a press conference in the morning. Then we're out."

"A press conference? Christ, aren't things bad enough?"

"It's necessary."

"JJ thought it would be helpful," Ian explained. "To announce the end of the campaign in his own words."

Charlie shook his head and led Chelsea by her hand upstairs. "Whatever."

Chelsea desperately wanted a shower, but when they got to the landing, Charlie put his finger to his lips. *Shhh*. The master bedroom was booming with loud, arguing voices.

They tiptoed quietly along the hall and stopped halfway to listen. It didn't feel right to Chelsea to eavesdrop, but Charlie held her hand with such force that breaking away wasn't an option.

"You are insane!" Patty yelled from the other side of the door. Something slammed like a drawer, and then another. "I can't believe you're considering this."

"Patty, my dear," John Senior said. "This could actually be an *opportunity*. We could be the campaign of total transparency and humility. Voters love fallibility—you know that! We could go out there tomorrow and make this a historic comeback story."

"No. Absolutely not. I won't even discuss this with you."

"But Patty—"

Another drawer slammed. "John, have I ever—*ever*—said no to anything you've wanted me to do? Have I ever objected to any of this?"

"Patty, please keep your voice down."

"Goddamn it, have I?"

"No, you have not."

"Right, I have not. But I'm doing it now. Because our family needs some time out of the spotlight. We owe that to our sons. We owe it to Philip. Poor Philip, look at him out there!"

Charlie's hand clamped harder around Chelsea's, and she thought she could feel his heart beating through it. His eyes didn't stray from his parents' bedroom door.

"John, please..." Patty's voice was softer now. She may have been crying. "I'm begging you. Please just let this go. Use tomorrow's press conference to say goodbye with dignity."

No one said anything for a long time. There were muffled sounds and a few of Patty's sniffles. Chelsea imagined that they were hugging, but it wasn't easy to picture. Then someone whispered something that sounded like "okay." And that was the end. No one said another word.

Charlie stayed for another minute, then pulled Chelsea into their bedroom.

She was ready for whatever he needed to do: yell, cry, have

sex (again). But he didn't do any of those things. He just stood there for a moment with wide eyes looking stunned, then walked to the bathroom and slammed the door. Chelsea heard the shower turn on a moment later. He was gone.

She wished to be invisible for the remaining time until the moment of her escape to the airport. It was such a short period of time, but the entire house felt as if it might burst into flames at any minute. She just happened to be caught up in the fire, a bystander and near stranger.

42

"I still can't believe he's going to do it," Spencer said from the bed. He had the sheets pulled up to his chin. A fan blasted cool evening air at him from the window.

Ian sat beside the bed in an armchair, making notes in a textbook. He was hoping to get some course planning done while Spencer slept. But Spencer, it seemed, never slept anymore.

"Do what?"

Spencer sat up in bed. "I just don't believe he's going to announce that the campaign is over tomorrow. Like, I'm not sure he's capable of it. I'm worried he won't really do it. Is that crazy?"

"Not crazy, but improbable."

"Ending the campaign is—to my dad—an admission of defeat. He hasn't had to do that in decades. I'm not sure he *can* do it."

"He'll have to figure it out, I suppose."

"Or not."

Ian put his book down and looked up at Spencer over his reading glasses. "Are you serious? Didn't your mom tell him that he had to end the campaign?"

Spencer scratched his scalp through messy hair. "I don't know. I feel like he's been trying to make some wiggle room for himself."

"What does that mean?"

"He wouldn't let me write him a speech, and he wouldn't let JJ confirm the purpose of the press conference. It feels like he's hedging."

Ian sighed. "I'm sure you're right that this is killing him. But he doesn't really have any other options at this point. He'll do it because he has to do it."

Spencer fell back onto his pillow and looked at the ceiling.

It hadn't occurred to Ian that his father-in-law was seriously resisting the plan to end this campaign, but it wasn't such a crazy theory. There might be a way to spin all this family drama into something heartwarming and relatable and almost winnable, but that's not what made the theory plausible. It was John Bright's ability to be selfish that made it plausible.

Spencer and his brothers had always joked about how their father could be a bit narcissistic. Ian had heard it said several times in loving ways over the years, and it was plainly obvious to any observer. But it wasn't until this trip that Ian realized John Senior was something more wicked than simply a charmingly vain patriarch. He was incapable of seeing this moment through the eyes of anyone else, including his own children. Their pain wasn't going to interfere with his plans.

"Maybe you should try again tomorrow morning," Ian said. "Ask him again if he'll let you write a speech. I'm sure everything will be fine, but it can't hurt."

"Maybe."

They sat in the cool silence for another minute. And then Ian set down his book, turned out the light and crawled into bed. He hoped for his husband's sake that they were both just crazy.

Tomorrow would be the last day of all this madness, because it had to be.

43

Farah hauled the last of all the cameras down the garage steps to the driveway. She arranged them in a circle in the gravel where she could make a plan for each. Two at the front gates, two facing the podium, one looking down from the second floor, and the smallest camera would stay with her as she roamed. Farah wanted to catch everything from every angle today. The press conference would begin in a few hours.

It was early, and all the Brights were still inside drinking coffee. Farah could see them talking excitedly through the window. A woman from a local salon was applying foundation to Patty's face while another woman painted highlights into her hair. Spencer was reading something aloud to them from his laptop. They were more animated than they'd been in several days, almost happy. The press conference was keeping everyone busy and purposeful.

Even Philip was inside now. He'd agreed to abandon his

post at the oak tree and get cleaned up for the press conference. Farah imagined him standing under a running showerhead as ribbons of dirt and sweat ran down his long body toward the drain.

They hadn't discussed the previous day's kiss, and Farah was trying to keep it out of her mind for now. There would be time for that later. Maybe, hopefully, there would be another kiss. But today, she needed to do her job and ignore the nagging feeling that her job was at odds with Philip's well-being.

Farah wanted to be done with the work. She had the sinking awareness that the footage she'd been gathering in those weeks would come together nicely into a tidy story arc. It had hubris, suspense, revelations and destruction. Wayne would love it. Farah salved her moral anxiety by convincing herself that she could keep Philip out of the final product as much as possible, to make it about John Senior and Patty alone. She vowed to protect the innocent in postproduction. The alternative was quitting the project, and that was just too professionally dangerous.

Farah picked up two medium-sized handheld cameras and two mounting clamps. She put one under each arm, threw the clamps into a backpack and set out down the driveway. She walked along the gravel, through the lush wooded drive and down toward the road. When she got to the gate, she mounted the cameras to trees on either side of the entrance. The plan was to get footage of incoming cars as they arrived. Farah could mount a camera to anything: the face of a mountain, the back of a goat. She had bungee cords of every size in the trunk of her car and an affinity for the challenge.

As she adjusted the position of the second camera on the fat part of a branch above her head, a Mercedes passed slowly, the driver craning his head. Farah waved, but the man accelerated again and kept going. Gawkers. Local people didn't want to be too obvious about it, but they'd been snooping in their own way—canoeing too close to the Bright beach and flashing cameras outside the gate. It was all pretty gross.

Farah had to remind herself that she was not the same as those people. She didn't need to feel bad about doing her job. The Brights were the ones who'd called a press conference. They *wanted* to be watched—excepting Philip, of course.

Do not think of Philip. Not today. Today—just work.

Farah walked back up the driveway under the canopy of evergreens and maples. The humidity had broken, and there was a welcome breeze. She pulled her hair off her neck and let it cool her, realizing as she did that she was going to miss all this when it was over. Somehow, despite being a person who craved the dynamism and energy of a city, she had grown to appreciate the quiet woods. She wouldn't miss the staged perfection of the little downtown or the uninspired whiteness of it all. But she'd miss the swaying trees and the way the air coming off the lake was always five degrees cooler than everything else. She'd come back here someday, maybe.

As she came around the bend at the top of the driveway, Farah found Spencer, JJ and Charlie locked in a hushed discussion. They stopped talking and looked at her with forced smiles, waiting for her to pass. They were talking so close their shoulders were almost touching, shaking their heads and wiping sweat from their temples as they did. Something was going awry.

Farah carried the rest of the cameras into the house and set them down along a wall in the kitchen. She poured herself coffee and made small talk with Ian, who was reading the newspaper.

"When does the press start arriving?" She already knew the answer to this, but she couldn't think of anything else to say.

Ian looked up. "They will start setting up in about an hour, I think. Charlie's manning the gate."

"And is everything still on track?"

Patty breezed into the kitchen at that moment in a form-fitting pale yellow shift. "Everything is great, Farah. I trust you'll be outside with the rest of the camera crews?"

"Uh, yes, of course." She nodded at Patty. This was her reminder that she was more help than family. "I'm almost finished setting up."

Ian smiled apologetically and went back to his paper.

Farah took her coffee out the back door and sat on the deck stairs. She pulled her phone out of her pocket and scrolled through her email. There were a dozen messages from Wayne already—suggestions for which cameras to set up where, early footage she should be getting and maybe doing some confessional-style sit-downs with the family members in the aftermath.

She just needed five minutes to drink coffee. Then she'd get to it all.

Behind her, a screen door slammed, and Philip emerged looking fresh and clean. He smiled and sat down beside her. "Hi!"

"Hi." The cheerfulness of this greeting unnerved Farah, who'd been hoping for something more intimate, less general. "How does it feel to rejoin civilization?"

He shrugged. "Not so different. Showers sure are nice, though."

"That's true." Was this intimacy or was it generality?

They sat for a moment in silence, alone.

Finally, Farah said, "So that thing that happened yesterday..."

It was his sentence to finish. "Right. That thing..."

"We don't have to say anything about it if you prefer not to. There's a lot going on right now."

"No, no, we probably should..." He was speaking slowly and from a distance. He cleared his throat. "Farah, I... I have a lot to think about now... You've made me think about things...which is good...but not necessarily easy..."

She waited.

"What I'm saying is that I'm not quite sure what to say just yet..."

It was excruciating and Farah wanted it to end. Whatever he was trying to say, it wasn't good. It wasn't *I want you*. It wasn't *This changes everything*. She couldn't watch him bumble his way through it any longer.

"Philip, I shouldn't have brought it up. Forget it." She wanted to sound breezy, but her voice was high and pinched.

"No, I don't want to forget about it. I just don't know what to *do* about it. Not yet, anyway."

Farah snatched up her coffee mug, sending a wave of warm liquid over her wrist. "You don't have to do anything! Let's just move on, okay? I think that's the right call."

She walked quickly back inside, dropping her mug in the sink and heading toward the door. Ian tried to say something to her as she left, but she didn't give him time to finish. She went past the guys still huddled together in the driveway and up the garage stairs to her room.

Fuck this. Fuck these people. And fuck these feelings. This was exactly what she didn't want to do today. How could she have been so foolish as to think that Philip was available to her? What kind of self-loathing lunatic falls for an aspiring priest?

Farah unlocked her door and fell face-first onto her bed. She cried as she hadn't in a long time—deep, wet sobs. They were the sobs of a foolish woman who makes terrible, embarrassing choices. The sound of Philip's tortured, stilted explanation was still ringing in her ears. She was gutted.

When Farah was drained of everything, she lay still on the bed, facedown, for a long time. She could have fallen asleep.

Instead, she stood up and went to the bathroom to wash her face. She applied mascara and changed into a new shirt. And then she went back downstairs to do her job. Her job was to watch these monsters as they blew themselves up. She was just there to record it.

44

The press conference wouldn't start for another thirty minutes, but parked cars already snaked down the length of the driveway. Sweating men and a few women set up video cameras in the grass while polished on-air personalities touched up their makeup in palm-sized mirrors.

The setting couldn't have been lovelier. John Senior was scheduled to speak from a small podium in the garden with a view of the glistening lake behind him. The exterior of the house had been adorned with flower wreaths, and an enormous American flag hung like a banner along the front of the garage.

It all seemed a bit much to Mary-Beth, who thought the setting should be more reflective of the somber occasion. But Patty said this didn't need to feel like a funeral, so that was that.

But of course, this *was* a funeral. The press conference had been called to announce the death of John Bright's campaign and, it seemed to Mary-Beth, the death of the long-standing myth of who the Bright family really was. Something had died here. Philip's previous understanding of himself—of his family—was gone. And no matter what her mother-in-law said, Mary-Beth was sure that this should look more like a funeral than a wedding.

"You think I need a tie?"

Mary-Beth turned from the kitchen window to her husband, who looked expectantly at her in his crisp shirt. Little sacks of exhaustion hung from beneath his eyes.

"No, I don't think so. What's your dad wearing?"

"I don't know. I haven't seen him yet. He's been in the study all morning working on his remarks. I really wish he'd let Spencer review them first."

"Your dad's a good writer."

"It's not that..." JJ rubbed his face. "Spencer thinks he's having second thoughts about this press conference."

"What? There are sixty people here already. It's too late for that."

"No, they think he's having second thoughts about ending the campaign. It seemed crazy to me until I started thinking about it. I wouldn't put it past him."

Mary-Beth closed her eyes and tried to breathe deeply. Now was not the time to say all the things she was thinking about John Senior. Now was the time to do as Patty did and just smile. "I need to check on the boys. I'm sure you'll make your father do what he needs to do."

JJ nodded and pulled her toward him. "Hey, I love you. This is almost over."

He kissed her lips with a restorative force, and she kissed back.

"*Hopefully*, this is almost over."

"Ha."

But JJ wasn't laughing and neither was Mary-Beth, because nothing about today was funny. The campaign would end

(probably) and they would go home. But JJ would be returning to an uncertain professional future. And Spencer would
go back to torturing Ian with his own insecurities. Charlie
would be unemployed indefinitely. And Philip…poor Philip.

They would get to the other side of today, but things were
still irrevocably broken for the Bright family. That wasn't
going to change overnight. It was hard to think beyond this
terrible morning, but eventually they would have to, and
Mary-Beth had the feeling that things were going to get worse
before they got better. All because of John—John and Patty.
Mary-Beth had grown accustomed to blaming everything
around them on her father-in-law, but it was now clear that
Patty was implicated in all this, too: the lies and secrets, the
cold ambition. They'd been working together all along.

Mary-Beth took another look outside. Ian and a cable camera guy were trying to fix the mult box out in the garden. God
bless him, Ian was on his knees plugging and unplugging wires.
Chelsea was carrying a doughnut wrapped in a paper towel
down the driveway, presumably to Charlie, who was checking press credentials at the gate. And dozens of media people
were milling around the Bright family vacation compound,
cracking jokes to the voices in their earpieces, putting cigarette
butts out in flower pots and waiting for the circus to begin.

Mary-Beth thought it was all so ugly, these vultures here
to feast on a family's downfall. But it was what this family deserved—not her, or her boys or JJ. Certainly not Philip. John
and Patty Bright deserved it all. Mary-Beth had no sympathy
left for either of them.

As she made her way to the boys' room, Farah passed Mary-
Beth on the left, a blinking camera held out before her. Mary-
Beth pretended not to notice, because that's what they had
all been conditioned to do. Behave as if you cannot see the

camera (but stand just so to avoid blocking the shot). It was second nature to her now.

Farah seemed like a nice girl. She wasn't like the reporters outside, not exactly. She'd been invited here on happier, more high-minded terms. But she still evoked in Mary-Beth the same urge to grab the recording device and send it flying through an open window.

If it were up to Mary-Beth, she'd have sent Farah packing two weeks ago when the boys were stuck in Spain. She'd have closed ranks around her family and hunkered down privately. But it wasn't up to her, and that was a thing that she was fed up with, too. From here on out, they would leave nothing in the hands of JJ's parents. Too much had been left to them in this life.

Spencer appeared in the hallway and looked around. "We ready?"

Mary-Beth shrugged.

"Let's huddle up!" he shouted.

Two minutes later, they were all there in the kitchen: Philip, Chelsea, Spencer and Ian, JJ and Mary-Beth, Cameron and Lucas. (John and Patty were still holed up in their room.) They stood in a tight circle, waiting for their marching orders. The din of outside voices and ringing phones was all around them, but for now it was just them, the Brights and their extras.

JJ rolled up his sleeves and put his hands on his waist. "Okay, so here's the game plan—Dad takes the podium in five minutes. At the start, I want Mom up there with him, and all of us standing behind them so we're in the shot. Dad will give a short, sweet speech, then take two or three softball questions from friendly reporters—he knows who they are. Then Spencer will send out the press release and we'll kick these animals out. That's the whole show. Got it?"

Everyone nodded.

"Where's Charlie?"

"He's still down at the gate," Chelsea said.

"Can you get him up here? I think all the press on our list are here now. Maybe someone can stand in for him for a few minutes. We need all Brights present for the speech."

"I can do it," Chelsea said.

JJ was skeptical. "Can you spot a fake press credential?"

"Probably not."

"Farah can do it," Spencer said, and everyone turned to her.

"Farah, can you watch the gate for, like, five minutes? You've got plenty of cameras on us up here, so you won't miss anything. All you have to do is let credentialed press in, and make sure the gate latches behind them, until Charlie is back."

"I, I really can't do that," she sputtered. "I should be up here with the—"

"It's just five minutes. C'mon, I think we've been more than accommodating, considering everything that's happened here. Help us out."

Farah swallowed and looked around. Mary-Beth almost felt bad for her as she squirmed. Finally, she nodded and left the house. She checked each of her cameras, which were mounted on tripods around the grass, then left for the front gate.

Seconds later, the sound of John Senior's heavy steps and Patty's heels clattered down the stairs. They looked great— disturbingly so. If either of them had missed an hour of deep sleep over the drama of their family, they didn't show it. Mary-Beth hated them.

"Are we ready?" John boomed. He had the look of a child who knows he's supposed to be frowning but can't suppress a grin.

JJ folded his arms tightly. "Do you have remarks?"

"I do."

"May I see them?"

"It's standard pablum…just like we discussed…apology, contrition, lessons learned…"

"Resignation?"

"Right," his father said.

JJ looked at his mother, who revealed nothing.

"If he doesn't resign, I'll do it for him," Patty said.

JJ rubbed his tired eyes. "Okay, then. Time for the firing squad."

They filed through the screen door one by one, out into the bright summer day. Charlie joined them outside and they formed a sort of procession to the garden, with John and Patty at the front.

Mary-Beth walked in step with her husband, trying to hold a pleasantly blank expression as she watched her sandals move in the grass.

As they approached the roped-off section of the garden, conversation among media people ceased, and all eyes turned to the Brights. The machine-gun clatter of cameras began firing all at once. Photographers stretched their bodies out over the rope, trying to get as close as possible with their lenses.

The Brights did just as JJ had instructed: waited for John and Patty to reach the podium, then formed a tight row behind them.

Mary-Beth wished she'd worn her sunglasses. The glare made it difficult to see into the crowd. JJ put a hand on the small of her back, and she smiled up at him. Big circles of sweat were already forming at his armpits. Maybe he should have worn a tie after all. Mary-Beth could feel Lucas bouncing on his heels to her other side, a nervous habit he'd had since toddlerhood. She wanted to tell him to stop, but that would only make it worse. She shouldn't have agreed to let her children stand up there. What sort of mother would submit her children to this? Everything about that moment was more humiliating than she'd imagined it would be.

Cameras kept going off, and it wasn't clear whether they should be smiling or not. Which would look worse, Mary-Beth wondered, a frown or a smile? Which would make them look less like liars and opportunists?

John and Patty were smiling. They were standing at the podium now, holding hands. John was enjoying himself.

Spencer cleared his throat in an apparent effort to get his father to stop preening and start talking. *Let's get this over with*, they all begged silently. But John Senior made a few more turns, a few waves and a personalized hello to three of the reporters he recognized in the crowd.

Finally, he adjusted the microphone and took a deep breath. "Good morning!"

Patty let go of her husband's hand and took one step away from the podium.

"Thank you for coming out today to the lovely Berkshire Mountains in the great Commonwealth of Massachusetts!"

JJ looked over at Spencer, who avoided his gaze. Mary-Beth knew they were thinking this was too cheerful, too boisterous. It wasn't the right tone. They all held their breath as their father went on.

"As you all know, the past few weeks have been trying for my family and me. We've had to do a lot of soul-searching. *I've* had to do a lot of soul-searching. Because in the long story of my life, I haven't always been the man I want to be. I haven't always been the spouse or father that these people deserve."

John Senior looked back at his family, and they all smiled as the cameras clicked.

"I've made mistakes in the past for which I'm deeply sorry—to my wife, my children and my constituents. There are no excuses for my transgressions. That's not what I'm here to do. I've asked for my family's forgiveness—and today, I ask for the public's forgiveness."

He paused to take a long slug from a water bottle.

Mary-Beth could feel her husband relax slightly beside her.

"Now, as for some of the other stories you've read about my wife and son, I take responsibility for everything. I violated my wife's trust years ago. I am responsible for the wayward path our marriage took. I hope you will spare them the public scrutiny that I deserve. All four of the accomplished Bright men who stand behind me are my sons, and I am their father. Please respect our privacy on the matter of Philip's patrimony."

Mary-Beth thought that was a nice touch.

"I hope, too, that there is room in the public's heart for forgiveness. I've spent every day since those early dark days reforming myself, improving my commitment to family and faith and country. I've redeemed myself in the eyes of my family, and I believe I can redeem myself in the eyes of my fellow Bay Staters."

JJ wiped his sweating forehead with the back of his hand and looked down at Mary-Beth, whose heart was racing now. This wasn't right. John Senior wasn't steering this speech in the right direction. She turned to read the expression on Patty's face, but Patty wasn't there any longer. Where had she gone? Spencer was whispering to Ian, who was trying to maintain a smile for the cameras. In the press scrum, Mary-Beth could see Farah and her camera looking back at her from the crowd. Charlie must have seen her, too, because he made a breathy little gasp. If Charlie was there, and Farah was there, then who was at the gate?

Meanwhile John was still talking about his reinvented self, and all the cameras were still rolling.

Mary-Beth squeezed JJ's hand, and he held on for dear life. They were trapped up there, for however long John talked, no matter what he said.

"And so I've brought you here today," John continued, "to

ask for your forgiveness and understanding, to tell you that I'm not the foolish young man that I once was, and to announce that—"

At that moment, a whooshing roar blasted them all from the western side of the lawn. It sounded like an enormous sucking of air and felt like a hot breath from the gods.

John Senior stopped talking and every head on the compound turned to the place where the sound originated: the driveway. It was then that they saw it: the billboard-sized American flag that hung down the face of the garage ensconced in flames. Every inch of the polyester writhed in fire.

For half a second, the crowd was frozen and silent. They felt the heat from the flag on their stunned faces and struggled to understand what they were seeing. Then a woman screamed, two car alarms went off and the flames jumped from the wick of the flag to the garage itself. It was swallowing the building whole.

"Someone call the fire department!"

People were screaming and running now, hurdling over the ropes that penned them in. Some went down the driveway toward their parked cars, others toward the water.

JJ herded his wife and two children to the lake without a word. Mary-Beth nearly tripped trying to kick off her shoes, but Lucas caught her with the strong arms of an adult she hardly recognized. "I've got you," he said as she planted her feet back on the ground.

Another car alarm joined the cacophony.

Someone pushed her as he rushed past.

Mary-Beth held more tightly to Lucas.

She didn't know where all the Brights were, but she knew where hers were.

45

Farah sank to the base of the oak tree and let her head rest against the trunk. Her wet cheek pressed into the cell phone as Wayne spoke softly from the other end. She couldn't remember crying, but she must have.

"Are you sure you're okay?"

"I'm okay," she said. "I mean, I feel like a fool, but I'm okay."

Most of the yard had cleared out by then. Only the firefighters were still walking the grounds while the cops talked with the family. Everything smelled like campfire.

"I'm so glad you weren't in there when it happened. God, Farah, I can't even think about that! I'm so glad you're okay. I nearly had a heart attack when I saw it on the news."

"Thanks. It's lucky, I guess. I didn't know you watched cable news, Wayne."

"You couldn't miss it today. Coverage has been wall-to-wall."

Farah had the feeling that, although she'd lived through the fire and watched the garage burn to a blackened shell, she hadn't been standing on her own feet while it happened.

"I'm so sorry to have to ask this, but..." Wayne hesitated. "Is our footage all gone?"

"It is. I'm so sorry, Wayne. Everything except what's on the cameras from today is gone. I kept all the storage in my room above the garage. Some of it was on an external drive, but most of it was on SD cards. They were in a shoebox." A choking laugh escaped her. "*Everything's* gone. I don't even have a wallet anymore."

"Well, I guess that's that."

She had to fight back tears and the overwhelming urge to keep apologizing to Wayne. His concern for her was genuine, but so, too, was his disappointment that all this work— all this prime drama—was lost now. It wasn't her fault that the garage had burned down and all her efforts went down with it. But there were a million things she could have done to protect her work. She could have stored everything in her car, or sent the memory cards back to the office. She could have backed up her computer or emailed the files to herself. It was the dumbest sort of bad luck.

Still, there was the good luck of being unharmed. The garage was a charred skeleton of itself, but it was lucky none of the nearby cars had blown up and no one had been hurt. The house would need a new paint job, but it was basically fine.

It was confounding, the entire episode.

In the distance, the fire marshal emerged through the back door of the house and made a gesture toward Farah.

"Wayne, I think I have to go talk to the authorities. They're interviewing everyone."

"About what? Why do *you* have to talk to them? The networks are all saying it's probably domestic terrorism."

"Jesus, is that what they're saying? I didn't know that."

"I'll call you later. I'm so sorry, Farah."

"No, *I'm* sorry."

She shoved her phone into her pocket and hoisted her stunned body onto her feet. As she walked toward the house, she forced herself to consider the possibility that the cops might think *she* had done something to cause this. That was the part she couldn't bear to tell Wayne: she was maybe a little responsible for the fire.

Farah had done two things while she was supposed to be manning the entrance gate, two things that she desperately regretted now. First, she'd let Jeff—from the hack news site—in. He was a marginally legitimate journalist, but he didn't have any real credentials when she'd asked for them. It hadn't seemed like a big deal at the time. The second thing she had done was simply walk away from the gate. She'd forgotten to make sure it latched after each entrant. The gate was probably open when she left it.

Why did she do those things? She was not sure. She didn't want to sabotage the Brights, not consciously. She just wanted to get back to work and look out for herself. She was still bruised by Philip's rejection. *Fuck it*, she'd said at the time, and then she walked back up the driveway. *Fuck it.* It seemed a relatively harmless infraction, a quiet act of protest. But the facts of the situation weren't looking so good for her now.

Farah followed the man through the screen door to the kitchen. Inside, a policeman was sitting at the table with the Brights. They were all drinking ice tea. Farah noticed that the puppy was curled up in the dog bed in the corner. She was glad it had survived.

"Are you Farah Dhaliwal?" the sitting officer said. He had an open notebook before him covered in chicken scratch.

"Yes."

"You're the documentary filmmaker."

"Yes, though I'm obviously not making *this* documentary anymore."

"And why is that?"

Farah looked around at John, Patty and the rest of them. She couldn't tell if maybe *they* thought she'd done this, too. It might make sense to these people. She wasn't family. They didn't really know her. She'd rebuffed one son and was secretly obsessed with another. She had brown hair and brown skin and long-dead relatives from a part of the world that Americans think all terrorism originates. It suddenly felt like everyone in the room (except Philip, the one she wanted to hate) was looking expectantly at her now, open to the possibility of her guilt.

"Nearly all the footage I've taken here this summer was in the fire," she explained. "It was all up in that room. About fifteen thousand dollars' worth of equipment, too. It's gone."

The cop looked at the fire marshal and made a note on his pad. "You should be able to file those claims with your employer's insurance. Be sure to itemize thoroughly or they'll really screw you."

She nodded. Was that a thing you'd say to an arson suspect? Maybe he was trying to earn her trust.

"And you were down at the entrance at one point?"

"Yes, for most of the speech."

"Did you let anyone in who wasn't a credentialed journalist?"

"No." Was she was really doing this? Was she really lying to local authorities?

He nodded, made a note. "Then, I understand, you walked away from the gate. When did you leave? Did you push it closed when you left?"

"I left right before the speech, um, ended. I thought I heard it latch behind me."

Another note on the pad. "You *thought* it latched?"

"Yes, I thought so, but I don't—"

And then Patty spoke up. "It did."

Everyone turned to her.

"I snuck away from the speech about halfway through, as you know," Patty explained. "It was difficult for me, and I needed a little air. So I walked down to the gate and then turned around and came back up. When I got down there, Farah was gone and the gate was locked."

The cop exchanged another look with the fire marshal. Farah couldn't tell if they believed Patty or not. Why was she covering for her?

"Do you have anything to add to that account, Ms. Dhaliwal?"

Farah swallowed. "No, that's my recollection, too."

"Well, then, it seems whoever did this must have gotten here some other way, maybe on foot or by water. We've interviewed all the press people, and they all have corroborating footage or witnesses who can attest to their presence in the garden. We'll need to take a look at all the footage you gathered from today as well, Ms. Dhaliwal."

"Of course."

"It's pretty rare that you have a dozen cameras running while a crime is committed, so we'll likely find something when we go through it all. The fire team believes this to be a highly suspicious incident, but we have no evidence to support that yet."

John Senior shook his head and slammed a fist on the table. "This is an act of domestic terrorism, goddamn it! I've been very outspoken on this issue in my career, and I'm a logical target. It was an American flag they set on fire, for Christ's sake!"

"Yessir, that's what it's looking like. But, of course, we can't comment on the matter until we know more."

"Maybe the video footage was the point of all this," JJ suggested. "Maybe they had some reason to sabotage the production of the documentary."

"It's a possibility," the cop said. "Do you have any idea of who might want that?"

"Of course not," Patty snapped. "Can you just tell us what happens next?"

The cop looked at the fire marshal again. "Federal investigators are on their way here now, so this is probably the end of the road for us. They'll have more questions for you."

"Well, are we safe here?" Mary-Beth asked.

"We'll keep a squad car at the end of the driveway through the night, ma'am. The feds will have further instructions after that."

She looked stunned. They all did.

As the cop and the fire marshal collected their things and shook everyone's hand, one of the firemen stuck his head in the front door to tell them they were leaving, too.

Everyone went outside to watch the firemen roll up their hoses and steer their trucks down the driveway. The police cars went next. Cameron tried to capture it on his cell phone, but Mary-Beth snatched it from his hands.

As the last vehicle disappeared around the gravel curve, another car pulled up. It was a black sedan with a middle-aged man at the wheel.

"Did someone call a car?"

Ten seconds later, Chelsea emerged from the house with an overstuffed frame pack over one shoulder. The driver got out of the car and hoisted her pack into the trunk. And then the entire family tried to avert their eyes as Charlie kissed her, hard. They were both crying. Charlie's face pressed into Chelsea's as hair matted against wet cheeks and more tears fell.

Finally, they separated. Chelsea thanked John and Patty for their hospitality. She kissed Ian and Mary-Beth on the cheek, and offered a fist bump to each of the boys. Lucas held the puppy out to her face, and Chelsea let it lick her skin as everyone looked on.

Farah was last in line for goodbyes. Chelsea wrapped her arms around her in a great bear hug, and as she did, she whispered into Farah's ear: "Go home."

Farah wanted to keep holding on to Chelsea. They'd been outsiders here together. Extras. Mary-Beth and Ian thought *extras* was their little secret, but Farah had always known about it. It was her job to know everything. Chelsea smelled like grapefruit shampoo and burning wood in her arms, a memory of good and terrible things.

They said their goodbyes, and Chelsea went back to Charlie for another long, shamelessly handsy, public kiss.

She cried and wiped her nose, waved to the crowd and got into the car bound for the airport. It was time to go home.

Farah assembled a makeshift bed on the couch in the living room that night. She showered and changed into clothes borrowed from Mary-Beth. Tomorrow, she'd be gone, too. And the strangest thing happened as she lay on the big, soft couch of the Bright vacation home: she felt okay with it all. She was better than okay; she was relieved.

Farah didn't want to tell this story. She didn't want to convince herself she wasn't in love with Philip and spend the next six months sorting through footage to find the most humiliating moments of his family life for the world to gawk at. She just wanted to walk away and let them have all their terribleness—and their undeniable goodness—to themselves.

Maybe it meant she wasn't great at this work. Maybe it meant she was a soft documentarian, but a decent human. She could live with that.

Just as Farah was ready to surrender to sleep, she heard footsteps coming toward her in the dark.

"Hey." It was Philip.

"Hey."

"Are you okay down here on the couch? We could set up an air mattress in the study if you want something more private."

She sat up. It was so dark in the room that only the whites of his eyes and the glow of the moon through the window were visible. "No, this is fine. I just want to sleep."

"My mom said you're leaving tomorrow."

"Yeah. First thing."

A pause.

"I guess you have to get back to your life," he said.

"I do."

"Listen, Farah, I'm really sorry about everything that happened. I mean, to all your work. This must be really bad for you."

She sighed. "It's not that bad...considering everything. What I mean is... I'm sorry for *you*. Philip, what are you going to do now?"

He sat down at the end of the sofa and put a hand on her socked foot.

"I don't know. For now, I'm still going to the seminary in a few weeks. Maybe while I'm there, I'll figure out how to think about my father...and my other father. And my mother, too."

"Your mother did a nice thing for me today, you know. She covered for me about the unlocked gate. I don't know why she did that, but it was nice."

"Yeah, she's a surprising person sometimes." Philip seemed to already know about the gate. He knew more than she did.

"But about the fire. I just don't understand how—"

"It doesn't matter how. It's over. Don't worry about the fire."

Farah didn't understand how he could say this, how it could be over. But she thought she saw a faint smile on Philip's face, and it was enough to make her feel slightly better about it all. No one blamed her.

"Farah, I just wanted to tell you that I'm leaving next week. I'm sticking with my plan. But I do have feelings for you. That part was true."

They sat in silence for a long time after that. Her chest pounded.

Finally, Philip spoke again. "I wish I knew what to do or say. I'm so sorry." He put his face in his hands and wept silently.

Farah leaned toward him and put a hand on his back. She wanted to do more. She wanted to throw her arms around him and hold on until he stopped resisting.

She also wanted him to just go, and let her mourn the end of this in peace. She was surer now that she would be okay without Philip. She understood that she could take some of this experience with her, and that might eventually be enough. She could take some of Philip's vulnerability, his faith in others and his moral endurance with her into the next chapter of life. She would be sad, but she would survive this.

"Let's stay in touch, okay?"

He nodded. "Definitely. And I'm sorry."

She smiled. "Don't be. Really, Philip. You're maybe the only person in the world with nothing to be sorry for."

46

Patty Bright

Nobody knows what they're going to want in the future. It's impossible to know, so you make choices based on the things you want now. You plan your life on the assumption that *future you* will be exactly like *current you*. But nobody is the person they start out as.

When we were in college, I wanted John Bright more than I've ever wanted anything. He was dazzling then, the absolute *most* of everything. He was the most charming and the most handsome, the most idealistic and the most ambitious. I harbored not a shred of doubt that this man would go on to realize all his dreams—and I was right about that. What I didn't know then is that realizing one's dreams changes a person. Ambition becomes success. Wanting becomes deserving. And the humility of desperation yields to hubris.

John could probably say the same about me. I didn't know that I wanted to be the wife of a successful politician (or I wouldn't admit to knowing), but I liked all the trappings of it. I liked the parties and accolades, the name recognition and the spotlight. The only thing I didn't like about the job was that it forced me to know that I am the sort of person who likes such things.

So maybe we were both a little taken aback by our slight distaste for each other in this otherwise successful life. We were enjoying almost everything about the path we'd created except for the mirror we each forced the other to look into. Which is why, ever the optimists, we turned off that reflective function of our psyches and forged ahead as partners; a sort of romantic collusion. It wasn't intimacy exactly, but it was symbiosis, and it worked extraordinarily well for us.

It didn't happen overnight, of course. The transformation took years, and it was broken up by the ceaseless schedules of parenting, fund-raising, campaigning and more parenting. The slow transition from lovers to coconspirators was felt as a series of quiet betrayals and disappointments. He didn't want me anymore, and so he went elsewhere. And when John's affairs got to be too much for me, I turned off the part of my heart that could keep breaking, and I decided to break his in turn. Revenge isn't a pleasurable motivation for sex, but it's an emotion, which is sometimes the best you can hope for.

We told ourselves that our children didn't see any of this, but I suspect they did, in their own way. We didn't submit them to any explicit traumas, but nor did we demonstrate a life of love. We didn't provide a marriage to emulate. I'll never know how regretful I should feel about my choices because the only thing I'm sure of is that parenthood is a job no one gets right. I don't know if I should wish I got it wrong in some other way or if this way is comparable to all the other wrong ways. Maybe a more sensitive mother would know the answer to this. I know I sacrificed some feeling on this path. I suppose I regret that: the dulled senses.

And so the person I've become is a surprise to me. But I'd grown so accustomed to this strange person that I was most surprised when, this week, I discovered a razor-sharp edge inside myself. Years after all the feelings and appetites had been dulled, a raging passion revealed itself.

I'm not proud to have burned down the garage. There may have been other ways to change course. But I did what had to be done for my family, and that's a thing I can't say I've always done before. It felt good.

This week—when the truth about Philip's father was revealed, and the press swarmed and John recommitted himself to his campaign—I realized that, this time, I would sooner die than let my children suffer. It was as if all my repressed doubt about the harm we inflicted on our children throughout their lives surged up as one great fireball of remorse. And I said *no more*. No more campaign—which John was clearly planning to move ahead with—and no documentary about my family. No more pain for my children. No more pain for Philip…or *less* pain, anyway. I wanted to take our story back, and that required something radical.

It's a strange thing, to set fire to your life to mend it, but I still think it was the best way out. It worked. John acquiesced and officially ended the campaign. The documentary that would ruin our lives was effectively murdered. All the pending catastrophes were thwarted. We get a reset.

It's certainly a reset for me. I can already see that my husband and children treat me differently. They regard me with the sort of cautious respect one holds for powerful lunatics, which is interesting and new. Maybe I'm imagining it, but my children seem to like me just a little bit more this way.

My younger self might expect that I'd be done with John, too, after all that has happened between us. But my younger self knew nothing about me. I'm not as good as I thought I was, and I'm not as brave. I summoned all my strength for that moment of fierce righteousness on behalf of my children. There wasn't much left after that.

The truth is, we made this life together and it works. So we'll go back to our pretty house and powerful friends. John will retire, but he won't disappear. We'll use our clout to have the authorities drop further inquiries into the fire and let it all fade into the past. You don't have to blow up your whole life to save one piece of it.

I didn't become a good and brave person this week. I just became a mother. I wish I'd done it sooner, but I'm not dead yet.

47

Three Months Later

When the last round of stuffing had been passed, and the cranberry sauce was gone entirely, JJ leaned back in his chair and put his arm around Mary-Beth. She was nursing a glass of port from Spencer's special collection.

"Thanksgiving is my favorite holiday," Ian said.

Everyone agreed.

It was just the four of them—Mary-Beth, JJ, Ian and Spencer—sitting around the dining room table in Ian and Spencer's apartment. The twinkle of city lights illuminated the dimming room. Their place looked just as Mary-Beth remembered it, with bookshelves that overflowed onto threadbare rugs, art competing for space on the walls, and elegantly aged furniture. It seemed a shame that in all the years they'd lived there,

Mary-Beth and JJ had visited only a few times. Until this year, all the holidays had belonged to John and Patty.

"Has anyone heard from them?" Spencer asked, one hand on his belly.

"Not yet."

No one had spoken with John or Patty since their call two weeks earlier to announce they were going to Tulum for Thanksgiving and would have to miss the festivities. Of course, there were no festivities planned. Everyone was still recovering from the drama of summer. It was a wry move on Patty's part—declining to attend a party she wasn't invited to—and everyone played along. The Bright sons wished their parents well on their vacation, and said it was a shame to miss them this year. But their relief was plainly obvious. Surely Patty could see it.

The previous three months had brought unexpected opportunities for all of them, and they were in no mood to look backward. The fire itself, the one that crazy Patty Bright had started, had ignited new and good things in their lives. Things were changing for the better, and they were all a little nervous that reconnecting with their parents would break that spell.

The changes happened first for Spencer. Mary-Beth wasn't aware of it at the time, but he'd made his television breakthrough as the now infamous fire was still roaring. When reporters were scrambling to cover the blaze from the Brights' front lawn, Spencer had offered himself up as an international affairs expert. He went on every major network that morning, providing measured analysis of the fire and its potential links to terrorism. He was lauded for his depth of understanding and evenhanded presence as hysterical theories were taking off. He was also lauded for his strong jaw, great hair and winning smile, becoming something of an internet sensation. After that, Spencer was offered a contract as a regular national security analyst on CNN, and he'd appeared on TV weekly ever since. He seemed happier than ever.

JJ's opportunity came days later when he received a call from the other Democratic candidate in the Massachusetts race for governor—his father's former primary opponent. Mary-Beth had been reading a book in the living room when she heard her husband take the call from the kitchen. *Thank you*, he'd said three times. *Yes, we felt strongly about that strategy*, and *Well, I don't think I can take credit for that*. It went on like that for a while, until JJ ended the call and came in to tell his wife that he'd just been offered the job of campaign manager for the other team. He was beaming. Apparently, they'd been impressed with the early strategy of John Senior's campaign (despite it all) and thought that JJ had a good understanding of the political climate. They thought John Senior was out of step with the voters, but that the message and mechanics were on point. *Your father wasn't going to win*, the man had said, *but your approach was smarter than ours*. JJ liked the guy. He was more liberal and less polished than his father. He wasn't a natural onstage, but he was genuine up close. He was kind of like JJ.

Mary-Beth never brought it up, and JJ never suggested it, but she knew this was more than a great job opportunity for her husband. It was a breaking with his father, a declaration of his detachment. JJ was free.

Spencer looked around the table. "Are we ready for dessert?"

They heard Lucas laugh from the other room, where he and his brother were watching Christmas movies. It was just like all the other Thanksgivings in this way: Mary-Beth's boys were still there; they were still hers. That would change soon, but for now, they were still hers.

"Let's wait," Ian said. "I'm so full."

"That's a good idea." Spencer looked out the window and smiled. "Did I tell you I invited Farah?"

Mary-Beth looked at him. "Really?"

"Yeah, she doesn't live that far from here. Too bad she couldn't stop by. She said she was going to her folks' place for Thanksgiving, then flying out tomorrow for some documentary about coral reefs. She was very polite about it, of course. Told me to say hi to everyone. She's a good kid."

JJ raised an eyebrow. "You know she had a little thing with Phil, right?"

His wife laughed in disbelief. "What? How do you know that?"

"It's true. I saw them kiss under that tree of his. I must have forgotten to tell you guys." He shook his head. "God, what a week that was."

"Do you think that's why Philip is changing his plan?" Ian asked.

Philip, who'd said he couldn't be there because of mid-term exams, was in the process of transferring to a different theological program in the Boston area. In a brief email to the group, he'd said he wanted something more flexible and socially engaged, a mainline protestant denomination probably. He didn't elaborate, but it was clear he was moving toward something that allowed for the possibility of a family someday. Maybe that's why he was making the change. Or maybe that's just what his family hoped. Either way, Mary-Beth was glad for him.

"I didn't get the sense that things were going to continue with Farah, but who knows," JJ said, "maybe she was part of that calculation."

Spencer laughed. "Charlie still thinks Philip's gay."

"Maybe Charlie's gay."

"Charlie's everything," Spencer said. "He's in love with everyone."

"None more than himself."

They toasted with admiration for their absent brother. At that moment, Charlie was in Costa Rica working on a conservation project for a new international development company. When Spencer invited him to Thanksgiving, he'd cheerfully claimed to be too busy, but they knew the real reason he wasn't coming home: Charlie was in love. This new woman was Costa Rican, some brilliant botanist who lived in a yurt. Their brother's capacity to fall frequently and intensely in love was a wonder to them all.

Charlie was elsewhere. And Philip was elsewhere. And it occurred for the first time to Mary-Beth that they weren't at opposite ends of some Bright family spectrum, but quite alike one another. They were both out in the world in search of beauty: physical, emotional, spiritual beauty. Mary-Beth remembered what her mother had told her as a child: that everything beautiful was proof of God's grace. And if that was true, then Charlie was exactly like Philip—giving up everything, over and over, in search of God's grace. You had to believe it existed to search for it. And you had to believe it was worthwhile to follow it to extreme places. They both believed.

There seemed no stronger proof to Mary-Beth of God's grace than the fact that hopeless cynics could beget great believers. All of them were proof: Philip, Charlie, Spencer and JJ. They were seekers of something beautiful. Patty and John shouldn't have made believers of their children. And yet. What possible explanation for their goodness could exist but God's grace?

Mary-Beth was happy with the thought.

The phone rang and everyone hesitated. Ringing phones produced anxiety in all of them. Even as the events of their summer faded from the public spotlight, the Brights were all still subject to random calls from magazine writers looking to do profiles and opinionated strangers who'd tracked down their numbers. The most anxiety-producing possibility of them all was the idea of a call from their parents.

No one was quite ready to talk to John and Patty. Patty was trying to rebuild their relationship in her own way. What she had done for them all—setting fire to the garage to kill the documentary—was breathtaking in its maternal heroism. They loved her for it. But their past was still there, complicating things. The Bright men needed time to redefine the concept of their family, to understand the new role that their flawed parents should occupy in their psyche. Mary-Beth thought it was emotional work they should have done in their teens, but better late than never, she supposed.

Ian picked up the phone. "Hello? Hey Philip! Hang on, let me put you on speaker."

He set the phone at the center of the dining table and opened a bottle of pinot noir as the group greeted him.

"Hey guys! How was dinner? I'm sorry I couldn't be there this year. Tell Lucas and Cam I miss them." Philip's tin voice talked excitedly about the program he'd be transferring to in January, about the friends he'd made in Boston and the studio apartment in the North End that he'd be moving into. Spencer and JJ took turns firing questions at him about when he was going to see a Pats game and who he'd bumped into from high school. They wondered if he was too wimpy now for East Coast winters and whether he owned a snow shovel. This was something new for all of them: genuine interest in Philip's life. They wanted to *know* their brother.

Mary-Beth smiled to see Philip there—in absentia—at the center of the room, the center of the conversation. It was what he'd always deserved and never had. The revelations about his life were unimaginably difficult, and yet they were the things that freed Philip and his brothers to really see each other. It took their father's fall to reinvent their relationships on their own, without their parents' gaze. And so it was sad, but it was also not sad at all.

And now it seemed that they appreciated Philip in a new light, as the only one among them who hadn't been under the spell of John Senior; the one who'd known who he was all along. In the end, being a Bright who isn't defined by his Bright-ness had been a wise path. The others were still catching up to Philip.

"Phil, tell me you're not just eating takeout in your living room," Mary-Beth said.

"No, actually I have plans. I should go. We're having a little Thanksgiving dinner over at my classmates' house, for all the Thanksgiving orphans."

A pause.

"Ha," he added. "You know what I mean."

A few laughs.

Spencer leaned in toward the phone. "We miss you, brother. It's too bad you couldn't be here."

"I miss you guys, too. There's still Christmas."

"Absolutely."

Everyone said goodbye once more, and then Philip was gone. He was their half brother now. Or maybe he wasn't. The expression on JJ's and Spencer's faces looked sad in that moment, as they sat around the dirty plates and empty glasses, the ghost of Philip's voice still there with them. But there was also an unmistakable sense that things were changing for the better.

The world had not blown itself up. It felt for a while as if it might, in those weeks after the Madrid attack, when they were counting their blessings and paying attention to every wrinkle on the world stage. But they'd been wrong about that. The world was no more or less dangerous now than it had been a year ago. Only their proximity to danger had changed, and only temporarily. Mary-Beth was sure now that, like joy, all the pain we endure in this life is almost always inflicted by those closest to us. All the comforts and threats are right here.

Ian stood up.

"Go relax," Mary-Beth said. "You guys made everything. We've got the dishes."

And so he and Spencer went to their couch that slumped at the center, where the paisley fabric had faded to a blur. The twins, who sat in armchairs on either side of their uncles, had briefly forgotten about the phones in their hands and were watching Linus deliver the Christmas monologue they'd seen dozens of times before. Spencer put his head on Ian's shoulder. Ian put his arm around him. And Mary-Beth wanted to cast them all in amber forever because they were perfect.

JJ went to the kitchen with a stack of dirty dishes and began scraping what was left on the plates into a garbage bin. They had to get it all off because there was no garbage disposal and the old pipes in their building tended to get blocked up on busy days like these.

Mary-Beth filled the kettle at the tap and put the pies in the oven to warm.

It must have been eighty degrees in that cramped little kitchen. JJ took off his sweater and cracked a window. The heat in that old building had a mind of its own, but all you had to do was open a window and let the outside air in. Elegant solutions abounded.

JJ went to the freezer and tried to reorganize its contents to make room for more Tupperware. Mary-Beth crouched down below him as she wedged containers of sweet potatoes behind stuffing, and applesauce above that. "We'll be eating leftovers for days," she murmured.

JJ attempted to close the freezer just as Mary-Beth stood up, and in the moment before her head collided with the door, he put a gentle hand upon it, steering her to safety.

She felt the gesture as a reflexive two-step in their perpetual dance. She was conscious of it, but only barely. These were the things they did for each other every day—each one forgettable on its own, but when you added up all the averted collisions, fleeting squeezes and private looks, you got a marriage. And it was better and bigger than the periods of passion, the grand statements. Sometimes these moments were almost too breathtaking for Mary-Beth to fully consider, too beautiful to take in with her open eyes. She had to go just a little numb to survive the devastating beauty of it all over the course of a lifetime.

When the kitchen was clean, Mary-Beth and JJ joined the rest of their family in the living room. The movie had ended, and Spencer had fallen asleep in Ian's arms. Below them, the boys were playing checkers on the rug.

They could hear the sounds of other people's Thanksgivings through the walls and cars passing on the street. Someone was playing piano in an apartment above. The distant cacophony of a hundred different lives at the same moment.

There is no way to know what a marriage should look like; no way to know how a family is supposed to be. No one can be sure what they are going to want in ten or twenty or sixty years.

But neither are we mysteries. Ours are the needs of children.

And so we hold on to each other. We block the incoming threats. And we open a window when it's time to let the outside air in.

★ ★ ★ ★ ★

ACKNOWLEDGMENTS

For this book and the ones that came before it, I am incredibly grateful to my agent, John Silbersack; my editor, Kathy Sagan; my publicist, Shara Alexander; and everyone at MIRA Books. Time flies. Thanks for everything.

I also want to thank the literary community of Vermont. This work wouldn't be possible without our thriving ecosystem of booksellers, librarians, arts journalists and readers. I'm lucky to call this brave little state home.

Thank you to my beloved colleagues at Bennington College for making the daily work of writing so joyful and surprising.

Thank you to Liam for keeping me sane, but not too sane.

And, as ever, thank you to the loves of my life: Annabelle, Josephine and Dan.

THE MISFORTUNES OF FAMILY

MEG LITTLE REILLY

Reader's Guide

QUESTIONS FOR DISCUSSION

1. Are the Brights sympathetic as individual family members? How would you describe each of the brothers' strengths and weaknesses?

2. How would you define their family dynamic? Do you find elements of their dynamic relatable?

3. Do you recognize universal themes of marriage in this story? If so, what are some of them?

4. All families have secrets—some darker than others. What do you think about the secret Patty and John Senior have kept from their sons?

5. Should they have told Philip about his real father at some point earlier? How about the other sons?

6. Does Patty Bright, in your view, redeem herself at the end? Is her behavior more defensible or less?

7. Which of the relationships in this story—romantic or familial—do you root for, and which ones do you view as irredeemable?

8. What do you think of Farah? Do you think she and Philip have things in common? Do you think there is a chance they might get together?

9. Some families can stretch and grow while others are more rigid. How would you characterize the Brights?

10. What role do you think the camera's lens is intended to play in advancing the story or illuminating the characters? Is it effective?

What was the inspiration for this story?

I knew that I wanted to write a story about love and marriage. Love is the most difficult thing to write about—or at least, to write well—because when it is good, it is earnest, sincere and gentle. I knew that my way into good relationships would be through trying experiences, things that test couples. Family conflict is the ultimate test.

Each of the Bright brothers, in my view, is capable of great love, but they need to learn how to create it on their own. They cannot fall back on the model provided by their parents. John Junior and Mary-Beth's marriage, and Spencer and Ian's marriage, are successes in this way. I enjoyed being inside their intimate moments and all the quiet habits of their loving relationships. The other siblings' romantic relationships are on shakier ground, but they are exciting and steamy, which I enjoy, too.

This story surprised me as it unfolded because it became largely about the unique quirks and codes that define a family. We learn them from our parents, and we reinvent them in our adult relationships. And then we all have to find a way to make these intersecting identities of chosen and biological families work.

In the end, this was a story about what we choose to inherit, and what we make for ourselves.

Are these characters based on real people in your life?

All of the characters in this story are fictional. In every way, they are inventions. But I also believe that there are universal experiences of parents, siblings and in-laws that put us all on common ground. And I am grateful to my big crazy family because, without them, I could never write stories about big crazy families.

The most direct inspiration for these characters was my ten years living in Washington, DC, working in national politics. John Bright Senior is an amalgamation of all the fantastical and archetypal characters I was exposed to in my political years. I love writing about Washington people and their world because everything is big—operatic even. The stakes are high, the appetites strong and the egos enormous. The rise and fall of powerful people will always be an irresistible story line for me.

Why did you tell this story primarily from the perspective of the spouses and partners?

I think the most honest assessments of our own families can only come from outsiders. We have all been outsiders to other families at one point or another, and it's a strangely disorienting experience, like visiting a foreign country. I wanted to give the reader the benefit of a critical eye.

I was also interested in the gender dynamic of this family. The women in the story are allied as "extras" in the Bright household. And the hubris that all Bright men share is undeniably male. And yet it would have been too simplistic to make this a story of stereotypical gender dynamics. As it unfolds, the question of who has the most agency, and who is most vulnerable, is far more complicated than gender alone.

What is the significance of Farah and the camera's lens in this story?

The vanity that motivates John Bright Senior—and, to a lesser degree, the rest of the Brights—is both a motivating force and a sickness in this family. It makes them charming, successful and magnetic, but it's also their Achilles' heel.

Farah's watchful lens helped illustrate just how performative the Bright experience is, how difficult it could be to distinguish between sincerity and affectation in this family. They are actors in their own lives.

The cameras were also an opportunity to explore the universal appeal of being watched and the allure of fame. Even the characters in this story who were critical of the documentarian's presence were not immune to the camera's pull. I like stories that exist in a particular time and place, and I was interested in the narcissistic impulses of contemporary culture.

Is there an overarching message or takeaway you want readers to have from this story?

Love is messy and so very worth it.